WHITE SUICIDE

SIMON GAUL
WHITE SUICIDE

First published in 2023 by
Simon Gaul, in partnership with Whitefox Publishing
This paperback edition published in 2024

www.wearewhitefox.com

Copyright © Simon Gaul, 2023

ISBN 978-1-916797-49-9
Also available as an eBook
ISBN 978-1-915635-61-7

Simon Gaul asserts the moral right to be identified
as the author of this work.

All rights reserved. No part of this publication may be reproduced,
stored in a retrieval system or transmitted in any form or by any means,
electronic, mechanical, photocopying, recording or otherwise,
without prior written permission of the author.

While every effort has been made to trace the owners of copyright
material reproduced herein, the author would like to apologize for any
omissions and will be pleased to incorporate missing acknowledgements
in any future editions.

Designed and typeset by Typo•glyphix
Cover design by Dominic Forbes
Project management by whitefox
Printed and bound by CPI Group (UK) Ltd, Croydon CR0 4YY

For Christopher J. Little,
1941–2021

CONTENTS

Author's Note	*viii*
Prologue	*xv*
Part One	1
Part Two	27
Part Three	59
Part Four	85
Part Five	105
Part Six	123
Part Seven	157
Part Eight	175
Part Nine	201
Part Ten	223
Part Eleven	239
Part Twelve	265
Part Thirteen	283
Part Fourteen	305
Part Fifteen	321
Part Sixteen	345
Part Seventeen	391
Epilogue	415
Afterword	*429*

AUTHOR'S NOTE

White Suicide is a novel that mixes fact and fiction with conspiracy theories. However, the historical backdrop, in Italy and the USA, and spanning a period from 1944–1987, has been carefully researched in the public and private domains. Some of what may seem implausible, is in fact true. Where public statements made by real people are used, they are done so in quotes and/or italics. More comprehensive explanations, notes etc., can be found in the Afterword; to reveal any more here would detract from the fictional elements of the book.

Simon Gaul
September 2023

DRAMATIS PERSONAE

In Sicily

Angelina Albassi a young unmarried Sicilian woman
'Nonna' the village of San Cipirello's elderly nurse
Dr Carlotto physician to the 14th Duke of Salaviglia and all who live on his estates
Father Albert Fiero Roman Catholic priest whose congregation spans the Salaviglia estates
14th Duke of Salaviglia head of the feudal Salaviglia dynasty, the largest landowners in Sicily
Victor Salaviglia the 14th Duke's only son and heir born in September 1944. His mother, the Duchess Constanza, died of typhoid in 1944 from a Salaviglia well, poisoned by the retreating German forces
Pietro Albassi an orphan born in San Cipirello in September 1944. Father unknown, his mother, Angelina, died in childbirth
Gaspare Pisciotta (1924–1954) a notorious Sicilian outlaw and bandit
Interior Minister Mario Scelba (1901–1991) became 33rd prime minister of Italy (1954–1955)
Maurizio Forte proprietor of La Tavernetta, Porto Portopalo, the southernmost tip of Sicily; a fisherman's *trattoria* frequented by Joshua Padden and Pietro Albassi

In Rome

Antonio Spiriticchio an itinerant Roman florist
Aldo Moro (1916–1978) President of Christian Democracy (DC), Italy's majority political party. Twice prime minister of Italy (1963–1968 and 1973–1974), Moro was a highly respected Cold War world leader and renowned statesman
Eleonora Moro (1915–2010 *nee* Chiavarelli) married Aldo Moro in 1945; they had four children

Marshal Oreste Leonardi Carabinieri, head of Moro's five-man security detail.

Domenico Ricci Carabinieri, Moro's driver.

Francesco Zizzi, Giulio Rivera, Raffaele Iozzino police officers assigned as Moro's bodyguards

Mario Moretti (1946–) national leader of the Red Brigades terrorists who commanded the eleven-person kidnap and murder squad. Arrested in 1981, confessed to, and was convicted of, Moro's murder; released 1997, whereabouts unknown

Giulio Andreotti (1913–2013) firmly on the right wing of the DC party, became the most powerful of all Italian politicians. Served as prime minister in seven governments between 1972 and 1992 during sixty years in Parliament

Enrico Berlinguer (1924–1984) General Secretary of Italian Communist Party (PCI) 1972–1984

Pietro Ingrao (1915–2015) President of the Italian Chamber of Deputies 1976–1979

Licio Gelli (1919–2015) Venerable Master of Propaganda Due (P2) the clandestine and powerful, anti-communist, fascist Masonic Lodge, which became, essentially, a criminal organisation. P2 was implicated in multiple crimes from plundering the Vatican Bank to numerous murders. Recognised as 'Italy's shadow government', P2 was banned in 1982

Tina Anselmi (1927–2016) was a WWII anti-fascist resistance fighter, and the first woman to hold a ministerial post (Health) when promoted on 11 March 1978, 5 days before Moro was kidnapped. She was Pietro Albassi's most trusted DC ally, go-between and friend of Eleonora Moro

Romano Prodi (1939–) a Christian Democracy (DC) politician who in 1978 rose to notoriety for his fantastical story of attending a Ouija board séance during Moro's incarceration, during which the address in Rome where Moro was being held was 'divulged'. The story dogged Prodi's career, but he went on to become prime minister of Italy twice (1996–1998 and 2006–2008) and president of the European Commission 1999–2004

Nicolai Sentini incarcerated in Rebibbia prison, Rome, for murder; one of the four Commanders of the Red Brigades

In the Vatican

Alessandro Cuci a P2 member and Director of the Institute of External Affairs (IEA) – *Istituto per le Opere Esteriore* – the Holy See's covert information and 'research' organisation for all foreign relations. The IEA's nominal head is the Cardinal Secretary of State of the Holy See

Pope Paul VI (1897–1978) University friend of Moro, he personally interceded with the Red Brigades in an attempt to save Moro's life and was rebuffed

Pope John Paul I (1912–1978) a surprise choice as the new pope after Paul VI. John Paul I vowed reform upon his election. He died in his sleep whilst in the Vatican under mysterious circumstances after only thirty-three days as pope

Roberto Calvi (1920–1982) a P2 member known as 'God's Banker'. He was found dead, hanging under Blackfriars Bridge, London, on a sunny June morning

Archbishop Paul Marcinkus (1922–2006) a US citizen was made president of the Vatican Bank (1971–1989) despite having no banking experience whatsoever. A P2 member, he was an associate of Calvi; both were alleged accomplices in the 'murder' of Pope John Paul I in 1978. Resigned all Vatican posts in disgrace in 1990 to return to the US

In Milan

Pietro Albassi a graduate of University of Milan is a mid-level lawyer at Scampidi & Rusconi; hard-working and a skilled *avvocato* who handles only criminal cases

Ruxandra Albassi Romanian by birth, she has a part-time job in a Milanese art gallery when not being a mother

Salvatore 'Toto' and Paola Pietro and Ruxandra's eight-year-old twin children

Dottore Enrico Scampidi vastly influential septuagenarian lawyer and political 'fixer'. A P2 member

Ispettore Lorenzo Massina, Criminalpol, Milan, investigates cynically and with formidable intuition crimes other officers won't touch. Near to retirement – a prospect he dreads – he smokes to excess and dislikes life almost as much as he does his downtrodden assistant, **Luca Pezzoli**

In Malta GC

Joshua Padden Rhodesian by birth, a widower with no evident shadow. Lived in Southeast Asia from the 1950s to early 1970s, and profited from its conflicts and wars. Later shipwrecked in the Malta-Sicily Channel, he found refuge on the small island of Gozo where he writes pulp-thrillers under the pen-name P.J. Fowler

Tony Grech (1950–) proprietor of the fabled Gleneagles Bar. Trusted friend of Padden

Palalu (1920–2014) Gozitan fisherman, low-level smuggler and Padden's friend

In America

President James Earl Carter Jr. (1924–) 39th president of the United States 1977–1981

President Ronald Reagan (1911–2004) 40th president of the United States 1981–1989

Vice President George H.W. Bush (1924–2018) 43rd vice president of the United States 1981–1989

President George H.W. Bush (1924–2018) 41st president of the United States 1989–1993

George H.W. Bush (1924–2018) 11th Director of Central Intelligence Agency 1976–1977

Admiral Stansfield Turner (1923–2018) 12th Director of Central Intelligence Agency 1977–1981

Henry Kissinger (1923–2023) 56th US Secretary of State 1973–1977, previously 7th National Security Advisor 1969–1975 to 37th president of the United States, Richard Nixon

General Alexander Haig (1924–2010) 7th US NATO Supreme Allied Commander 1974–1979 and 59th US Secretary of State 1981-1982 in President Reagan's first administration

Robert McFarlane (1937–2022) 12th US National Security Advisor 1983–1985 to President Reagan. Ensnared in the Iran-Contra affair (1985–1987) he pleaded guilty to four counts; attempted suicide in 1987 and was later pardoned – with others – by then President H.W. Bush in 1993, who had been President Reagan's VP throughout the entire Iran-Contra scandal

Casper Weinberger (1917–2006) served as 15th US Secretary of Defence (1981–1987) during both Reagan administrations. He too was indicted over his involvement in the Iran-Contra affair, only to be pardoned by President H.W. Bush in 1993, three weeks before Bush Snr. left office

Admiral John Poindexter (1936–) 13th US National Security Advisor (1985–1986) conspired with Lt. Colonel Oliver North in all aspects of Iran-Contra affair: covert arms sales to Iran, aid and money. Convicted of five felony counts in 1990, all reversed in 1991 on technicalities. Last heard trumpeting 2020 election was stolen by the Democrats

Manucher Ghorbanifar (1945–) Iranian ex-SAVAK agent who first proposed the arms-for-US hostages deal in 1985 during President Reagan's second term. He sold missiles to Iran with support of Poindexter and North in the Iran-Contra affair (1985–1987)

Adnan Khashoggi (1935–2017) key Saudi Arabian middleman and financier with Ghorbanifar of the Iran-Contra affair (1985-1987)

Judd Barings CIA Head of Rome Station during 1970s; later Deputy Director Central Intelligence Agency

Carlos Marcello (1910–1993) head of New Orleans *mafia*, **Santo Trafficante Jr.** (1914–1987) head of Florida *mafia* and **Salvatore 'Sam' Giancana** (1908–1975) head of the Chicago *mafia*, were all *'two sides of the same coin'* (*Mafia* and CIA). In 1979 the HSCA (United States House Senate Committee on Assassinations) concluded that JFK *'was probably assassinated in a conspiracy and that Oswald did not act alone'* on 22nd November 1963

Saxon Monteleone originally of Italian descent; his forebears settled in Louisiana in 1790. The Monteleone business empire has industrial and financial interests across all the Southern US states; his influence reaches 1600 Pennsylvania Avenue, whomever the incumbent. A private man, a widower with one son. He delights in speaking Creole

Anthony Bianchi a bachelor who lives alone in the French Quarter of New Orleans, he is Monteleone's Chief of Staff, *consigliere* and family confidant

Joey Thibodeaux Monteleone's fulltime gofer and sometime valet

Dawn Loubiere a fourth generation Louisiana lady who befriends Anthony Bianchi

Stevie Conn Technical Director of Tipitina's, a storied New Orleans music venue in which the Monteleone family has an interest

*'The two most important days of a man's life
are the day on which he was born
and the day on which he discovers why he was born.'*
                                                            Anon.

PROLOGUE

San Cipirello, a village in the west of Sicily.
Friday, 1st September 1944. Early afternoon.

A *scirocco* had blown for ten days and nights. The arid north African wind was relentless, the air seared with red Saharan sand. The earth baked as opaque mirages shimmered into one with the horizon. Neither the meditative cool of the old church, nor the shade of the olive terraces offered sanctuary. Stray mutts, mouths parched, lay motionless in the deserted streets. In the small and irregular-shaped piazza, flies feasted on a dead donkey. It was graveyard quiet, and apart from a broken shutter slapping against a wall, the only sound was that of a young woman screaming from the depths of her very being.

In Sicily, they say that when the *scirocco* blows for more than eight days all crimes of passion are absolved.

* * *

The young woman lay on her back. Her legs trembled as she gripped the iron bedstead in an effort to steady her body. Blood trickled down her chin from where she'd bitten deep into her lip.

As the afternoon wore on, her screams became reed-thin. Beside her, an elderly woman gently dabbed at her lip and brow, sweat mingling with blood.

"Sssh, sssh, *piano piano*…"

She rinsed the cloth in a chipped enamel basin and the water ran pinker. Locked in her agony, the young woman couldn't see the concern in the old lady's wrinkled and weathered face.

"*Cara*, try and breathe deeply and slowly…" she whispered.

The young woman nodded. She knew she was weak from losing blood and breathing deeply meant taking the Devil's furnace inside. An icy fear acted like a tumour in her windpipe. She couldn't do it. The old lady smiled at her as she threaded her rough hand through the young woman's matted, reddish hair. The young woman's green almond-shaped eyes creased in gratitude.

The village was unnaturally silent. Usually, even on the hottest of summer days, carts jiggered over the cobbled streets and scavenging dogs chased pedlars – just out of kicking range – as they knocked on doors. Perhaps it was the vicious African heat that kept the village quieter than an undisturbed tomb, the old lady thought, or, more likely, curiosity as to the fate of the young woman. She may have been spurned, but she was still one of them. The old lady cursed God and Dr Carlotto for their absence.

A tiny body, finally, bloodily, slipped out from between the young woman's thighs and into the old lady's hands. The old lady, deprived of not only Dr Carlotto but his instruments too, gnawed through the umbilical cord, then slapped the boy into life. She placed the wailing infant beside the young woman's head. She smeared blood from her face and mouth with the back of her hand. Her only wish was that the wailing might arrest the young woman's spiral into oblivion.

Sinister shadows had played across the wooden floor all afternoon. The old lady angrily jabbed open the broken shutters with her elbows. In the distance she caught sight of Dr Carlotto shambling across the piazza. She squinted through the rising heat haze at the battered medicine bag – the villagers called it *'il portautensili'*, the toolkit, as it thumped against his short, unsteady legs. She cursed aloud.

The front door opened and Dr Carlotto stumbled up the stairs. A threadbare linen suit stretched across his overweight frame. He caught his breath and kicked *il portautensili* across the floor. The old lady didn't ask him what had delayed him. Cards, wine, or the 14th Duke of Salaviglia – it could have been all three.

"The boy's alive, but the mother is done for." Dr Carlotto bent over and looked at the near lifeless body on the straw mattress. Her green eyes were closed. Not even the cries of her new-born son sparked life.

"Yankies! Americans! What is it their soldiers love about our women? Get me fresh water, Nonna," snapped Dr Carlotto as he peeled his frayed shirt, translucent with sweat from his forearms.

* * *

"Father Albert! Wake up! Wake up!"

A skinny, barefoot young boy shook the priest's shoulder as he dozed in the shade beneath his favourite almond tree in the cemetery.

"Pronto! Dr Carlotto is dying."

Father Albert woke with a jolt and fastened his cassock. He stood up, shaking his tall, rangy body free of dust and earth. He slicked perspiration into his grey-flecked hair and strode ahead silently.

The boy's mission accomplished, he scampered over the dry-stone wall into the olive groves beyond.

Father Albert knew he wouldn't have to administer the last rites to Dr Carlotto; the Carlottos of this world don't die convenient or tidy deaths. His heartbeat quickened with his pace. He had an idea of what the truth was. There was nothing that made him doubt God more than the death of a new-born.

The young woman's torso pivoted upwards. Her blood and sweat-stained muslin garment clung to her loose flesh, soaked in the darkest of honeys. Her green eyes were open and her pupils were alert. Her eyes implored a promise from the old lady and Dr Carlotto. Their expressions must have returned what she'd desired, for as she sank back in slow motion, her gentle, young mouth smiled as if all was good in the world.

"The boy's survived." Dr Carlotto paused. "Premature ones rarely do…" His words tailed off. "Who's going to look after him…?"

He leaned into the young woman's left ear. "Who's the father? Can you remember his name? His rank? Anything?"

The young woman moved her head from side to side. Dr Carlotto felt her wrist for a pulse, then turned to the old lady. "It's weak. She's dying."

Father Albert kicked the door open, sweat dripping off his unshaven face. The scene before him stopped him: an iron cot-bed upon which a young and beautiful Sicilian woman lay. On the floor was a worn rattan Moses basket, which held a baby. Dr Carlotto, ruddy and perspiring, was only a pace away, behind him stood an old lady. There was a bowl of crimson water on a trestle. "Americans! Americans!" Dr Carlotto blurted out in self-defence. Too many times he'd felt the iron grip of Catholic guilt around his throat when simply fate, disease, hunger, murder had caused a death. He didn't need more of the same today, of all days. Everyone in the village of San Cipirello had known – and liked

– the young woman now bleeding out on a lice-infested straw mattress in front of their very eyes.

"She's dying, Berto. Nonna and I did what we could, believe me."

The priest looked at the old lady for confirmation; he had never liked the gambling dipsomaniac doctor God had sent to San Cipirello. The old lady nodded and closed her eyes. He knelt down between the bed and the basket. It was not supposed to happen this way. Babies died. Yes. Strong, healthy young women did not. He looked up at Dr Carlotto. The old lady moved away from the window to gather up the infant to cradle him in her arms, and he stopped crying immediately.

Father Albert removed from the folds of his cassock an old leather prayer book, a small phial of oil and an ancient ebony crucifix, silky to the touch; it had been a gift from his late father on the day he had been ordained, some ten years ago. He administered the last rites with a compassion neither Dr Carlotto, nor the old lady had ever witnessed before.

Saharan dust, pregnant with sickly-sweet fresh blood, mingled in the air and danced in the light's stilettos. As the young woman passed into the afterlife, Father Albert remained vigilant at her side.

When he stood up, his tall, muscular build towered over them all. His face wore only anguish.

"Nonna, fetch some fresh water. It is time for a baptism."

The cemetery of San Cipirello, the west of Sicily.
Saturday, 2nd September 1944. The following morning.

Two skeletal dogs took it in turns to piss on the bald tyres of Dr Carlotto's age-old blue Fiat. They scampered from wheel to wheel, as if they too had become demented by the *scirocco*. They were the only attendants at the cemetery so there was no one to witness their game.

Let the dead bury the dead. There was none of the pomp, music and families that are normal at funerals, and no children to run behind the funeral cortege. The young woman had succumbed to the charms of an invader, so her interment was not a traditional Sicilian affair.

The cemetery lay along a narrow track beyond the last ramshackle stone building on the outskirts of the village. It had spread, like so much else that was Sicilian, haphazardly, down the southwest facing hill upon which San Cipirello sat. In the distance, yet somehow almost close enough to touch, the Tyrrhenian Sea winked in the sunlight. The graves, with their humble wooden crosses, were shaded from the pains of summer by peering, haughty cypress trees and by a grove of biblically old olive trees. In the lower corner of the cemetery stood a solitary almond tree, under which Father Albert was often to be found.

Like most things in a land steeped in ignorance and fearful of change, the cemetery had evolved out of necessity. For over 500 years, whilst tending olive groves and citrus trees on the vast estates of their feudal overlords, peasants were buried in the unforgiving ground where they had fallen.

The task today for the gravediggers was unexpectedly easy. During the night, a Divine thunderstorm had finally rendered apart the blanket of African heat that had brought death to San Cipirello. The storm had gathered over the Tyrrhenian Sea and speeding south and striking the mountains behind Palermo to the north, then fleeing inland towards Trapani. The ceaseless thunder may have stopped a few hearts as the lightening played its own *festa*, but the arid soil had gulped thirstily upon the rains. At least the young woman's interment would be easy.

In the shadow of the almond tree, the two gravediggers leaned on their long-handled shovels. Huddled a few metres away from the tree, and beside the fresh grave, was a pitiful congregation. Father Albert prayed silently. Dr Carlotto perspired into his linen suit. The old lady gazed down at the infant as he slept the sleep of the innocent in the rattan Moses basket. Only Signor Albassi, the young woman's father, with a smile drawn by senility and a body broken by a lifetime's toil, stood to a buckled attention.

"It should be him in the box, Berto. He won't see the year out." Dr Carlotto nodded in the direction of Signor Albassi. Treating the remark with contempt, Father Albert coughed and began the service. Within fifteen minutes, God had pronounced Godspeed to Heaven. With loud 'Amens', the two gravediggers revealed themselves to be the only believers present.

Signor Albassi, statue-still, remained where he had stood. He was confused. The priest had told him they were to bury his daughter, his only child. But he recalled that they had done just that earlier in the year when she could no longer hide the swelling in her belly. His little girl had died then: the same little girl he had taught to swim in Golfo di Castellammare: the same little girl who had broken his heart and tarnished his family honour when she had informed him that she was pregnant by a man she had refused to name. In pity, Dr Carlotto smiled and took the old man's arm, leading him away as the gravediggers shovelled clods of earth onto his daughter's flimsy coffin.

The dogs waited for their audience to return. When they saw Dr Carlotto approach, they bared their teeth and managed one final squirt of piss before hurrying off. Uneasily, Father Albert stood in silence beside the decrepit Fiat with the old lady, the new-born, Dr Carlotto and Signor Albassi. There was nothing to add, and less to do.

Nonna would, of course, look after the infant until Father Albert could cajole his bishop, or perhaps the 14th Duke of Salaviglia, into securing a place in an orphanage. Dr Carlotto would return to his wine and games of *scopa*, and Signor Albassi would wait with all the stoicism he could muster for the cancer that was devouring his insides to finish its hungry work.

The sun edged over the tops of the cypress trees into the hard, blue sky. The ground beneath them began to steam like a huge cauldron and the aromas of wild herbs, soil, olive trees and soft almond hinted at a rebirth of life. The boy remained blissfully asleep. Dr Carlotto began to shift his weight impatiently, and mud squelched beneath his feet.

Nothing remained of the summer of 1944: with the birth of an orphan boy, and the sorry funeral of his beautiful young mother, it had become just a shadowy memory. All that lingered were the many immense and grotesque flies.

The rains had swept everything else away.

INTERNATIONAL Herald Tribune

THURSDAY, DECEMBER 14, 1950   Compiled by Our Staff from Dispatches

San Cipirello Massacre

Outlaw Responsible Found Dead

ROME---Gaspare Pisciotta, cousin, lieutenant and blood brother of the most notorious Sicilian outlaw of all time, Salvatore Giuliano, died yesterday from a massive overdose of strychnine in his coffee, 'enough to kill forty horses' according to unnamed sources. The poison was administered within Ucciardone Prison, officials in Palermo, Sicily have also confirmed.

It was only six days ago that Pisciotta 'confessed' in a statement to having had Salvatore Giuliano murdered in, he alleged, collaboration with Interior Minister Mario Scelba. It is thought that Giuliano's men had long sought revenge on Pisciotta for the slaying of their leader and the disastrous rout of their gang following the horrific massacre five months ago in the piazza of San Cipirello, a small village adjoining the vast estates of the Dukes of Salaviglia in the impoverished west of Sicily.

Pisciotta, in a power struggle for command of the rebels, had led three other renegades into the tiny village, home of Father Albert Fiero, priest and confessor to the current 14th Duke of Salaviglia. It is believed that Father Albert Fiero's influence with the elderly Duke was the reason Pisciotta targeted the hitherto backwater village. Pisciotta had wished to demonstrate his ruthlessness in front of Sicily's most influential, but disparate powers: the 14th Duke of Salaviglia and Salvatore Giuliano. An endeavour he failed in, and Giuliano swore revenge on the innocent victims of San Cipirello, a Salaviglia village.

The massacre, the bloodiest this century, when 27 men, women and children were killed, took place on August 24th, 1950 in the village piazza. Eyewitness statements show the first victim was Nino Camporele, the proprietor of the Bar Lombardo. The second to die was the Duke's personal physician Dr Carlotto. The killings were entirely random, the victims described as 'falling within the line of sight of Pisciotta, who would point and someone would shoot.'

Apart from those who were able to flee, there was one wounded survivor, a six-year-old orphan, Pietro Albassi. In the maelstrom of gunfire, a bullet struck his left temple and he was blinded in that eye. He is being cared for at Bonnera, the Salaviglia's Castello. Together with the bandits' discarded American carbine guns found in the piazza of San Cipirello, the young boy, Pietro Albassi, has come to symbolise the Italo-American debate over war reparations still raging in the US Congress and the Italian Senate.

PART ONE

CHAPTER 1

**A nondescript building in via Brunetti,
a street behind Piazza del Popolo, Rome, Italy.
Thursday, 16th March 1978. 06:40.**

"I don't believe it! Who the hell did this? I'm never going to make the market, let alone make any cash. Fucking vandals!"

Antonio Spiriticchio, dressed in his work clothes and a rumpled red smock, rubbed his stubbled chin and walked around his Ford Transit van kicking each of the four slashed tyres in turn. He shook his head in disbelief. For years he'd been selling flowers from his Ford van on the corner opposite the Olivetti Bar, where via Fani crosses via Stresa, in the well-heeled residential district of Monte Mario and Camilluccia in Rome.

"Just my luck…"

It was a beautiful, bright early spring morning and it would have been a good day for selling flowers, but since the owner of the swanky Olivetti Bar had gone bankrupt, business had not been so good. There was no way he was going to get from home, all the way across to the right bank of the Tiber to the flower market, and then up to the crossroads where he had sold flowers for years. Today was going to make him as much money as last week's dead blooms. Worse, he had to find 600,000 lire for four new tyres.

Antonio Spiriticchio needed a good day, and with money so tight, life had not been easy at home. He groaned and booted one of the tyres again. He looked up at the cloudless sky. He had always said the sun married in spring, and honeymooned in Rome.

Today the sun was very much in love. Dammit.

CHAPTER 2

No. 79, via del Forte Trionfale,
the Camilluccia district, Rome, Italy.
Thursday, 16th March 1978. 07:45.

Aldo Moro woke up with a start at the shrill sound of the alarm clock. President of the Christian Democracy (CD) party, twice prime minister of Italy, he was an influential and powerful political figure. He silenced the alarm, his bloodhound-like eyelids drooping. Every tissue of muscle, blood and water that constituted his ageing frame felt very used. Very second-hand. Even his mind ached.

"Do you think every sixty-one-year-old man feels this bad in the morning?" he grumbled aloud to Eleonora, his beloved wife of thirty-three years.

"No, *caro*, only Italian politicians, it's part of their job to look haggard. Imagine how few votes you'd get if people believed that you had a cushy life." She glanced at him. "Don't fall asleep again, Aldo. Today is the day you've worked so hard for. Now, go and shave while I put your clothes out."

Moro felt warmed by the tenderness of her voice. He swung his legs out from between the sheets, scratched his distended stomach and smoothed down his luxurious shock of white hair.

"Please be careful with the tie, nothing exuberant today. Parliament will expect more from me." Moro had a love of silk neckties and usually selected his own.

"Alright, *caro*, how about the dark grey suit, the one with the waistcoat?" she asked, as she drew back the heavy brocade curtains to let the sunlight flood in. He blinked and his wife shivered involuntarily.

"Are you alright?" Moro caught her troubled expression as she drew on her robe tightly.

"Yes, *caro*. I just remembered something Julius Caesar said: *'It is the bright day that brings forth the adder.'*"

"What's that supposed to mean?"

"Just look where you tread today, Aldo. Now hurry into the bathroom," she said, clapping her hands. He shook his head from side to side, more in affection than exasperation about women in general before closing the bathroom door.

Standing as erect as his weariness would allow, he felt the scalding jets of water pinprick his poor circulation into life. Moro grinned sheepishly to himself. He was a proud southern man, one who had never been hollowed by conceit. Not even his enemies – and there were many – would have levelled the crosshairs of self-importance at him. But alone, wet and naked, he allowed his adrenaline to massage his vanity. He had been prime minister of Italy twice: from 1963–1968 and recently from 1973–1974. Now, perhaps even more influential, he was president of the Italy's ruling Christian Democracy party and the de facto Head of State.

Today was the culmination of his life's political work. The 'Compromesso Storico', the plan to bring Italy's Communist Party (PCI) into a governing alliance with his Christian Democracy party in order to promote national stability in these troubled times, was finally to be signed at 10:00 this morning.

Parliament's business for the day, Thursday, 16th March 1978, was public knowledge, but only he fully grasped what had gone into ensuring that it had *actually* reached Parliament.

It had been he, and he alone, who had brokered this deal between Christian Democracy and the Italian Communist Party, the largest and most powerful Communist party in Western Europe. No one else had danced, sung and acted as he had through the long and sometimes operatic set-changes that were Italian politics. Italy, his Italy, would be the first Western alliance country to treat with 'Eurocommunism', an ideal that promised to eschew closed-door excesses, and to be acceptable and independent, and sport the fresh smile of liberalism. 'Eurocommunists' did not wear the dour, craggy and bearded expressions of those who hailed from the cold steppes of the USSR.

In the bleak aftermath of the Second World War, Moro had dreamed of uniting the two parties. Not even the Americans, who had long viewed

Moro's ideals – and the man himself – as an enemy, had been able to scupper this alliance, try as they might. America's Cold War credo held that the Italian Communist party was, *'at all costs'*, to be kept out of any Italian government. Unwanted, ill-advised and dogmatic interventions by the Americans had only helped Moro's cause; only two months ago, on 12th January 1978, President Carter's spokesman announced that: *'The US State Department would like to see the Communists hold less power, not more,'* and on the 6th February 1978, US NATO Commander General Alexander Haig stated: *'Highly sensitive military information within the framework of the NATO Alliance would be endangered if the Communists gained power in Italy.'* A few days later, Henry Kissinger had leaked falsehoods that Moro himself was in the eye of the storm of the 'Lockheed Aircraft Bribes' scandal. In fact, Moro was expecting to read his name again in connection with the bribes, paid by Lockheed, this very morning.

"To hell with Carter and the damned Americans. Today is my day," he said aloud as the water ran like a waterfall over his thickset body.

CHAPTER 3

No. 79, via del Forte Trionfale,
the Camilluccia district, Rome, Italy.
Thursday, 16th March 1978. 08:55.

"*Ciao*, Papà!" shouted Giovanni Moro.

Aldo Moro waved at his son, who hurriedly kickstarted his motorcycle. Despite being twenty years old, Giovanni was terrified of dentists and that was why he was running late.

Sunlight fingered its way through the surrounding green of the pine trees in the driveway and Moro, usually a punctual man, was an apprehensive five minutes early. He detected a complacency in his security detail. Sighing, he tossed his grey homburg onto the back seat of his dark blue Fiat 130 and climbed in.

He tapped an affectionate *Buongiorno* on the left shoulder of Domenico Ricci, his driver. Ricci, a plainclothes paramilitary officer in the Carabinieri, was forty-three and had been with Moro since he was twenty-five, when Moro had formed his first government in 1964. He was of peasant stock, as were all of Moro's five-man squad. They all felt safe protecting him, and the old Italian saying that '*no one ever touches the truly mighty*' was lore. Besides, if anyone did try, there were three police bodyguards, with an arsenal of Italian machine guns – Beretta M12s – locked in the boot of the cream-coloured Alfa Romeo Alfetta escort car, which always followed Moro's larger dark blue Fiat 130 saloon.

Oreste Leonardi sat beside Ricci. Known to his colleagues as 'Judo', he was also Carabinieri paramilitary. Leonardi had headed up Moro's security for fifteen years and was known as 'The President's Shadow'. Muscular and dependable, but at fifty-two early retirement had its attractions.

"Let's go," announced Moro impatiently.

Leonardi and Ricci looked at each other and nodded blankly at their boss. Both men disliked Moro's official Fiat 130 saloon and cursed it daily. They – and neither man had ever quite worked out who 'they' were – had taken far too long with the manufacture of Moro's new and bulletproof car; Leonardi had been informed there were *'inexplicable delays'*. How was a man supposed to guard one of the great post-war Western leaders if he didn't have the right equipment? And this regular Fiat 130 simply wasn't up to the demands of the job in today's troubled Italy.

More than three weeks had gone by since Leonardi had filed a report of suspicious activities outside the Moro family home, activities that had followed a warning issued by the Red Brigades terrorists: *'Our No. 1 Enemy is the personnel of the Christian Democracy party...'* Yet no one seemed to care apart from him, Ricci and of course Signora Moro.

Leonardi steeled himself with the knowledge that it was only a twenty-minute drive to parliament, and behind him was the unmarked Alfa Romeo escort car, driven by Giulio Rivera. His walkie-talkie continued to crackle. He switched it off and lowered the window.

"Giulio, Giulio," Leonardi shouted, "my walkie-talkie isn't working. Santa Chiara as usual. OK?"

"*Si*, Judo," Rivera replied.

The two other bodyguards, Raffaelle Iozzino and Francesco Zizzi, both young, and with swarthy southern features, looked at Leonardi from the Alfa Romeo. It was Zizzi's first day on the prestigious Moro detail and everything was unfamiliar. But Iozzino knew that whichever one of Moro's four offices he would attend, the day would begin with twenty minutes of private worship at the Church of Santa Chiara.

The church, a modern brick confection, was only four minutes' drive away from the pine and cypress trees of Moro's courtyard. As with Moro's prayers, the route from his home to the church had barely changed in fifteen years. Both drivers, Moro's Ricci and the Alfetta's Rivera, could have driven them blindfolded; and except for the closure of the ritzy Olivetti Bar, the scenery never seemed to change.

CHAPTER 4

**Crossroads of via Fani and via Stresa,
the Camilluccia district, Rome, Italy.
Thursday, 16th March 1978. 08:58.**

Spiriticchio had begun the task of buying four new tyres when three cars parked adjacent to his corner 'patch' at the STOP signs on via Fani and via Stresa.

On the via Stresa side of the intersection, a blue Fiat 128 was parked. A slender young woman who wore faded jeans, with long hair which fell either side of her large round glasses, sat beside a tall man, who wore a green Loden coat. Together they talked as the car ticked over in neutral. Fifty metres behind was Mario Moretti, the leader of the Red Brigades, who sat in a white Fiat 128 Estate car on fake diplomatic number plates.

On the via Fani side of the intersection, a white Mini Minor Estate car was also parked. Opposite Spiriticchio's 'patch', beside the unkempt flower pots of the closed Olivetti Bar, stood four men, two of whom had alighted, at about 08:40, from a fourth car, a dark blue saloon, a four door Fiat 132, which was parked *against* the oncoming traffic flow.

Each of the four men at the intersection were dressed in Alitalia uniforms. They wore braided caps and carried Alitalia flight bags. One held his cap in his hand, while the youngest fidgeted with his collar; it could have been an excess of starch or even a flurry of pre-flight nerves? None of the four men appeared out of the ordinary.

Further down the via Fani, the news vendor's son sat on a stool beside the kiosk and read a football comic. He too was unaware of a Honda motorbike and yet another car, a white Fiat 128 saloon, in which two other men sat.

No one, not even the couple who were walking their dog took any heed of the eleven strangers, multiple stolen cars and one motorcycle in their midst. Unbeknownst to all, the telephone lines in the immediate area had been cut, and several trucks were spread out, their engines idling, all ready to run interference and block the main arterial roads should any Carabinieri reinforcements arrive. The only person to look up when Aldo Moro's modest motorcade sped down the via Fani was the news vendor's son, momentarily glancing up from his football comic.

CHAPTER 5

**Crossroads of via Fani and via Stresa,
the Camilluccia district, Rome, Italy.
Thursday, 16th March 1978. 09:03.**

From the first second, when the woman with the large round glasses slammed her blue Fiat 128 into reverse and drove straight across the via Fani and via Stresa junction and crashed into the bonnet of Moro's oncoming Fiat 130, the entire – precision – operation took less than 180 seconds. Moretti's white Fiat 128 Estate rammed Moro's car from behind and blocked the Alfa Romeo Alfetta with its three bodyguards.

The woman and the man in the green Loden coat, leaped out of their car spraying bullets at Moro's driver. Ricci and Leonardi were killed instantly. Fourteen bullet holes peppered their bodies. They died slumped across each other. The submachine pistol shots were an immaculately rehearsed crossfire drill; other than an insignificant thigh wound – from a ricochet – Moro was unharmed.

Two of the 'pilots' executed the three bodyguards in the unmarked Alfetta using the same methods. Rivera died whilst the new man Zizzi was mortally wounded. Iozzino was able to draw his pistol and fire off two rounds, blindly. The Honda motorcycle pulled up alongside the Alfetta, and the rider calmly put a bullet in the back of Iozzino's skull; he later died in hospital.

In the hurricane of lead coming from the Italian FNAB-43 and Beretta M12 weapons, the two other 'pilots' grabbed Aldo Moro – their timing was also split second rehearsed – and rammed him into the footwell of the waiting dark blue, four-door, Fiat 132 saloon parked in front of the Olivetti Bar.

All around Spiriticchio's flower 'patch' was death and ghostly silence. Stonework and cars were acned from the ninety-one bullets loosed off by the assassins. Spent brass casings and submachine gun magazines littered the ground. An Alitalia flight bag lay upended with one of the 'pilot's' caps. Shallow rivers of gore found their own course through the carnage and debris of bodies and smashed cars.

Sheaves of unread newsprint from the back seat of Moro's car fluttered across the streets like outsize butterflies. Both Moro's briefcase and his grey homburg lay on the tarmac battleground like the destroyed totems of a nation that they were.

Only when someone noticed that the security detail's new man, Zizzi, was still just about breathing was the alarm was sounded. Too late for Zizzi. Too late for Moro. And to no avail.

Apart from the coincidence of an ex-policeman eyewitness, who attempted to give chase, the kidnapping assassins getaway was as flawlessly executed as Moro's abduction and the murder of all his five-man security detail.

The kidnapper's dark blue Fiat 132 saloon, with Moro in its rear footwell, turned left at high speed off the via Fani and into via Stresa, followed by the other cars. A few hundred metres away all the getaway cars, and an ex-policeman pursuer, were caught by a red traffic light on a pedestrian crossing outside the Church of San Francesco.

For nearly as long as the entire operation took – less than three minutes, it was all over by 09:05.

Aldo Moro's hard-fought coalition between his Christian Democracy and the Italian Communist Party could not, and would not, be signed at 10:00 that morning as had been planned. The historic pact could not, and would not, become enshrined in law without him.

At 10:00, Pietro Ingrao, president of the Italian Chamber of Deputies, closed the parliamentary session, announcing that Aldo Moro had been kidnapped. Which meant that his formal DC/PCI coalition wouldn't be inked by either party. Prime Minister Giulio Andreotti, due to the emergency, would hastily pass a vote in the afternoon denying the Enrico Berlinguer's Italian Communist Party any role in the new coalition Italian Government Andreotti would now form. The Americans also had the result they so desperately wanted: a communist-free NATO government.

The Red Brigades, and those to whom they ultimately answered, finally had their prize.

CHAPTER 6

**No. 5, Largo Claudio Treves,
the Brera District, Milan, Italy.
Thursday, 16th March 1978. 09:20.**

Pietro Albassi wiped his hand across the mirror and looked at himself through rivulets of condensation. He had weathered the storms of big-city ageing well. His not-so-classical Sicilian features had survived Milan's tension, bustle and grime. He tugged at his right eyelid to check just how far the tiredness went. It went all the way down to his soul. He'd been putting in too many hours of late. But this morning, he had no appointments, and decided to take some time off, a rare occurrence for him.

He was a hard-working, mid-level lawyer at Scampidi & Rusconi, a highly respected Milan law firm. Defending criminals was his forte. He liked his criminals more than his employer, a conundrum which rarely troubled him, for Scampidi & Rusconi redefined the meaning of autocratic it was, in truth, a tyrannical place to work. There had never been an Avvocato Rusconi, there had only ever been Dottore Enrico Scampidi.

In his mid-seventies, Dottore Scampidi had written not only The Bible, but the Italian Constitution as well, or so he believed. 'Ask' was not a word he ever used: tell, order, command and demand were his four rules. There wasn't any spectrum of Italian business, political or religious life (and they were so intertwined as to be identical triplets) that Dottore Scampidi didn't dominate as an *éminence grise*. Thankfully, Pietro and his secretary, Angelica, were left alone to ensure that even the truly guilty were set free. That was the high bar the *dottore* had set Avvocato Pietro Albassi on the first day of his employment, fresh from his years at UniMi, the renowned University of Milan.

Pietro soaped the shaving brush and studied his face, one that had been bred in adversity for adversity. The Sicilian world he had been born into was not one where love, or anything else for that matter, rights wrongs. And it showed. His forehead was prematurely lined, resembling a clenched fist. He had a weathered and olive-tanned complexion from the scorched earth that was his Sicilian DNA, and perhaps his age too; he still couldn't believe he was going to be thirty-four in September. His black hair was as slick as a raven's. Salt white flashes streaked lightly at his temples, like those of a badger, emphasising the depth of his lake-green eyes. He frowned. He rubbed the deep scar scalloped above his left eye where the American bullet – fired by a Sicilian – had struck him in the San Cipirello massacre, back in August 1950, one week before his sixth birthday. Apart from being the only survivor that day, the Parcae, the Sicilian Fates, had further blessed him, for they had led the wounded boy into the arms of the Salaviglia family who had nurtured him; he grew up as if he were a scion, not an orphan.

Pietro's left eye had a faint milk-hue and a permanently dilated pupil, evidence that he was 100 per cent blind in this eye. But it was a small burden after all that he had been given by the 14th Duke of Salaviglia after the massacre. Wounded and blinded, the duke had taken him away from the orphanage to grow up at Castello Bonnera, on their vast estates in the west of Sicily, with Victor, the duke's only child. The duke had raised him and protected him, and taught him the ways of the world. He educated him and cared for him just as he had his son Victor. Being the same age, the boys became as inseparable as twins. Aged eighteen, the 14th Duke had astutely despatched Pietro north to Milan to study law. Victor remained in Sicily to live his preordained life as the future 15th Duke. Pietro knew that the west of Sicily was no place for a young, and orphaned, man to prosper.

He grabbed his robe and pulled it tightly around his athletic 6'1" body, and headed out to the kitchen for a cappuccino, and to catch the morning news. Same old, same old he suspected. These were the *anni di piombo* – the years of lead – so, which city had the terrorists struck this time?

He slid the kitchen door open, fired up his old Gaggia coffee machine, and smiled his open smile. This morning was to be a rare few hours where he could enjoy the company of his beloved wife, Ruxandra, with his mutt Enzo, now that their eight-year-old twins were at school. They could both relax and all would be tranquil at their home. He clicked on the radio.

Like all of Italy, and most of the free world, he could never have conceived of what he would hear.

CHAPTER 7

The Vatican State.
Thursday, 16th March 1978. 09:40.

The view of the Piazza San Pietro from Alessandro Cuci's office was superlative. Ignoring the looming presence of the largest church in the world, the Basilica San Pietro, it was the chemistry of the stone, and the artists who had built it, which gave it an unidentifiable something he could never quite come to terms with.

Cuci was the definition of a paradox; he was two truths that were forever in competition. He both despised and marvelled at his incredible view. So what if Caligula and Nero had turned the Piazza into their own personal circus ring? Did anyone really care that its central obelisk bore witness to St Peter's crucifixion? No, of course not.

Cuci walked the tightrope between savagery and civilisation. He was feral and ice-blooded, yet also an extraordinarily civilised man. The atheist that he was, he saw no reason whatsoever why St Peter should have insisted on being crucified upside down. (Jesus Christ, right way up – St Peter, wrong way down. Martyrdom was martyrdom. Dead was dead. Surely?) All that did stir his stone heart were Michelangelo's walls. The Holy See, the Universal Government of the Vatican City, all forty-nine hectares of it, with a population of 700 or so souls were all, in effect, that held him. Too true the old Roman saying, *'Faith is made here and believed elsewhere'*. The Holy See and the Vatican State were, he reminded himself, his personal fiefdom across the Tiber.

Cuci spoke seven languages fluently, and dressed the same each day: a single button, single-breasted shadow-blue tailored suit, each cut in three different weights of cloth for the changing seasons. His crisp white Egyptian cotton shirts – cutaway collars only – were made for him in Naples, as were his black silk knitted ties and black calfskin loafers.

Nothing varied, not even his simple platinum cufflinks, or his platinum Patek Philippe Calatrava watch. Cuci had his own aesthetic and it never changed. His love of Russian literature didn't change either; and on rare, dark days he would read the classics in Cyrillic as a sop.

Apart from a handful of chosen staff, no one had such a commanding and awe-inspiring view; not even Their Eminences, who lived in the old servants' quarters of the Apostolic Palace. It was a panorama that invoked in all, save one Alessandro Cuci, a sense of humility, of one's true position in His scheme of things. But at just forty-one years of age, it couldn't intoxicate him the way a heady Tuscan wine did as he lay in his lover's arms. The view, however, did make him feel as if he commanded the universe, and not just the Vatican's *Istituto per le Opere Esteriore*, the Institute of External Affairs, the IEA.

During the six years that he had been its head, he had, in his Machiavellian way, turned the IEA into his own political machine, his own financial hub and subsequently an incomparable and altogether sinister powerbase.

There were more than 750 million Roman Catholics in the world, a goodly percentage of whom had a vote in the democratic world: no one from the slums of South America, to Capitol Hill, to the parliamentary offices in Rome, and all via *his* Vatican State, dared challenge the IEA's wishes, silences or secrets.

Cuci possessed two of the rare attributes a man of power must be endowed with: a position of true global influence while maintaining almost total invisibility. Out of sight, unphotographed, hidden from a world even as he shaped it. Members of the Curia whispered that the IEA had become God's Left Hand. So much so that Cuci's superior, the Cardinal Secretary of the Vatican State, trotted behind Cuci's heels like a mute lapdog.

It was a historic day, with Moro being kidnapped. Cuci knew the truth, of course. And he was now set to become his own *éminence grise* in his own state, one that wasn't confined to the Vatican. The thought delighted him, for he had just received the confirmation telephone call he had been waiting for: Licio Gelli had just telephoned him from the Hotel Excelsior, sixty metres from the US Embassy, where P2 members had been meeting in secret. Gelli was the Venerable Master of Propaganda Due, P2, aka the Frati Neri – the Black Friars – the most powerful fascist and clandestine Masonic Lodge in Italy – and counted the heads of all three Italian intelligence agencies as members. Gelli had confirmed to Cuci that, "the most difficult part is done…"

Beaming at the good news, he toyed with his goatee, and then fidgeted with his tie. He had two telephone calls to make following Gelli's news.

* * *

"*Pronto!*"

"*Ciao*, Enrico. How's the weather in Milan?" Cuci asked.

"Why are you always concerned about the weather, Alessandro? It's so English," Enrico Scampidi said. "What's the news?"

"Licio called to tell me what I already knew," replied Cuci, "that the weather here in Rome is pleasant indeed."

"OK, you win. Good news I take it. So, what do you require, Alessandro?"

Cuci let a silence come between them. He'd known Dottore Enrico Scampidi for many years. A fellow P2 member, he was vehemently anti-communist down to his expensive bootstraps; it was all he had in common with the CIA. The *dottore* was a highly capable, snake-like Milan lawyer who held more secrets than the cemeteries in Italy, who was as infamous as he was renowned. A political and financial fixer who'd dodged all manner of scandals over decades with footwork so deft he made Fred Astaire look like a drunk. Cuci required a favour, but he didn't want to be in Scampidi's debt. However, he had no choice. He had to turn to the maestro.

"Please Alessandro, I'm busy. What do you need? It must be important for you to call me at such a time."

"I want a go-between."

"Can't the IEA find one? You know very well I'll require a quid pro quo."

"Of course." Cuci took a deep breath. "In the meantime, here's what's needed, Enrico. A cut-out who can operate as a go-between amongst the following: the Red Brigades. Andreotti. The Communists. The Moro family. The Christian Democrats. The Press. The IEA. He – no women please – must have credibility with most, if not all, of them. He'll report directly to you, and you'll report back to me. A difficult request I appreciate."

"That's a tall order. Why do you want such a person?"

"To know what all the players are thinking, all of the time. I'm the one dealing with CIA in this joint operation, and I must be one step ahead of them."

"That makes sense," replied Scampidi, matter-of-factly. "I'll consider it and we'll speak before lunch. *Ciao*." Scampidi ended the call without further ado. He didn't like Alessandro Cuci, in fact he didn't know *anyone* who did, but Scampidi held him, and his IEA, in very high esteem. Cuci was the most dangerous, ruthless man he'd ever met. And he'd met and worked with them all.

* * *

It was the middle of the night in Virginia, USA, but Cuci just couldn't help himself. He dialled the US. His winter-grey eyes, like those of a husky, mean and unblinking, searched out the last four digits from his diary. Finally, the line crackled and echoed.

"When are you returning to Rome?" Cuci asked crisply.

There was a grunt and then a pause.

"It's 3.30 in the mornin'!"

The voice, a weighty Lone Star drawl, was thick with sleep.

"When are you returning to Rome? The weather is lovely here," Cuci repeated.

"End of the week. Everythin' OK?" The question was calmly rhetorical, but the voice alert.

"Yes, *tutto bene*, and thanks to you, all went fine. Call me on my secure line when you get to Langley. There's one detail I think we could finesse. Sleep well Judd."

Cuci replaced the receiver and smiled at his own impertinence. The call could easily have waited until a civilised hour, but he enjoyed waking one of the CIA's most powerful station heads at an ungodly hour. All morning the echo of his late grandfather's voice in the walled garden of his tumbleweed Umbrian palazzo had been ricocheting in his mind. As an only child – of an only child – and from a family with more pedigree than wealth, he had paid great attention when his grandfather cautioned him. And this morning he couldn't shake off his Nonno's nudging words: "*Alessandro, the lemons always ripen before the cherries. If a fruit is going to go bad, it usually does so quickly.*"

* * *

Judd Barings fisted his pillow and cussed in heavy Southern tones. The finest agents he'd ever worked with had been assigned to this operation, not men who couldn't hit the ground with their own hats. Of course it'd gone to plan; CIA had used their best. Unbeknownst to Cuci, he'd stationed two agents, astride Vespas, on via Fani to be his eyes and ears.

What he didn't want was a jumped-up, pint-sized wop telling him what he already knew. Christ, what the hell did Cuci think this operation was? It wasn't exactly Martin Luther King. If this was a real big deal, he'd have been awake *and* in Italy. So, what was the purpose of the darned call? The first rule of any conspiracy, is y'all don't *ever* talk about the conspiracy.

OK, the target was Aldo Moro, Italy's Commie lovin' head politico, but that was in itself no problem. He knew Texan businessmen with better personal security than Moro. Besides, this was not a coup. No, there really had been nothing to worry about.

"Really, Alex?" Barings grumbled, "it's yer Red Brigades that are going to kill him, y'all just keep to yer end o' the deal."

Usually, neither the Cuci's nor the Moro's of this world caused Barings to lose one minute of sleep. The only thing that ever did was a pretty girl, and she had to be hotter than a June bride in a feather bed. And where he came from, they dressed in short skirts and purred husky bourbon breath too. Now partially awake, he began to recall in detail the conversation he'd had at Langley with CIA Director Admiral Stansfield Turner.

Turner had blown nonchalantly into a steaming mug of black coffee. His tone held contempt for anyone other than his superiors. In this case, there was only one such person. Number 39. President James Earl Carter Jr.

"Judd, tell me about Alessandro Cuci."

"Cuci thinks the sun comes up just to hear him crow, sir."

"Please, Judd, the Confederate drawl is hard enough, but your colloquialisms are beyond me."

"Well sir, he sure has a high opinion of hisself. He's as timid as Napoleon, has the hide of an armadillo, the blood of a polar bear, an' lies like a tombstone." Barings' deep Southern accent – part Texas, part Louisiana, part Alabama – sounded exaggerated in the Director's seventh floor office. "The man's darned ruthless an' dangerous, like an army of Texan fire ants. But more important, Mr Director, intel-wise Cuci could find a whisper in a whirlwind."

Turner knew why he instinctively liked Judd Barings. However garbled, he received accurate opinions from a highly skilled CIA field agent, not the usual blather.

"When I was appointed director last year, I took over from Director George H.W. Bush, who had, and still has, a strong anti-communist approach. Director Bush was a militant director, and he'd just started a policy of funding General Noriega down in Panama. Noriega's a thug, and Bush showered him with money and support. The reason I'm telling you this, is that I've inherited just *half* of Bush's allies, but I'm landed with *all* of his enemies. So, what I'm saying is that Cuci had better be good, I've got enough enemies out there already. You understand me?"

"Sure do, Mr Director. Y'all want me to keep him on a tight leash?"

"Precisely, Judd. I'm not Director Bush. I'm US Navy, more of a 'good hound-dog, good hound-dog' man." He paused. "So I always carry a big stick." The director's brow creased with anxiety. Barings knew to remain silent. "This is one of those rare occasions when the US State Department agrees with a CIA report. Like the General Noriega anti-communist policy which Bush stuck me with, I'm now stuck with Cuci and the IEA. Let me remind you of what Director Bush said only last year: *'We are making sufficiently alarmist assessments of Soviet might, and that no Communist is going to form any part of any government coalition in Italy, however small, because the Italian Communist Party poses a threat.'* Turner swigged his coffee before continuing. "All this is according to the Bush CIA and US State Department. Director Bush was open about what had to happen to Moro. This is NATO Italy for Christ's sakes! It's not a mosquito-infested swamp with a ditch in it called Panama. Judd, you keep me closely informed on this operation."

The tape replayed with Barings now pop-eyed awake, and that ticked him off big time. He liked his sleep, and there was no slumbering, foxy redhead he could stir into life to help take his febrile mind back into a deep sleep.

CHAPTER 8

The Vatican State.
Thursday, 16th March 1978. 12:05.

The intercom buzzed. Cuci stabbed the flashing button. Who now?

"I have Dottore Scampidi for you," announced Angelo, Cuci's PA, with more trepidation than normal. The telephone lines had been fizzing red-hot since the Moro news had broken two hours ago. Angelo's end of shift – he was one of two PAs – was still six, dauntingly long, hours away. He clicked the call straight through.

"The weather has cleared up in Milan before you ask," chuckled Scampidi impishly, before continuing. "I've given your request quite some thought, Alessandro. I've circled the globe and I've found a good solution. Right at my front door too."

"I'm listening," Cuci replied eagerly; he'd been waiting for Scampidi's call.

"For what you require, I decided to look outside all the normal channels. So, no P2 associates, no law-enforcement officers, no politicians, no priests, no bankers. What you need is an ingenue and a virgin. No one we've ever used before. I've a lawyer in mind. Better still, he works for me."

"Go on," interrupted Cuci.

"His name is Pietro Albassi. Sicilian by birth and lives here in Milan where he went to university. He's in his mid-thirties, married with two young children, twins, and he's worked for me since he graduated." Scampidi let a beat pass. "Here's the main reason why I like him for this role. Albassi is a criminal lawyer – he's a worker, thorough, skilled and the only criminal lawyer in my office. About two years ago he defended two Red Brigades *brigatisti* after a shooting in Turin. Both were as guilty as the original sin, but on a corkscrew-like technicality Albassi got them both off. Of all the parties you need information from, the Red Brigades are going to be the hardest. Albassi has an 'in', as well as their trust, after the Turin verdict. The Red Brigades believe Albassi can feed 5,000 with two fish and a handful of *grissini*."

"Anything else I should know, Enrico? What about his personality? Weak points? Strong points?" Cuci asked in measured tones as he wrote copious notes. Much hinged on the intel this person was going to relay to his fellow Freemason.

"Albassi was born an orphan in 1944. His mother died in childbirth. Father unknown, rumoured to have been a US soldier. The Salaviglia family raised him as their own, until the 14th Duke sent him north to university here in Milan. Again, all on Salaviglia's lire."

"What would the Salaviglias be doing with a Sicilian orphan?"

"You know of the family, Alessandro. They believe they're responsible for anything and everything that happens on their lands. Been like that for centuries. Don't forget, the Salaviglias were in Sicily when the Normans invaded in the eleventh century. Albassi was shot in the San Cipirello massacre back in 1950 when he was a child, which explains his scar, and the fact he's blind in his left eye. There's no part of the west of Sicily the Salaviglia's don't rule over, so looking after him after he was shot would have been a debt of honour. Also, Albassi is the same age as the old duke's only child, Victor – the next, and the 15th Duke. They grew up together on the Bonnera estates," concluded Scampidi.

"The Salaviglias have held all the *real* power in Sicily for centuries, Enrico," replied Cuci. "In 1810, King Ferdinand decreed that any boar-poacher caught in the forests around his Ficuzza hunting lodge, would have both their hands amputated – on the spot – by his soldiers. Most died of shock straight away. The Salaviglia's far larger estates bordered the king's, and the wily duke, I forget which one, immediately pronounced that any *paesano* who hunted on Salaviglia lands got to keep not only the boar – but their hands too – and were able to feed their families. So, for the sake of some wild boar, the entire west of Sicily became forever a loyal Salaviglia dominion. Not even the Mafia dare go near their estates. They're sovereign." Cuci, a mine of historical knowledge, finished by saying, "O, you *are* a lucky man, Albassi, to have had the Salaviglias as guardians, and I like lucky men, Enrico. Bravo." Cuci paused. "Other than his wife and children what are Albassi's weaknesses? Mistresses? Boys? Girls? Drugs? Hookers? Gambling? Everyone has skeletons."

"No, happily married by all accounts. He's a loner, but well liked here. He's not social. Doesn't travel. He's clever, diligent and has an instinct, a feel, too. I witnessed that in the Turin case. He persuaded me to take it pro bono, only because of the legal twist in the case. I suspect he is apolitical too."

"OK, so, who will he liaise with at Christian Democracy? Andreotti is already on side and he's not going to let up on Moro now, so much for his party loyalty."

"Good. That makes my Christian Democracy contact Tina Anselmi an excellent pick. Andreotti promoted her to Health Minister five days ago and she has his ear. She's anti-P2 and she told him so when he promoted her. So, Alessandro, tell me who one of Anselmi's best friends is?"

"It's my place to know, but I confess I don't," Cuci replied.

"None other than Eleanora Moro."

"You have done your homework. *Grazie*. Who's in the crosshairs at the Communist Party?"

"You'll like this. No one."

"What?!" exclaimed Cuci.

"Calm down, young man. Think laterally."

"I am. Who is it then?"

"Their paymasters of course. The Soviets. There's nothing the Communist Party doesn't pass on to Moscow via their embassy in Rome. I have a senior contact in the Soviet Consulate here in Milan, and a KGB colonel in Rome."

"All the bases seem covered, Enrico. No more than I'd expect," stated Cuci.

"It's my job. I'm your counsel after all." Scampidi chose his words carefully. "This service is going to cost you and the IEA at some point, a fact you're already aware of, Alessandro. The CIA are your affair, they're your partners. Don't ask me for help, you won't get it."

"I'll manage the CIA. I've been working with the head of their Rome Station for some time."

"To conclude. I'll hand Albassi the task as soon as I put the phone down and certainly before he leaves for home. I'll personally ensure that I pass the fruits of his labours to you. He'll only report to me, as I will to you. So, *ciao*, Alessandro."

The line went dead. Used to having the final word, Cuci was more than prepared to let Scampidi have it this time. This Pietro Albassi sounded the perfect candidate for what he had in mind. Bravo Enrico, he thought as he slowly replaced the receiver.

* * *

"*Pronto*, Avvocato Albassi's office. How may I help?" Angelica Cortone saw the call was coming from Dottore Scampidi's office.

"Tell him to stop what he's doing and have him come to my office right away. I have an urgent new, complex dossier for him." The line clicked off before she could inform him he was engaged with a client.

Angelica reflected what had just happened. She was Albassi's gatekeeper, and he was in a meeting with another in the steady stream of criminals – from lowlife thieves to highlife fraudsters – who came through her office. They were his clients and it was her job to protect them as well.

Avvocato Pietro Albassi only acted for the criminal fraternity, and was fiercely successful at his job. He was a legal defender and he never judged. Guilty or innocent, it didn't matter to him, and that was, perhaps, one of his secret constituents. That, and hard work. Angelica decided, from the *dottore*'s obvious impatience and tone that whatever it was the *dottore* wanted to see 'her' *avvocato* about was not going to be good news; he had mentioned a 'complex dossier', not a 'case' or a 'client' as he usually would. She took her powder compact from her handbag, patted her flushed cheeks and elected to disobey the *dottore*'s bullying command until the meeting was over. Whenever that might be.

* * *

Alessandro Cuci decided he would lunch alone and in his office; the only distractions he wished for were those of his own making. His favourite seventeenth-century French theologian, Blaise Pascal, had said, "All of humanity's problems stem from man's inability to sit quietly in a room, *alone*."

Today he needed quiet, and to be alone. It was not a day to be spoiled by inconsequential talk. Besides, he had to speak with Barings later. And very soon, there wouldn't be a single shepherd in the Apennines who didn't know every detail of what had taken place at 09:05 this morning in Rome.

Delaying the gratification of ordering his lunch, Cuci rearranged his desk: a small silver frame with a black and white picture of his faithful wife, a Morocco bound English-Italian dictionary, a solid piece of nineteenth-century ivory from Cameroon sculpted into a crocodile – it was his paperweight – and beside it an out-of-place proprietary blotter, and a priceless jewel-encrusted seventeenth-century silver goblet that had once belonged to Pope Innocent X was full, of all things, with sharpened Blackwing HB pencils. Having inched his sparse possessions into a form of symmetry that satisfied him, he buzzed his outer office.

"No calls whatsoever, Angelo. Bring me a salad, a *penne arrabiata* and a half bottle of chilled red Burgundy at 12:45. Sharp." Cuci released the button and didn't wait for a response.

Slowly, he rearranged all the notes, arrows, question marks, connecting the lines he had jotted down during his conversation with Scampidi. When they were in chronological order, he wrote at the top in bold, black ink: 'ALBASSI, Pietro'.

He then settled deep into his chair to read, and to *'sit quietly in a room alone and decide which part of Albassi was a lemon and which was a cherry'*, knowing full well that one couldn't pick cherries with one's back to the tree.

By the time Barings returned his call, his thoughts would all be in order. Playing God was a cheerful pastime for Alessandro Cuci.

PART TWO

CHAPTER 9

**No. 5, Largo Claudio Treves,
the Brera District, Milan, Italy.
Thursday, 30th March 1978. 06:10.
Two weeks after Moro's kidnap.**

"Air rat time," Pietro whispered to himself as he crept out of the bedroom. Ruxandra, who slept the sleep of the righteous, breathed calmly. He smiled at her like a brother would a sister. Their relationship was no longer one of fire, but one of deep love and profound friendship. He had grown up in Sicily knowing that harmony and passion rarely coexist, while she had learned early that love was so easily confiscated. However, it was the necessity of each other, of filling each other's void, that was their currency. Now, alone and stranded on the barbed wire of Moro's kidnap, he was too preoccupied to recognise that she was the only friend he had.

Pietro dressed quickly, and for a few heartbeats longer than usual, he lingered to gaze at her again; even her name was like a lover's whisper. He needed to take courage from her gentle curves before he crept along the bedroom corridor where Paola and Salvatore dozed on.

Unlike his wife, he was an anxious sleeper and always the first to wake. He cherished the solitude of dawn. Ever since his involvement in Moro's kidnap had been wreaked upon him by Dottore Scampidi, his solitary rituals had returned some normality back into his strained life. Silently, he cursed his conniving boss for forcing this hateful job into his life. Pietro had used all his not inconsiderable courtroom wiles to decline the *dottore*'s direct, and bullying, orders on the very afternoon Moro had been kidnapped. All his Sicilian instincts told him to walk away, but all of his entreaties had bypassed Scampidi's fancy hearing aids and he was having none of it. He'd been firmly placed on the 'down escalator' that afternoon. He was a criminal defence lawyer, and a very good one, and he missed his crooks. Political intrigue was a big players game, not one for bit players like him.

Pietro reached the kitchen sporting an impatient smile. Enzo waited excitedly in his basket, sensing his master's footsteps. There was no recognisable pedigree – or known age – for the short-legged ten-kilogram mutt with fox-like striped fur and a looped tail. The dog was part dependable VW, part temperamental Fiat, part zippy Lancia, part curvy Alfa Romeo, and when it was cold or raining, a wholly defunct Vespa. The only Ferrari part of Enzo was his name, that and his astronomical speed and cornering skills when chasing Milanese pigeons. Pietro scooped him up in his arms, grabbed his worn Zippo and a pack of yellow corn-paper Gitanes, and headed for the roof and the pigeons, his air-rats.

They lived on the top 6th floor of a classical nineteenth-century apartment building in the unfashionable neighbourhood that was the Brera District. Their home was a patrician affair indeed, and the Albassi family cherished it. No. 5, Largo Claudio Treves was the largest building in the confluence of streets that formed Largo Claudio Treves into a miniature garden square, with a solitary hackberry tree and several wooden benches. The stone balconies were all filled with colourful flowerboxes that gelled with its faded yellow masonry, and behind the two outsized oak front doors, there was a small cobblestone courtyard. The hunched caretaker, Cesare, passed the daylight hours endlessly polishing brass door handles and sweeping the courtyard, pausing only to sift the residents' mail into their pigeonholes. He rarely set foot outside – the fear of being a wartime deserter had never left him – and he had been No. 5's resident caretaker since Italy's surrender in 1943.

Pietro's fifteen minutes on the large flat roof in the grey light of Milan's dawn with only his thoughts, a slow-burning cigarette and Enzo for company, was the *real* start of his day. He had a view of the city's disjointed limbs stirring, its soul and energy accelerating into the day ahead. A northerner now, but the Sicilian country boy lived on in his heart-of-hearts, and it was more out of an old Sicilian tradition that he continued to feed the pigeons who nested in the rudimentary coop he'd fashioned. Enzo, with the slow-beating heart of Fangio's Maserati, stared with hunter's eyes at the pigeons. These pigeons were his master's and must therefore never be chased. Stared down, yes. Hunted, no. Even Enzo knew that these flying vermin he loved to menace belonged not only in his master's life, but in the city's too.

Milan and pigeons were ideally suited and Pietro found solace in the purity of their scavenging greed, amoral behaviour and meaningless squawks. These were not like Sicilian pigeons. Their complete disregard for loyalty – far worse than a cat's, hence Enzo's interest – fascinated him. Ruxandra loathed them. She refused to feed them when Pietro was away. It amused him just how inefficient the Milanese pigeon jungle-drums were. It sometimes took more than a week for them to flock back; neither the drunk's vomit, nor the corn dispensed by gullible tourists in the Piazza del Duomo, were ever in short supply. Rarely, and then only on Milan's dazzling and smog-free summer mornings, would the country boy surface. City-dwelling pigeons weren't good for anything at all, not even shitting on cars.

The first hit of the strong black tobacco reassured Pietro like a true friend. He was, and he knew it, an addict. Calmly, and with a cigarette clenched in the corner of his mouth, its corn paper burning slowly, he broke stale bread around his feet. He watched as the birds gathered, fighting for each crumb. When the supply of bread had been exhausted, the birds retreated sullenly towards their coop, and Enzo peed, disinterestedly, against a chimney stack on the far side of the roof and waited for his master.

Pietro ground his cigarette out on the brickwork, picked up Enzo and shivered as if someone had walked over his grave. Hastily he returned to the warmth of all that he held, and had ever held, true. His family.

**

Pietro pulled up a kitchen stool, which made a scraping noise as he did so. He grimaced. Then, as usual, he flicked the switch on the Gaggia coffee machine. He'd nursed its chipped red enamel in the same manner that he cared for Enzo, and thankfully its loud hisses wouldn't stir the twins – their bedroom was at the end of the long, wood-floored hallway. His cappuccino made, he broke a biscuit in two, dropped a morsel into Enzo's eager mouth and dunked the rest into the froth. He flicked through the previous day's copies of *La Repubblica*, *Corriere della Sera* and the *International Herald Tribune*, tearing out the leader column on Moro in the latter.

In a practised manner he then laid out bowls and cereals, glasses of juice and a jug of fresh milk. Speedily he reached for a sheet of notepaper and sketched a cartoon of a fat cat on it; he lampooned the animal with eyes so crossed the poor thing could not possibly have even seen its own nose. He drew a ridiculously long, striped curly tail around its feet and fashioned its whiskers into plaits simply to make it look even more demented. He named it 'Ubaldo' and scrawled *'Paola and Toto, be good at school, Love Papà xx'*. It was another ritual for the days when he left the apartment before the children were even awake. He liked to think that a smile would help lift their sleepy and reluctant pre-school eyes. What he didn't know was that Paola had kept every single animal cartoon her father had drawn in an old shoebox under her bed.

He patted the Gaggia again. Ruxandra never, ever, drank her espresso, but he knew she loved to wake up to the aroma of fresh coffee, a luxury she hadn't experienced in Romania before she'd met him. And one of his greatest pleasures was spoiling her. He tiptoed into their bedroom, placed the espresso on her bedside table and kissed her, his lips barely touching her forehead. Silently, he mouthed "I love you" before he crept away.

With his slim black briefcase tucked under his arm, he knelt by the door to stroke Enzo's head. He stepped out of their apartment, gently closing the door to take the elevator down to the humourless streets, nodding *buongiorno* at Cesare as he did so. A feeling of contentment came over him when he purchased his newspapers from the vendor in the middle of Largo Claudio Treves, after which he strode twenty more paces to the Il Tabaccaio Cafè in the via Solferino, for a *ristretto* and a leisurely smoke before the ensuing tram or bus ride, complete with their inevitable queues and pickpockets. Through the smoke-stained glass café window, he looked back at No. 5, Largo Claudio Treves. His home and their castle.

With all the turmoil and terror surrounding him, his mind drifted back to Bonnera. What he wouldn't give right now to be sitting with Victor, in the palliative shade of his father's prehistoric olive trees, chatting and playing melodies on their *scacciapensieris*. Sicily had never seemed so very far away.

* * *

"*Ciao*, Mama!" shouted Toto and Paola in unison, and Enzo added his yap too.

Ruxandra heard the lock on the front door slam shut. Her nose twitched like a mouse at the aroma of the cold espresso on her bedside table. This was her favourite time of the day. The apartment was peaceful and the morning light filtered through the curtains. Groggily, she swept her hand underneath Pietro's pillow in search of his T-shirt. Having found it, she drew it close, and inhaled deeply on its fabric. Loving Pietro was consuming, but she wouldn't have it any other way. Today, her mind brimming with their history, she decided Enzo could wait a while for his walk.

She and Pietro had met more than ten years ago at an English seminar at the university in Milan. He was studying Law (specialising in criminal law), English and European Literature, whilst she was immersed in Art History and English. A mutual lust with the swarthy Sicilian, who kept himself very much to himself, had developed instantly. He appeared to be everything she expected a Sicilian to be: demanding at times, yet passive too. He was sensual, funny and compulsive. She had sensed early on that they could both create their own history where there had been none. She felt that he could answer unanswerable questions. And from the day they had met, she had hoped she could do the same for him.

As for Pietro, Milan was her adopted home. She had arrived on a blustery winter's day from Romania. More the exile than the refugee. An outcast of a political and sexual ring that had taken a fatal turn. She had been just fifteen when her parents were mysteriously hustled into one car from their farm in Timişoara, while she was escorted to another. She never saw her parents again. Ever. For three years she didn't see anything apart from the inside of Romania's state and government houses. Didn't feel anything except the chill flesh of sweaty politicians. Didn't smell anything except the dank breath of those who would abuse her.

She, with six other young girls, were passed around like toys in a playground, until one December evening, in a Bucharest blanketed in crisp snow, a youthful Nicu Ceausescu and a corpulent official from Arad, went just too far. The obese official's heart imploded from Ceausescu fils' concoction of American amyl-nitrate, Peruvian cocaine and Irish whiskey.

For a reason she still didn't understand (and had long since given up trying to) she had found herself the following morning being escorted to the Ceausescu's private BAC 1-11 jet. Destination unknown. A little more than two hours later, the aircraft touched down at Milan Linate Airport and its solitary passenger was disembarked by a muscular female flight attendant who handed her two envelopes: one contained an Italian passport, drivers' licence and a new identity, whilst in the other envelope were two centimetres of crisp $100 bills; enough to last several lifetimes in Romania, but barely a year or two in Italy.

The memories had all but faded away. The palette of her life had painted over the greys of hurt and coloured in the white spaces of loss. She liked herself now and the years had been kind too. She was no longer the felix-faced energetic girl who had fallen in love with Pietro. Now aged thirty-two, her pale blue-grey eyes, under arcs of thick, unplucked eyebrows still flashed with confidence. Her fresh, middle-European complexion gave her the charm of seemingly perpetual youth. Although Milanese men were more attracted to her long, bronze hair rather than her tall, taut body. That, and her gravelly voice – one octave below normal and one above hoarse – kept them as curious and playful as Labrador puppies. Yes, life had been kind, maybe too kind, she thought as she nuzzled into Pietro's old T-shirt.

Instantly, and for no reason, she shivered as a familiar fear bit her empty stomach. Her husband's involvement in the Moro affair terrified her. She saw, with her third eye, the stresses and dread being heaped on him every day. Bless him, she thought as she clung to his T-shirt, he tried so hard to camouflage it all, which only made her love him more, if indeed that was even possible. With Pietro she never had to articulate a rising panic. His presence somehow used to soothe it away like a gentle caress. It was as if he could calm the wind and waves. But there was an emptiness in him which frightened her. She'd suspected it had been with him always, and she had been his mother, muse and lover ever since. There was no more she could do; she felt powerless in penetrating the vacuum inside of him. And she knew nature abhorred vacuums.

She shuddered again, threw back the sheets and jumped out of bed. Standing tall, she shouted curses in Romanian about the fallacy of self-fulfilled prophecies.

From the recesses of a childhood corrupted with superstitions and drenched in terrors, she remembered what the gypsies had always said about fearing things too much.

CHAPTER 10

The University of Bologna, Bologna, Italy.
Monday, 3rd April 1978. Lunchtime.

Nineteen days after Aldo Moro, President of the Christian Democracy, had been kidnapped, Romano Prodi, a colleague, paced up and down metronomically on the threadbare rug in his small office at the University of Bologna.

The smug, dull politician without any identifiable charisma – but lashings of self-satisfaction – had a story to tell. And what a story! At thirty-nine he was a centre-left academic tipped for a government ministry before the year was out. If he played his cards right, he would soon be Minister of Trade, Industry and Crafts.

Cautiously, he adjusted his thick black spectacles on his nose. He normally didn't drink at lunchtime, but today was different. Very different. No one would believe his story, of that he was sure. A story of a devout Roman Catholic attending a séance to experiment with a Ouija board? He was almost forty years old, not twelve. Who would believe him? No one.

Prodi's ploy, his story, was just too fanciful for anyone to credit, and it was to be told by a dreary economist. That alone made it preposterous. But what he was about to recount was all his stunted imagination could come up with. Not known for a fecund ingenuity, the only plausible tale he could invent was pure and unadulterated rubbish. It wasn't even a tissue of lies, it was a cashmere blanket of bullshit.

Prodi had thought of telling the truth but dismissed that fanciful notion; he was an Italian politician after all. *'If in doubt, lie,'* was the mantra of his prime minister and mentor, Giulio Andreotti. Andreotti, was now acting president of the Christian Democracy party, whilst Moro was enduring Lord knows what privations at the hands of the Red Brigades.

Prodi reached for the telephone on his desk. Before the red wine's faux courage wore off, he dialled a number in Milan. The phone rang and rang and rang... Prodi gripped the receiver so hard the colour of dead flesh seeped into his knuckles. There was, he grasped, true operatic horror in the newsreel footage he'd seen long ago of a Second World War Italian infantryman juggling a live grenade after he'd inadvertently dislodged the pin.

Prodi looked at the receiver again. It felt like a pin-less grenade in his hands.

CHAPTER 11

**No. 18, via Durini, the Law Offices
of Scampidi & Rusconi, Milan, Italy.
Monday, 3rd April 1978. Lunchtime.**

Pietro Albassi sat behind his desk and stubbed out another cigarette, watching the ash fall to the floor. He *hated* this assignment of being tangled up in a web of political intrigue. He moved his files aside and noticed his *scacciapensieri* – a small harp – played between one's teeth – and hand-sculpted in fine nickel. His was an object of beauty, one of a matching pair, a Salaviglia heirloom. It was a treasured possession, another gift, like so many others the Salaviglia family had bestowed on him. Both he and Victor had each been given their *scacciapensieri* as Christmas presents, by Victor's father when they were both eight years old.

The *scacciapensieri* is a symbol of Sicilian culture, the island's identity, and it has been the soundtrack of all Sicilian melodies and songs since the fourth century BC. It was played by the wandering storytellers of their childhood, who had taught the boys how to play the instrument. There wasn't a typical Sicilian *tarantella* that he and Victor hadn't mastered as the years had passed by. Pietro picked his up, placed it between his teeth, closed his eyes and plucked out of his childhood a nostalgic melody. Transported back to Bonnera, he considered just how far he had travelled from his homeland, and how much he missed Victor, when the days and nights were simple, honest and true. Now, he was just a mediator being shuffled between the multifarious cabals warring over Moro's life itself; this was not his way of staying sane. The haven of regular crime that had been his day job had gone. Having played a short *tarantella*, he replaced his cherished *scacciapensieri* back on its wooden stand. He knew in his heart that its twin sat on Victor's desk at Bonnera.

Pietro's boss, the politically savvy, septuagenarian Dottore Enrico Scampidi, had turned his life upside down with this dossier. Yet, there had been something tempting about the task Scampidi had forced him to take on. In the end, Pietro *could* have refused to take the assignment, but that might have cost him his job. However, Pietro's nous had detected that Scampidi had already bargained away his soul, such was Scampidi's determination to immerse him in Moro's kidnap. As much as he liked his drumbeat of criminals, there had been a temptation to be a central player. And Scampidi was offering him just that. Pietro's secret desire to assist, to be at the core of it all, was what had drawn him to grasp Scampidi's apple. The idea that he could be a part of saving Moro's life tugged at his own damaged soul; watching Moro walk free would be a redemption for the twenty-seven who had died that day in San Cipirello. Politics were too northern for him – he was from Sicily not Lombardy – and in truth he had been lured by the challenge itself. But that was then, nineteen days ago. If only he hadn't allowed himself to be devoured by Scampidi, who had led him ultimately to take that fork – the wrong fork – in the road. The regrets were his to own, his to be mortified by.

* * *

From bitter personal experience Pietro understood that involvement in a crime, any crime, leaves a heavy bruise and at worst, a deep scar which never heals. Moro had been held captive for almost three weeks and there was not a scintilla of a lead. Not one clue as to a region, let alone a city, as to where he was being held captive. Thankfully, searching for clues wasn't his job. Pietro was a subordinate who carried information between the different players – be they politicians, terrorists, press – only to empty the mixture of innuendo, lies and suspicions onto the *dottore*'s desk. Pietro had never asked, for it was not his place, just who the *dottore* passed this hard-won information onto. Someone, some organisation, was conducting this opera, and he was just a stagehand. All he had worked out, was that the Moro affair was not being orchestrated by the Red Brigades. The reason, to be a part of freeing Moro, was why he'd acquiesced to Scampidi's entreaties on the day Moro had been kidnapped. Looking back over his shoulder now, that had been a quixotic decision, made by man who was not quixotic.

Some 38,000 police and soldiers, auspiciously and publicly, were crawling all over Italy: on the streets, in the hills and the slums, they were the ones searching for clues. Or were they? What were they *actually* unearthing? Nothing. In truth, less than nothing.

Pietro shuddered, as if someone had again trespassed on his grave. His principal conundrum had always been with the physical execution of the kidnap operation itself. As an Italian, he knew it was axiomatic that anything executed with precision, skill, punctuality, expertise and efficiency could not, by any definition, be of Italian origin.

Moro's kidnapping – in broad daylight and under armed guard – had been textbook. In the maelstrom of the ninety-one bullets which had killed all five bodyguards, Moro was unscathed. The Red Brigades just weren't that good. They never had been, and they never would be.

This was a kidnap and murder operation *summa cum laude*. At 09:05 on Thursday, 16th March, the Red Brigades were more than good, they were superb. Their plan – daring and complex – yet very simple – was military blackboard theory actually working in the field. And, as for the accuracy of their shooting, it was as if they were marksmen. Impossible. Now, if the Red Brigades, a ragtag organisation if ever there was one, had been trained by the Mossad, the US military... Fanciful notions.

Unexpectedly, the telephone on his desk rang. It shook him out of his reverie and back into the cold present.

* * *

"*Pronto!*"

"Signor Albassi, we've not met, my name is Romano Prodi."

"No sir, but I am familiar with who you are and your reputation. How may I assist you?"

A Christian Democracy politician, known for his ability to sit on a fence and sway with whichever wind was blowing, calling a mid-ranking criminal lawyer of a prestigious Milan firm out of the blue? No, Romano Prodi didn't need his help for a traffic infraction. The Sicilian in Pietro distrusted coincidences as not-of-this-world.

"Thank you, Signor Albassi." Prodi paused. "Your name has cropped up in conversations several times over the past ten days, as... perhaps... someone to speak with." Again, Prodi stalled, willing the conversation to be over. Pietro remained silent. "Well, yesterday, Sunday, I was here in Bologna, the rain was terrible, and I stopped for an espresso, where by coincidence…"

Pietro coughed involuntarily. There was that word again. "Excuse me, please continue," he said.

"… where I bumped into a friend. We left the café and decided to join some colleagues at Professore Alberto Clo's country house. The rain was so bad I just wanted to sit it out, the weather that is."

Pietro wondered where this conversation was going.

"One thing led to another, there were eight of us there, and one bottle of Chianti led to another, you know how it is, all sitting around a kitchen table. I'm not sure how to say this, but we decided to make a Ouija board out of the table top. The table was rectangular you see." Prodi let the words trail away, hoping the details would infuse his fanciful story.

"Ouija! Isn't that a game where you try and contact the spirits of the dead?" Pietro asked, truly fascinated now.

"Yes, Avvocato, that's right. We made the individual letters from a notepad and placed them on the table. We used a coffee saucer as the Ouija's messenger boy, so to speak."

Perspiring, Prodi cackled nervously. He rammed his large spectacles onto the bridge of his nose and ploughed on.

"As I said, the rain was sheeting down, and we all decided to call on the spirits of the Christian Democracy."

Pietro burst out laughing. He just couldn't help himself. "I'm so sorry, I meant no offence. I'm a Sicilian first and a Catholic second, and I find the notion of Christian Democracy spirits in the afterlife just too, well, absurd. Please continue. I apologise."

"Perfectly understandable, if I'd not had a few glasses of wine, I, too would have found the notion ridiculous, you know how it is, no?"

Pietro didn't, but he didn't say so.

"So, what did these long dead political spirits reveal to you via your coffee saucer?" Pietro asked, deadpan.

"Avvocato, as I said earlier, you're respected as a, how to say, a trusted emissary in this Moro affair. All I'm asking you to do is pass on to those who need to know, what I am about to tell you. Perhaps the Interior Ministry, or someone who… That's all I ask of you."

Pietro detected a tremor of desperation in Prodi's speech.

"I'm not sure I like being compared with a coffee saucer, but rest assured that I will do my best, Signor Prodi. So, please tell me, what did this saucer of yours reveal then?" Under the circumstances, 'Signor' was rank enough for Romano Prodi today.

"The letters and numbers spelt out on the Ouija board were 'G R A D O L I' followed by the numbers '9' and '6', and then '1' and '1' again. All in that precise order."

Pietro scribbled the letters and numbers down on a notepad.

"Yes, but what was the question you, and your saucer, asked these Christian Democracy spirits, Signor Prodi?"

"Oh, I'm sorry, yes, yes," stammered Prodi. "We asked the spirits for the exact address of where Aldo Moro is being held captive."

"Of course you did, of course..." It was all Pietro could manage by way of a response.

Then the line went dead.

***

What on Earth had been the purpose of Prodi's telephone call?

Pietro shook his head in disbelief, tore the piece of paper from his pad, scrunched it tightly into a ball and lobbed it at the wastepaper basket against the far wall. It missed.

"Damn!"

He stubbed out his cigarette and picked up the discarded message from the afterlife. The message where spirits had so kindly detailed Moro's exact address, which had contrived to land on his Milan desk via a coffee saucer on a Ouija board in Bologna.

And why not the desk of just one of the 38,000+ police and militia who were conducting house to house searches? Too easy Pietro mused. Christian Democracy spirits, like their living counterparts, needed their tasks to be clandestine.

Every fibre in his body told him that either: a) Prodi had had a breakdown, or b) Prodi was blind drunk or, c) Prodi genuinely had a story to tell for his own reasons; and it was anyone's guess as to what they might be or d) Prodi had a credible lead as to where Moro – or his kidnappers – might actually be or e) all of the above and none of the above at the same time.

Pietro inclined to b) but dismissed it. Prodi didn't sound drunk. Fearful, anxious, yes. Drunk, no. That troubled Pietro, so he reopened his notepad, and like the professional lawyer he was, he made a contemporaneous note: he annotated the time, the duration of the call, the name of the caller and what the caller had said. He wrote down in block capitals: GRADOLI 96 & 11 and then signed and dated the document. Before he filed it in his 'Moro' file, he studied GRADOLI 96 & 11 as if it were a cryptic clue. The letters *could* be Italian shorthand for an address: 96 via Gradoli, Apt 11. Christian Democracy spirits evidently didn't like longhand.

He lit another cigarette and paced around his office deep in thought. Finally, knowing Angelica was on a lunchbreak, he stepped into her office to use her direct-line telephone; he'd long ago stopped trusting the office switchboard and its operators.

"*Ciao*, Claudio, it's Pietro." He wavered before continuing. "What was the weather like in Bologna yesterday? Big clouds full of spring rain?"

"Pietro, what are you going on about? Yes, I'm fine and thank you for asking. Yesterday was a beautiful day, like today," his friend Claudio sighed. "Pietro, have you called me simply to ask about the weather in Bologna?"

"Yes, I have actually, Claudio, sorry. *Grazie*."

Very, very slowly, Pietro cradled the handset and blew onto the tip of his cigarette until it crackled white-hot.

CHAPTER 12

The Embassy of The United States.
121, Palazzo Margherita
via Vittorio Veneto, Rome, Italy.
Monday, 3rd April 1978. Afternoon.

The CIA Station at the US Embassy in Rome was located in the chancery at the rear, and oldest, part of the Palazzo Margherita. Queen Margherita of Savoy had called her elegant *Cinquecentesimo palazzo* home from 1900 until she died in 1926. After her passing, Mussolini's fascist government commandeered her home for offices. Needless to say, the Americans had taken a shine to the large palazzo in 1946, and 'purchased' it for cents on the dollar from the defeated and bankrupt Italy. The new US Embassy soon meshed into the rubble and politics that was post-Second World War and the Cold War, so much so that its fabric became part of the United States itself.

Judd Barings' office was soundproofed with no windows. Its decor was cheap wood panelling with soft furnishings in rich, primary tones. The walls groaned with numerous framed photographs and diplomas. The only humour came from the two outsize American flags behind his desk and his nameplate: Office of the Chief Cultural Attaché.

Barings had just been handed a typed manuscript by a clerk from Operational Communications. He stared at the file with wide eyes as he flipped the pages. After he'd read it a second time his eyes narrowed, as if cheap cigar smoke had drifted into his corneas. In disbelief, he whistled loudly.

How in Jesus. H. Christ's name did that halfwit Romano Prodi get the *exact* street name in Rome – and the building and apartment numbers – where Mario Moretti and his Keystone terrorists were holding Moro prisoner? A 'safe house' they'd called it. Ha-darned-not-so-ha.

Barings swivelled his chair around to focus on the folds in the flags that stood behind him like improbable guards. He needed to think before acting. His gut told him to move in one direction, but his training said the opposite. He ran through a checklist of options which ranged from moving Moro to a CIA safe house, to setting up a secure conference call with Director Turner and Cuci, to – and he had the authority – having two bullets fired into Moro's cranium before sunset.

His sixth sense told him to play it long. Play it *very* long.

Yet his training also commanded him to be proactive. If he did it his way, he might be able purge the sociopath Cuci *and* his information-gathering stooge Albassi from this joint op. He was convinced that Cuci was using Albassi to spy on the CIA's involvement via all manner of sources, especially the P2 masons. Barings understood the way the Italians used cut-outs, behind the scene movers. Heck, all those caught in the middle, died in the middle. Expendable souls, the lot of them. CIA had been killing cut-outs for years, as had the Cosa Nostra.

But right now, his immediate problem was that Albassi also knew where Moro was being held. Apt. 11, 96 via Gradoli. Just a twenty-minute drive across town from the US Embassy. The principal issue that concerned him was what the hell Albassi was going to do with his new information.

The mission from Day 1 was that Moro was to be killed after single figure weeks whilst in captivity. No Communists – ever – in a NATO Italian Government had been the order. Full stop. And killing Moro was the easiest way for the CIA and IEA to achieve that. No Moro. No Communist alliance. However, before Barings could make a move, he'd have to see how Albassi was going to deploy the information Prodi had given him.

Barings' reflex told him Albassi would do nothing at all for the simple reason that Prodi's 'story' was stupider than a lizard eatin' cat. Christ Almighty, a two-bit Sicilian lawyer – Cuci's middleman – knew precisely where Moro was being held captive.

Then an idea came to him, Wile E. Coyote-like. He stood up with a sly grin.

Grab the lizard eatin' cat by the tail, then toss the critter into a gaggle of Italian geese and see what happens. Now, that was a plan, an' one without a Road Runner too. Create some chaos. He liked chaos, but it had to be *his* chaos. So, after a blind CIA tip-off, the Carabinieri would be chasin' geese for days.

Barings had long known – simply because he was that good – that there was a medieval village about eighty kilometres north of Rome called Gradoli. So, let's give Prodi's dumbass Ouija board some credit. Trot out the Carabinieri up-north to the irrelevant Gradoli, an' let them literally tear the place apart. Everyone'll be jumpin' like cookin' fat on a hot skillet for a few days.

Barings needed to buy time, and raiding the village of Gradoli was his best play. This would free him up to either move Moro, or if indeed-y needs must, kill Moro. It would also throw a Coyote-sized spanner into anything Cuci's messenger boy, Albassi, might be thinkin' of doin'. Whatever the hell that might be.

CHAPTER 13

**Il Tabaccaio Café, Largo Claudio Treves,
the Brera District, Milan, Italy.
Monday, 3rd April 1978. Evening.**

Today had been one of the most bizarre days of Pietro's life. The clamour and white noise of his local café was exactly what he needed to untangle the mesh of nonsense of the last few hours.

"Freddo, another glass of red and a ristretto, *per favore*."

He wasn't going to sleep tonight anyway, so he might as well enjoy being awake.

"*Momento*, Pietro!" grunted Freddo, the surly proprietor.

Pietro looked around. The small bar was almost empty. Freddo had only a handful of regulars rash enough to pay for his customary rudeness. The other customers were all strangers, and Pietro had always felt secure in the company of outsiders.

The phone call had left him feeling very uneasy. From his initial dismissal of Prodi's ridiculous story, Pietro had convinced himself that there might actually be a grain of truth in it. The decider was not the words themselves, but the tone, the timbre. Being a criminal lawyer, Pietro had long ago learned how to read tone; he knew when he was being lied to: liars tell simple stories, they hedge, they lack confidence and are too earnest. Other than the foolish untruth (and that's what it was) about the weather in Bologna, Prodi was not lying in the *purpose* of his call. The last time he'd heard the clarion call of a lie was in Scampidi's office whilst he was being briefed in the aftermath of Moro's abduction.

Prodi knew something, he had information for sure. But the man had neither the wit nor the experience to know what to do with it. Had someone planted that information – misinformation even – on him? If so, who? Which part of the jigsaw-plot did this piece fit? Other than Scampidi, who was Pietro supposed to tell? His most trusted Moro contact was Tina Anselmi; was he to call the Health Minster or was he supposed to ignore Prodi's call altogether? Were his office phones tapped? More alarmingly, was his home being watched, his home phone tapped? If so, who also knew what Prodi had told him? What could – and would – be drawn, and by *whom* (Pietro *really* wanted an answer to that question) by either his *failure* to relay the details of Prodi's call, or the *speed* with which he passed the information on? And *if* he were to pass this address on, then – other than Scampidi, whom he didn't trust at all – who should he tell?

He lit another cigarette, toyed with the vinegary red wine and switched to another thought-tape.

There had been rumours about US involvement since the 16th March. Such rumours were no real surprise, Pietro figured, this was Italy, where conspiracy theories were served with the pasta course. What about just informing Scampidi in a 'I'm-just-doing-my-job' way and be done with the whole Prodi/Moro/Ouija matter? But, he still came back to the question, "Why me?". Pietro's rational thought process had ground to a halt with Prodi's call – the whole episode was sugar in the fuel tank. However, there was *something* in *what* he had been informed about and *how* he was informed by Prodi that bristled all his instincts. Pietro was sure about that.

None of his questions had any answers. All he knew was that he was too deep in Scampidi's imbroglio, and wanted out. The trouble was no one had the desire, the will or the ability to drag him out of the quagmire that this assignment had become. The hope had all but evaporated. There appeared to be no way out. Even if he fed Prodi's Ouija info to Scampidi, he'd still be stuck, sinking and expendable. An anonymous call to the *Corriere della Sera* and RAI TV wouldn't work any more than the police would help. Prodi would simply deny it all.

Pietro laid a 10,000 lire note on the bar, horsed his rough wine and headed out of the door. He decided to do nothing but sleep on his dilemma and keep Prodi's fantastic tale to himself for the time being. If Moro *was* being held in Rome in Apt. 11, 96, via Gradoli, then one more day wouldn't matter. Perhaps in *his* silence lay the possibility of his rescue, he reflected as he strolled home. Then again, perhaps not.

When he reached No. 5's imposing oak doors, he stopped dead in his tracks. He dropped his briefcase on the pavement. His mind flashed back to a January weekend family trip to Pisa. In mid-winter there had been more pigeons than tourists at the Leaning Tower. A biting *maestrale* was howling in from a squally Ligurian sea. The twins were wrapped up in their ski-jackets and wore glum and perplexed expressions: *'Mama, Papà, what* are *we doing here?'* Together, and in single file, they trudged ever up and up the claustrophobic 296 spiral stone steps. Ruxandra was the elephant's trunk, the twins its tummy and Pietro the tail. Thirty minutes later they finally reached the *campanile's* summit and its meagre circular viewing gallery, 56.87m above the Piazza del Duomo below.

Halfway up though, Pietro had begun to feel unwell: dizzy, anxious, faint and weak. The shot-blast of cold wind which greeted him briefly, chased away a queasy unsteadiness. He looked around and saw that they were the only visitors on that bitter Saturday morning. Starting on the high side of the *campanile*'s 5.5-degree tilt, he sucked the *maestrale*'s salty medicine deep into his lungs. He propped himself up against the four skimpy metal rungs of the circular viewing platform. All he took in were his immediate surroundings: the Piazza dei Miracoli, the Cattedrale and the Piazza del Duomo, for he dared not lift his eyes to seek out the Pisan Mountains to the north, or the River Arno to the south. He found he could only focus on the immediate foreground.

Edging away from Ruxandra and the twins, Pietro white-knuckle gripped the top guardrail, and sidled down slowly to the leaning side of Pisa's *campanile*, a steep 4.5m off the perpendicular. He was a strong, confident man – mentally and physically – but his call to move to the lower side was a serious mistake. As he inched his way along, a detonation of vertigo unexpectedly struck him down as if it were a bolt of lightning. Panic and terror garrotted his throat. Oxygen was sucked out of his lungs, and his calves were suddenly drained of all strength. Sirens shrieked inside his skull, as blood vaporised from his frontal lobe, which shut down all his neural pathways. Frozen in body, thought and action, all he could visualise was the sweet temptation of a soaring escape from what his brain misinformed was *not* certain death. He placed his right foot on the first rung. Paused. It held his weight. Then his left foot involuntarily trod on the second rung. Only one more to go before he would be in the air, free and safe...

Ruxandra caught sight of him just as his right foot moved up to the third rung. And, with a banshee scream, she sprinted around the circular platform and threw herself at his lower body, grabbing his waist in a tackle. It was all she could do. His body hit the platform's stone floor in a heaving, convulsing mass of flesh. Ruxandra planted herself on top of his quaking foetal shape as if she were a Pisan gargoyle. The twins stared on, bewildered.

Trembling at the horror of the memory, Pietro reached down to gather up his briefcase. He wiped sweat from his brow, exhaled to temper his racing heart and fumbled his key into the door. It swung open and he slumped onto Cesare's bench. Short of oxygen and short of ideas, he realised in that petrified moment, that he *had* to tempt that ravenous wolf called fate and go to Rome to ring the doorbell of Apt. 11, 96, via Gradoli himself.

Mined into the core of every Sicilian was a dark fatalist that now cautioned him: going to via Gradoli could be as much an error as climbing Pisa's idiotic leaning *campanile* nearly was. Conversely, it also informed him that if he didn't personally verify Prodi's statements, that could also be a betrayal.

The 14th Duke of Salaviglia had taught him that duty was all. Standing in the entrance hall, Pietro understood that he did have a duty, and that to abandon one's duty would mean betraying the code that had long ago been instilled in him.

CHAPTER 14

**Via Gradoli, 'Tomba di Nerone' District, Rome, Italy.
Tuesday, 4th April 1978. Late morning.**

Pietro stepped off the train at Roma Termini. He stretched out his legs on the platform, pleased that he'd not taken the Alitalia shuttle from Linate airport. The long train journey had granted him the time to organise his thoughts. At Milano Centrale, just after 06:00, he had left a message for Angelica, his loyal secretary, on Scampidi's new gadget, a 'Robofone' answering machine, to say he wouldn't be in the office today. She knew only too well that meant he would be out on manoeuvres with the Moro case. Having cleared his day, he had purchased – using cash – a one-way ticket to Rome, and hustled his way past the junkies, vagrants and beggars to the station's main café.

He shook his head; Milan was the financial centre of Italy, its richest city, yet still the derelicts endured. Behind the zinc bar, the barman served up two espressos. Pietro threw them both down in rapid succession, sprinkled some coins in the saucer and strode off to grab a forward-facing window seat at the front of the train for his 500 km, five-plus-hour journey.

Rome's ranked-up cabs were plentiful, customers scarce. Pietro tossed his raincoat – you never could trust Roman weather – onto the back seat and gave the driver a simple command: *"Tomba di Nerone, per favore."* He wound down the Fiat's window and lit a cigarette. It was a twenty-minute drive northwest to Nero's Tomb where he was going to alight. Not so much as to see where they had *not* interred Emperor Nero (Proconsul Publius Vibius Marianus had that dubious honour) but to throw off anyone who may have tracked him from Milan. He'd trained himself to spot 'watchers'; the hapless Red Brigades were an easy snare.

His plan was to loiter, and to study, the sepulchral monument as if he were a tourist, and then saunter northwest towards No. 96 via Gradoli, some 850 metres away. He would pause to examine an architectural detail, then cross the street only to look in a window to catch a reflection perhaps. Pietro had learned that, like a muscle reflex, 'watchers' couldn't help but hesitate should their target stop abruptly.

Satisfied he wasn't being tailed, he walked past No. 96 and carried on around the corner to be extra careful. As good fortune would have it, via Gradoli was a long, circular street. The second time, he climbed the front steps of No. 96, brushing aside the overgrown foliage. He sought out the apartment building's intercom. He pressed the button for Apartment No. 11. It rang. No answer. He pressed it again, this time for a full count of three seconds. No answer. For a third and last time, he held the button down. Again, no answer. He hadn't expected there to be one, so he turned on his heels and simply walked away. His obligation to all, including himself, had been satisfied.

Vigilant though he was, Pietro hadn't noticed the teenager in jeans, and a filthy singlet, crouching in the street as he fixed a beaten-up red Vespa; his tools and bits of a dismantled exhaust spread around him. This was an everyday sight, on every Italian street, from Turin to Bari. Nor did Pietro detect the four, single, elderly people with their shopping bags full of groceries who had been criss-crossing the entire length and breadth of via Gradoli all day, in a fluid symmetrical ballet. Or the sharp glint from a prototype Nikon F3 camera, with its 500 mm telephoto lens, which caught the sun from the fifth and top floor of No. 51 via Gradoli. It only struck Pietro's blind eye.

The Red Brigades had Pietro Albassi marked. The IEA had four witnesses to confirm his presence in via Gradoli. But worst of all – and unknown to all – the CIA had black and white photos of the entire cast: Cuci's stooge, the four IEA agents, and the Red Brigades urchin *brigatisti*. Only the CIA had the full picture.

None the wiser, Pietro hailed the first taxi he saw and headed to Roma Termini to buy a cash ticket to Milano Centrale. He had fulfilled his duty. Little did he know that that by following his Sicilian upbringing, and the beliefs of the Salaviglia family, he had unwittingly set in motion forces darker than he had ever experienced or could ever imagine experiencing.

CHAPTER 15

Café Cordino, via dei Condotti, Rome, Italy.
Tuesday, 4th April 1978. Mid-afternoon.

Situated part way down that most elegant of Roman streets, the via dei Condotti, stood Café Cordino, a discrete fortress for the *cognoscenti* since 1760. Directly opposite BVLGARI, it was lost – gratefully – amongst the peddlers of fine jewellery and haute couture.

Alessandro Cuci strummed his manicured fingernails on the table as he stared at his surroundings. He admired the quintessential Roman-ness of the ageless café – from its seams of Carrara marble, via the staff's double-breasted white linen jackets and razor-creased black trousers, to the improbable perfection of their sweetmeats; the only ingredient to outstrip the desirability of a seat at one of its nine tables were the stratospheric prices. It all added weight to his personal supposition that there was a fifth element in the universe: Cuci had always believed that fire, water, air and earth were never enough. He knew the scented mystique of Café Cordino's reputation alone was capable of tarnishing even the bold brass of Americans. And that was why Cuci had requested it as the venue when Barings had called an urgent meeting.

He sat at his regular table tucked away in the corner and speared the olive in his empty martini glass, then impatiently checked his platinum Patek. Barings was ten minutes late, and Cuci's irritation was increasing with each passing second. A waiter removed the empty glass and took the faint crease of a smile at the corner of Cuci's small, thin-lipped mouth as a signal for a second martini.

Deprived of conversation and bored by the newspapers, he once again wondered why Barings had wanted to see him.

Just as his irritation was morphing into anger, he saw the tall, muscular

All-American silhouette of Judd Barings through the window. He noticed his large hand hesitate on the two solid brass entwined 'C's' of the glass door. Cuci smirked – Café Cordino could do it to anybody.

"Judd, *per favore*," Cuci beckoned him to one of the three empty chairs.

"I'm late. Sorry."

Cuci didn't respond.

"Get me a bourbon, Alex." His broad shoulders heaved. Barings looked as if he needed a drink. There really was no escaping the spell Cordino's could cast thought Cuci, as he raised his right eyebrow indicating his desire for service.

"To what do I owe the pleasure, Judd?"

"You're more Limey than the darned Limeys. I'm not in the mood."

"We'll see," replied Cuci.

Barings glanced around for any lonesome ears. There were none.

"What would y'all say if I told you we intercepted a conversation in which an address in via Gradoli was discussed? Mean anything to you? Pluck any yer banjo strings?"

Off guard, and with the bile of surprise in his throat, Cuci's eyes flickered.

"Thought so. I'm gonna tell you just once, so listen up. Y'all keep intel like that from us again and we, that's Langley and me personally, well, y'all wish you were born sorry. Y'all need to whistle *real* loud before walkin' into our camp, Alex."

Barings stared at Cuci as he sniffed the aromas of home in his glass: oak, vanilla, sweet butterscotch, caramel and pecans. He savoured his bourbon in silence.

"You knew where he's being held. Please don't insult me. Tell me my partners in Langley are not *cretini*? The Red Brigades we know about, but you too? No please," Cuci laughed with a grating whine in his voice. "And the conversation was between…?" Cuci let his question go unfinished.

"Y'all surprise me, Alex. Content to let me do the espionage an' the leg work an' assume that I'd simply let it all slide? It's not like we're best buddies. We've howdied, but we ain't shook yet, as we Southerners say."

"I thought it was implicit. Langley has the men in the field and the technology, while I have the local expertise, no?"

"Fair assumption. One was a politician, the other, well, y'all should be able to guess if you think hard enough."

"Did this person pass the information on?"

"Not that we can tell. His home and office numbers are tapped, an' he was followed home yesterday an' he made no calls from any public phones. The conversation has stayed with him. All I will say is your politician put a crock o' hog-shit 'round his story as to Gradoli that no single human would've believed it" – Barings smirked – "'cept of course, another Italian." Barings sipped his bourbon, unsure just how long he could keep up this charade. The CIA had black and white photos of every player since 16th March, shots Cuci would kill for. That's what pig-arrogance does to a man, thought Barings as he drained off his drink.

"OK, we're up to speed. I'm outta here, Alex. Just remember what I said. Do *not* keep intel from me, understand?" Barings stood up and left without saying another word.

Cuci didn't know about the telephone call from Prodi to Albassi, because Albassi had evidently not informed Scampidi. And that explained the mysterious visit Albassi had made to via Gradoli a few hours ago. The IEA had had multiple agents watching via Gradoli 24 hours a day since 09:00 on 16th March. Cuci had deployed agents of all ages, genders and ethnicity. The IEA were 101 per cent convinced the CIA had no presence whatsoever in the area; the IEA had it swept cleaner than the pontiff's bedchamber. The Red Brigades antics caused him no concern. So, outside of the Red Brigades, Barings now had the names of two other people – Pietro Albassi and Romano Prodi – who knew where Moro was being held captive. Not welcome news.

Albassi. Always secretive. Always the loner. That's why Scampidi and Cuci had chosen him. What to do with him, he reflected as he chewed an olive. Albassi prowling around via Gradoli obviously had an agenda all of his own – Scampidi was in the dark – and he posed an immediate and present threat to all Cuci's plans. Yes, what to do with Albassi he pondered, as he ordered a third martini.

Then an afterthought: Barings' unblinking eyes had held a glare he hadn't seen before.

CIA withholding information too?

CHAPTER 16

Café Lolita, via Durini, Milan, Italy.
Wednesday, 5th April 1978. Dusk.

Alessandro Cuci had long mastered the power of fear and the fear of power. He'd learned few lessons from his late father, an undistinguished academic and somewhat tragic figure. It had always amused Cuci, in a heartless fashion, that the childhood lessons he could recall (other than those of his beloved Nonno) had been put to work in a way his father would never have condoned. Cruelly, it made Cuci savour them all the more.

One of his favourites was when his father had described the behaviour pattern of an African silver-backed gorilla: essentially the anthropoid was harmless to its very distant cousin, *Homo sapiens*. An eighty-five kilogram man dressed in fatigues walking in a crouching position poses no threat to a 300 kilogram gorilla. However, and this was the part Cuci had always delighted in, should the same eighty-five kilogram man in fatigues approach the shy beast clutching a tube of steel with a wooden handle, the huge gorilla will recoil into aggression. It will either flee or attack. Such was the power of man's subliminal body language when armed, whatever the intent might be.

Cuci sat alone at a 1960s Formica table in the unbeguiling Café Lolita, opposite the entrance of Scampidi & Rusconi. Twenty minutes after his earlier meeting with Barings, he'd elected to go on a safari of sorts, and boarded the pontiff's new twin-engine Agusta A109 helicopter – in its white and yellow papal livery – for the one hour, forty-five-minute flight to the Vatican helipad in Milan.

And, as he sipped a gritty espresso he mused on the irony of this new hunt. Albassi had not informed Scampidi of Prodi's call, and worse, he'd set off on his own secret mission to via Gradoli for as yet unfathomable reasons. Albassi knew exactly where Moro was, and he was keeping that information a secret – a possible bargaining chip? – or so Cuci assumed. But why?

Cuci liked to study the behavioural traits of certain species. Today, he believed that seeing Albassi in the flesh for the first time would give him a greater insight. His very presence in Milan also told him that he had seriously underestimated Albassi, and that he didn't *really* understand what made him tick. He had thought he did, but evidently not. Albassi (who had direct access to the Moro family via Tina Anselmi – as well as the DC hierarchy itself – the Communist Party and the Red Brigades) held standing orders to immediately disseminate all information he harvested from all sources to Scampidi.

Albassi, not having done so, could skewer Cuci's plan to bring Langley to heel, or worse, release into the public domain the whereabouts of Moro's prison. Albassi posed a real threat to all his scheming. Equipped since birth with a sense of self-preservation sharper than an assassin's stiletto, the invisible line from ally-to-adversary had been crossed. Cuci wiled away the time wondering which animal Albassi was: an impala perhaps? Vulnerable like all antelopes, the animal grazes and breeds. A peaceful creature, its place in the food chain is to offer its weakest up to the quicker cheetahs, savage lions or rabid hyenas. Initially, he had viewed Albassi as a doe-eyed impala. From other sources, Cuci had latterly recognised that Albassi could also be portrayed as a grey wolf: an intelligent monogamous animal that mates for life, with well-developed communication skills. An alpha grey wolf lives within a rigid social hierarchy, one where he fiercely protects and guards over his mate and their cubs.

Albassi wasn't an impala, and he felt threatened by Albassi as a grey wolf. Brushing the thought aside, Cuci reminded himself that it is the clever who take from the strong, as they feed only off the weak. It will always be thus, as his weak father had often reminded him.

The oak doors of Scampidi & Rusconi swung open. A tall, striking man with dark hair stepped out and looked left and right. Erect, purposeful and with an ominous tilt to his head, he marched westwards down via Durini. The man had a long, muscular stride Cuci noted as he put his espresso cup down. With unforgiving and hostile eyes, he continued to stare after the man who powered ahead into the other, shorter, strolling pedestrians until he melded into the distance.

Albassi, he had recently discovered, came with an insurmountable problem. One that not even Cuci could overcome. After Scampidi had Albassi deep in the Moro affair, Cuci had begun an in-depth research into his background. An interest prompted by an alarm-bell that Albassi appeared to have no vices whatsoever. Cuci found that incomprehensible; viceless humans didn't exist. Cuci subsequently unearthed that Albassi was regarded as a Salaviglia son. He knew of the family, but he hadn't realised how profound the relationship was when Scampidi had proposed Albassi. The Salaviglia family had saved the orphan's life after the San Cipirello massacre, which meant, according to their own lore, the Salaviglias would forever be accountable for his protection and well-being. And that made Albassi off-limits; a fact he too would be ignorant of. Astute as Albassi was, he wouldn't have been able to grasp just how deep veined, subterranean even, the centuries old Salaviglia alliances went. Such unspoken concords governed every aspect of the Republic – life, politics, religion, the arts, business – and Cuci knew that Salaviglia influence travelled far beyond any mapped Italian borders too. It was a straightforward fact: Albassi was untouchable. Cuci understood all this and more, which meant his nemesis was not a grey wolf, he was a North African white rhino, unknowingly protected as he safely roamed the savannahs.

Cuci had figured out a workaround though. He knew precisely what he was going to do. And fast, before it was too late, for he had no time to lose. Albassi could decide at any time to scatter about like confetti the intel he'd secretly withheld from Scampidi. The man was a danger. Another straightforward fact.

Cuci tossed a few coins on the table and slunk out through Café Lolita's shabby doors, hailed a taxi and headed back to the luxury of the pontiff's new helicopter.

PART THREE

CHAPTER 17

The Brera District, Milan, Italy.
Thursday, 6th April 1978. Mid-afternoon.

There can never be any justice in certain acts.

Paola didn't see the green Volkswagen Golf as it accelerated aggressively into the traffic flow. All the tunnel-visioned driver registered was the little girl's wide-eyed stare as the car crashed into her. The VW's front-end punched Paola's small, brittle frame high into the air, and her body launched over the car's roof. She had landed in the road as the car sped away, leaving her crumpled with broken limbs splayed out disjointedly, as if she were no more than large rag doll.

Toto saw it happen. Was a witness. Scarred for life. His twin sister had gone to cross the road after school was out. He had hesitated at the traffic lights with their friends – as twins they'd been in the same class since nursery school – but Paola, always eager, pushy even, had run on ahead. There had been no stopping her. There never had been and now there never would be. Before anyone had called an ambulance, Toto knelt beside her and cradled her head in his young arms.

Paola bled from both her ears and mouth. Even aged eight she still had milk-teeth but somehow the last of them had been torn from her gums and were in the wool of her cream-coloured cardigan. A deep gash in her cheek pulsed blood onto her white school shirt. Her right arm and right leg were twisted and broken like trampled saplings. However, she was breathing, and Toto never stopped whispering – he knew not what he said – in the hope that her eyes might flicker a hint of recognition. They didn't. Yet his words still flowed, even as the paramedics plucked them both, Siamese twin-like, from the bloodstained tarmac and away from the bedevilling onlookers, both young and old.

The car and driver – believed to have been a woman – were now deep inside Milan's intestinal back streets, before anyone could register that the car was the sole reason that Paola's shattered body lay in the arms of a young boy with dark, tousled hair.

* * *

Whichever side of the tracks you are born – and there's dirt on both sides – can and will, immutably, affect your ability to make decisions. Or so Pietro Albassi had always believed. As a young child, Father Albert and his benefactor, the 14th Duke of Salaviglia, had taught him that was just a fact of life. Words from the village priest and a nobleman held the granite of truth, no?

Despite being the same age, Pietro understood that he *was* different from his best friend Victor, the 14th Duke of Salaviglia's son. They played in the scorched fields of summer, they swam in the cool waters off Castellammare, they caught lizards in and out of the dry boulders and afterwards played their *scacciapensieri* together. After school, and from dawn to dusk at the weekends, they worked hard alongside the many hundreds of Bonnera's dedicated labourers during the harvests: February to March they picked (and ate!) the 'Moro' variety of *Arance Rosso* unique to Bonnera; the Salaviglias had brought the sweet blood orange to Sicily in the eighteenth century. And in the autumn, they gathered, for days on end until the November rains came, plump olives from the estates' infinite groves. As they grew older, their voices deepened, their muscles thickened, their hair grew unruly and long and they both found themselves drawn to the same Sicilian girls. Not one dispute ever arose, for their unspoken devotion to each other meant, simply, that the girl in question would choose who to step out with. They were closer than any two brothers could ever be, and their different birthrights mattered not: to Victor, Pietro, or even the 14th Duke himself.

Or so Pietro had believed, until he stared down at the shattered body of his beloved daughter. So fragile. So small. So delicate. So invaded by tubes. So disfigured by wires and dwarfed by an old, rusting oxygen tank beside her bed. An endotracheal tube was taped into the corner of her mouth, her miniature veins were breached and plumbed by IV drips. Her pale skin – she was very much her mother's daughter – was clothed in what looked like a shroud. But the heart monitor broadcasted the news that she was alive. There was, quite simply, nothing else that mattered. Her heartbeat. The pulse of her strong Albassi heart.

Pietro ran his hands through Ruxandra's long hair. Her eyes had shed the puffy redness of tears and were now hard and marble-grey, no longer pale blue. Toto was outside the Intensive Care ward with a nurse who was doing her best to keep him calm.

"Every sentence Paola ever spoke always began with 'Let's', didn't it, Ruxandra?" Pietro volunteered. Ruxandra ignored him. The dark side of her Romanian psyche told her this was no accident. She was sure that her husband's work in the Moro affair was the trigger *and* the bullet.

"Tell me this was an accident, Pietro? I need to know it was. For me. For you. For Toto. Please."

"The police and the witnesses said she ran out across the road to get to the other side first. You know Paola, second place is last place. It was an accident," Pietro replied, fearfully.

"I spoke with them too, *caro*. I need to hear it from you."

Pietro scratched his scarred temple and turned away from his wife to hide the look in his one, seeing eye. He'd had enough of coincidences. Deep down he distrusted the policewoman who had told him that this was 'a commonplace traffic accident'.

"My darling, she *will* recover, I promise you... you... you..." unusually, he stammered. "Do you mind if I go out for a cigarette?"

"No, smoking always calms you. Then go home, rest too. You look shattered. I'll stay here with Toto and look over Paola. *Vai caro!*"

Pietro nodded mutely at her command. He couldn't find the words to respond. Instead, he crept past the numerous tubes to lean over and kiss Paola on both of her bloodied, stitched cheeks. When he did so, he made a silent, Sicilian, oath to protect his family at any cost.

Once in the corridor, he looked left and right, scanning for Toto. He caught sight of him sitting alone with a nurse. They were holding hands, and the nurse had put her other arm around him. Pietro walked slowly up to them. He smiled at the nurse, and knelt down so he and his son were eye to eye. The father and son's eyes held onto each other very tightly.

"My darling boy, have you any idea just how brave you are? I've never met anyone with as much courage as you, Toto," he spoke directly to him, *sotto voce*, ignoring the kind-hearted nurse.

"Thank you, Papà. I only did what Paola would have done, if it had been me."

"Your heroism was everything, Toto. By holding her, you kept her alive. You *were* her knight, her sword and shield against the chaos that surrounded you both."

"If you say so, Papà."

"I do say so. I'm very proud of you."

"Where are you going now, Papà?"

"Home to feed Enzo and take him out. I suspect he's cross-legged in his basket," Pietro chuckled, and Toto rewarded him with an easy smile. "I'll be back later, then Mama will take you home and I'll spend the night with your sister."

"Give Enzo a hug from me, and from Paola too."

"I will, you can be sure of that. Brave and fearless aren't big enough words to describe you, Toto. I love you very much."

Pietro leaned forward, took Toto's head in his hands and kissed his forehead as if he were a priest anointing him. He stood up and silently mouthed *'grazie tantissimo'* to the nurse.

He walked away and put a Gitane in the corner of his mouth, not lighting it. As he strode to the nurses' station, he registered a man, small, young and lithe, wearing a black rollneck sweater, black jeans and work boots who was engaged in conversation with an orderly. A black woollen cap was pulled low over his forehead, his head hidden. Pietro's antennae went up. He slowed down and overheard the man ask a little too loudly, "*What is Paola Albassi's condition?*" Pietro slammed on the brakes and spun around as the orderly flicked over the pages on her clipboard. He stared at the stranger and took a mental Polaroid of him, his heart thumping at the centre of his very being. Who was asking about Paola and why? Twin responses detonated simultaneously inside him – one in his head and one in his heart – rush to Paola's side or shadow the man? Shadow, his Sicilian instinct shouted.

The man signalled a toothy *'grazie'* when the orderly replied that unless he was immediate family, she couldn't answer him. He inched away – backwards – turned on his heels and sinewed through all the other families towards the emergency stairs. Pietro glanced to his left and saw the elevator doors were about to close. The elevator was empty. The arrow flashed down. Pietro was far taller than the man, who had reached the emergency double-doors and, on the balls of his feet, he vaulted like a cheetah into the elevator's closing doors, where he stabbed the ground floor button. It was a speedy elevator, and with only three floors he reckoned he'd be able to track the man in the hospital's main entrance.

The man swivelled his head, sniffing at the air like a fox, sensing a threat, a something. Pietro stayed still, and alert, before hustling through the revolving doors onto via Ettore Majorana. He cupped his hands to light his cigarette and to recce the man's options unnoticed; he was determined to trail him wherever he went. Without a waiting car, the man had two choices: run across the very busy main road and head north across the park, or turn right to via Graziano – 500 m away – and then turn left or right to catch one of the trams which ran north or south. With over 180 km of track, Milan had one of the world's biggest tram systems and once on one, vanishing like a white rabbit into a black hat would be too easy. What Pietro hadn't accounted for was the dense throng of people, most of whom also seemed to be wearing black; it was as if the small man had faded to black. Pietro saw the man meld into the crowd milling around Milan's largest hospital, and then caught a glimpse of him as he sprinted towards via Graziano – Pietro had been 'made'. That didn't stop Pietro, who ditching his cigarette accelerated after him. But he hadn't bargained on the statue-still crush of humanity or the small man's nimble speed. And the last Pietro saw of the man was a turned-head, evil smirk shot back at him as he jumped on a speeding southbound tram. Defeated, Pietro put his hands on his knees and heaved a heavy sigh, knowing that his breath was all he was going to catch now. The man was long gone, Milan was a huge city.

* * *

Pietro lit another cigarette under a dense shroud of low, grey clouds eager to spit drizzle over the city. He drummed his right foot nervously on the pavement and wondered what to do. The man wasn't going to risk returning to the hospital, that was for sure; whilst Pietro had been 'made', so too had the small man. Having smoked his Gitane, he ground it out and elected to walk home – fifty minutes or more – to try and clear his head. There, he would sit on the roof with Enzo and let the pigeons – his Sicilian ones, not his Milanese ones – help him determine what he should do next to protect those he loved.

CHAPTER 18

**No. 5, Largo Claudio Treves,
the Brera District, Milan, Italy.
Thursday, 6th April 1978. Late afternoon.**

Pietro arrived home and found the two oak doors to their apartment building wide open. Cesare stood in the middle, like a sentry on duty. He was a few centimetres inside the building he was in charge of; once a deserter, always a deserter.

"*Ciao*, Cesare," Pietro greeted him with a thin smile, for nobody knew what had happened earlier. Pietro detected a furrowed brow with furtive eyes. This was not No. 5's usual caretaker. "Everything OK?"

"I don't know, Avvocato. Something's not right."

"What do you mean?"

"I haven't forgotten everything the army taught me. When I'm not cleaning or sweeping, I'm observing our home. I'm its guardian too, Avvocato."

Pietro was mystified, but also intrigued. He'd never seen him in this role before.

"A woman came by, about an hour ago. Thirties, I guess. A *cozza*. She asked if you or your wife were at home."

"What!" exclaimed Pietro. "Describe her to me?"

"Ugly, thirties, jeans, long greasy hair, piggy little grey eyes, bad skin, big hips. No tits. Broad shoulders, swimmers' shoulders. Strong, mean-looking too. Not nice. Wore an anorak. Zipped up. Bulge on left side. Gun, I'm sure."

"You should have been a Military Policeman, Cesare, not a foot soldier," said Pietro, with as kind a frown as he could muster. "Carry on."

"I watched her park the car over there." He jutted his chin to a place 25 m from where they were standing. "It was green. Milan plates. Foreign.

Dent on the front end. Filthy dirty too." Cesare replied in staccato phrases, as if he was emptying his memory as quickly as possible, lest he forget any details.

Pietro was shocked. Speechless. And worst of all, he was terrified. Not for himself, but for his wife and son and daughter. He'd long been fair game, and he'd reckoned on that from the day Scampidi had inveigled him in the Moro affair. Family are out of bounds; that's the Italian way. So, who were the forces of evil trying to get at him through his family?

"Is there anything else you can tell me, Cesare?"

"Yes. The bench opposite. The new one. You read your newspapers there sometimes. Underneath the hackberry tree."

"What about it?" Pietro asked. He'd clearly underestimated the vigilant Cesare.

"She sat there. Staring at our building. Silent. Chain-smoking. She threw all her butts into the grass. Messy bitch. Left without saying anything about ten minutes ago. Headed east."

Christ, so, if I'd taken a taxi home from the hospital, as I would have been expected to do, and not walked for an hour, I'd have caught – or more likely *been caught* – by the woman who ran down my daughter, thought Pietro. Whoever was behind this was employing dangerous amateurs. And his profession was understanding the working minds of criminals.

"Thanks, Cesare," he repeated as he daze-walked into the courtyard. He pressed the button for the elevator. Next stop, the roof with Enzo and a packet of cigarettes. It was time he started to scheme too.

* * *

Milan's usual ability to deliver rain in April had thankfully failed to materialise that afternoon. It was neither cold, nor warm on Pietro's roof. He went to his small wooden shed, grabbed a striped canvas deckchair, unfolded it and loaded the weathered pine side table with ammunition: a large bottle of cold San Pellegrino – it tasted better straight from the bottle – a windproof yachtsman's ashtray Ruxandra had given him for a birthday years ago, a yellow packet of corn-paper Gitanes, and a small bowl of treats for Enzo. His primed, febrile mind was now prepped to play chess against an invisible – and unknown – adversary.

Pietro understood immediately that he had drawn white. It was a matter of how to exploit his upper hand by a process of elimination, of who had ordered the trigger to be pulled? Whoever was behind this was foolhardy to have made an attempt on his, Ruxandra's or Toto's lives by sending the same assassin straight to his home. That mistake made him move his queen straight across the chessboard. Solve the problem boldly, or lose forever.

Whoever it was who'd ordered his daughter maimed or killed had made a momentous miscalculation. In doing so, they had removed any ambiguity. They had made it devastatingly clear that this was a campaign of escalation. And that was just a hygienic term for a foul and potentially tragic reality: perhaps his entire family could be wiped out.

Pietro swigged deeply from his San Pellegrino, lit another cigarette and tossed a biscuit at Enzo, who caught it neatly before folding himself back into a circular ball of brown fur. Pietro sucked hard on the slow-burning cigarette, scorching his lips as he did. To find his 'present' he knew he would have to delve deep into his past. Not something he wanted to do, but had to. The massacre at San Cipirello, 1950. He was six. That was as far back as he dared go.

After an hour or so of reflection, of studying the moving parts, of kaleidoscopic memories dragged out of the darkness, Pietro solemnly concluded that there were three core reasons behind the massacre in the piazza of San Cipirello, in that stifling Sicilian August twenty-eight years ago: 1) A ruthless power struggle between two men, two forces. 2) A perceived betrayal. 3) A pre-emptive strike of revenge.

Twenty-seven men, women and children had died that afternoon. One child had survived, wounded, but alive. The survivor's chess pieces were now in position. What he had to do was determine the following: 1) Who were the two people – entities – engaged in this power struggle? 2) Who perceived that he – Pietro Albassi – had committed an act of betrayal? 3) Work that out, and the person(s) who had committed the act of pre-emptive revenge on Paola would become self-evident. Whoever it was knew no fear, or wasn't thinking straight, or both, for they'd just sent the same assassin undisguised to his home, for Heaven's sake.

As the ruthless Sicilian bandit Salvatore Giuliano had said, before he too had been slain violently in that very same year: *'I can look after my enemies, but God protect me from my friends.'*

With that recollection from his past life booming inside his head and heart, Pietro got up from the deckchair, stretched out his rangy limbs, stubbed the half-smoked cigarette into Ruxandra's ashtray and whistled Enzo awake. He had a bishop to move in order to protect his queen and her two neighbouring pawns. And he had a plan too.

* * *

Pietro settled down into the large sofa in the sitting room. He arranged the telephone and a notepad on the coffee table. A fresh bottle of San Pellegrino was on the side table, beside framed photos of the twins, and a beautiful black and white studio shot of Ruxandra; that too had been a birthday present from her. He plumped a cushion and Enzo hopped up.

His first call was to the hospital to check on Paola's condition. An ITU nurse informed him there was no change, her vitals were stable. That was the good news. But she was still unconscious, and the doctors were apprehensive that she might fall into a coma. Pietro replaced the handset and glanced at the photos next to his elbow. He dialled Tina Anselmi. As much as he trusted anyone in this triage, he trusted her.

"*Ciao*, Tina. Have you got a few minutes? It's Pietro."

"Of course. Always for you," she replied warmly.

"I have some bad news."

There was a pause, the line crackled.

"What is it, Pietro? Please."

Pietro proceeded to report the tragic events of the afternoon. In order to find out what he needed to, he would withhold no detail, except his motives for calling.

"I am so, so very sorry, Pietro." Anselmi was horrified. "You've suspected that you might have been in danger ever since the Red Brigades assassinated the head of the Milan prison guards after the information you'd gathered. Do you think this was another dreadful warning?"

"No, I don't. Maiming children isn't the Red Brigades', Christian Democrat's, or the Communists' style…" he hesitated "… it's not even Italian. Children are off-limits, you know that, Tina. It's someone's style though." Pietro let his words hang.

"You think it was deliberate?"

"Yes, I do. You know what I think about coincidences."

"Accidents *do* happen, Pietro."

"Really?" he replied bitterly. "No! The assassin WENT TO MY HOME AFTERWARDS, TINA! UNFINISHED BUSINESS!" Pietro shouted, then caught himself. "I apologise, Tina, I'm sorry, I shouldn't have raised my voice."

"That's OK, Pietro. Don't worry. What can I do?"

"I need some straight answers to some straight questions. I trust you, Tina."

"Fine, ask away. I'll do my best."

"Who's fronting for the CIA?"

"What do you mean?"

"It's a simple question. Who in Italy is running the CIA side of the Moro affair?"

"Why? I don't know. How would I know?"

"Because the Red Brigades didn't pull this off without external help, they're simply not capable. It can only be CIA or Mossad, and Mossad don't care about Italian communists. The Americans do, and they've wanted Moro, and his deal, dead for a long time, or so I have unearthed. So, your best and informed guess please, Tina?" Pietro asked, before continuing. "The CIA went into business with the Mafia back in the 1960s to assassinate Castro. Moro is just another communist. We all know governments sanction assassinations through their alphabet agencies. CIA work with partners, share the workload with local intelligence wherever they operate. And at the end they send in kill teams to clean up any loose ends." He laughed, nervously. "The CIA call them 'auditors', can you believe that?"

"I have heard talk of the IEA being especially busy in the last few months. That's from our intelligence here in Rome. But there's always talk about the IEA when anything happens."

"More information."

"Don't speak to me like that, Pietro. We're on the same side, remember?"

"Not any more, Tina. Unless your daughter's about to fall into a coma in Niguarda Hospital. Which means, I'm on no one's side other than my family's," Pietro replied politely, but with a steel tone.

Tina Anselmi took a deep breath. Pietro waited for the exhale. Many a truth came with an exhalation, as all razored lawyers knew.

"The head of the IEA is a man called Alessandro Cuci. You won't have heard of him."

"True. I know nothing about him," replied Pietro.

"Cuci has spent his entire life hiding in the shadow's shadow. That's his secret. He's not of our world or even this world, Pietro." She inhaled deeply again. Another 'tell' of a solid lie – or a solid truth – about to be spoken. Pietro knew that whatever came from her lips would be a truth. Anselmi spoke in a whisper this time. "If anyone is the CIA's partner in this, it will be the IEA. Not even the Pope knows what Cuci does or what he controls. He's that invisible. But under his command, the IEA has influence everywhere, it's far more than an intelligence network. The IEA has become a powerhouse."

"OK, I'm astonished I've never heard of him."

"I'm not, Pietro. The IEA are so influential that they decide much of what happens in Italy. Like P2, it's a state within a state, a shadow government. And all behind closed doors too. Cuci is far more than just another Vatican ghost," Anselmi concluded.

"Well, I know something more about him now."

"The man is amoral, lethal and feared, with tentacles everywhere."

"Thanks for the warning, Tina."

"If the IEA are involved, you'll need to be careful, Pietro. Very careful."

"I will. Anyway, whoever is responsible won't touch my family ever again."

"What are you going to do, Pietro?" she asked nervously, sensing even more tragedy.

"You'll know when I've done it. *Ciao*, Tina," answered Pietro enigmatically. He replaced the handset before she could ask any more questions.

* * *

Pietro let the phone ring, and ring, and ring... He knew someone would answer at some point in time. Finally, someone did.

"Bonnera."

"May I please speak with Victor Salaviglia?"

"Who is asking for him *per favore*?"

"*Un vecchio amico che vive a Milano. Grazie tanto.*"

For what seemed like an eternity, Pietro listened to all the hisses, static and general mayhem that was the orchestra on long-distance calls in Italy.

"*Ciao*, Pietro, good to hear from you. I've missed you." Victor Salaviglia's speech was not just rich and generous in tone, it was imbued with warmth. It was ever thus with Victor.

"They say that Africa begins south of Rome, so, what's it like in Africa today?"

Victor went to laugh, then shivered. He knew Pietro better than he knew himself. Something was off. He could tell from the intonation and pitch of his words; and it wasn't just the usual bad connection.

"What's wrong my brother? Tell me, Pietro." Only a Salaviglia could make a direct command sound like a polite request for a biscotti, thought Pietro.

"It's to do with Paola. She was involved in a hit-and-run this afternoon. She's borderline comatose. Her body and bones are all broken. I need your advice, Victor."

Was it what he said, or was it hearing Victor's voice, or was it the floodgates of bygone years suddenly opening that made Pietro lose an element of control? He didn't know, and much less cared. Victor knew to remain mute as he listened to his dearest friend tremble, then break. A man's dignity is all he has in the end, and Victor remained silent for he could see the tears coursing down his brother's cheeks.

At last, Pietro composed himself and Victor saw him smile.

"Africa is lovely in April, you know that," laughed Victor.

"Yes, I do. I really do," Pietro breathed in. "I don't believe Paola's accident was an accident."

"How so?" Victor was a man of few words at times.

And for the second time, Pietro recounted, over the rollercoaster connection, the A–Z of it all: how he had become unwittingly involved in the Moro affair – he hadn't told Victor – all that he knew, all that had happened, all that he had suspected, and more importantly, all that he had just learned from Minister Tina Anselmi.

"They always strike at those you love, *caro*. Leave this with me. Enquiries will be made. No names, fear not. Godspeed to you all. We'll speak tomorrow."

"And a warm embrace for your father, please."

"Always, Pietro, always."

The call ended between the two brothers just as it had begun. With unspoken love.

* * *

Pietro reflected that Hell is an easy place to get into, but a difficult place to escape from. He glared at the telephone. A conversation, even the tough one he'd just had with Victor, was always heart-warming. Days, weeks, months, it didn't matter. There was no place to pick up from, for there was never a place they had ever left.

This was a Hell Pietro had fallen into, been dispatched to, and he wasn't going to let Victor be dragged down into that inferno. It was bad enough that his wife and the twins looked like they were sinking with him, but there would be no one else on this road with him. This was his journey now, one he had to make alone. He knew Victor would offer them all sanctuary at Bonnera, but Pietro had decided he would refuse, not least because it would be impossible to move Paola. And if he was right about who was playing Lucifer, not even Bonnera would be safe. No. After all the Salaviglia family had given him – they had rescued him too – he would rather die than have them brought low by his actions. Not even sacrificing his own life could expunge the lifetime debt he felt he owed the Salaviglia family.

* * *

Dottore Enrico Scampidi was next. Pietro had been dreading this final call before he had even spoken with Tina Anselmi earlier. His instinct told him that this would be the denouement. He dialled Scampidi's private office number, the one used for information he disgorged on a daily, sometimes twice daily, basis, and usually made – upon Scampidi's orders – from shadowy payphones. How *does* one un-remember a telephone number?

"*Pronto!*" Scampidi answered even before the second ring. "Pietro, how are you?"

"I've been better, Dottore."

"Why, what's happened, young man?"

"My daughter Paola was involved in a car accident this afternoon after school. She was run over at a pedestrian crossing. She's in Niguarda

Hospital. Unconscious. She's on life support." Pietro was matter of fact, exactly as he always was when he spoke with Dottore Enrico Scampidi. This was business. The fact that it was Pietro's *personal* business, didn't change anything. Business was business; that much he had learned over the years.

There was a long silence. Pietro wondered, as the seconds ebbed away into darkness, if he was telling Scampidi something he already knew. And the longer the silence continued, a wheezy, unhurried breathing emanated from Scampidi which grew louder. It was the sound only a devil could make. Scampidi knew alright. It was all Pietro could hear. Let the guilt and horror consume you too, you *bastardo*.

"I am so sorry to hear that, Pietro. Is there anything the firm or I can do?"

"Yes, there is as a matter of fact, Dottore. Thank you for asking. Would you mind if I asked you to hold a moment? I'd like a glass of water."

Pietro needed no such thing. He placed the receiver on the sofa to make Scampidi wait. People like Scampidi corroded one's beliefs in not only justice, but in the goodness and integrity that existed in this brutalised world. The Scampidis, and so, so many others, conspired to reward only anger, suspicions, and the very meanest of instincts. Sixty seconds for Scampidi to reflect on his own evil was a token – not a price – he had to pay before Pietro asked him questions, ones he already knew the answers to; but a lot depended on *how* Scampidi answered them. Calmly, he continued stroking Enzo who lay beside the receiver.

"*Grazie*, Dottore. Thank you for your patience," Pietro said politely, as he finally lifted the phone off the sofa. His bishop had the king in check.

"I'm a busy man, Pietro, what is it I can do? Let's move this along." Scampidi sounded peeved, which is exactly what Pietro had wanted.

"Answer me this, *per favore*, who are you feeding my intelligence to?"

"That's my business, young man, not yours. How dare you ask?!" Scampidi shot back.

"Not anymore, Dottore. It's now my business too."

"Last time I looked at *my* building, *my* writing paper, they all have *my* name on it, not yours."

"Would you like my immediate resignation in writing, or will this telephone call suffice?"

"You can't quit. I will *not* give you permission!" exclaimed Scampidi.

Pietro laughed aloud. "I just have, with all due respect, Dottore." He paused. "Unless of course you care to tell me where the hard-won information I provide you with ends up? The decision is yours. Just like the building and the writing paper are yours."

Scampidi went silent. This was a move by Albassi that he'd not anticipated.

Eventually, the silence was shattered by a raspy, grating cough.

"You understand I cannot name the individual for client privilege reasons," Scampidi snarled, sensing he was cornered. He needed Albassi. Even an inkling that Cuci and P2 discovered that his underling had disobeyed orders, and had then walked out the door, could be ruinous to his own reputation; Scampidi's most valued article of trade.

"The name of the company, or the organisation, will be good enough, Dottore."

Pietro knew straightaway that everything depended on his employer's reply. And that Scampidi would take his own ungodly time to deliberate. Never, ever, give a man an ultimatum, Pietro reminded himself, especially if that man was named Dottore Enrico Scampidi.

"The Vatican."

"The Catholic Church is neither a company, nor an organisation, Dottore, it's a religion." Pietro teased out his words. "Who precisely in the Holy See do you report to?"

Again, Scampidi puffed out his frustration with hesitation. Pietro heard it clearly, and welcomed it. Subordinates like Albassi did not address him in this manner. Only he dictated. "The Vatican IEA," responded Scampidi at last.

"Thank you, Dottore. Would you like my resignation confirmed in writing or would you prefer for me to continue in my post?" Pietro asked, hiding all rhetoric. He knew the answer.

"Continue working as usual, Pietro. Report only to me. My best to your wife and daughter."

Checkmate. Scampidi thumped his receiver into its cradle. How typical that he couldn't even recall the names of his subordinate's wife or daughter. Pietro frowned as he nestled the receiver into its cradle and stroked Enzo's fuzzy head. It was time for him to leave for the hospital for the nightshift, and Ruxandra and Toto could return home for supper and rest.

Pietro appreciated that tired though he was, he'd put the sleepless night ahead to good use. The eerie quiet in the hospital's pale green light, with the rhythm of Paola's steady, unconscious breathing beside him would help. With the information he'd reaped he'd be able to plot an escape route off this road to Hell he'd put his family on.

As he headed to the front door, he knew that their route off the road to Hell would probably not include him. He was no longer concerned about himself. This was only about Ruxandra, Toto and Paola's survival.

CHAPTER 19

Bonnera, the west of Sicily.
Friday, 7th April 1978. A little after sunrise.

Victor Salaviglia woke, as always, at sunrise. He hadn't slept well. The cotton-stuffed mattress atop his seventeenth-century mahogany bed – high off the ground and not on account of cold draughts, for there were none in the suite of rooms that constituted his bedroom – had been as enveloping as always. The linen sheets were both cool and warm. This morning, however, his head ached and he was anxious; troubled, in fact.

He pressed a button on his bedside table and hauled his indigo-blue silk robe over his muscular frame. He ambled barefoot onto the age-old slabs of hand-cured terracotta of the west-facing terrace. He never closed the shutters, nor ever drew the damask curtains. The saturated light of the Sicilian dawn was his first espresso of the day.

Unsettled and tense, he leaned on the stone balustrade and stared out over the Tyrrhenian Sea. He hoped it would be a salve for the difficult task which lay ahead of him. He doubted it. His valet placed, ghost-like, an espresso beside him; he had looked after the future Duke long enough to know when not to speak. He slipped away to draw the claw-footed copper bath full of warm salted water, and to prepare his badger-hair shaving brush with lemon-scented camomile soap. As the bath filled, the valet laid out, in the adjoining dressing room, the clothes that would be worn this morning.

Victor buzzed for another espresso and drank the tepid, thick brew in one swallow. A lengthy soak in warm salt water would surely help his unease. He folded his robe and pyjamas and laid them on a bluey-grey Carrara marble plinth. He lowered himself into the deep bath and pondered an old phrase his father sometimes used, and always with a customary, wicked chuckle: *'Man plans. God laughs.'*

Today, God was, with any luck, not going to laugh at his plans.

* * *

Annexed to Victor's bedroom suite on the ground floor was his private study. It had been his grandfather's study. The 13th Duke had gifted it to him on his deathbed, bypassing his son, the 14th Duke, who had long preferred a cowshed he had begun converting as a teenager into what was now a remarkable private museum. One charged full of treasures dating back to the Roman Empire that the 14th Duke had curated during his lifetime.

Victor's study was a panelled, formal affair. It was a large and rectangular room with three walls, the fourth being massive, glass panelled doors which opened onto Bonnera's western terrace. The dark oak floor was covered with an array of different-sized Persian Isfahan rugs, all dating back to the late 1600s. The desk was purposeful, and had been constructed in African blackwood a hundred years or so ago. Its only accoutrements were: one of a pair of *scacciapensieri* his father had given him and Pietro when they were children, sheaves of notepaper made for the family from a papyrus colony in the Ciane River, near Syracuse on the Ionian coast. There were also a handful of assorted fountain pens, two inkwells, a silver box of Turkish cheroots, a Venetian glass ashtray, a striker full of English Swan Vesta matches and a simple rattan armchair with a tapestry cushion. The only item Victor had added was a black Bakelite telephone.

On the study walls his grandfather, a man of contradictions, had hung in a seemingly haphazard manner framed drawings he had spent decades collecting. The southern wall displayed a series of original lunar drawings by Galileo, and a telescope built in Padua in 1611. On the eastern wall, facing Victor's desk, were drawings by Michelangelo, including early studies for what became *The Creation of Adam* and *Vitruvian Man*. A random selection of Michelangelo's horse sketches filled the few gaps. On the third wall, the northern one, hung a compilation of preparatory sketches – all in charcoal and red chalk – by Leonardo da Vinci for his failed attempt at painting the 1440 Battle of Anghiari in Tuscany, between the forces of Milan and the Republic of Florence.

Victor stood in front of da Vinci's work and examined them as he rehearsed what he was going to impart to Pietro in a few minutes. The Florentine forces may have defeated the Milanese that day, but Victor was determined to secure a different outcome today. Besides, his dearest friend wasn't Milanese; he just worked there. Pietro was a blood Sicilian.

* * *

"*Pronto!*" Pietro answered the kitchen telephone. He was sitting alone on a barstool sipping a cappuccino with Enzo at his feet waiting for his share of his master's sweet biscuit.

"*Buongiorno caro*, Pietro."

"Victor, how good of you to call."

"Are you alone?"

"Yes. Ruxandra and I swapped over this morning. I spent the night at Niguarda, so she and Toto could come home. They're both at the hospital now."

"How is Paola?"

"She's still unconscious. The prognosis is not good."

Victor took in a deep breath. He waited for his ancestral courage, ingenuity and strength to surface. They all failed him. He had no alternative but to wade toward the deep waters and power into the waves ahead.

"I have more bad news I'm afraid. I made enquiries after we spoke yesterday." He picked up a cheroot, the Vesta's phosphorus stung his eye as he lit it. "I started, anonymously, with a connection we have inside P2. This led me to question all that I'd previously heard, which I didn't like."

"What was that?"

"Let me finish, Pietro, I know this is difficult. I spoke with a Minister in Andreotti's inner circle who was of little help. Later I tapped into two people at the Communist Party of all places. They were more forthcoming with information."

"So, where did that lead?"

"Precisely where you predicted, *caro*" – Victor broke off momentarily – "the IEA's front door."

Pietro felt numb as he dropped Enzo's half of the milk-sodden biscuit into the mutt's jaws.

"I also cross-checked with various intelligence personnel we know in Rome and the Vatican, all of whom are able to translate Italian whispers."

"What did they say?" Pietro asked.

"That dead men make the very worst enemies."

"That's actually good news."

"Yes, it is, but you're a marked man, brother," Victor puffed his cheroot. "I want you to listen to me very carefully. According to our sources, you have information to quake the very fabric of the Republic itself and no one will permit that. I don't have to translate that for you. You *were* right all along. An injured Paola was meant to be a warning, but it seems amateurs were hired at short notice, and when that happens mistakes are made. It was to be a scare to muzzle you, and it went horribly wrong." Pietro did as Victor had asked of him; he ground his teeth in order to remain silent.

"We're dealing with Hydra, Pietro. Our family *can* get to those who would harm you, but if we do decapitate that head, two more will reappear. And yes, you're correct, the CIA are involved." He paused again. "I repeat, you're a marked man, Pietro. That's the problem."

"I can't go on the run with the family. It's impossible. As you say, even if Hydra's head is cut off, I'll have another one to deal with. Cuci is behind all this and I can't stalk him and then kill him. I'm a lawyer, a father, for God's sake! You remember, I never even liked hunting rabbits when we were young," Pietro added. "Any ideas I can work with, Victor?"

"This is Italy. Politics is always urgent, justice seldom so. However, there's a crumb of hope in this idea, but how it's executed is another matter." Victor broke off and waited a beat. "The Salaviglia family have been guaranteed that Ruxandra, Toto and Paola wouldn't be harmed if you no longer pose a threat."

"What am I supposed to do? Blow my brains out in St Peter's Square?"

"I don't have an answer to that, Pietro."

"Victor, I do know where Moro is being held captive. I kept that information to myself. My mistake. I did it to protect my family, and all I've achieved is the opposite. Posing a threat means *what* really? And we both realise that any deal with Lucifer is going to be flawed," concluded Pietro.

"Listen, with the pledge I obtained last night we've been granted time. How long I can't guess. Days, a few weeks perhaps, but time for sure. The proviso is that we in turn had to guarantee your silence. I assume I have your word, Pietro?"

"Our bond was written in blood many years ago. Of course, you have my word."

"My next move will be made after this call. Two men will leave Bonnera today for Milan. Their families have worked for us for generations. They'll know what to do. Be aware, you won't even sense their presence. No one will. They'll look over Ruxandra, Toto and Paola until you decide what course of action you need to follow. It's not a permanent solution, but it is protection whilst a decision is made. This'll blow over I suspect, but when, I daren't speculate. Remember what father used to tell us, *'fear finds weakness'*."

"Your family put wings around me as a child, Victor, and now you're doing the same for my family." A stillness came over Pietro. "I'll figure something out. I always do. You know me."

"To give advice can be dangerous. However, the faster you go underground the better. Italy is too small a country for you. You need to vanish, Pietro, like only a Sicilian can do." Victor dropped his dead cheroot into the ashtray. "This'll change in time. You'll be able to return. That's a fact, just as I know our olives have grown for centuries, and will continue to grow for centuries more. Trust me, brother, and fear not."

Pietro heard Victor's counsel, but remained far from convinced. He had an outline of a plan, and had analysed its multiple risks – of which there were many. Nevertheless, his idea had gradually taken hold. It was Victor's father who had also taught him as a child that if nothing makes sense in daylight, then search in the night's darkest shadows.

CHAPTER 20

The Vatican State.
Friday, 7th April 1978. Mid-afternoon.

Alessandro Cuci placed the report he'd been reading back on his desk, removed the rimless *pince-nez* from the bridge of his nose, and cursed. Loudly. Something he rarely did. Then he crossed his office to his ornate French Second Empire drinks' cabinet and mixed himself a Campari and soda. More Campari than soda this afternoon. Just as he did so, the phone rang on his desk.

"Alex, y'all wouldn't have heard anything 'bout a girl being slammed into by a car yesterday?"

"Good afternoon, Judd."

"Jesus! Are y'all ever gonna let up?"

"Shall we begin again?"

"Just answer the darned question."

"No, I don't know anything about a young girl being hit by a car. Why should I?"

"Y'all said she was young? I surely didn't." Barings held his breath. "Not tellin' me somethin', Alex? Because y'all right. She's Albassi's eight-year-old daughter, Paola, and this is jus' the kinda half-crazed stunt you'd pull. You know, mow down a child to scare off her daddy."

There was ice in Barings' Southern twang to 'daaa-ddy'.

"Don't ever lecture me on methods. The words 'black', 'kettle', 'calling' and 'pot' come to mind. Rearrange the words into your own stupid *patois*, Judd," snarled Cuci, "and don't ever call me a child killer, especially when you've no evidence."

"Who said she was dead?" Barings' words circled the air like a vulture. "Y'all better pray to whichever God's cock you're suckin' on that I don't find yer fingerprints on her body."

Cuci's pallid complexion began to match his drink. "We Italians don't put pigtails in white coffins. Only Americans kill children."

"Bullshit, an' I don't believe a natural born liar like yerself, but I'm gonna cut y'all some slack, until I know more."

"*Grazie*," and with a snake-hissed voice, Cuci asked, "so, the little girl, is she dead or alive?"

"Neither. She's in a coma."

"That'll keep Albassi from meddling anymore. We're nearing the endgame now."

"Don't y'all ever forget this ain't my first rodeo, Alex, an' that's no threat, it's a Confederate promise."

"A promise of *what* precisely?"

"Y'all the genius, Alex, go figure it out. Y'all on *very* thin ice, an' the sun is a-comin' up real hot." Barings forced out a laugh as he hung up. He'd heard enough lies for one day.

PART FOUR

CHAPTER 21

Mġarr Harbour, Gozo, Malta GC.
Thursday, 4th May 1978. Midday-ish.

"Jesus!"
The telephone hit the terracotta floor and bounced under the bed.

"Maria! Maria! Help me find the bloody phone. What's the time? The clock's busted," bellowed Joshua Padden.

He flopped back onto his rickety brass-framed bed, shut his bloodshot eyes and clutched his chest. As quiet as a field mouse, Maria, his long-suffering maid, stole into the bedroom to mosey through the prodigious debris of the previous twenty-four hours: she counted eleven empty bottles of Heineken, the splintered remains of a bottle of Smirnoff Blue Label, three school exercise books, a dozen or more pencils, and a telephone amongst the wreckage.

"Sir, it's after twelve o'clock."

"Midnight already, Maria," groused Padden, playfully.

With a self-conscious smile, she handed him the phone and turned away, so as not to be caught looking at her employer's naked body. With his free hand, he grubbed around the ashtray on the bedside table for a half-smoked Players.

"Whoever you are, hang on, I can't find my matches!"

Padden rolled off the bed like a slumbering bear, and crawled around on all fours until he found a matchbox. He slumped against his old dresser and flared up a few matches. He sucked in a lungful of stale tobacco, and, with a smile long famous for its irascibility and charm, managed, "OK, who are you? What do you want?"

"A polite greeting, Josh. Have you any idea how long it takes to get a call through to your godforsaken little island!"

WHITE SUICIDE

"Hey, Pietro, good to hear from you, *amico*," Padden coughed and laughed at the same time. He was pleased to hear his voice.

They had been solid friends for over six years, ever since they'd met on an aircraft: for three hours they'd drank and talked. And talked and drank, telescoping their lives with an intimacy reserved only for strangers. However, life had turned from bad to worse of late for one Joshua Padden, and Pietro was apprehensive of what to expect today.

Before he'd placed the call, he reminded himself of the last time the two of them had met. It was just three months ago at a funeral in England. A pewter February sky had hung like a low drape over a nondescript suburban cemetery; the drizzle faint and mysteriously warm. A light wind had whipped over the crumbling red-brick wall as a lay priest murmured implausible pleasantries about a woman he'd never met. The woman's name was Annie Padden and she'd been Joshua Padden's wife for all her adult life. She would have been twenty-six on her next birthday.

One day she had had a headache. The next day a migraine. Two days later she was in a London hospital. And three days later she was dead. On the day after she died, a devastated Joshua Padden had checked into a seedy hotel in Kings Cross, where he'd boozed himself back from the precipice of suicide. It wasn't for him that the two bottles of Mogadon he'd snagged from a bent Greek pharmacist had remained intact. Ultimately it had been, yet again, Annie who'd saved him; her shrine in his soul still had a lifetime in which to burn.

They had been together ever since she'd visited the small, rural island of Gozo in springtime. She was in her twentieth year when they met. Lithe and beautiful, with bobbed chestnut hair and hazel eyes that twinkled with the cycle of optimism, hope and expectation that rarely accompanies youth. He was a hooching, burnt-out thriller writer approaching forty-five who'd traded on past glories with a history which could have come from one of his more fanciful plots. They'd married in the local village church in the September of that year, and the first time they had ever truly been apart was three months ago on that grey February morning in England.

Joshua Padden's life had begun somewhere in the African veldt, and had continued via Hong Kong, Vietnam, Cambodia, Laos and finally the French Concession in communist Shanghai, until something, nobody knew what, spurred one of life's true loners to buy a wooden sailboat (he named her *Innamorata*) and point her westwards. One year later, as the sun rose on the 1970s, he sailed the Suez Canal and fetched up in the central Mediterranean, and unintentionally, on the island of Gozo.

A fierce *gregale* had cooked up over the Balkans, and the storm had swept down through the Adriatic into the Malta-Sicily Channel. Within hours the spry *Innamorata* had sunk somewhere between Malta and Sicily. For three days he was tossed in his flimsy life-raft until a Maltese smuggler returning from Sicily rescued him and took him to Mġarr Harbour in Gozo.

The insurance company coughed up some money in the end. With the meagre proceeds he turned his back on the sea and acquired a ramshackle farmhouse – complete with chickens, mice, rats and lizards – on one of Gozo's flat-topped hills overlooking the fisherman's harbour. It was to become his home.

Joshua Padden knew only too well that history turns on a dime, and so contentment came at last, and easily, to him. He had seen far more than his share of horrors in the chaos of Southeast Asia, and he recognised that anyone who comes, by whatever force of nature, to an island, does so as a refugee. And every refugee needs a refuge, and Mġarr Harbour was just that to him. His refuge. As the damp first winter turned into a verdant spring, Joshua Padden, the mysterious Sino-African trader passed on, and P.J. Fowler the thriller writer was born. Even the pseudonym was 'borrowed'; P.J. Fowler had been a childhood friend from Rhodesia who had ended up a dead mercenary in the Biafran War.

Padden had always been one of life's true chancers: too honest for his own good and too dishonest for the good of others. A likeable chameleon, a great raconteur and a hard drinker who had explored the phenomenon of the hangover with a diligence that bordered on the heroic. Annie had changed all that. After the success of his very first book, *The Iceman*, he had floundered like his little sailing boat, dictating (he'd given up on the 'writing' part) increasingly implausible books, until Annie had rescued him. She subtly watered the vodka, his beers were often in 'short' supply, and from her (and his) efforts two, new, credible thrillers quickly emanated from the porous school exercise books in which he scrawled late into the night. And P.J. Fowler once again found life in airport bookstores. The tragedy, as Pietro knew, was that alone, utterly heartbroken and now in his fifties, there wasn't much that anyone could do for Joshua. He also knew there wasn't much Joshua could do for Joshua either.

"Are you awake?" Pietro asked.

"Sure, sure, what's it like in Italy? Is your bloody politician dead yet?"

"No, he's alive, but only just. It's been seven weeks since they kidnapped him." The terrible connection hissed static, hurriedly Pietro added, "Josh, can we meet up?"

"Tell me when your plane arrives and I'll try and make it to the airport. No guarantees though…"

"No, Josh, this has got to be on Italian soil, and can you get there the 'old way'?"

"Sure, Sicily is only fifty some miles away, and the day the Maltese stop smuggling will be the day shit won't stick to fur." Padden sucked on the cigarette end. "Let me check my schedule," he joked to buy himself thinking time.

"Sounds urgent, so, how about tomorrow, Friday, Porto Portopalo at La Tavernetta. I'll be there all day from dawn onwards. OK, Pietro?"

"Thanks, I'll get there when I can. Be patient and wait for me, Josh. I *will* be there."

Padden replaced the handset warily and ground the hot stub into the terracotta floor. He knew Pietro was not a man with an overdeveloped sense of drama; he wasn't anything other than a clever Milanese lawyer with a nutcracker brain and a devoted family. Or that's what he had always appeared to be.

Joshua Padden and P.J. Fowler had both heard enough tongues in their double-lives to recognise the pitch in one which asks politely: "Please, no questions."

What perplexed him, as dehydration took control and a vice-like hangover began to kick in, was that – his friend, the unassuming lawyer and family man – had a tone in his voice which screamed: "No questions!"

CHAPTER 22

**Milan Linate Airport – Ciampino Airport, Rome, Italy.
Thursday, 4th May 1978. Late evening.**

The air brakes on the Alitalia DC9 whistled Pietro out of an uneasy catnap. His stomach was queasy and empty. He'd stopped at the hospital en route to Linate, and he certainly had no appetite for aircraft food. Almost one month to the day had passed since Paola had been run over. She was still in what the doctors insisted on calling a *'deep state of unconsciousness where she is unable to feel, speak or move'*. Why use thirteen words when 'coma' would do? The prognosis was bleak, and there was little hope of any change.

He looked out into the dark night and saw only more thick, angry clouds. He tugged at his seatbelt as the aircraft bounced through pockets of turbulent air, and ran through his schedule. By the time he'd rented a car, disconnected the odometer cable and was clear of Rome's traffic heading south, it would be 22:30. Porto Portopalo, a fishing village at Capo Passero, the very southernmost tip of Sicily, was over 950 kms from Rome. And he had to cross the Strait of Messina too. It was going to be a very long night.

He flicked through the day's telexes: that afternoon had bought yet another shooting in Milan, and a couple of hours earlier, an industrialist had been shot in Genoa. This wasn't terrorism any more, it was civil-war levels of political violence between left and right. Open warfare in fact. Or were they the desperate actions of cornered men?

All his sources told him there was real dissension over Moro's fate, held prisoner for over seven, long, weeks. It was binary: to kill him or not to kill him. The very skin of the Red Brigades organisation seemed to be splitting apart like overripe fruit. Both his and Tina Anselmi's suspicions about the CIA and IEA were becoming ever clearer, and he continued to feed, without filter – for he'd given Victor his word – all the intel he gathered straight to Scampidi. Whatever the final denouement, Pietro knew he *had* to be a part of the endgame. Someone, anyone – Cuci, Scampidi, P2, CIA, Andreotti – might reveal their hand.

The aircraft's tyres squealed as they hit the runway hard. The captain applied the reverse thrust too enthusiastically, and the aluminium body shook in anger at its mistreatment. Pietro reached across to the next seat and undid the seat-buckle from around his holdall. It contained a neat bundle of thirty $100 bills he'd had stashed in the bottom drawer of his desk, four packets of the best Italian spaghetti, a toothbrush and eight identical black and white headshot photographs.

All he intended to return to Milan with was the toothbrush.

CHAPTER 23

**La Tavernetta, Porto Portopalo,
Capo Passero, Sicily.
Friday, 5th May 1978. Lunchtime.**

"How are you, Josh?"

Pietro hugged Padden's wracked, bearlike body, and stared, affectionately, into his friend's bloodshot eyes. He placed his hands on his unshaven cheeks and kissed each in turn.

"I've been better, Pietro, truth to tell, so have you too, huh?"

Padden took a step back. The weeks had galloped by and Pietro hadn't noticed the deep greying under his own eyes, that his hair had lost its well-cut sheen or that his gentle smile had faded.

"Any clue how long the drive is from Rome to Portopalo? With only one eye, you don't have any peripheral vision."

"So, it's the drive and your dud eye, eh? Come on, sit down, let's eat. Everything will look better after lunch."

Padden linked his arm through his friend's and led him past the fish tank towards a table in the far corner. The harbourside trattoria was completely deserted save for the owner, Maurizio Forte, and his solitary waiter, Pepe – once a proud fisherman who now hobbled between tables crippled with arthritis. Outside, in the little harbour, the stained white topsides of run-down fishing vessels gathered the sun's rays and shot them in flashes around the bleached buildings. The quay was deserted, apart from three fishwives swathed in layers of dark cloth. They were scrubbing stone stalls with coarse brushes where the meagre catches were to be laid out. At the end of the quay, a swarthy teenager, hair all thick and curly, fished with a cane pole and simple bob-float, his feet dangling above the still waters.

For the first few minutes the two men enjoyed the silence of friendship and sipped beakers of blood-red Sicilian wine, each alone with their private memories. Porto Portopalo was that sort of a place; the small fishing village, on the southernmost tip of Sicily, was somewhere you *swore* you could see Africa on a clear day. Porto Portopalo had the power of the past, for it had no future.

Joshua Padden hadn't been to La Tavernetta since Annie had died. They used to visit regularly during the few springs, summers and autumns of Annie's short life. La Tavernetta had been their shared secret. Together, in the veiled blue-hour before daybreak, they'd steal away from Gozo like the Barbary pirates had when they'd plundered the island for slaves. As they chugged north in their *luzzu*, they trailed fishing lines for small tuna or *lampuki*, and six or so hours later they'd be sitting with Maurizio at La Tavernetta. After they'd lunched and laughed, and drank, and laughed some more, and as the exhausted sun had taken cover in Africa, turning the few clouds a deep brinjal, they would ham-fistedly untie the *luzzu*, and with Padden gripping the wooden tiller they headed due south. Weary yet exhilarated, with fresh *lamupki* for a fish-pie they had somehow caught on their voyage, they'd always safely reach their refuge. For each trip was a unique voyage to Joshua and Annie. Only Pietro could have brought me back here, Padden thought. And as he drank his wine, he wondered what peculiar, hypnotic power his friend must have. He'd never understood it in all the years they'd known each other and he wasn't about to try now.

"What's going on?" Padden asked.

Pietro fidgeted with his Zippo and lit a Gitane, dark smoke enveloping his face. "How about the present?" Pietro replied. He was too tired to lie, and too canny not to know better.

"Good a place as any."

Padden remained silent as his friend recounted all the details of the ongoing Moro affair, and his own ever deeper involvement in it, sparing neither secret nor theory. Medieval Italian politics intrigued the writer in Padden, as did conspiracy theories, but the very dangerous company his friend had been keeping, and struggling to stay ahead of, shocked him.

"You're in a tangled web here, Pietro. When trouble is looking for a partner it's usually my bell that's rung." Padden reached for his own cigarettes and lit up. "I've lived through enough violence to have figured out that violence leads to times of nonviolence, odd though that may sound. It stops. It's nature's way." He inhaled hard. "Anyway, why did you have to see me so urgently? It sure as hell wasn't to tell me your theories about your megalomaniac boss, P2 Freemasons all the three-letter agencies teaming up with the usual suspects at that criminal enterprise you call the Vatican." He ground out his cigarette as if it tasted bad. "Your haywire Italian politicians, with all their right-wing fascist murderers make it sound like *'The Borgias meets 60 Roman Senators on The Ides of March'*."

"Eloquent, Josh" – Pietro managed a grin – "the only people you can rule out are the Communists. They needed Moro's political deal more than anyone." Pietro hesitated. "But you're right, there's more. Much more."

"Go on..."

"It's personal now."

"Why, Pietro?" Padden added, "I'm not sure I'm going to like what's coming."

"Four weeks ago, Paola was mowed down in a hit-and-run outside her school. She's still in a coma. Usual doctor talk, which means they don't have a prognosis."

"What! Christ, Pietro, why didn't you start with the important part? That part!"

"I've worked out who is behind it, had it confirmed too."

"By whom?" Padden interjected.

"The Salaviglia family, Sicilians, I told you about them. They brought me up."

"Even I've heard of them. Farmers west of the island, no?"

"Farmers is a good way to describe them, Josh. They'd like that." Pietro smiled at the memories of toiling on Bonnera's estates.

"Because it's the end, not the beginning. It was an attempt to scare me off that went badly wrong."

"The Red Brigades are Marxist terrorists, Pietro, they're not child killers any more than CIA are..." Padden faltered. "No. Forget that, I saw too many dead children in 'Nam and Laos." A childless widower, he was lost for words, so he tacked hard to wind. "How are Ruxandra and Toto?"

"Bearing up. I'm not being the best husband or father at the moment, but I'm trying in other ways."

"You've got more bloody riddles than the Sphinx. English, Pietro, English. So, who did it? Who's behind it?"

"The IEA."

"They're just the Vatican's PR department."

"Not any more. They'd like you to think that, but they're far from Vatican PR in today's world." Pietro leaned across the table in a conspiratorial manner. He continued. "What I don't get for *certain* is who's behind the Moro affair. CIA are involved, and the IEA are running CIA operations in Italy. I should have seen it earlier. Communists in an Italian government? Never. NATO is America's domain, so of course CIA are involved, as are the American State Department. I was ordered by my boss to gather information from all the known players and feed it back to him: the Moro family, the Red Brigades, the press, the Vatican, the Democrats and Andreotti, the Communists, you name it. I'm right in the middle of it. I'm the trusted, nameless and faceless source. My boss feeds my intel to the IEA. I'm supposed to be everyone's Switzerland."

"This is becoming darker by the minute. Even I understand that politics and crime are one and the same in Italy. Carry on," ordered Padden, with a hard stare.

Pietro then recounted the entire Romano Prodi Ouija story of five weeks ago. How he'd figured out that Prodi had given him the precise address of where Moro was being held. How he'd disobeyed Scampidi's orders and not passed on this information, and kept it to himself. Then, obviously as a diversion, the old village of Gradoli had been torn apart as if Roman Legions had been hunting for escaped slaves: no scent of Aldo Moro in the village of Gradoli.

"Phoof! That's some tale, Pietro. Fill in the blanks for me about the IEA and CIA."

"The head of the IEA is a man called Alessandro Cuci."

"Not heard of him."

"Nor has anyone else. He's the mysterious man behind all the shadowy moves in the Philippines, South and Central America. Every Catholic country takes IEA Communion on Sundays and pays alms too."

"Tell me more about this man Cuci?"

"I know almost nothing. This is the Cold War and I'm up against a Berlin Wall. I've spoken with people, but no one is saying anything. And that tells me everything." He drank off some wine and lit another cigarette. "You see, Josh, we Italians love to talk and gossip. About anything: football, politics, religion, girls, food, cars. You name it. And when no one is prepared to talk about someone, then there's something being well hidden. Trust me here."

"I do. So, where's Cuci fit in with what happened to Paola?"

"I'm not 100 per cent sure yet, but he's suspect number one. I've established that Scampidi and Cuci are both P2 members. Their Lodge is a nest of corrupt, merciless Masonic fascists, and it was Scampidi who ordered me to take this job. He was probably asked to do so by his fellow mason, who's partnered with the CIA, one Alessandro Cuci." Pietro paused. "Ever since the Prodi call, I've seen and heard far too much. With hindsight, I should've just passed the information on to Scampidi. But I didn't, and they found out that I knew where Moro was."

"Is there a suspect number two?"

"Only Andreotti and his people. They wouldn't sully their hands with what happened to Paola. Her being run down was a warning for me to stay silent. I expect the rest of my family to be targeted and my job is to protect them. The Salaviglia's have brokered a temporary truce. Don't ask me how, the old families work in mysterious ways. In exchange for Ruxandra, Toto and Paola's safety, I have to be dead or in the wind."

Padden whistled aloud. This was language he understood. He remained silent to gather his thoughts. Finally, he ducked his head and whispered through a haze of cigarette smoke. "You're in very deep shit here, Pietro."

"For sure, and that's why I'm talking to you. I'm an ordinary 'Joe'. I'm not a murderer or a detective. I can't stalk and kill Cuci, and Andreotti has more bodyguards than a Sicilian dog has fleas."

"I get it. Don't say any more. Enough already. There are those beyond reach and redemption: CIA, IEA, P2, Cuci, Andreotti, they're all bulletproof." Padden sighed before carrying on. "Just to put a dent in the Kennedy family, the entire US Mob had to unite, and from what I heard Jack-y boy had it coming anyway." He swigged his wine back. "So, where to now, St Peter?"

"I need your help. No, let me rephrase that, my *family* needs your help."

"How?"

"What I do know, and what they suspect I know, *can* hurt Ruxandra and Toto. It's as clear as day after what happened to Paola."

"So, how much is too much?" asked Padden.

"I need a completely new identity. Passport, driving licence, in fact, I need the life of someone who's already dead."

"There you go with these riddles again, Pietro."

"I intend to fake my own death when they kill Moro, which is inevitable."

"What are you talking about? Faking deaths. What's all that about?"

"I've got to disappear without a trace. Die. But there'll be no body. So, it has to be a white suicide. There is no orthodox way to vanish, Josh." Pietro wavered, buying time. "A left-wing group, probably the Red Brigades, will get blamed. No one will ever be arrested and my insurance policies will pay out in spite of there being no corpse. I'll have faded away, just another footnote in this tragedy. The Salaviglia's truce has lasted longer than I thought it would, but that's only because Moro's still alive."

Pietro's stare tightened. He remained calm, as if steel had replaced his bones and iced water coursed through his arteries. Padden swigged another throatful of wine, and raised his furry eyebrows.

"Just like that, Pietro! PHOOWF! You arrive, and then evaporate into thin air on a magic carpet from *'Padden's Souk'*. You're nuts! What about a thought for those you'd leave behind?" Padden refilled his glass again. "You didn't drag my bleeding-raw memories all this way just to inform me, over a bowl of bloody calamari, that you're going to blow your brains out, metaphorically speaking of course, now did you?"

Pietro touched his scar. "Yes, Josh. Actually, I did," he whispered in reply.

"My God!" A sarcastic tone crept into Padden's delivery. "I don't care what you call it, black, white or fuckin' scarlet, suicide is something you do on your own. You want to end it all, pal, you pull the damned trigger. Alone. Suicide isn't a team sport, it's a solo sport," he added, as he felt a twinge in the centre of his chest. "How dare you ask me to hold the damned rifle while you squeeze the trigger."

When anxious, Padden's eyes blinked furiously. "Listen up," he continued, "there are one-way doors and there are two-way doors. One-way doors are irreversible, no coming back through that door. Two-way doors you can always walk back through them. This idea of yours is a one-way door, my friend."

"Josh, this is 'First Mover Advantage'. I'm making my move before any more are made against my family. You really think I want to abandon my comatose daughter, my son and wife? They're not just my sun and moon, they're all my universe." Pietro spoke calmly. "One life to save three. The numbers are compelling. I have *no* choice."

"Sure, but I never could count," Padden stammered. "There must be alternatives, Pietro?"

"None are workable. With Paola in hospital we can't all go into hiding or flee overseas. I thought about going public. There's a journalist at the *Corriere della Sera* who's in my inner circle. I trust her too, but the story wouldn't get past her editors. Prodi's Ouija story is too fantastical. Then there's the crazy notion of getting to Cuci himself…" Pietro shook his head at his own stupidity before continuing, "This goes beyond the top, trust me, Josh. I know who my nemesis is, and it would be OK if the target was me and me alone. But the ante got raised when Cuci went after Paola. It's a miracle she's survived this far."

Padden, never short of a word or three, just looked down in silence at his uneaten calamari. "There must be something else?"

"*Niente*. There are no alternatives. The Salaviglias told me that. Me, or the family. My fear is the car bomb with Ruxandra and Toto and me all go up in pieces, leaving Paola an orphan." Pietro was chain-smoking. "No, Josh, one Albassi orphan is enough. There aren't going to be any more. Cut out the cancer – me – from this situation and Ruxandra, Toto and Paola will be safe."

"Jesus H. Christ," conceded Padden. "I've forgotten more about death than you'll ever know. People kill – or kill themselves – for manhood, money, glory, pleasure, love, power, revenge, despair, jealousy, desperation, redemption… Millions of reasons, millions, and they're all valid, but they are *all* secondary. The only real reason is necessity. In my extensive experience, that's the sole reason people kill. Necessity," repeated Padden.

"Do you need more necessity than my daughter five weeks into a coma or the fact that it'll be Toto, or Ruxandra, or both next in line?" Pietro was composed, cold even. He continued. "Someone in a nameless department, somewhere in an airless room in Washington prepared a briefing paper that stated that Moro was going to let the Soviet-funded Italian Communist party into a First World European democracy, a NATO member too, and they were going to do this through the front door. Josh, Moscow directly funds the Italian Communist party which won 35 per cent of the vote in the last election! This briefing paper then got passed through God knows how many US channels, including CIA and the IEA, and now Moro, the architect of this political pipedream, will soon be dead. I'm like the man in the airless Washington office who started all this. That man didn't matter, and my family don't matter either. My family and I are insignificant. Minute details in someone else's big picture. 'They' kidnapped a world statesman in broad daylight, and have kept him imprisoned for nearly two months. The only people who know where he is being held are Prodi, CIA, Cuci, probably Andreotti and the man you're having lunch with. So, what the hell do you think they'll do to be rid of the small-time Sicilian lawyer and his family? I need to save them, Josh."

Padden was numb in the face of such determination. He studied his friend in silence. Pietro held a determined expression, one that gave little away. Yet, there was something hollow in his eyes, even his blind one. It struck Padden that looking into it was like peering over the edge of a precipice. An almost irresistible urge to throw himself into the void began to tingle in his calves.

"How do you think Ruxandra will feel when she loses her husband, and when Toto and Paola lose their father?"

"I don't have those answers, Josh. This isn't one of your books where I can skip to the end and rewrite it. Ruxandra is strong, she loves the twins, and as you know, there's a nobility to women which men lack. Toto, well..." Pietro caught Padden's stare and averted his eye. "No, I don't know how he'll feel when his father dies any more than I'll cope with how it'll feel to lose my wife, my son and my daughter. My flesh and blood."

"I'm not Catholic or a Buddhist, I'm a simple man, Pietro. I think Darwin's wisdom was spot on. No God could create a creature as magnificent as a horse, or an eagle, or a tiger or an 'anything' for that matter in six or seven days. You need hundreds and thousands of years to master the creation of a living creature. There *is* no force, no God, out there. Believe me. The horrors I've witnessed make that a bankable fact.

We're just made of water and other stuff, that's all. We've been evolving for millions of years, and it's because of that, and that alone, that I find the idea of what you're saying so inherently repulsive."

Padden, alternating swigs of wine with nicotine, went still. The slit-openings out of which he peered shuttered like a powered iris on a camera.

Finally, he said, "but that doesn't mean I won't help you, my dear friend." He frowned in resignation. "Pass me another cigarette. We've got to work it all out. If we're going to do this, we need to plan it to six places of decimals. OK? Remember the six 'P's of Padden? *'Prior Preparation Prevents Piss Poor Performance'*."

"So, you'll help us?" Pietro knew that without Joshua, his stratagem – however flawed – was doomed. Padden was a truly anonymous man. He had survived in Southeast Asia by being invisible. He knew the rules and how to game the game. Pietro grasped that whilst the Salaviglias had the power, they didn't have anonymity, which would be his safeguard. Besides, Victor had kept him alive thus far; he couldn't ask him for anything else. Pietro and his family were in Joshua's hands now. That was the *only* plan.

There were many quadrants on Padden's moral compass-rose, and he paid scant attention to societal whims or bureaucratic rules. He knew the value of a secret and expected people to keep their word, and woe betide them if they didn't. He was one of life's outright survivors. Pietro knew, beyond peradventure, that for Ruxandra, Toto and Paola to remain alive he would have to slipstream Padden's wings. He'd recognised, after he'd spoken with Victor almost four weeks ago, that he was already in the wind.

"Every day above ground is a good day, Pietro, so I don't have a choice, do I? The killings, the bombings, are getting worse and with you below ground, metaphorically, those above ground will be safer. You make a compelling argument, Counsellor," Padden shook his head and carried on. "You're either the bravest man or the stupidest man I've ever met. For the time being my money is on brave." He toyed with his wine glass and nibbled a grissini. "When I was in Shanghai in the early '70s I taught myself Mandarin. The Chinese word for 'crisis' is represented by two symbols: one symbol means 'danger', the other symbol means 'change or opportunity'. I really hate the bloody Chinese, but they've been around for a long, long time. So, we now have a 'crisis' for sure, but we'll start work on 'change, opportunity' first." Padden grinned. "We'll worry about 'danger' later, alright?"

Pietro shook his head in relief as the light began to fade. The sun would soon dissolve into the Mediterranean leaving in its wake a gentle sea breeze to lip over dark cerulean waters. They ambled out of the restaurant in the direction of the harbour. Padden wheezed for breath as they settled on top of a rough wall near the harbour's entrance. They listened to the phosphorescent waves fold into the barnacled concrete below, and watched small brown crabs scamper out of the cracks. Venus glowed neighbourly at her crescent moon, low on the horizon. The street lamps cast ochre shadows that danced like disembodied marionettes on the ebbing breeze.

Padden looked into the clear night sky for a long minute – he took it all in – then turned to his friend, breaking the silence.

"Know this, Pietro, you *can* run, but you'll die in the end, and you'll die very tired too. That's what happens to people who run." Padden let his gaze drop back to the water's edge.

"I'm OK with that, Josh, just so long as it's me, and me alone, who dies."

CHAPTER 24

Reggio Calabria – Naples – Rome *autostrada*, Italy.
Friday, 5th May and Saturday, 6th May 1978. Night-time.

Initially, Pietro hadn't understood why Joshua had refused the $3,000. It was meant for bribes, *'to spread some green'* as Joshua would have said. He figured his friend didn't take the cash in order to preserve his own integrity with Ruxandra, Toto and Paola. Pietro didn't want to ask. He'd learned at an early age that you didn't ever tamper with the pride or courage of others.

The burning problem was one of timing. Pietro reckoned Moro didn't have long to live. The Americans were impatient and wanted him dead, and the Red Brigades were beyond reason. With Moro's death, the clock on his own mortal timeline would begin counting down rapidly. He *had* wanted to try and save Moro, yet after they'd killed Moro, Cuci would assume that Pietro would release his own story, the uncut version too, linking his death to Moro's.

Pietro understood that Padden's contacts with the Malta police department were first-rate; they'd been soft-soaped by P.J. Fowler over the years with his research-led questions. Padden had explained to him how he had an almost free run of the Malta Special Forces HQ in Fort St. Elmo, Valletta, and he'd told him how it would play out: a series of seemingly innocent enquiries to a senior officer about what happens to someone's file when he dies? *'Let's suppose a Maltese man didn't die in Malta, but, in a boat or car accident, in, say, Sydney, Melbourne or Toronto? A man in his mid-thirties, single, who'd attended Malta University?'* The answers would have been detailed. P.J. Fowler would then have added something like: *'I need to flesh this out for a new character. Let's see if such a case happened recently?'* From the way Padden had told it, the archaic records system in Malta sounded naïvely operatic, even when compared to Italy.

If, and it was a substantial if, such a person had died, it would not be beyond the bounds of possibility to bring him – complete with passport, driving licence, etc. – back to life. He had further convinced Pietro that in Malta, the left hand had no idea of what the right hand was up to, so obtaining a passport, with the identical numbers from an altogether different department would only be mildly problematic. The risky part would be keeping the deceased man 'alive' until such time as the heads of the departments changed. Padden had said that there was a General Election in Malta in two years, so he'd have to spin his research out, which wouldn't be a problem. The senior officer in question (he had an individual in mind) would be asked, politely, if his name and rank could be used as a character in the forthcoming book. *'Death by flattery, Pietro. It never fails,'* Padden had chuckled.

The Malta police departments enjoyed the attentions of their homegrown thriller writer. Novels take time, and bureaucrats always get shuffled after an election, irrespective of which one of the two political parties claimed victory. After the new head of department had changed, the old files would be forgotten and the deceased would be alive again. It was that simple, and that complex. If anyone could pull this off, it was P.J. Fowler.

Before they'd said their goodbyes hours ago, they'd agreed to meet at La Tavernetta seventy-two hours after Moro's corpse was found. If the conspirators were to preserve any standing at all, Moro's dead body would have to be delivered up.

Padden had promised a comprehensive Maltese identity – complete with its green passport, red driving licence and a full backstory – at best. And at worst, a solitary Maltese passport. With that promise, front and centre, Pietro drove faster and deeper into the darkest of Italian nights he'd ever known.

PART FIVE

CHAPTER 25

Central Rome, Italy.
Tuesday, 9th May 1978. 08:20, approximately.

Aldo Moro elected not to shave his two-day stubble. He also decided to skip breakfast.

On his small iron bed had been placed the very clothes he had been wearing, fifty-four days ago, when he had been kidnapped. Unexpectedly, they had all been returned, freshly laundered and pressed. The blue and white tie Eleonora had picked out that bright March morning had been cleaned and wrapped in cellophane.

He dressed with care, as he always did: first, two layers of underclothing, the second set being long-sleeves and long-johns; it had been a bright, but chill, March when he had last worn them after all. He then pulled on his calf-length, dark blue hose. He unfolded the crisp blue-lined, white shirt made by his shirtmaker friends at Ninarelli in Bologna, all of which sported his simple monogram: A.M. He removed Eleonora's chosen tie from the cellophane and, for what he knew would be the last time, he knotted it with not only precision, but with love.

Then, he threaded his cufflinks, and completed his morning dressing routine with his tailored dark grey three-piece suit. He checked the turn-ups on his trousers for fluff – a habit only – as he attached, and then pulled, his white braces over each shoulder. Even his black Oxfords had been hotel-shined. He slipped them on and laced them just-so. Finally, he stood up and checked – for he had no mirror – that each of the twenty plus buttons were fastened acceptably. They were. He smoothed down his shock of grey hair, now longer than usual. Perhaps it was the dim light, or simply the effluxion of time in solitary confinement, but he didn't notice that he'd put his socks on inside-out. There was a more serious problem which he did notice, however. Nothing fit as it once had. Everything was loose, like old sackcloth. Moro smiled his sardonic smile, and then sat down to write.

Today was Tuesday, 9th May 1978 and he understood that this letter to his family, would be his – and their – very last communiqué. The sentences he now crafted were ones he had begun to plan on the morning of Tuesday, 16th March 1978, when fifty-four days ago he lay trodden under the Red Brigades' boots in a car's footwell. He suspected even then what his fate would be.

Aldo Moro hadn't wanted to die, but he had refused to succumb to demands of his captors with dignity, duty and valour. Thus, he had defeated the terrorists and those who had truly masterminded them. They had never understood that he had always been *ready*, prepared even, to die, especially after treacherous Andreotti had steadfastly refused to negotiate for his release.

When he had finished his letter to his wife, Eleonora, he placed his fountain pen next to it and re-read his words.

'I die, if my party so desires it, in the fullness of my Christian faith and in the immense love for an exemplary family that I adore and hope to watch over from on high in the Heavens. A kiss and a caress for everyone from me, face by face, eye by eye, hair by hair. To each I send an immense tenderness through your hands. Be strong, my sweet, in this absurd and incomprehensible trial. These are the ways of the Lord…'

CHAPTER 26

**No. 8, via M Montalcini,
Southwest Rome, Italy.
Tuesday, 9th May 1978. 08:55.**

Aldo Moro was escorted, respectfully and with eyes-down gravity, by two men – Mario Moretti and Germano Maccari – for the last time from what had been called The People's Prison into a cold and desolate underground garage. The walls cramped around a small red car. The boot, or rather hatchback, of what was a stolen, and very second hand, Renault 4 had already been lofted open.

Moro looked at the space the *brigatisti* Maccari instructed him to climb into. He was 1.80 m tall, and the width of this treacherous old French car was half that. Moro took his time to study – as he did everything – the small space to see how best he could squeeze himself into such a car boot. A tatty orange blanket covered its floor. There was a spare tyre, and two sets of rusted snow chains to contend with as well. He was as powerless as a man can get. No student of yoga or origami, and dressed impeccably, Moro calmly folded himself – bending and twisting and curving – into the least uncomfortable position (he was Italian, even in death) of the boot of the Renault 4. He put his head on the left, and laid back onto the soiled orange blanket. He neither sighed, nor protested.

Before he could become agitated or uncomfortable, the two men looked at each other and then focused stony eyes on their prisoner. In the split second before the first of eleven bullets were fired, Moro jerked his right hand over his chest as if to protect himself. Moretti fired the first bullet from his 9mm Walther PPK pistol. It tore through Moro's thumb and drove bone and flesh into his left lung. The second bullet went straight into his chest. Then the Walther PPK jammed. Bleeding like a stuck pig now, Moro was still very much alive as Moretti reached for a second gun, a silenced 7.65mm Škorpion machine pistol, and rained nine more bullets into Moro's chest.

Aldo Moro died a slow and excruciating death from massive internal haemorrhages. Yet, not one of the eleven bullets had touched his heart. The men – for a reason they, and only they, alone could know – then plugged the mortal wounds which had just been inflicted with four large handkerchiefs, in a morbid effort to try and absorb the gushes of blood as the fetor of death, gun-smoke and cordite hung heavily in the air of the poky garage. Maccari tossed a plastic bag beside the dying body. It contained Moro's wristwatch, his wallet and one of Eleonora's bracelets he had always kept close.

Moretti sneezed, then waited a minute for the air to clear before he heaved and wedged Moro's bleeding body into something approaching a foetal position, shoving the dead man's left shoulder into the spare tyre. Why was it that dead bodies seemed to weigh more than live ones? Funny that. Moretti had killed many people and he'd never been able to square that circle. Having repositioned Moro, he stepped back, lit a cigarette and jutted his chin at his *brigatisti* to close the car's boot. Before he did so, he folded a corner of the orange blanket over the plastic bag of Moro's few possessions, and threw an overcoat on top of the body of the man who until a few minutes ago had twice been prime minister of Italy and the President of the ruling Christian Democracy party. Moretti looked dispassionately at the corpse bleeding out. He ground his cigarette – an MS – into the garage's concrete floor.

Finally, he slammed the rickety car boot shut so hard that Aldo Moro's coffin literally shook.

CHAPTER 27

No. 8, via Camillo Montalcini,
Southwest Rome, Italy.
Tuesday, 9th May 1978. 09:05.

The butt of his 9mm Walther PPK pistol poked out of the back pocket of Mario Moretti's jeans like a mechanic's wrench. The Red Brigades' leader, who had commanded the entire Moro operation, twitched his nose. Gunsmoke always made him sneeze and he wondered if he had an allergic reaction to it. Now that would've been ironic he thought, as he sneezed again. And again. James Bond's 9mm Walther PPK had never jammed when he shot the baddies. He laughed out aloud. Lucky they'd had a spare weapon.

Moretti knelt down to pick up his brass: eleven spent cartridge cases. He counted each one in turn as he dropped them into his jeans' pocket. Then he unscrewed the silencer from the muzzle of the 7.65mm Škorpion machine pistol. He could just as easily be slicing pizza such was his nonchalance. Pizza, God how he'd come to hate it! The very first thing he was going to do (the second was to get laid) this evening was eat a decent meal. Ossobuco. He could feel his tongue sucking the marrow out of the bone.

Before those rewards could come to pass, he had to deliver the car, and Moro's corpse, to its pre-destined place for the grand finale. A specially chosen location, about twenty minutes away – traffic depending – between the Square of Jesus and the Street of Dark Shops, as the Romans used to call them. Or rather more specifically, it was a hand-picked parking space opposite the Palazzo Mattei in the via Michelangelo Caetani, equidistant from the Communist Party HQ and the Christian Democracy HQ.

Via Michelangelo Caetani was just over seven kilometres from the underground garage where Moro's execution had taken place. The journey didn't take Moretti more than fifteen minutes as the traffic was light. He parked the car, badly, in the via Michelangelo Caetani, and it stuck out into the traffic flow due, not only to his lousy parking, but to the nearby scaffolding the Red Brigades had overlooked. By 10:00 he was finished. Quickly, he abandoned the red Renault 4 in the anointed space, a space which had been 'held' by another of his *brigatisti* on a motorcycle, who sped off northwards as soon as he saw Moretti arrive.

Despite a slow but steady flow of tourists heading to the Palazzo Mattei, with its three libraries, no one looked into the rear of the badly parked red Renault 4 for over four hours. If they had, they would have spied not only rusty old snow chains but some hefty lumps, like discarded garbage bags covered by an old overcoat. They'd also have seen a scruffy orange blanket, from which a shock of unkempt grey hair protruded incongruously.

Had anyone bothered to glance in the hatchback's rear window, they would have been the first to bear witness to the cold-blooded execution of Aldo Moro. A murder most foul.

CHAPTER 28

**No. 5, Largo Claudio Treves,
the Brera District, Milan, Italy.
Tuesday, 9th May 1978. 14:35.**

Three-wheeled Piaggio Ape vans scuttled frantically about the streets of Milan like liberated hamsters, their earnest bee-like exhausts grated on Pietro's shot nerves. He was sitting on the roof in his old beach chair with Enzo at his feet, chain-smoking. He needed some time alone. Ruxandra was at the hospital, and Toto was at school.

About thirty minutes ago, he'd received the news of Moro's death in a regular call to one of the many phone booths he and Dr Nikolai – his opposite go-between in the Red Brigades – used. And all before Moro's body had even been officially identified. Dr Nikolai informed him that the red Hammer and Sickle flag, which hung outside the Italian Communist Party HQ, had been lowered to half-staff. This was a signal both men understood as they said their own goodbyes.

Pietro knew it wouldn't take long for his wife to hear the news. News in Italy, especially bad news, had the unnerving habit of travelling faster than the swallows of summer. It stemmed from the unruliness of the race, or so he convinced himself. What had Mussolini said? *'It is not impossible to govern the Italians. It is merely useless.'* How right the despotic madman had been, he thought.

Pietro had hoped for something better. Something more subtle. Italians have been murdering their Caesars for over 2,500 years, they should've had enough practice by now, he reflected. This time it wasn't a dagger on the Senate floor, it was the Red Brigades, who having held a world statesman captive in Rome for fifty-four days chose to *execute* him in the boot of an old, and stolen, French car. Whose idea was that detail? CIA or IEA? It certainly wasn't the Red Brigades.

Yes, these were the *anni di piombo*, the years of lead: of terrorism, of bombs, of slayings, and of innocent death. This year alone, bomb attacks, shootings and assassinations were happening twice a week and in Milan alone there'd been three in four days.

The *anni di piombo* for sure. However, Pietro had never figured out, even during many sleepless nights, how more than 38,000 Carabinieri, police, Italy's armed forces and its three intelligence services – deployed for nigh on two months – and helped by civilians who'd searched their own towns and villages for him, couldn't catch so much as a scent of the man. Their orders had been to comb the length and breadth of Italy. Yet not one trace, not even a slug's trail of slimy evidence as to Moro's whereabouts had been unearthed. Try hiding President Carter in Washington DC, Prime Minister Callaghan in London, President Giscard d'Estaing in Paris, or even President Marcos in Manila for fifty-four minutes, let alone fifty-four hours. And as for fifty-four days, well, that would've been as impossible an act as an Italian Government balancing its books; simply inconceivable.

Pietro had learned of the Vatican and American involvement in the whole sordid affair. And he had thought – to his shame he now accepted – that by keeping tight-lipped he would be protecting his family. In the end, he concluded, it was *so* inevitable. History would repeat itself; the assassination had been carried out in the centre of Rome, in plain sight. The Italians were to have their own Zapruder moment, with the photos of Moro's bullet-ridden body in the boot of an old red Renault 4. This was Italy's, no Europe's, John F. Kennedy assassination.

Aldo Moro's death had been a slow, painful, nasty fifty-four days of a mock trial followed by a tawdry execution. It was the mealy behaviour of depraved street thugs, backed by other conspiring nations and forces. Whatever truisms history often spoke about death, there was no such thing as a *good* death. He should know, as a child he'd witnessed many a death.

The 'why' of who had ultimately placed the metaphorical dagger over Moro's heart no longer mattered: the CIA because of Moro's power-broking with the Italian Communist Party? The Vatican IEA in collusion with the P2 Masonic Lodge? The Red Brigades' own idealism? Mossad, on account of Moro's pro-Arab sentiments? NATO's own secret Operation

Gladio, with their anti-Warsaw Pact/anti-communist paramilitary army based in Rome? There were so very many – too many – players in this tragedy.

Moro was dead, and with him died his optimism for Italy. That was all that mattered. This crude finale was just a bad Italian drama dressed up to be a powerful work of political symbolism. Pietro's mind was a melting pot of emotions: anger, sorrow, remorse, confusion, rage, sadness, terror, all of which served to seal the canister on his fears for the survival of his own family. He knew the *whole* story, and that was far too much.

He lit another cigarette. The brisk north wind clipped his ears as the May sun warmed his bones. A plague of pigeons perched strangely silent in the coop. He gazed out blankly over the city and smoked in silence. The precarious sinew which kept him alive, had been cut. He was all but dead too, his tracks would need to be covered. And quickly.

He stubbed his cigarette into the concrete wall and noticed a couple of drops of blood fall too. He hadn't even felt the pain as he'd bitten into his own lip; a habit, a tic of late. He looked over the wall at the non-stop bustle of Milan's traffic that drowned out his impatient and unwanted questions. For that, he was grateful.

Time to go and confront the new world – with its new rules – which awaited him.

CHAPTER 29

Niguarda Hospital,
Piazza Ospedale Maggiore, Milan, Italy.
Tuesday, 9th May 1978. 15:25.

Pietro stared through the large ICU 'windows'. Ruxandra was beside Paola's bed and hadn't noticed his arrival. She too was looking at the shattered Meissen doll that had been her daughter. Knowing what he had done, he felt fraudulent even breathing the same air as mother and child.

Suddenly, as if she had sensed her beloved Pietro's spirit, she turned towards the 'window'. She smiled; a tear streaked her eye makeup. Slowly, he opened the door and fixed his gaze on her dreamy almond-shaped eyes, forever alert and inquisitive, even now. He loved her eyes and they would accompany him forever. Wherever.

"*Caro*, I am so sorry, so very sorry," Ruxandra said, finally.

"Moro died a very brave man. We southern men need to be brave, Ruxandra, remember that."

Pietro forced a smile out of his dark mood. There was nothing he didn't adore about his wife. He knew then, as he drank in every detail of her face, that he was at fault. Whatever the demands forced upon him by Scampidi, he was at fault. Whatever the alternatives, he was at fault. And he knew, from her silence, that she knew too. Too late now.

"Did you hear how they killed him?"

"In Romania we treated the gypsies better." She paused. "Moro is dead and you have to leave his family to mourn. I love you, Pietro, but you must bury him too."

She placed her long index finger over his bloodied lip and drew his head onto her angular shoulder. It was as near to surrender as he had come for fifty-four days.

Or for that matter, thirty-three years, fifty-four days and more.

CHAPTER 30

The Vatican State.
Tuesday, 9th May 1978. 15:25.

Alessandro Cuci slouched in his chair, tugged lightly at his goatee and sipped his Campari and soda. He loved the bitterness masked in its sexy red colour. To him it tasted sweet. Not as sweet as his current success though. The sweetest taste of all: an enemy's downfall. And the combination of the two was heady indeed.

Cuci had found that enemies are always faithful, and there was comfort in that fact. He couldn't decide just how many enemies had fallen with Moro's death (an insignificant act as far as he was concerned) which had only served to further promote his influence. There wasn't one senior member of the coalition who could not be 'moved' anymore. By 'move' he meant blackmail. Of course, his standing with the CIA was also beyond doubt. Had he not delivered, Salome-like, via the boot of an old French car (that detail was personal, he reviled the French) not on a silver salver it had to be admitted, the head of the man who was set to allow communism into a Western democratic government? Yes, he had. There would be time enough for American gratitude and for multiple favours to be called in.

All of a sudden, his phone rang, gate-crashing his gloating triumphs.

"*Pronto!*" Upon hearing who it was, he put the Campari on his desk and sat up. It was his most trusted field agent, who'd been Albassi's invisible cloak for over three weeks. Cuci listened without saying a word. The news was not good. The IEA had a tap on the payphone outside the Il Tabaccaio Café in the via Solferino, and Albassi had telephoned Dr Nikolai ninety minutes ago; the transcript wasn't available yet. Cuci thanked him, replaced the receiver and hoisted his Campari down in one. The *very* last thing he needed was Albassi and Dr Nikolai teaming up. It could've been an innocent call between two go-betweens, but between them they did own the whole story.

So much for his daydream of a holiday, somewhere warm, banal and far away from Italy. That had vanished in an instant. He was fed up with Rome, and the inevitable, upcoming protestations and rife hypocrisy over poor dead Aldo Moro, it would all be too much to bear. What was it his Nonno had taught him: *'The fires of Hell burn hottest for hypocrites.'* It was probably true, save for one minor detail.

There was no Heaven or Hell. Cuci had that fact on very good authority.

CHAPTER 31

The Embassy of the United States
Palazzo Margherita
121, via Vittorio Veneto, Rome, Italy.
Tuesday, 9th May 1978. 17:15.

"Thank you for the cable, Judd. Sorry for not getting back to you sooner. Another operation, you know how it is."

"I do, sir, but we need to speak."

Director Turner pricked up his ears when he heard that tone in his Head of Station's voice.

"So, Judd, what's it about?"

"Excuse me if I talk my mind, Mr Director. I was just wonderin' if w'all had another agenda? The operation is over. Moro is as dead as a buzzard's dinner, an' the local political fallout is not for us to manage. Correct?"

"What is it you want to say, Judd?"

"I've never been on a mission as confusin' as this one." Barings checked himself. "In joint operations, we're the ones in charge. We map our moves and they're well-rehearsed. More important, w'all plan *our* exit *before* we kick the darned front door down. Anyone on our side, as sure as guns do smoke, is on *our* side. I just don't get that feelin' here. It's like we're the plug-ugly sister who just happens to have a trunk full o'silver dollars." He paused. "I'm outta' turn here, but it's just a gut-feelin'. That, or I'm gettin' rusty."

"I doubt it." The director would take Baring's rust over marine-grade stainless any day.

"Cuci is like a lotta gals, he wants the very first lick of the lollipop, an' only then mind, is he happy to pass the lollipop around. However, y'all are *never* allowed to forget just whose lollipop it is."

Director Turner was finally grasping Barings' predilection for Southern colloquialisms.

"I've worked with many people in my years of service, but no one like him. Cuci has more hat than cattle, an' he's so darned twisted that when they bury him, they're gonna need a corkscrew to get him into the ground."

The director smiled to himself. He too felt the same way about his counterpart (if you could call him that) at the IEA: small-time operation, big-time crooked chief. Seen it all before, he just couldn't have put it quite so accurately.

"What do you want to do, Judd?"

"With permission, sir, I'd like to stay on in Rome awhile. Maybe prepare another, or a different, exit perhaps?"

"Your call, as ever. Come home when you're good and ready."

"Thank you. Y'all have a good day, Mr Director."

Barings clicked the phone off and listened to the satellites' static. His mind was a clenched fist of concentration.

Task No.1: Establish all the facts about hit and run car accidents in Milan; there was somethin' off for sure. Coincidences stuck in his gullet like furballs in a bobcat's throat.

CHAPTER 32

**Torrita Tiberina, a small village in the Tiber Valley,
50 kilometres north of Rome, Italy.
Wednesday, 10th May 1978. Late afternoon.**

"*The family retreats into silence and requires silence. As to Aldo Moro's life and his death, let history judge.*"

With those words, the widowed Signora Eleonora Moro made public her intentions upon hearing the news of her husband's murder the day before.

She, with her four adult children, had instructed politicians of all castes – including Christian Democracy – the press and the simply curious, be barred from attending the private funeral service the Moro family had planned. It had been her husband's dying wish that there be *'no national mourning, no state funeral, no medals in memory'* and she would honour those wishes.

Signora Moro neither needed, nor sought, anyone's permission. Yesterday, ninety minutes after the University of Rome's Coroner had completed his post-mortem examinations, she had simply whisked her husband's corpse away in a private hearse: no Carabinieri vehicles or motorcycle outriders. There were just three cars of close relatives to escort the body from the morgue to the village of Torrita Tiberina, fifty km north of Rome, where the Moro family had had a modest retreat for many a year.

The ceremony, an afternoon Requiem Mass, was attended by a hundred or so villagers and the Moro family relatives. Signora Moro knelt with her four children in front of the white oak coffin. The local parish priest officiated, and said prayers for the dead and for the living. The only flowers in the church were a simple bunch of red carnations which Signora Moro had placed on the coffin itself, content in the knowledge that the message was all her late husband would have ever wanted: *Your wife and children.*

When, finally, and as the reaper's twilight beckoned, Aldo Moro, *Il Cavallo di Razza* – the Purebred Horse – as he was affectionately nicknamed, was to be lowered into the vault in the nearby cemetery, Signora Moro was seen to touch the coffin for one last time and heard to say, "*Goodbye, Aldo...*"

PART SIX

CHAPTER 33

Mġarr Harbour, Gozo, Malta GC.
Friday, 12th May 1978. An hour before sunrise.

"You sure you want to go, Josh? It's going to get rough out there, and on the return trip we'll be smacking into the wind and waves. This *scirocco* means business."

Palalu, in the crisp predawn light, held the forward line of the *luzzu* as his boat bucked in the relative calm of the harbour.

"Fuck you, Pietro!" Padden shouted at the demons who awaited him; both Pietro's and Neptune's.

"Does that mean we're going, or not?" For a Gozitan fisherman, Palalu had rare flashes of dry humour.

"We're going. You, me, the damned wind and the rough seas. My hangover and this vodka bottle are going to keep me company, and I'll keep you safe, Palalu. This stretch of sea had its chance to take me years ago, so we're going to be just fine, my friend."

Padden belched. He looked spent, but like many long-term drinkers he neither weaved as if he'd been filleted, nor spoke English as if it had become his second language. Even at his most inebriated, he could stand erect and coax his tongue into tricks that made powerful orators sound monosyllabic. He was that rarest of animals, a drinker who had been kitted out at birth with a tungsten liver and hollow legs.

With a white-line gait, he stepped adroitly off the fisherman's quay and on to the *luzzu* and rubbed his temples. The previous night, and it had been one to stretch even his famous resolve, had begun in the local church, an alien place to him, talking to an alien man. Never in his entire life had he felt the desire (let alone the need) to confess before a God he knew, for sure, did not exist. He was his own best priest and he'd long ago forgotten the definition of faith. Yet last night he'd sensed his own mindset shouldn't hear his own confession. The ear of the vodka bottle was not a suitable confessor when a friend's life was at stake. The vodka bottle confession would come later, as indeed it did.

Padden had known the village priest in the way everyone knows each other on a small island. There was no hint that Padden's confession was to be any different from the usual fare of adultery, thieving and incest. When he'd finished, the priest had blessed him and offered up a prayer for his nameless friend and then vanished, leaving a bewildered Padden behind a velvet curtain in a cold church. He'd needed to hear words more robust than generic prayers; in that simple fact he'd found a vestige of comfort.

Padden planted his strangely angular bottom on the *luzzu's* wooden bench. He wrapped a woollen blanket around his old, yellow oilskin jacket and patted his inside breast pocket for reassurance only; the thick wallet, sealed in plastic with duct-tape, was over his heart. He then nestled the unopened vodka bottle securely between his legs.

Truth be told, in all his years he had never wanted, let alone needed, a true friend. People had come and gone. Dead or alive. They'd been vassals to bring him contracts, armaments, uniforms, anything to trade, anything to profit from. Again, Annie had changed all that. But now she too was dead. As dead as his friend Pietro would soon be.

Last night, he'd realised in that wretched church, that apart from Annie, Pietro was the first real friend he had ever had. It *was* true, only the good die young.

CHAPTER 34

**No. 5, Largo Claudio Treves,
the Brera District, Milan, Italy.
Friday, 12th May 1978. 05:45.**

Pietro Albassi had passed what seemed an endless night. He was woozy from lack of sleep. What little rest he'd been able to steal came only after his eyelids had surrendered to physical exhaustion. Even then, sleep hadn't comforted him. Ruxandra had sensed his uneasiness, and at 03:00 she'd nestled into his body to make love in the alarm clock's half glow. Gently she'd nursed him as he drifted in-and-out of restlessness until he'd drifted off into a deeper sleep.

05:45. Fully awake he glanced sideways. He'd given up counting the number of times he'd stared at the numerals. Daybreak would soon be upon the city. He propped himself up against the padded headboard and scratched his chin, while Ruxandra continued to sleep. Of late, his first waking image was always of Paola as a baby. It was strange how he only dreamed of the twins as babies, never as the children they now were.

Pietro thought ahead to tomorrow. He'd learned that a reluctant Pope Paul VI, and Cardinal Ugo Poletti, were to celebrate a State funeral for Aldo Moro in the Archbasilica of St John's in Lateran. An unassuming university chaplain had met one Aldo Moro, the university's student union leader, and they had become firm friends. Over forty years later, the university chaplain, now a frail, eighty-year-old Pope Paul VI, would wear the traditional scarlet papal mourning cape especially for his old friend's funeral Mass.

The pontiff's gesture was unprecedented. Pietro recalled that during the kidnap Pope Paul VI had made a personal plea – *'on bended knee'* – to the Red Brigades to spare the life of his friend. Out of gratitude, and love, Signora Moro had decided that Moro's sister, Maria Rosaria and his brother Carlo, would attend the ceremony where the heads of state of more than 100 nations would be represented. It had been a shrewd decision by her.

Pietro had toyed with the idea of going to Rome, for somewhere in the congregation would be the person(s) responsible for having Paola run down. Surely the proximity of evil would manifest itself in such a holy setting? He rubbed his eyes again – 05:55 – nailed his stare to the ceiling and waited for another five minutes to elapse. 06:00 was the time he rose every day, except Sunday.

Warily, he moved the bedclothes moments before the alarm was due to sound. His legs pimpled from the sudden temperature change and he rubbed his arms. He swung his legs onto the ground and stole across the bedroom floor to the bathroom. Every step laboured. Every breath agitated and shallow. Every thought elevated. Every noise deafening.

He rushed his shower and shave. Then, he dressed for work and hurried to the roof for a cigarette. His air rats squawked greedily. He and Enzo were late, and as with all wild animals who've been marginally domesticated, they'd become demanding and dependent, just like the junkies who loitered in the shadows and seedy espresso bars of the Mussolini's Stazione Centrale, Milan.

"I'm afraid you're all doomed to return to a life of scavenging, dodging cars and annoying tourists," he tried to joke as the pigeons crowded noisily around him. He threw generous handfuls of seed and stale bread about the flat roof. They didn't notice when he ground his cigarette out, grabbed Enzo and closed the door on them with purpose.

Once back in the apartment he toured each room in turn, with Enzo at his heels. Ruxandra had decorated it with a certain élan. His gaze fell upon the various surfaces like a wandering gypsy. A small group of photos ranked on the mantelpiece caught him off balance. There was a history there, of course there was, but not one that could save him. Snapshots taken on holidays: the twins throwing coins into the Fontana di Trevi, Ruxandra with her arms outstretched, somehow dwarfing the Eiffel Tower in the background, another shot – a self-timed one – where he and Ruxandra squeezed the twins like slices of cheese in a sandwich. And of course, with young children, beaches and lakes various: Ischia, Forte dei Marmi, Riccione, Lago Maggiore all featured. There were so many and he noticed that there weren't any shots of anyone other than the four of them. No friends. Just his family. The photos themselves had mostly faded from sunlight, heartlessly turning their faces an indelicate pale yellow. There was the faintest whiff of complacent neglect to them. He was sure they were no different from photos that lived on many a mantelpiece or piano. Yet, these Kodak moments of their bygone days somehow spoke too. He could hear their voices – Ruxandra's, Toto's, Paola's. They were as natural and as effortless as Sicilian birdsong. He locked on to each one in turn, to study and to listen. There could be no immediate past – this he recognised. And if there were to be secreted keepsakes and stolen memories, Ruxandra, Toto and Paola's very survival could be doomed. His survival was not what mattered. All that mattered was *their* survival.

Pietro gently pushed the children's bedroom door open. The hinges squeaked. He froze and prayed the little boy would carry on sleeping. His son lay on his side, a sheet folded loosely over his small shoulder. A half-light filtered through the curtains. Members of the Ferrari Formula 1 Racing Team glared down at him accusingly as he stood in the doorway. On Toto's small corner desk, he saw unfinished homework spread out. The floor was littered with toy cars and shoes. He stared at Paola's empty bed and caught a flash of her in her hospital room. His heart was slowly breaking. And as the father stared down at the son, Pietro passed the time of reason, and reached the limit of the forces of self-preservation required of him. With slow deliberation he wiped the first, and last, tear he would shed on this day from his right cheek. He took its warm moisture onto his finger, kissed it, and placed his finger onto Toto's left cheek. The little boy stirred, an eye cracked open, and recognising his father's familiar silhouette, a happy smile creased his face before he drifted back into his dream: a dream, an adventure dream, one he promised, promised, promised to remember so he could tell his father about it when he saw him after school later that day.

CHAPTER 35

The Law Offices of Scampidi & Rusconi.
No. 18, via Durini, Milan, Italy.
Friday, 12th May 1978. Late morning.

The intercom on his desk buzzed. The flashing light told him it was Angelica.

"*Ciao,* Pietro, the Alfa garage just called to change the time of your appointment. They need your car today at 12:00 not 16:30, I told them that would be OK. I've arranged for Joseph to drive it there for you." With nowhere to park near home, his car lived at the office, rarely driven.

Pietro had to think very quickly.

"Sure, that's OK, but I'm behind on some research. Can you call them back and tell them Joseph will deliver the car before 12:30?" He checked that his breathing and speech remained even. "He can drop me off at *Gianni's* on the way, I'll have lunch early today."

This Friday would be an ordinary working day for Pietro Albassi, *avvocato,* and it was the one day a week he allowed himself to lunch out alone. He took his index finger off the intercom's button. His body shivered as if all of his nerve ends had suddenly leapt outside of it. The heart really is dead centre of the chest he thought, as he lit yet another cigarette. Breathing deeply through his nose, he counted the butt ends in the ashtray. Eight. Four more than normal. He placed four in an envelope, licked it down and dropped it in his briefcase. Eight would be more like his normal tally for a working morning. There could be no difference in anything, not even his quota of cigarettes, and there was still some smoking yet to do.

Thanks to a clerk at the Alfa Romeo garage, who probably wanted to skive off early on a Friday, his detailed game plan was now irredeemably altered.

"It was Napoleon who wanted lucky generals, not good generals," Pietro muttered, as he reworked his strategy. So much for good plans. So much for good luck, on a day when he needed a little luck to ensure it was the unluckiest day of his life.

He reminded himself of The First Rule of Law: *'You* will *get caught'*, no matter how meticulous your planning: be it adultery, robbery, fraud, murder, you name it. He should know. Nearly all of the people he'd defended had ignored The First Rule of Law.

Only two alternatives came to mind: ring the garage himself and reinstate his 16:30 time, or stay an extra day. Neither were acceptable. For him to change the garage's new time would undermine the credibility of the day. Any decent investigating officer would sense it immediately: *'Hmm, that's odd now that you mention it…'*

To stay one more day was psychologically beyond impossible. There could be no turning back. He would have no alternative but to think on his feet and use his honed instincts. At whatever the cost, he was resolved to die. Today.

CHAPTER 36

The Law Offices of Scampidi & Rusconi.
No. 18, via Durini, Milan, Italy.
Friday, 12th May 1978. 11:50.

"*Ciao*, Angelica, I'll see you later. Don't be too long at lunch, I've letters that must leave this afternoon."

Angelica had been his secretary for five years, ever since being widowed unexpectedly young. Hers had been a childless marriage, and despite no apparent shortage of suitors, she'd chosen to lead a solitary life as a single woman in her thirties. Pietro wondered momentarily to himself if Ruxandra would go back to full-time work. Before the notion could take hold, he smiled a secret farewell to Angelica.

The corridor that led away from her neat outer office to the elevator was dead space. It had a neglected and musty air about it. Vintage maps lined its drab green walls where people had knocked into them and forgotten to straighten them. The carpet, a mushy brown affair, was curling at the edges, and the lights hung as depressingly low as the bulbs that illuminated it. Their offices were not ones visited by Dottore Scampidi.

Pietro waited for the elevator. His mind couldn't help but absorb the impedimenta of everyday objects which had, until today, slid by ignored or simply unnoticed. Whether he liked it or not, this cornucopia of mental debris would accompany him: Angelica's smile. Her unflattering purple skirt. The green coolie-hat shaped lampshades. They would all be stowaways.

The elevator delivered him directly into the basement car park, where alone in his subterranean aluminium and glass cubicle, Joseph Zangretti sat for his mandated time slowly clogging his lungs with carbon monoxide. He was, even as Milanese security men go, as effective as a toothless poodle. However, Joseph was a kind and gentle man, and as he'd aged, he'd become agoraphobic. So, for him to pass his working day in a cramped, darkened underground space, with only a radio and inanimate pieces of machinery for company, was an ideal existence.

"Avvocato, if you give me your keys, I'll fetch the car."

"*Grazie,* Joseph."

A minute later the modest red 4-door Alfa Romeo Giulietta came to a halt by the booth, and Pietro climbed in to the passenger seat.

"Tell me, how are you, Joseph?"

As he asked a seemingly innocent question of the firm's elderly Security Guard, a seed-germ of an idea formed in his mind.

* * *

Joseph slipped the clutch anxiously and edged the car towards the steep ramp which would lead them out to via Durini, daylight, people, and the traffic he so dreaded.

"Hold on, Joseph! I've forgotten something upstairs. I'll call Angelica from your office."

Joseph stood on the brakes forcefully, the car jerked to a halt and Pietro jumped out and let himself into Joseph's cubicle.

Pietro dialled Angelica's direct line and opened his briefcase. Inside was a weighty file marked 'IEA/Moro'. In addition, it contained a ring of keys, attached to which was a Swiss Army penknife. There was also a black peaked cap, and a fat aluminium cigar-tube of tightly rolled US bills totalling $5,400. At the bottom of the case was an old, and loaded, 9mm Beretta pistol and silencer. He studied the pistol contemptuously. It had been an odd gift from the two Red Brigade terrorists he'd successfully defended two years ago after a shooting in Turin. An anonymous messenger had delivered it wrapped in an UPIM shopping bag with a servile note of gratitude. He'd thrown the letter away, and was about to do the same with the pistol, when for no reason he could recall he'd dropped the UPIM bag in his bottom drawer, where it had languished ever since. He had supposed it to be a totem of surrender – not a gift of protection – from both defendants who knew their bright young lawyer was too much the fatalist to have had a use for such a weapon, especially one with a silencer. It was bizarre then, and bizarrely ironic now.

"Angelica, I think I've left an IEA/Moro file in my filing cabinet, you know where the spare key is. Will you check for me please? *Grazie*." He paused. "Don't worry if it isn't there, I've got so many of these files in my case, it's going to split, it might have slipped inside one of them."

"Sure, Pietro, hold on."

He gripped the phone between his shoulder and ear and removed the red Swiss Army penknife from the keyring. He opened the blade and palmed it in his hand.

"Sorry, Pietro, the file isn't there, only your personal files are left. You must have all your IEA/Moro files with you. Enjoy your lunch." Without waiting for further instructions, she clicked the line dead.

He already knew that; he was simply baiting the hook. All his IEA/Moro files had stayed with him at all times. These files contained facts, suspicions, ideas, schematic sketches of possible links, general notes he'd made, intelligence reports on the status of the IEA, CIA, P2, Scampidi, Andreotti and all their links to the Moro affair. Suppositions, but also hard evidence to kill for, like his contemporaneous Prodi notes, all of which he'd kept secret, even from Scampidi. However, what if both the IEA/Moro files, and their author, disappeared? For a conspiracy theorist – and Milan's criminal investigating officers were either speechlessly corrupt or speechlessly moral – it might prove to be a diverting plot.

Pietro tripped out of Joseph's pokey aluminium-framed booth, and landed almost facedown on the dusty ramp, falling beside the rear of his car.

"Damn it!"

Quickly, and with stealthy precision, he rammed the penknife's blade into the wall of the rear passenger-side tyre. It hissed foul air at him as he folded the blade back into the knife.

"I'm OK. I just stumbled, come on let's get going," Pietro picked himself, and his briefcase, off the concrete.

All he could think about as Joseph nervously crawled the car up into the sunlight and the congested streets, was that he had no idea just how tough tyres were.

The pre-lunchtime traffic ground its way forward as if each car was a scale on a huge snake that had entwined itself through Milan's streets. The car radio hummed in the background. Neither of them listened, but the breathless gabble stemmed the abuse from the weaving Vespa drivers. Joseph, his face a study in uneasy concentration, stared straight ahead as he white-knuckled the Alfa's wooden steering wheel.

Within two kilometres, the first-gear-only traffic had thinned out, and Joseph made his way through the cobbled one-way streets towards Gianni's.

"Avvocato, I haven't driven your car for a long while but it doesn't feel right."

"What's up?"

"I'm not sure, feels like it could be a flat tyre."

"If it's a puncture don't change it here, we'll be lynched!" Pietro laughed, and focused ahead like a ship's captain searching out land – a cul-de-sac or a quiet side street.

"There, Joseph, turn left just after the green Ford, before the large apartment building."

Obediently Joseph pulled into the narrow residential dead end: all firmly shuttered windows, communal refuse bins, chained bicycles and an open garage ramp like the one they had just left. Both men got out of the car and instinctively looked at the front tyres and shrugged.

"Here it is," Joseph said, pointing at the rear passenger's-side tyre, which was as flat as a black rubber band.

"The spare is in the boot." Pietro's tone held a faint, but unmistakable command. "I'm going to get an espresso."

Pietro grabbed his briefcase and turned to make direct eye contact with Zangretti.

"Tell me, Joseph, am I imagining it or did you notice anyone following us after we left the office?"

"No, sir."

"I've this strange sensation we were being followed, watched. It's unnerving. I kept seeing this dirty white Lancia in the wing mirror. I studied it. It copied our every turn. Are you sure you didn't see it, Joseph?"

"I was busy looking where we were going, Avvocato."

"I could swear I saw it," he sighed, "I'm sure I did. That white Lancia was shadowing us."

Pietro walked away to the end of the cul-de-sac and turned left towards the apartment block which fronted the dead end. He rushed to the main glass front doors and urgently shook the tarnished handles. Locked. His heartbeat was now well into three digits as he pressed a doorbell at random. No reply. Another. No reply. A third. Again, he needed a little luck to be unlucky.

"*Pronto!*" A shrill voice boomed out of the loudspeaker.

"A delivery for No. 4a. There's no reply and I need to leave the parcel inside."

Pietro's breathlessness must have made him sound like a delivery man. The door buzzed open. He immediately darted to the lift, slid back the concertina gate and pressed the button to descend. The old lift-cage shuddered when it reached the basement. He stepped out and breathed mildewed air into his lungs. He had, he reminded himself, not committed a technical crime. So far. So why was he feeling and behaving like a fugitive? He wasn't a fugitive. Yet. A heinous crime in which he was peripherally, and innocently, involved had made him behave like one.

Now, he had to run. Hard. Fast. And without regret if the lives of his family were to be preserved. He knew nothing would ever be the same, but at least they would all be alive: albeit in different corners of the globe. Given the circumstances it was the best he could orchestrate.

Pietro laid his briefcase by the exit-way ramp. He removed the 9mm Beretta and gripped the pistol firmly by its silencer and barrel. Fifteen metres away, and directly in front of him, Joseph knelt with his back to the building's exit ramp and struggled with the jack, the wrench and the wheel nuts.

Without realising, Pietro made the sign of the cross and crept forward. He needed just a little more luck.

* * *

Joseph only found out the next day as he lay in his hospital bed, what had caused him to black out, and what it was that had torn through his fleshy thigh: the butt of a hand gun and a solitary bullet from a 9mm pistol. He also remembered the first question he'd asked when he came-to in the ambulance.

"The Avvocato, how is he?"

The doctors had refused to tell him at first, but he had found out from one of the nurses. There must have been a struggle, she had told him. In addition to the bullet that had passed right through his thigh – no more than a flesh wound – two more bullets had pierced the car, and yet five spent brass shells were found in the gutter. Which meant that two bullets were presumably somewhere inside the Avvocato. Traces of a rare blood type, AB-, were found splattered on the spare tyre, the passenger seat and some legal papers. Anxiously, the nurse continued: there were no witnesses, no one had heard gunfire and no one had come forward or had yet been found. More significantly, no organisation had claimed responsibility or made any demands, so, there was hope. This really was the *anni di piombo*, she'd said. Joseph sighed back into sleep once he heard all that she had told him. He liked the Avvocato, he was a good man.

Before he shut his tired eyes, he reminded himself that he must remember to inform the police about the dirty white Lancia that he'd seen following them all the way from the office, as he'd weaved his way through the back streets of Milan.

CHAPTER 37

**No. 5, Largo Claudio Treves,
the Brera District, Milan, Italy.
Friday, 12th May 1978. 20:35.**

There were times when Ispettore Lorenzo Massina hated his job. And hate was not a word he often used. There wasn't a mention of the host of extra duties he had to carry out for his measly salary. This was one of those jobs. What with the new car, and his wife's wolverine appetite for clear potato-based liquids marked 40% proof, life was none too enjoyable. Be thankful for small blessings, Massina thought, at least both daughters are married. But the boy.

He dismissed the memory of his son's junk-hollowed face before it sent him into a tailspin of despair. The problem with life in Italy was not so much the left wing, it was the left arm. It was dark outside, and he really didn't want to be where he was right now. He scratched his temple and pressed the intercom again.

"Two out of three. It could've been worse I suppose. At least their husbands are good men with steady jobs," Massina muttered noisily to himself.

"*Si, pronto*, who is it?"

"Oh, oh, I'm sorry, talking to myself, hazard of the job. I'm looking for Signora Albassi."

"I am Signora Albassi. What can I do for you?"

"My name is Ispettore Lorenzo Massina, Criminalpol. May I please have a word with you? I won't take up much of your time." He regretted those last words the second he uttered them.

"It's late, Ispettore, and my husband isn't home yet, can it wait?"

And he's not coming home either Massina nearly replied.

Ruxandra caught her breath. Surely, she had left the gypsies with their superstitions in Romania's ghostly forests?

"I'm afraid it can't wait, Signora."

"Then of course, Ispettore. Top floor, apartment 6a."

She buzzed open the heavy main doors. Massina rubbed his chest to ease a jolt of pain. Questura HQ, in the via Fatebenefratelli, was about 500–600 metres away; he wasn't sure whether it was the modest exercise or the task which lay before him that had caused the chest pains.

"Whoever this man Albassi was he's done alright for himself," he reflected, as he stepped into the courtyard, his mind forever active.

Once in the elevator, he adjusted his trousers around his outsize stomach, groaned and turned to face the gilt mirror. Cracked veins shot off his bulbous nose onto his fleshy cheeks. His hanging jowls, as plump as a chipmunk's and softened by cream and pasta, were mottled with livid red blotches. Then he stuck his tongue out and cringed; it looked like an old Turkish prayer mat. In fact, his whole face resembled a month-old potato both in colour and texture. And forty years of smoking had stained his thick grey moustache a bitter gravestone yellow. At least he'd finally quit smoking. He turned away in disgust. Everything about his life depressed him, right down to this assignment. But there was a worse hell out there. He was at the blunt end of his late fifties and could retire soon on a meagre pension, but if he did, he'd be forced to spend more time with his wife. No assignment could be that bad. Death would just have to catch him unawares, or in the line of duty. A coronary would be good. A chest-imploding one of Vesuvian proportions. Anything, so long as it wasn't a debilitating stroke. The thought of his wife pushing him around in a wheelchair as he drooled into a teacloth was an extravagantly cruel fantasy that only a handful of his criminals could dream about. Noisily, he groaned again.

The elevator slowed to a halt as the doors juddered apart. Ten metres away, standing sentinel in her doorway, and dressed in tight beige trousers and a navy cashmere sweater, which only served to accentuate her slim figure, was the comely Signora Ruxandra Albassi. A stripy brown mutt sat beside her, silent and still. It stared at him with hangdog eyes.

"He *did* do alright for himself," Massina caught his inner voice, so the words remained inside his stale mouth. He raised an eyebrow instead.

Ruxandra Albassi greeted him with an outstretched hand, as warmly as she could, desperate to delay the news she sensed the policeman was about to impart. Massina took her hand. He smiled too, and his last vestige of vanity made him bow his head so as not to expose his stained teeth.

"I've heard your name before, from my husband perhaps? Pietro Albassi, he's a criminal lawyer."

Massina didn't reply. Despite his years, he didn't trust himself. Her husband's body had not yet turned up.

"May I please come in?" He opened his identity wallet, trying to avoid her bloodshot and puffy-eyed stare.

"Of course, how rude of me." She led him into the sitting room.

Massina's facial veins throbbed as they blushed. He'd never understood his success as a detective. He'd have taken bribes if he could've been bothered. He'd have done actual legwork if he hadn't been so lazy. Nevertheless, the truth of his numerous accomplishments as a detective was both simple and secret. He was bone idle. An Ispettore who preferred to exercise his formidable, and cynical, intuition from behind his desk. That, and good fortune, had solved his cases. Shoe leather and hard work certainly hadn't. Let everyone think otherwise. Who cared? For sure he didn't.

"May I get straight to the point, Signora Albassi?"

Ispettore Lorenzo Massina was a man of unusual sensibilities (another explanation for his accomplishments) and he hesitated for a moment to breathe in the scented air of her sitting room for the first, and the last, time. He had been a policeman long enough to realise the words he was about to utter would forever leave an impermeable odour.

"We think your husband has been kidnapped. We don't know by whom. We're hopeful he is still alive. His car was found east of here in a cul-de-sac with his driver..."

"His driver?" Ruxandra asked, coldly.

"Yes, his driver, Joseph Zangretti from his office. Anyway he, the driver that is, was found unconscious with a bullet wound in his thigh. Zangretti is expected to make a full recovery. You see..." Massina paused, this was not going as planned. "May I please trouble you for a glass of water?"

His eagle stare followed her as she left the room. Up close she looked dreadful, not 'Massina dreadful' he admitted to himself, somehow worse, if that were indeed possible. Her watery blue-grey eyes were empty, soulless. She wore no makeup, her skin was dry, her hair unkempt. Only her clothes looked the part. While she was in the kitchen, he recalled the brief file on Pietro Albassi he'd read earlier when his stomach muscles had tightened in a way they hadn't for a long time. The missing *avvocato* was up to his neck in the quagmire of the Moro affair, and he hated – that word again – the octopus-knots in his stomach. They always meant trouble, and trouble meant work. And terrorist cases always bought out the truly apathetic in him. What perplexed him was that Signora Albassi had obviously been grieving in order to end up looking like she did. Yet, the husband had only just disappeared… He dismissed his train of thought as she returned with the water and sat back down, her posture rigid.

"You see, Signora Albassi," Massina continued, "they'd stopped to fix a puncture." He sipped the glass of cloudy tap water hoping it would dissolve the knot in his stomach. "I'm sorry to inform you we've no leads at present, and no one has yet come forward to claim responsibility, which is not unusual. Traces of your husband's blood type were found at the scene, and we've verified it with medical records. AB-, only 0.7 per cent of the population have that type. It's the rarest in the world."

"Is there anything else you can tell me, Ispettore?"

"No. I'll call you in the morning and we should know more by then. Meanwhile, I would like to station an officer here tonight to monitor any calls."

"Absolutely not, Ispettore. My son is asleep and I will not permit him to wake up to a policeman. Our family has endured enough lately," Ruxandra spoke forcefully.

"From your tone, Signora, I take it that's your final word?"

"*Si.*"

Massina hauled himself awkwardly up from her sofa and marvelled at her poise. He had rarely seen anything like it before. He had just told her that her husband had been kidnapped – possibly murdered – a few short hours ago. Yet her eyelids had not fluttered, and she neither sniffled nor cried. In fact, she looked cried out. There had not even been one miserable jaw-quiver from her. She had behaved as if he were telling her something she *already* knew. When he reached the front door, he held out his card.

"If anyone does contact you before we speak tomorrow morning, you're to call me immediately. Whatever you do, do not talk to the press. I don't need grieving wife stories fouling things up." Massina spoke with a grind of aggression. Maybe it was her cool, and her refusal to observe Criminalpol's kidnap procedures that did it, he thought.

He glanced at the two children's bicycles propped against the hat stand. She caught his look.

"Twins. One boy and one girl. My daughter is in hospital."

"I'm very sorry to hear that, Signora Albassi."

"Thank you, Ispettore Massina." She closed the door firmly before he could say another word. Pietro had gone graveyard quiet before, sometimes for two nights during the Moro business. But she *knew* this time was different; what had occurred this afternoon was definitely connected to Paola. Her mind smothered Massina's facts until they vanished into that quadrant of her psyche that stored only trauma.

Before returning to the sitting room, she looked at the photographs in their frames on the hall table. Tears edged slowly down her cheeks, not for her husband, not for the twins, and certainly not for her. The warm salt tears edged into the corner of her mouth and her tongue flicked at them. Their taste bought back memories of twisted and harrowing nightmares. They were someone else's tears. Someone else's youth. A past she had buried and never wished to exhume. A past that had now returned to haunt her.

Gospels in Hell. Lies in Paradise. So, the Romanian gypsies had been speaking the truth after all.

CHAPTER 38

The Vatican State.
Saturday, 13th May 1978. Early evening.

The sun dropped wearily behind the Basilica Papale de San Pietro. It had been a hectic day for Alessandro Cuci. Earlier, Aldo Moro's – empty coffin – State funeral had been held in the Archbasilica of St John's in Lateran, just five kilometres from the Vatican State. What a ceremony it had been, in the oldest basilica in the Western world. All that it had promised to be, and more. He took personal credit for pressing the Vatican's Sistine Chapel Choir into service. They were Heaven's angels sent to sing. Cuci had likened the entire day to an American Embassy Independence Day cocktail party, except everyone had dressed in black, with smells, bells and Latin all thrown in for good measure.

Heads of State, and representatives of more than 100 nations, had been present he'd been informed earlier. Apparently, that number was more than the ninety-two Heads of State who'd attended John F. Kennedy's Arlington funeral, fifteen years ago. Cuci wondered if it was in fact true, but still smirked when he'd found out. A Southpaw's jab at the US and CIA was long overdue.

Outside St John's in Lateran in the piazza of St John, red Communist flags co-joined the white Christian Democracy flags. All were massed along with 100,000-plus workers and citizens throughout Rome to hear the papal ceremony. Several hundred soldiers in grey battledress with navy berets and submachine guns guarded the piazza, with more stationed throughout the entire city of Rome. In quiet homage, the people of Italy had assembled in bars, cafés, homes and public spaces to hear Aldo Moro's old friend, their pontiff, Pope Paul VI, address the world. Quite a show, Cuci mused as he fixed himself a second, more robust, Campari and soda.

At first His Eminence had refused to officiate out of respect for his friend's last wishes. It had taken Cuci's forceful cajoling to humbly suggest that His Absence, after His Eminence's offers to mediate during the deceased's incarceration, would give the wrong signals. And Beelzebub himself, Prime Minister Giulio Andreotti, had been quite insistent with Cuci, irritatingly so. The Pope *must* attend. Pressure *must* be brought to bear. *'You have to see to it, Alessandro,'* Andreotti had whined.

The dilemma, as Cuci had tried to explain to the querulous prime minister, was that Moro was a layman, and it would be an unprecedented gesture for a Pope to lead the service. Besides, He was not someone who could just be ordered around. And certainly not by Andreotti. His Very Aged Eminence Pope Paul VI was a man of the Church. Admittedly, Cuci had hoped that by now he might actually have understood his role in the world. Nevertheless, Cuci had won him around in the end and silenced Andreotti. Another favour in the Andreotti bank, an account Cuci would be sure to collect on. In Italy you only need to bribe a politician once. After that, it was plain vanilla blackmail, such was the fear of losing power, especially to Il Papa Nero – The Black Pope – to use another of Prime Minister Andreotti's apt monikers.

Cuci stroked his goatee beard and grinned conceitedly. His real coup had been to persuade His Eminence (within two hours of Moro's body being found) to have Cardinal Poletti deliver – directly into the hands of Signora Moro – his personal Papal Rosary. There could be no better way to build a bridge, and Cuci never knew when he might need the widow Moro's help. Pope Paul VI's very own rosary was indeed a calling card. That *was* a platinum deposit in yet another favour bank.

Cuci suddenly felt a wave of tired gloominess descend over him. He leaned forward and rested his chin in the cup of his scaly, dry hands and allowed his mind to drift. Home to his wife after a brief but soothing drink at 'the club' with Tonino, his boyfriend of the moment. That was to be the evening's plan. He had earned a little rest and recreation. Moro was really dead. Pope Paul VI had said so.

The job of positioning Moro's memorial in the mind of the general public could wait a few more days. Thursday 16th March 1978, to Saturday 13th May 1978 was far longer period of time than it looked on the calendar. Furthermore, the planning of this joint CIA/IEA operation had started eighteen months before the kidnap itself: President Ford's

CIA Director, George H.W. Bush, had been much easier to deal with than President Carter's CIA pick, Director Admiral Stansfield Turner. No, he deserved a couple of hours of quiet with Tonino, and he drifted off into a reverie of youthful fantasies.

His telephone's loud and anxious ring shot immediate holes in those dreams.

"*Pronto!*" snapped Cuci, aggressively.

"Alex, get 'round here now. Y'all got a major problem."

The sing-song was unmistakable, and the emphasis on the *'y'all'* unmissable.

"What problem? I've a meeting in twenty minutes with two Cardinals," Cuci lied. Even Barings knew certain appointments were inviolate. "I don't care if y'all shakin' dirty Martinis for yer Pope. My office, Alex. Soon as." Barings' pitch was as calm and black as Lake Pontchartrain on a still night.

The line went dead, and Cuci's budding erection promptly followed suit.

CHAPTER 39

The Embassy of The United States.
Palazzo Margherita
121, via Vittorio Veneto, Rome, Italy.
Saturday, 13th May 1978. Early evening.

The journey across the city from the Vatican to the US Embassy took longer than normal; Rome's streets still thronged with mourners. Initially, Cuci hoped he might still have time to catch up with Tonino later, but with his Vatican driver off sick he was forced onto the vinyl seat of a Roman taxi. The driver proved as impervious to Cuci's bleating as he was to the empty promise of a large tip. So, from the squalid back seat, he was left to study the eerie shadows cast by Rome's old street lights, the colour of tobacco-stained teeth.

It wasn't Moro's death they, the fickle Italian public, were distraught about, it was the very nature of the act itself. The point was never to make people *believe* the lie; it was to make people *fear* the liar. He knew Moro's ghost would be exorcised soon enough.

Cuci recalled telling Barings during one of the first planning meetings in Director George H.W. Bush's seventh floor office at Langley that Moro was no JFK. Cuci mistakenly chose to ignore then, as he elected to try and forget now, Barings' inscrutable response: *'JFK was no JFK until he was dead. Jack Kennedy was just an ass-chasing Catholic son-of-a-bootleggin' gangster, who liked to keep company with the Mob. Marcello, Trafficante and Giancana paid for the bullet that blew Jack's head open, but they shoulda' killed Bobby instead. Even Jack woulda' got the Mob's message loud an' clear an' fallen into line. Remember that Alex, an' this Moro operation will be A-Okay.'* Director Bush had smirked and remained silent.

The taxi halted at the embassy's heavily guarded perimeter. Cuci checked his watch and sighed. Tonino may still be on the menu tonight. He pulled a thin-lipped smile and handed the driver two *gettoni* as an empty tip.

"Mr Barings informed us to expect you, sir. Go right on through."

Cuci knew the way to the Cultural Attaché's office blindfolded. Rome Station was located at the rear of the building. Each time he'd attended the numerous meetings Barings liked to summon him to, he was confounded by their shallow imagination. 'Cultural Attaché'. What a title! Once, light-headed from wine, he'd remarked: "Why not just call yourself the 'Cultural International Attaché'." The scowl Barings had shot him finally convinced him what an overtly serious and humourless race the Americans were; CIA suits being the very worst.

Barings opened the door and dismissed the orderly.

"Sit down, Alex, I need to speak with y'all before we head out to Rebibbia Prison." Barings paused. "Ain't got none of that red fizzy drink y'all like. It's bourbon or Kenco? What's yer pleasure?"

Cuci had the presence of mind to not respond.

Barings rose from his chair, ranged himself up to his full 6'3" height and sluiced three fingers of Jack into a glass. No ice. In doing so, he knew that he embodied the might and swagger of the richest nation on Earth. The Vatican may be the smallest independent state in the world, but it could summon up the forces of discontent just about anywhere in the world, thought Cuci, deep in a low-slung chair; a cheap American gambit. He aimed a puckish smile at Barings. David and Goliath, infantile fable that it was, always comforted Cuci when he dealt with the Americans, especially patriotic, ruthless vipers like CIA Station Heads. Barings knew only too well just how strong the Catholic lobby was in US politics, and they did need Alessandro Cuci and his IEA.

"What was so important I had to cancel two cardinals, and what's this talk of Rebibbia Prison?" Cuci was determined to get into Tonino's embrace. And quickly.

"I'm very surprised. Call y'self head of IEA, shame on you." Barings' eyes widened. "Y'all lookin' wound up, Alex, pantin' like a lizard on hot desert rock. Y'all OK?"

"Judd, it's been a long and wearisome day," he replied, fed up.

"Alex" – Barings shot him another mean grin – "y'all got a face so long you look like you could eat oats outta' a churn, so I'll keep it sweet.

Albassi was shot in Milan yesterday afternoon, in a scummy dead-end alley. Yer type know all about dirty lil' dark alleys, don't they?"

Again, that white southern smile of Barings' dominated the room.

"Whoever ordered this, screwed up royally. Albassi's body is nowhere to be found. His driver is wounded an' in hospital. Albassi may still be alive, nobody knows, but AB- blood has been found all over the car. Less than 1 per cent of the population are AB-, Alex, an' that's his blood type. Ain't no corpse, not even any darned parts of a corpse. Albassi's gone. He's disappeared, just like a blue-jay on a Friday!"

Barings returned to his desk, rocked back into the deep comfort of his black leather chair. He gloated like a ravenous bear salivating over a trapped rabbit.

"Y'all want the best part, Alex?" Barings drawled.

Cuci stared.

Barings flashed him a wide grin, then he began to grind his jawbone. He scrutinised Cuci with an expression of menace and hunger.

"They did find somethin'. A clue perhaps? All manner of sheets of typed, white, an' bloodstained paperwork was all headed IEA/Moro."

The bear laughed with a deep growl as he ate the petrified rabbit whole. Bones 'n all.

CHAPTER 40

Rebibbia Prison, Rome Italy.
Saturday, 13th May 1978. Late Evening.

Even in the blanched hospital wing of Rebibbia Prison there was no escape from the nose-clawing gag of decay; of rotting souls. Barings opened a satchel and pulled out a black tape recorder and microphone. The room was 'clean'. Two CIA assets had verified that earlier whilst Cuci was at the embassy. He was still perplexed at the ease with which the prison governor had agreed to CIA's conditions. In addition to sweeping the secure room, he had permitted him to interview Nicolai Sentini, one of the four Strategic Commanders of the Red Brigades, alone and in private. Maybe it was because Sentini wielded even more power from behind bars; prison governors were targets too. Barings shook his head. He didn't know, much less cared. Italians were north of the Mason–Dixon line as far as he was concerned.

The door opened and Nicolai Sentini sauntered in. Uninvited, he sat down at the table where Cuci and Barings were seated. He pulled a pack of Nazionali from his shirt pocket.

"Don't even think of smokin' in my airspace," commanded Barings.

Sentini smirked and put his cigarettes back into his prison fatigues. Barings looked at Cuci and Sentini, and then repeated what he'd told Cuci earlier. There was an internal rift in the Red Brigades and it would be a damning irony if unknowingly Albassi had somehow split the Red Brigade leaders; a divided bunch of gun-toting, left-wing terrorists was not a jukebox favourite of his.

What were these darned files they'd found at the scene? The ones with IEA's and Moro's name on them? Barings didn't trust files any more than he did women in pantsuits. Anyway, how many files had Albassi kept? Everyone in Italy maintained files on everyone else, it was a national pastime. But how many did the kidnappers have and what information did they contain? The CIA could only manage just so many inadvertent and unfortunate mishaps. Screw you, Cuci, Barings thought again.

"Sentini, I'll keep it short. Did y'all order Albassi's kidnappin', or murder, or whatever the hell has been done with him?"

Barings inched forward, the steel in his expression pinned the younger man back. Sentini drummed his fingers on the table. Visitors of Barings' and Cuci's rank were infrequent. He was going to enjoy this.

"No, why should we? He was your man, not ours." His thick Anglo-Italian accent curdled with revulsion. "It was your idea to have someone convince Rome it was a genuine kidnapping. If you'd have listened to me, we'd have killed Moro on 16th March."

"Cut the history lessons. Is it possible the Red Brigades have split?"

"No! We're united in what we did. You paid well and thanks to you, Signor CIA, the kidnap itself went perfectly." Sentini tugged at the hairs on his forearm. Neither Barings nor Cuci believed him. They knew, from separate sources, about the Red Brigades' internal strife. Sentini looked at each man in turn. He sensed their mood.

"OK, so a few men, and one commander, not Moretti, felt there could be more to be gained by keeping Moro alive, but" – Sentini thumped the table dramatically – "we made a deal the three of us, and I keep to my deals. The IEA and CIA wanted Moro dead" – he nodded at Barings – "and you" – he turned to Cuci – "wanted Andreotti as head of the Democrats *and* prime minister. Well, that's what you've got. Moro's corpse and Andreotti."

"Then who took Albassi, Niki?" Cuci asked calmly.

"I don't know. We haven't." Sentini nodded in the direction of the phone on a side table. "I'll make some calls if you want."

"Start diallin'," Barings ordered.

"I will, when you're outside *my* airspace, Signor CIA."

Sentini got up from his chair, sat behind the rudimentary side table and lit a cigarette, deliberately. Barings and Cuci knocked on the door for the guard.

It took all Barings' resolve not to punch the wall. All the investigative and technological might of the CIA appeared to be useless: here he was in a stink-hole Roman prison, with the emotionally unbalanced thirty-year-old Marxist son of a Turin doctor, who was his pilot through a maze of armed cells which constituted the octopus of Italian terrorism. Sentini, a political pygmy in a world of giants, could tell him something he should've already grasped. The Red Brigade's engine is runnin', but ain't nobody drivin', he thought.

Twenty-five long minutes elapsed before a knock was heard from inside. Without even a nod to Sentini, Barings strode in and sat back down. Cuci followed suit.

"I don't have the full story yet, but the Red Brigades had no part in the Albassi incident." Neither Barings' nor Cuci's expression changed. "I contacted two other organisations, and they had no hand in it either." Smoke billowed out from Sentini's nostrils like an angry dragon. "There was one thing" – he turned to face Cuci – "your man Albassi was trusted and liked. Why I don't know, especially as he worked for you, and if you want to find him, help was offered. You figure it out. You men are the geniuses."

Barings shot him a bullet-stare. He said nothing. But he reminded himself that it takes all kinds of stupid to make a world.

Sentini couldn't hide the pride on his face. He was still a man with skin in the game; there'd be no moving him aside now. Barings looked at him as he grinned inanely. He wanted to punch him too.

"You may have cut the Gordian Knot, Niki. Who cares who's got Albassi? He's better off dead anyway," announced Cuci, his small mouth hardened as his smile fell away. He stared at Sentini and then at Barings, who held his tetchy look.

"You care, Alex, big time, so do you, Sentini. I just ain't figured out why yet. I will though. Even a blind hog can find an acorn once in a while, and don't y'all forget its hogs that get slaughtered whilst the pigs just get fat."

Sentini stared at Cuci again. His arms and neck tingled involuntarily. There's more evil in that man's eyes than in my entire organisation, the terrorist thought.

"So, do you want me to look for him?" Sentini knew the answer before he asked the question.

"No," Cuci replied quickly.

Barings kept his counsel: "I figured that." So, it was Cuci all along, his inner voice told him.

"We never had anything to fear from Albassi. He's a Sicilian with a young family – vulnerable – we could always have got to him." Sentini inhaled as he spoke. "Besides, he was a lawyer, and the only creatures closer to the filth of this earth are snakes."

"Y'all a darned ranch-hand, Sentini?"

"What do you mean?"

"Sentini, y'all full of hogshit." Barings rose and stood tall. "I'm outta' here."

The corridor's noxious stink of bleach and excrement had the heavy, still air of a swamp. Barings screwed up his nose.

"Don't underestimate Albassi," Cuci whispered in Barings' ear.

"Oh, bless yer heart, Alex."

"What?"

Barings threw him an 'aw-shucks smile'. "I don't much care for profanities, an' where I come from *'Bless yer heart'* means *'fuck you'*". He stared down the shorter man, drilling him into the ground. "Albassi wasn't my call, my cut-out, my go-between, my man on the inside. An' it ain't my name on any dumbass papers found in his bullet-ridden car in a Milan alley either. It was yours, Alex. We do what we Americans do best. W'all provide the money an' the skills on the ground. We leave you Italians to do what y'all do best. Provide the train wrecks."

* * *

The two men sat silently in the back of the US Embassy's Lincoln Town Car, protected by its diplomatic registration and the extravagance of its deep leather seats. Barings pressed two buttons on an overhead panel: one shone a low wash of light directly onto Cuci, the other raised a soundproof screen between them and his US Marine driver.

"Did we learn anything, Judd?"

"I'm not sure *we* did, Alex," he lied.

"Do you think Sentini had anything to do with Albassi's disappearance?"

Barings didn't respond. Instead he continued to look out of the darkened windows at Rome's nightlife, hustling silently by. When he did reply, his mood was solid with fatigue.

"I ain't sure 'bout much these days. For me to admit that, I'd have to find myself in the middle of Rome, plumb centre of a gaggle of conspiracy theories with people who're dealin' off the bottom o' the deck. Y'all are as rank an' as dark as ol' coffin air, Alex. Clear enough?"

Cuci, silhouetted in the chiaroscuro light, had nothing to say. His face looked troubled, lined too. His eyes weary and bloodshot, and for some reason that Barings couldn't work out, Cuci's ears twitched like a night-prowling mutt. He knew Cuci to be as sharp as a hooty barn owl, but the tensions in his face belied that.

"That doesn't take us much further down the road, does it?" Cuci said finally.

"Oh, I dunno. I feel better for gettin' that off'a my chest," mocked Barings.

What do y'all take me for Signor Alessandro Cuci, Head of the IE darned A? thought Barings, as the Revox tape machine that was his pin-sharp memory replayed the day's events. "Lissen' up, Alex, I'm beat. My Marine will take y'all home after droppin' me off, meanwhile let's observe some quiet."

They continued the journey in silence, each man alone: Barings with hypotheses, Cuci with random curiosities and lascivious homoerotic designs. By the time they arrived at the US Embassy, Cuci's head was nodding in and out of sleep. Barings grasped the chance to avoid a 'goodnight'. Nimbly, he got out of the car and instructed the Marine to head straight back to the Vatican.

CHAPTER 41

The Embassy of The United States.
Palazzo Margherita
121, via Vittorio Veneto, Rome, Italy.
Saturday, 13th May 1978. Almost midnight.

Barings walked towards the heavily guarded security gates. His overcoat collar was up and he took the night air deeply into his lungs. He was saluted crisply by the Marine guards as they raised the second barrier. He returned the salute, and headed straight through the main entrance to Rome Station where he poured himself a stiff bourbon and sat behind his desk to flesh out thoughts on a yellow notepad:

1) This operation is in danger of spiralling out of CIA's control, and there is no Disney ending.

2) Sentini is telling the truth. Albassi is not a Red Brigades hostage.

3) Albassi not only knew the Gradoli address where Moro was held. He suspected he had information on the joint IEA/CIA 'operation' too, and that he was way out of his depth.

4) Dead snakes can still bite, and it was Cuci who'd found and hired Albassi and orchestrated his disappearance. Beware.

5) The VW car used in the hit-and-run of Paola Albassi had been stolen two days prior to the incident, and the unknown driver had never been traced. Mowing Paola Albassi down had been Cuci's twelve-gauge scare shot. But he'd miscalculated. Cuci's fingerprints were all over the comatose girl, of that he was sure, he just couldn't find them. Yet.

6) Albassi had information on Cuci specifically, and as a result Albassi – with the Red Brigades perhaps – would set some form of trap for him. A trap that would inevitably spill over into CIA's arena, then the Italian, and finally into the bear pit of Washington politics. Everything he didn't need, and more.

All this because of two people: Alessandro Cuci and a half-blind, mid-ranking Milanese lawyer. Whoever it was who'd said, *'You're only as strong as your weakest link'* was right on the money. He put his Sharpie back on the notepad, sipped his bourbon and let his mind roam free to play out many more different scenarios. When it came to CIA tactics, he was as good as Bobby Fischer and Boris Spassky. Or so he believed.

* * *

Judd Barings was one of life's resolute bachelors. Born and raised in Texas, he was an only child to caring parents, both of whom had perished in a car crash on the very day he had graduated high school. With no kith or kin, he'd readily accepted a sports scholarship from Tulane University in New Orleans, Louisiana. A young, tall and energetic man, Barings was a loner with no shared hinterland, and suspected that was one of the reasons CIA had sought to recruit him. So, he quit Tulane to head north.

In Virginia, he became a CIA field agent with the emotional detachment of a savant. He understood, and held firm, that his life and work were based on many certainties, like: gravity held him on the Earth, the sun rose over Japan and set California-way, a blue-flame will burn you as sure as pack-ice will freeze you, no two fingerprints are the same, politicians lie as they breathe, cynicism trumps trust, and a highly trained sniper (bar a neutron bomb) is the single most efficient killing machine known to mankind.

Yet, for all his experience, honed instincts and sheer smarts, the truth, the why, the sole reason for Pietro Albassi's disappearance from Milan yesterday afternoon wouldn't have ever entered Barings' ordered mind. He was a man as quick as sin itself, as fearless as the first human who ever ate an oyster, with trained skills of self-preservation and a trough full of courage. So, the very notion of a wilful and a premeditated suicide, for the *possible* salvation of others – even family – wouldn't have registered with his intuitive thought processes, despite his reflexes being as fast as a prairie fire with a howlin' tail wind behind it.

However, and this was the measure of the man, and for a reason he couldn't yet fathom as he toyed with another bourbon, he was cognisant of a solitary buzzard flyin' high in a fire-hardened Texan sky. The buzzard was overhead, patiently circlin' the corpse of a dead Longhorn on the scorched prairie below, waitin' for when it was safe to descend and feast on charred carrion. He was certain Albassi and his files were in the wind. But somebody, somethin', was tryin' to block the darned buzzard from his view.

PART SEVEN

CHAPTER 42

Malta–Sicily Channel.
Saturday, 13th–Sunday, 14th May, 1978. Dead of night.

"How many more hours are we going to be stuck out here, Palalu? This old body can't cope with much more of this saltwater waltzing."

"I'm doing my best, Josh..." Palalu looked up from the oily bilge, his hands smeared in thick black grease. His proud face masked the seasickness brought on by diesel, oil, bilge water, sodden wood and stone-cold fear.

"You wait till I get my hands on that *bastardo* Tony. He sold me diesel cut with water." Palalu held up a copper fuel pipe, as if that were proof enough for the fact that his antiquated Perkins engine had simply conked out.

"Tony doesn't dilute my bloody vodka with water, Palalu."

Tony was Padden's barman, therefore a faithful friend who he needed to defend even here. But he wasn't sure where here was.

The sea, like all rough seas, looked more menacing in the moonlight as cresting white water crashed around them. The typically short, steep Mediterranean swell lifted and dropped the *luzzu* from roiling trough, to breaking wave, to deep trough again and again. A *luzzu* was a famously sturdy craft, but in any battle with any sea both men knew in their bones that the sea would win. It was just a matter of when. Lying a-hull in a rapidly building Force 7 was unlikely to bring about a safe disembarkation.

The engine had spluttered a death rattle sometime before midnight. He guessed they were about fifteen nautical miles south of Capo Passero, and, as bad luck would have it, the engine had died just as the storm had picked up. Their progress all day had been painfully slow, the wind building with each passing hour. Their silent hope was that the rhythmic *thwop-thwop-thwop* of the hitherto trusty Perkins wouldn't let them down, but it had. To make matters worse, the offshore current wasn't their ally. With each passing minute they were drifting away from Sicily, in a south-westerly direction.

Next stop: North Africa and then Hell, in that order thought Padden. Although seasick from smoking his last cigarette and drinking a bottle of vodka, he wasn't fearful for his own life. For the first time in many a moon, he found himself worrying more about the man he was going to give the documents and cash that he had stashed inside his old, yellow oilskin jacket – the one he had been wearing when *Innamorata* had sunk in the same stretch of water all those years ago.

"Hey, Palalu!" Padden shouted above the mean howl of the wind and waves.

The Gozitan's grimy face popped up again from the engine's cowling. He grinned. He had heard that tone in Josh's voice before. It was a good omen.

"Lightning doesn't strike twice, whatever they say. I've been pulled out of this bloody channel once before, and if your God had wanted me, he would've taken me then." A belt of chill spray spumed over the *luzzu*'s tall prow and soaked them a-new. "The flyboys in Cambodia used to say when both engines were sucking fumes over the jungle," Padden hollered, *"we're in good shape, Josh. Good shape."*

Padden was almost gleeful. His face dripped freezing seawater, the wind had crusted it into the deep lines around his eyes. Palalu nodded back at him with a Catholic smile, and Padden found that he actually believed his own words.

CHAPTER 43

No. 5, Largo Claudio Treves,
the Brera District, Milan, Italy.
Sunday, 14th May 1978. An hour after sunrise.

Ruxandra had forgotten just how long, how interminably long, one solitary night could be. Not since Bucharest, when her scrawny teenage body had lain naked and pop-eyed awake (while the pitiless, sweat-chilled meat that had abused her snored drunkenly on), had she remembered just how many seconds, minutes and hours constituted one desolate night. Then, she had shivered under sullied bedclothes and awaited daylight with a noxious mix of dread and hope. Only Pietro, her Pietro, had been able to somehow spirit all of those memories away, and now someone had spirited him away too. His essence, his laughter, his life-force, his moods – and so much more – had been the bedrock of their marriage; and with him silenced, something in her had died.

This time she had lain on top of crisp bedclothes and shivered until the sun delivered her from the darkness. With the faint rays of the dawn sun, she knew that Pietro would never again share a room with her. Pietro was lost, dead or alive. The instant Ispettore Massina had stepped over their threshold, she had sensed it. He was gone. The loose shards of shattered glass in the corners of her mind, where she secreted her past, formed a prism through which a spectrum shone. It was a piercing light. Her 'third eye', one that could foretell a future, was indeed a curse. An intensely vindictive Romanian curse, one as dark as the insides of a Transylvanian wolf.

Only once did she try to break her of chain of thoughts by creeping into Toto's room, after his confused sobbing had subsided into restless breathing. Pietro was still alive. Paola's and Toto's blood were her proof. Toto had not been a brave and collected boy when she had told him; and why should he have been? He had simply been an eight-year-old boy who wanted his father at home. Words like kidnap, terrorists, disappeared were abstract. She had been careful to tell him, despite her 'third eye', that his father was alive somewhere, and because of his dangerous work, other men, bad men, were keeping him.

First, Ruxandra thought, let him come to terms with absence then let it be his father's. The inevitable end of the story would come later. She had shuddered when she had sat beside him at the kitchen table and stared into his bewildered face. Toto had his father's striking green Sicilian eyes, and another shard of glass had fallen into place.

CHAPTER 44

Questura HQ, via Fatebenefratelli, Milan, Italy.
Sunday, 14th May 1978. Early morning.

"*Buongiorno*, Signora Albassi, were there any calls?" enquired Ispettore Massina.

"No calls at all. I would have rung you, Ispettore," Ruxandra replied icily.

"I see." Nonplussed by her abrupt tone, Massina sucked in the rancid air of his stuffy office, before continuing. "Fortunately, all the newspapers are full of Moro's State funeral yesterday, and it appears only the Milanese papers have picked up the story so far."

"Thank you. Toto and I will be going to the hospital this afternoon as usual."

"That'll be alright, Signora Albassi, we'll monitor your line from the Questura."

"So be it. You have your procedures. It's early, Ispettore, and I didn't sleep last night."

"Understandable indeed. Call me anytime, Signora. You have my direct line. Goodbye."

He sighed with relief as he hung up the phone, before staring across the files and general clutter on his grey metal desk at Luca Pezzoli, his young assistant.

"So, Pezzoli, the ice-maiden is indeed homoiothermic after all. I was beginning to have my doubts."

Glazed on Pezzoli's face, like the baked sugar on the cornetto pastry Massina had devoured for breakfast, was a combination of profound indifference and intense stupidity.

"For those who don't read the dictionary at bedtime, she's what exactly?"

"A mammal, *cretino*, like you and me. Warm blooded."

"Like you and me?" Pezzoli's thin top lip, with its trace of fuzz masquerading as a moustache, tried – and failed – to hide his sarcasm.

"Clever boy, Pezzoli. Let's just do a checklist of where your scuffed shoes are going today, shall we? I want answers by 16:00, is that clear or do you need a dictionary?" Massina sipped on a plastic beaker of coffee. It was vile. "First, I want the ballistic report, and second, when's the earliest time I can interview the driver. What's his name again?"

"Joseph Zangretti."

"Third, and most important, I need to know who hired our deontologist lawyer" – Massina grinned – "as the go-between in the Moro kidnapping and assassination."

"But it's Sunday."

"I'm well aware of that, Pezzoli. When you've done all that, you're to arrange, today, for me to speak with his secretary. I want access to his diaries first thing on Monday." Massina parted the grey and mustard-yellow hairs of his bushy moustache. "Go on, what are you waiting for? Go to work."

Luca Pezzoli got out of his chair almost eagerly. He disliked the thick, rank air of their shared office. His boss never opened a window, even in summer.

"Oh, and Pezzoli, get me all his bank records for the last twenty-four months, and any other financial details and his insurance policies. He's a lawyer, so there'll be a fistful for sure. Whatever you do, do NOT ask the grieving Signora, or anyone else who's close to him. And Pezzoli, do it the quiet way, just call our friends at the banks and make threats."

"But everyone is closed on Sunday..."

"You can read minds as well as comic books? So, start disturbing everyone at home, and since you're a mind-reader, locating all their home phone numbers will be easy, won't it?"

"Anything else, Ispettore?"

"There will be, you can count on it. If you're out of shouting range leave a number, or call in every hour. That's all, now scram, I've got work to do."

Ispettore Massina smiled amiably at Pezzoli as he heaved his feet onto his desk and picked up his pink newspaper: *La Gazzetta dello Sport*.

CHAPTER 45

Malta–Sicily Channel.
Sunday, 14th May 1978. Late morning.

The storm, as so often in the Mediterranean, had mysteriously died away just after sunrise, and as with all storms a hushed calm trailed in its forgiving wake.

It must have been a bad two weeks of fishing in southern Sicily for a large fishing boat to have ventured out as the *scirocco* churned the seas. The skipper had trusted his maritime lore, which told him this bad blow would abate. A lost day, even a Sunday, meant no money, and fishing in the increasingly barren, saline Mediterranean was already a hard life.

The *Santa Ana*, a once proud 55' trawler, her old wooden topsides indelibly stained with the blood and scales of a quarter of a century of catches, had struck out of Capo Passero in a south-westerly direction. She had run smack into the wind and cresting waves, hoping for a school of lazy – and valuable – swordfish sometimes found in deeper waters as the sun came up. Dawn had long broken, and still the skipper continued to plough into the rough weather; the swordfish were proving to be both energetic and elusive. With a climbing barometer, and clearing skies ahead, his fisherman's eyes caught sight of the primary colours of the stricken *luzzu* in the far distance, bobbing in the sea like a red, yellow and blue quill-float.

It had been Padden who'd caught the first glimpse of the *Santa Ana*, and had flapped his yellow oilskin like a flag, just as he'd done once before. Palalu, his hands now frozen wooden stumps from hours of cold and wet toil, jumped around like a demented puppy. He slapped his friend on the back several times, crossed himself even more times and swore on the sainted lips of the Virgin Mary, that he would never, *ever*, take Joshua out in a boat again, not even fishing for *lampuki* in the limpid waters off Comino.

"You're just bad luck, Josh," he shouted over and over again.

Within thirty minutes, the *luzzu* was being towed astern of the *Santa Ana*, on a reciprocal north-easterly course for Capo Passero, the *Santa Ana*'s home port. Fortified by strong, black coffee laced with two slugs of raw grappa, Joshua excused himself from the bridge. The captain understood the man's need to be solitary. He watched him head forward, where the man nested himself amongst the *Santa Ana*'s thick Manila ropes and old nets.

Being pulled alive, when death had been all but certain, from the same sea twice in one lifetime would do anything, to any man, even Joshua Padden.

* * *

With the *luzzu* safely tied up against the worn tractor tyres on the old harbour wall, Padden left Palalu to the impossible task of seeking out a mechanic on a Sunday. He had more important matters to attend to.

He ambled over to La Tavernetta, dragged an old wicker chair outside and let the sun warm his bones, as the grappa and coffee had his stomach. He ordered another grappa, but with no coffee this time. He felt as if he had won the lottery for a second time. Unlike Palalu, he had made no impetuous vows that would have to be broken. Gratitude, not a sentiment he was on speaking terms with, was due to the *Santa Ana*'s captain and his crew. Only they had pulled his carcass back from the watery grave he had stared into all night. For the time being no one disturbed him. The southern Sicilians knew how to read people he reflected, as he smoked, drank and nursed his precious plastic bag whilst waiting for his friend-in-need.

* * *

Pietro, wearing a peaked cap, stood silently in front of his napping friend and blocked out the sun. Suddenly, maybe it was the shade or the absence of sunlight, Padden woke with a start.

"Josh, you made it! I've been worried. I've been here since Saturday lunchtime. Almost the longest twenty-four hours of my life. I saw the storm and feared the very worst."

"I did make it, here's the proof," Padden said, standing up, laughing and stretching, "but that's another story, one for later. All I'll say is that this cat has used up all his nine lives. Christ, you look like hell, Pietro!"

"I'm sure I do," grinned Pietro, a perfect *mezzaluna* of white teeth contrasted with the deep shadow of his stubble. He was bone-exhausted. A fifty-two-card deck; the suits of fear, doubt, self-loathing and love had fuelled him since Friday afternoon in Milan, and that seemed like a lifetime ago. Which it was.

Sensing an exhaustion far deeper than his own, Padden threaded his way past the small bar, the restaurant tables and into the kitchen. Maurizio, the proprietor, sat on a stool beside his primitive range of cookers.

"*Eccolo*, Joshua. Food?" Maurizio asked.

"*Sì*, I've had enough of things that live in water and my friend looks like he needs meat too. I'll go find a table outside, you cook what you want. But no fish, OK?"

They chose a corner table up against the harbour wall, where they could observe, yet not be observed. Two label-less bottles were on the table. One contained tap-water, the other tap-wine.

Pietro pulled out a chair for his friend, then sat down and poured two beakers of blood-red wine, and offered him the last of his Gitanes.

"Never could stand those cigarettes of yours, but thanks. I'll get a packet from Maurizio." As Pietro lit his cigarette, crumpled the packet and coughed heavily, Padden returned with a packet of Marlboros.

"So, start, Pietro," he said lighting up.

With smoke billowing all around him – it had been a long time coming this cigarette – Padden wanted to get down to the reasons he'd returned to Sicily.

In a sure-footed manner Pietro recounted the events of the previous forty or so hours. Padden listened intently, never interrupting, occasionally picking at a plate of salami and olives which Maurizio had silently placed on the table.

His story told, Pietro squinted his seeing-eye at Padden. It implored him for something more than understanding.

"Whatever I say isn't meant to undermine your…" Padden groped for the right word "… improvised plan with your driver on Friday. It occurs to me that there's a couple of wrinkles which might turn into deep creases." He checked himself. "Your main problem is the absence of a ransom demand. You've put yourself in a living limbo. You've denied any investigation of motive, which means Cuci will be free to call the shots."

"I figured that, but it won't take the police long to trace the gun I used back to the Red Brigades. That'll give the authorities something to work with. No ransom note, a hallmarked Red Brigade 9mm Beretta pistol, and my AB- blood splatters everywhere should be enough. To actually close the case, they'll have to have me killed. Someone will be framed. I know the Italian way."

"That's one helluva gamble, but maybe you're right. Let's just hope you're not going to become a running sore. It's human nature, almost a reflex, to pursue that which runs away from us. Don't forget that."

"A lifetime of looking over my shoulder?"

"That might be the price tag." Padden let his words hang. "OK, enough crystal ball gazing, let's get down to business."

Padden reached down into the sealed plastic bag in his yellow oilskin. He cut the duct-tape with the meat knife and took out a thick paper wallet.

"This wasn't easy, but I've got to admit it wasn't that difficult either. Anyway, your new name is Anthony Phillip Bianchi, you're thirty-six years old and a graduate in, of all things, English. You received a BA from the University of Malta and emigrated to Australia soon thereafter. You left behind a widowed mother, long since deceased, and one sister who married a local Maltese businessman. Your father passed away when you were young.

"Carry on."

"Sure," Padden raised his wild eyebrows, lit another cigarette, downed a beaker of wine and continued. "Once in Australia you settled in a northern suburb of Sydney – a lot of Maltese emigrated to Australia. You went into business making spas and backyard crap. You later expanded into swimming pools, and figured out that maintaining the stuff you sold was more profitable. By the time you were killed in a horrific car crash…"

"Any details?" asked Pietro, genuinely curious.

"Sure, why not, if you want them. You were driving in the outback in some fancy German car and you hit a six foot red kangaroo, head on. You were doing in excess of 100 mph…"

"What's that in kilometres?"

"How the fuck should I know, I don't even own a car! It was mighty fast! Shut up, and remember you're *not* a lawyer anymore." Padden tossed back another half a glass of wine. "The marsupial went through the windscreen and decapitated you instantly. After they'd picked all the 'roo fur out of your headless carcass, it turned out you'd amassed quite a fortune. Your next of kin, your sister, and oh-so-lucky brother-in-law, scooped a lottery of over $3 million Ozzie bucks from your Antipodean enterprises. Clever guy, huh?"

Padden's pride couldn't quite disguise the sarcasm in his voice.

"Is it Tony, Anthony or An-tho-ny?" Pietro asked.

"No idea, but knowing the Maltese love for diminutives, probably Tony, but it's up to you, it's your life now after all. You weren't married, had no regular girlfriend, and it seems not much of a life outside of spas, pools and sacks of chlorine."

Padden slid a green Maltese passport, a scarlet Maltese driving licence and a sealed envelope across the table. His expression hardened as he did so.

"I ran anonymous checks on Bianchi. When I contacted the University, their records show him as being alive, as do the Malta Immigration records. A death certificate was issued in Australia. Your greedy sister used it to get her hands on the cash and business in Australia, which she then sold to your lawyer on the cheap. As your estate was entirely in Australia, and with an original death certificate, she didn't even bother to file for one in Malta. She had the cash, so why bother? That was a lucky break for us." Animated, Padden paused for breath. "As to appearances, you both have dark hair, but he was shorter than you are. On a telephone description you would pass muster, but not on a photographic one. The principle physical differences are: a large dimple in his chin and of course, two functioning eyes. The good news is the university don't maintain photographic records, nor do the Malta police unless you'd committed a crime, which Anthony Bianchi hadn't. The only people who know Bianchi, and who aren't dead, are the sister and brother-in-law. The Australian resident permit in this passport," Padden tapped it with his index finger, "is technically still valid, as is the US multiple re-entry visa. Stay out of Australia is my advice."

Pietro fixed his gaze on the two documents and the anonymous envelope. Tears welled in both his eyes, even his blind eye. Slowly he lifted his face and met Padden's hard stare.

"What can I say, Josh?"

"Nothing. You would have done the same for me. There's $10,000 in Benjamins in the envelope. You're going to need them."

"Benjamins?"

"A Benjamin is a $100 bill. These are from my war adventures. Don't try and say 'no' either. I know far more than you about how expensive it is being on the run. You're going to need it all, and then some."

Pietro nodded silently and Padden smiled, wrinkling his fleshy face. They both held the momentary peace. Lives would be saved, at a tremendous cost. This, they both knew.

"If you're going to survive out there, Pietro, you're going to have to train yourself to believe in nothing. And I mean *nothing*. Believing can be dangerous. There's only one Holy Trinity, and that's gin, vermouth and olives," he chortled.

"Cynical even for you, Josh. When I was young, a priest named Father Albert said the Old Testament taught you to strike at evil with vengeance, while the New Testament said you combat evil with forgiveness."

"I'm definitely an Old Testament man. Hellfire, thunderbolts, revenge, they've all had a bad press this century."

"I do have one more favour, Josh. It's to do with spirits, and I don't mean the drinking kind."

Pietro removed the cigarette from the corner of his mouth.

"Try and keep the evil spirits away from Ruxandra, Paola and Toto. Watch over them. Can you do that for me? Please."

"Do you intend to contact me?" Padden asked, deadly serious.

Pietro shook his head slowly from side to side. "Don't you see, I can't."

Now it was Padden's turn to look away.

"I can barely take care of myself, Pietro. Being a drunk is hard graft, it requires dedication and perseverance, it's almost vocational. Like all drunks I go to bars. I don't go to meetings, they're for alcoholics. There's an ocean of difference my friend. Besides, any self-respecting evil spirit would collapse in hysterics if I tried to shoo it away."

"Truth, Joshua."

Padden waited a while before answering.

"Truth, huh, that's something you only ever find at the very bottom of the bottomless pit, Pietro. Who was behind Paola's accident? You believe it was Cuci. You want confirmation? Then that's where you'll have to hunt. The bottomless pit."

"Back to my question, Josh."

"I couldn't look Ruxandra or the twins square in their eyes knowing what I do. I may not be able to find Anthony Bianchi, but he could find me, don't forget that. It's a small world and I'm not going anywhere, except the Gleneagles Bar of course."

"I understand."

Padden wavered, his mind weighing up an instinct play.

"Here's the best I can offer, top o'the head stuff, Pietro. If I need you, but *really* need you, then read my books. There'll be a message, you'll recognise it. I've hit a stride of about one a year. None are as good as when Annie was alive, but people still read my yarns. If there's nothing for me to tell you, just read the books anyway," Padden smiled warmly. "That do? That work?"

"It's more than enough, Josh. Thank you."

"Forget it. Besides, I've got a feeling you'd be there for me if the flame turned blue."

CHAPTER 46

Porto Portopalo, Capo Passero, Sicily.
Sunday, 14th May 1978. Dusk.

The sun arced gracefully down through the sky to hide beneath the waves. It wasn't until its final glow had been doused by the majesty of the Inland Sea itself, did they wring the last drop of grappa from their bottle. A solitary streetlight flickered alive, and as the moths gathered around, Padden noticed Palalu sitting patiently on a bollard beside his *luzzu*.

"There's never a good time to say goodbye. Now's as good a time as any. Where are you headed?" Padden asked.

"West with the sunset I suppose."

Padden reached across the table and gripped Pietro's wrist so tightly his knuckles whitened.

"Two pieces of advice, Pietro. First, never make a vow, it's something to aim at. Second, never give a man your back, it's something to shoot at." With those words Padden stood up, and held out his glass.

"*Cent'anni*, Josh," Pietro slid his chair back, and he too raised his glass.

"I've always loved that toast my friend. Here's to a hundred years."

"For us Sicilians *cent'anni* also means, 'A Sicilian never forgets'."

Padden gazed at his friend and repeated *cent'anni* in a gravelly whisper, as he placed his empty glass back on the table. Without another word, he gathered up his weather-beaten oilskin jacket, looked down the quay, and lolloped away from La Tavernetta like a lame camel to where the *luzzu* was tethered. Not once did he turn back; regrets had never been Padden's currency.

Palalu helped him climb over the tractor tyres hanging from the quay, and he sat down heavily on the wooden bench. Palalu caught a look on his friend's face he'd only ever seen once before.

"Who was that, Josh?"

"An old and loyal friend, Palalu. Someone we both knew died suddenly. Pity. He was a good man. Now is this bloody engine of yours going to work?"

"Only if you bring good luck, Josh."

"Good luck! What else do I ever bring you, Palalu!"

Palalu's face broke into a proud grin as the Perkins spluttered – on the third turn of the hand-crank – into some form of life. He slipped the lines and coasted his *luzzu* towards the mouth of the harbour.

Pietro walked to the high, whitewashed harbour wall and hoisted himself up using an old rope, scuffing on rough concrete as he climbed. He sat with his hands under his thighs, his legs dangling over the wall's edge, and stared out to sea in the manner of a young boy awaiting his parent's homecoming.

The sea's turmoil had abated and the Mediterranean was oil-calm now. The pulsing *thwop-thwop-thwop* from the *luzzu*'s engine was the only sound to be heard as it passed the red and green harbour lights. Slowly, like a dream fading with time, the quiet of the still evening returned. He watched Palalu, standing proud and tall, with his hand on the tiller, as he steered the *luzzu* due south on a Mediterranean frosted by the moon's light.

Pietro checked his watch. With Gozo fifty-plus miles away, they had a solid eight-hour voyage, and from where he sat, Neptune's watchful eye was going to shepherd them home. Not once did his friend look back over his shoulder. He hadn't expected him to, but not until the *luzzu* had misted into the horizon did Pietro take his eyes away from his friend.

In a darkened Porto Portopalo, Pietro contemplated the night sky. The moon was full, almost primrose in colour. A strong gust of a chill wind brushed past him and he shuddered. The preservation of those he loved was truly a mighty force untethered.

In this, the landscape of his past, where darkness stalked the edges of his mind, he felt neither anger nor bitterness. Bewilderment over what had transpired with such damning speed and permanence, yes, but not anger. The *salve* was the knowledge that there were those who were – who are – simply broken beyond redemption.

And he, Pietro Albassi, was not amongst their number.

PART EIGHT

CHAPTER 47

The Vatican State.
Wednesday, 17th May 1978. Early evening.

Alessandro Cuci's phone rang and jolted him out of his trance. He guessed who the caller would be.

"What is it this time, Judd? Any more bombs you'd like to detonate?"

Cuci's voice ebbed into boredom. Albassi's disappearance had already distracted him enough for the last couple of days.

"Y'all called me, remember? I'm just returnin' the favour."

"I wanted to talk to you about 'Milan'."

'Milan' had become Cuci's racoon-crazy codeword for 'Albassi', a game Barings simply wasn't going to indulge.

"I hear this man Massina at Milan Criminalpol is good," stated Barings matter-of-factly.

"He's capable, and I wasn't going to try and influence who got this case."

"That mighta' been the smartest thing you've gon' an' done in a long time, Alex."

"Massina is a bloodhound, even looks like one, and unfortunately his scruples are intact. My conclusion, Judd," he dithered, "is that we've both underestimated Sentini. Let me tell you what Massina has so far established."

Barings had already got his tail right up, an' he knew the kinda' bread Cuci was bakin', so his brain switched off the whining noise. CIA had a new policy towards the IEA, it was: *'Hear the Evil and See the Evil'* but *'Talkin' the Evil'* no longer factored. Director Turner didn't have to order Barings that damage limitation, followed by a one-way flight from Rome to Langley on a US Military transport aircraft, was the sole aim.

The CIA's objectives with the Moro operation had all been successful. The prime one being to kill the Euro Communism pact, which was now as dead as its mastermind. Barings was going to head straight out of the firestorm, towards the big green letters flashing EXIT EXIT EXIT. No more dickin' around with the IEA.

Cuci, oblivious to Barings' indifference, continued:

"One: All, and I do mean all, Albassi's sensitive files have gone, and there wasn't a break-in at his offices. Two: Ballistics in Milan and Rome examined the bullets taken from the driver and his car. They all matched a Beretta used by the Red Brigades in a Turin shooting a couple of years ago – a case Albassi successfully defended. Three: There's an identical blood match to Albassi's AB-. Four: No ransom demand has yet been made and Albassi has been missing for five days."

Cuci put the handset back in the cradle and switched on the loudspeaker. He walked over to his French Second Empire drinks' cabinet and listened to Barings' measured breathing as he poured himself a Campari and soda.

"Alex, it's simple. Y'all have one of two possibilities," Barings chipped in finally. CIA's prior intel of Cuci's four points had given him scripted responses. "Option One, the Red Brigades really do have Albassi an' plan to kill him for what they think he knows. That's hogshit an' y'all know it, yer idea is tougher to swallow than stewed skunk. Option Two, however, is my darlin' favourite." Barings hesitated for effect only. "There ain't no ransom demand, an' you should git I don't gotta ball of racoon shit as evidence, but here goes. Dollars to donuts, Alex, I figure Albassi has disappeared up his own asshole an' is in the wind, an' he's taken all his IEA files as insurance against anyone comin' after him or his family."

Barings, letting the tension seep out, then went quiet. "Y'all allowed Albassi to draw a line in the sand, an' that meant you gave him control, Alex. I can't prove a darned thing, but lissen' up. You harmin' his daughter was a mistake the size of Texas, an' if that ain't a fact, then God's a possum." Barings fought back the bile in his throat. "Y'all know somethin' else, Alex, y'all may have plenty o' notches on yer gun, but you mess with lil' ones in this grown-up world of ours, then life becomes even more goddamn' serious."

"He hasn't disappeared, Judd. I've checked his movements already and they're all accounted for. He left Milan only once, in the first week of May. He flew to Rome and rented a Ford at Ciampino Airport. He returned the car about twenty-four hours later having travelled less than eighty kilometres. Admittedly those twenty-four hours he was in Rome are unaccounted for, but he was obviously there to meet with various informers or sources. Albassi was just doing his job, the one we made him do."

"We? No. You." Barings growled.

Cuci had had enough of Barings' attitude. It was as if he and the CIA had forgotten just who the head of the IEA was.

"Judd, you have your opinion, which if I may say so is fiction. I think Sentini's got him and he'll plan on using him and his files as leverage against both you, and possibly me." Cuci was too astute to allow his implicit threat to sound like a direct threat.

"It would be too much to hope that Albassi would have gone an' packed his IEA files in his Friday lunchbox on the very same day he happened to be kidnapped," Barings cackled. "Y'all know Alex that coincidences only happen in Italy, right?"

"Albassi's secretary told Milan Criminalpol that he was in the habit of taking them home with him most nights."

"What about money? He sure can't run on empty for long."

"He was not the sort who took kickbacks, quite the contrary. His two accounts show no curious movements in the past six months, and no cash withdrawals more than 500,000 lire." The Campari and soda, combined with the replay of the facts helped Cuci to relax. "Sentini's got him, I'm convinced of it, there's no possible alternative."

The mode Cuci used to dress his case *made* his case, and sensing this, Barings was ready with his answer.

"Never dig up more snakes than y'all can kill, Alex," Barings drawled. "So here's what y'all gonna do. Nothin', absolutely nothin'. Diddly-do squat. If Sentini hasn't made a move in a month or so then we'll review it all." Barings exhaled calmly. "I learned from my daddy a very long time ago that there's a value to inertia. Sometimes, even when the fish are jumpin', it's best to sit back on the riverbank an' just watch the show. Don't even bait a hook."

"OK, Judd, we'll wait one month. Nothing will happen without your prior approval. It's agreed then. If you hear anything you call me. I have to go. *Ciao.*"

Cuci rang off and downed his Campari and soda in one. Deftly, he removed his buckskin moccasins and paced across his Aubusson rug;

the sensation of its weave on his stockinged feet was, for some reason, soothing. And he needed soothing. If Barings thought that he was going to sit around inert for one long month, while files about him and the IEA were out there, somewhere, then Langley's cohorts were very much mistaken. Cuci said out aloud, "I'm going to show you all the mercy of a Greek tragedy, Judd Barings."

A substitute 'Albassi' would have to be found. One who would then turn up – face down of course – with lungs full of the Tiber; the river had been an outstanding dumping ground for corpses for more than 2,000 years. Ten times longer than Baring's United States of America had been in existence. A dead 'Albassi' would close the case forever and the missing files would no longer matter.

Enough was enough decided Cuci, as he scrunched on his rosy ice cubes.

CHAPTER 48

No. 5, Largo Claudio Treves,
the Brera District, Milan Italy.
Wednesday, 17th May 1978. Early evening.

Alone, except for her thoughts, Ruxandra lay sphinx-still with her eyes closed in Pietro's favourite chair. Enzo, her ever-present shadow of mourning, lay at her feet. Forever silent, Enzo had shrunk into a ball-sized beating heart of remembrance to his master. She had yet to accept that Enzo's grief was hers too. Like every day since her husband had been kidnapped or murdered, or both, 7 a.m. to 7 p.m. was far more than just twelve hours.

Abruptly, the telephone shattered the silence.

"Oh, it's you Ispettore Massina. Do you have any news?"

There wasn't even a hint of eagerness in Ruxandra's question.

"None I'm afraid. The kidnappers have yet to make contact. Your husband's photograph in the newspapers has only solicited the usual cranks. An old lady did call to say she thought she had seen a man go into a large block of apartments adjacent to the scene, but frankly, she's a lonely widow who probably likes the company of police officers. We visited each apartment in the block, and found nothing. As I said, Signora Albassi, there are no leads at present." Massina hissed at Pezzoli, "Get me a coffee." He continued. "Did your husband take you into his confidence about his work?"

"No, not really. He was a private man who kept himself to himself."

Unintentionally her tone had a hard edge. She sensed Massina flinch.

"Did you and he ever discuss the Moro case?"

"No, as I said, he kept himself to himself, especially with his work."

As she answered his question, she recalled the very day Moro's body was found, Tuesday 9th May, a week ago yesterday. She'd sensed at the time that Pietro had wanted to tell her something. He never did though, for she'd been more interested in healing his wounds. Now, this police *ispettore* wanted to ransack her memories. Pietro was dead. She didn't need a police officer to tell her that.

"I'm sorry I can't be of any more help. Have you spoken to his secretary Angelica?"

"Yes, and she was no help either. I must say, Signora Albassi, your husband was a very secretive man."

"To you, Ispettore, maybe," Ruxandra snapped, "but to those who knew him, he wasn't a secretive man – he was a private man. There's a difference. You only think like that because people will not tell you what it is you wish to hear." Massina had interrupted her grieving, and it made her cross. "He was an ordinary, honest lawyer who minded his own business, that's all. There was no mystery to him."

"If that is indeed the case, Signora Albassi, then why has your husband, a man with no mystery and an ordinary, honest lawyer, been kidnapped by ruthless terrorists and possibly murdered in cold blood? Answer me that, Signora Albassi, and soon please. Good day to you." And Massina cut the call dead.

CHAPTER 49

Questura HQ, via Fatebenefratelli, Milan, Italy.
Wednesday, 17th May 1978. Early evening.

"Don't you dare look at me like that, Pezzoli. I realise that we've got no more leads than you've got living brain cells." Defeated, Massina scratched his temple. "Book me on the last flight to Rome tonight, and when you've accomplished that simple task, I want the governor of Rebibbia Prison on the phone. Now get out, Pezzoli. OUT!"

Massina jammed his little finger in his ear, rummaged aggressively for wax and proceeded to inspect his bounty while speaking out aloud to an audience of none. "Why the hell is no one offering us a chance to pay a ransom for Signor Ordinary Signor Honest Signor Private Avvocato? That's what I want to know."

Massina's stomach knotted again as he spoke.

"In fact, thinking about it, that's just what I *don't* want to know." He frowned and wiped his finger clean on the underside of his chair. "Albassi, you're a man with too many shadows. Damn you."

Then Massina had an idea. His friend, Dr Guillermo Osta, Criminalpol's Head Psychologist, was but a short walk away. An unannounced visit was in order. Besides, he didn't want to sit in his nasty office thinking about Rebibbia Prison. Decisively, Ispettore Massina threw his brown overcoat over his shoulder and strode off down the corridor in the direction of Dr Osta's far plusher suite of rooms on the far side of the Questura HQ. Massina was not a man who coveted material possessions, however he did hanker after a decent office. Like Dr Osta's. Five minutes later he knocked on the door and strode in uninvited.

"Guillermo, I'm leaving for Rome to interview Nikolai Sentini and I need some advice," he announced promptly, whilst taking a seat.

"Sit down, Lorenzo, won't you?" Dr Osta offered a welcoming smile. He liked and respected Ispettore Massina. "Ask what you like, Lorenzo, but if it's why do the sons of successful people become idealistic terrorists the answer is obvious and dull."

"No, it's more complex, and in truth I haven't fleshed it out yet. I've just got that old gut-tightening feeling again. You heard they've given me the Albassi kidnapping?"

Massina half picked and half stroked his right nostril as he talked.

"Yes," nodded Dr Osta, his shaven head glistened like a pink domed carapace.

"Let me recap it for you," Massina continued, "last Friday, 12th May, about lunchtime, an ordinary – well – so far ordinary, mid-level lawyer with a top Milan firm, disappears. All the signs are that he was kidnapped. The firm's driver, one mental rung above a grasshopper, is wounded and the lawyer's very rare blood type, AB-, is everywhere, as are a few spent cartridges from a handgun we've traced back to the Red Brigades. With me so far?" He paused, not waiting for an answer. "All the moronic driver remembers is having seen an old white Lancia following them. Now, all the obvious clues point to the Red Brigades. But there's one coincidence too many and it jars: the gun used in the Albassi kidnap was first fired a couple of years ago in a Turin shooting by two *brigatisti*. They were later arrested, and by some inexplicable legal wizardry both *brigatisti* got off and were freed. The lawyer in question, was, by all accounts, very talented. A man who could find and exploit ambiguity where there was none." His chest pains returned and he inhaled slowly. "Guillermo my friend, there's no cigar for guessing who their defence lawyer was."

Dr Osta remained silent and merely grinned. He did enjoy Massina's methods.

"In one! Anyway, lately our lawyer had worked tirelessly, and according to his secretary to the point of collapse, on the Moro affair. A fixer, a grey intermediary between the Christian Democrats, the Red Brigades, the Communists, Moro's family, and he had Minister Tina Anselmi's ear too apparently. I haven't got the full picture yet and I probably never will, but he was right in the very thick of it all." Massina paused. "Apart from blood and cartridges, some files were found at the scene."

He leaned forward, grabbed Dr Osta's water glass without asking, and drained it off before continuing.

"As to his personal situation, well, he's Sicilian, born an orphan during the war. Somehow, he ended up a ward of the 14th Duke of Salaviglia, and much later he left Sicily to finish his education in Lombardy. Now, he's married with eight-year-old twins, a boy and a girl. Unfortunately, the little girl was involved in a mysterious hit-and-run six weeks ago, whilst Moro was still captive. She's in a coma in Niguarda, and the prognosis isn't good," Massina added matter-of-factly. "Anyway, Albassi is a passive sort of a man, not violent. He's not in debt, and on the surface has everything to live for." Massina vacillated. "I just don't believe he was kidnapped, Guillermo. It's that simple. I can't see the Red Brigades being involved with this. Besides, my sources inform me that they've a lot of respect for him. As usual, my dear friend, I've saved the best for last." Massina smirked. "Those files I mentioned in the car, they were all Albassi's notes on the Moro affair. The papers had the names Moro, IEA and one Alessandro Cuci all over them. We call Cuci 'God's Gangster' at our end of the building. Heard of him?"

Massina's question was both theatrical and sarcastic. Dr Osta frowned as if to say, 'I know *exactly* who you mean'.

"So, Guillermo, what's it all about?"

Massina's bulbous nose twitched like a hungry animal.

"You're the detective, Lorenzo. You haven't exactly given me much to go on. Ask me a direct question."

"OK, do people just up and vanish into thin air for no apparent reason, or motive?"

"No, in a word. Very, very rarely. If they do, a deep amnesia has shut the brain down, like these new computers do when they've been overloaded. In nine cases out of ten they kick-start themselves and 'reappear' if you will, not always where you thought, but they do turn up."

"That's helpful," Massina replied, derisively. Then without thinking, he switched his index finger's attention to his left nostril.

"If it wasn't for the wounded driver, Albassi's rare AB- blood-type splattered over the crime scene and the papers with Moro, IEA and Cuci's names, I'd guess that's exactly what happened. But with the IEA involved, there's anything and everything to play for. The Curia, with the Pope's full blessing because of his close friendship with Moro, were up to all kinds of behind-the-scene antics during the fifty-four days Moro was imprisoned. So, it's safe to assume the IEA were up to their gullets in it too."

"From what I hear, Lorenzo, the Pope's Heavenly reign could begin any day."

"Who cares about him? He's been dead from the neck up for years, and all he ever did was ban the Pill. Do me a favour, Guillermo, think on it, and if you want my files ask Pezzoli, OK?"

As abruptly as he'd arrived, Massina sauntered out leaving his friend and confidant's door wide open.

CHAPTER 50

Porto de Lisboa, Lisbon, Portugal.
Thursday, 18th May 1978. Afternoon.

A tall, athletic man, who was neither tanned nor olive-skinned, blended in with the hustle and bustle of the Porto de Lisboa. The man hadn't shaved for five days, and his face was masked in thick, dark stubble. He wore jeans, scuffed trainers and a heavy blue sweater underneath a grey windcheater. His cheap sunglasses flicked away glimmers of afternoon sun. He could have been just another itinerant looking for work on a tanker, a cargo ship, a cruise liner or even as a stevedore – for he was strong enough – but he moved through the crowds with a single purpose.

Tacked on the edge of Iberia, Lisbon has one of the largest natural harbours in the world, a few kilometres from its spiritual heart: the Atlantic Ocean. The Porto de Lisboa's maze of docks was on the north side of the Tagus River estuary, and opened westwards – the direction of travel the man had chosen – into the Atlantic. The man had never seen an ocean before, and its grey, unimaginable rolling vastness sent a shiver down his spine. Until now the indigo waters of the Tyrrhenian Sea had been his only reference, and from where he stood, the Earth was flat.

It was a mild afternoon, and the chill sting of an Atlantic wind was yet to come. High wispy mares' tails of cirrus clouds painted the sky the colour of a fish's underbelly and blended in as one with the ocean. Seagulls, with incredible wingspans and bodies the size of a dog, circled everywhere. The man had never imagined a seagull could be so large, so predatory. Their incessant, greedy screeching, as they swooped in low to chance their luck, drowned out even the most brutal of the docks' persistent clamour. The man was searching out a particular quay where a cargo ship named *Straits Star* was docked; she was due to embark at

17:00. The ship was to be his passage away from all he'd ever held true and loved in his thirty-three years.

The *Straits Star* was a Malaysian flagged and crewed vessel. The westerly route from Lisbon was via the Azores to take on bunkers. The final destination was the Americas: North, Central or South. The bosun wouldn't say. The man was just going to have to take his chances; he was okay with that. His route to Lisbon, from the Italian port of Reggio Calabria, had led him, ironically and briefly, to the Grand Harbours of Malta, where, after a few hours, the Italian tramp ship had put to sea for Gibraltar. En route, the man had learned there was a contact in Lisbon who arranged passages for those who wished to remain invisible.

The man had met the bosun of a Malay ship in a bar in Lisbon's Alfama district. A bosun, the man had learned, was a junior officer in charge of equipment and crew. This one was clearly running a scam of his own. He had an inscrutable, icy anonymity. Short in stature with a wiry frame, unblinking eyes the colour of ebony, yellowed stubs for teeth and a reed-thin smile which told of betrayals past, and foretold of treacheries to come. There was only one answer to the green question the man had asked: *'Yes, I have a berth available for you, if you have $500 in cash available for me.'* The bosun's reply had begged no names; neither were requested, nor proffered. Such are the perfunctory transactions of smugglers, refugees and thieves, the man had thought, after their business was concluded.

The man checked his watch – 15:25 – and saw the *Straits Star* concealed amongst cranes in perpetual motion. The vessel, brick in colour as if to hide its rust, was immense and foreboding. Two steep gangways stretched up at a forty-five degree angle from the quay towards the ship's topsides. The man did as the bosun had instructed and climbed up the stern gangway.

Upon reaching the marred deck, he knew he would soon vanish without a trace. He dropped the small holdall which held all that remained of his worldly belongings at his feet. The man knew that going into a wilderness, one should leave no footprints and take only memories.

He turned to look over his shoulder and to seek out two realms far beyond the hills of Lisbon, lands he would never visit again, such was the price to be paid. The man searched for, and found, them both: a city very far away and the Inland Sea's largest island.

CHAPTER 51

The Vatican State.
Thursday, 18th May 1978. Afternoon.

"I've just received a curious phone call from the governor of Rebibbia Prison."

Of late, Cuci found it easier to deal with Barings by getting straight to the point.

"Thrill me, Alex, what's happenin'? Make my day, tell me Sentini has disappeared down the same rabbit hole as yer man Albassi?"

Cuci's diminutive frame winced as if a sciatic nerve had been tweaked. He despised the way Barings kept saying '*yer*'.

"Sorry to disappoint, but last night Ispettore Massina lodged a request to interview Sentini this afternoon…"

"Whoa…! Shut right up!" Barings double-tapped Cuci like a hitman. "I've just had an idea that might help *you* out of the alligator bayou yer sorry ass is in." He paused. "Tell me, does Sentini have to see Massina?"

"Legally, yes in reality, no. Sentini can just sit there and refuse to cooperate, something he does well." There was a high-pitched impatience in Cuci's tone. "Why?"

"Calm down, Alex. Walk to yer fancy drinks cabinet, pour yerself one of those fizzy Cherryade drinks y'all like, an' I'll walk you through this."

Barings' deep southern drawl became ever more languid. Obediently, like a castigated child, Cuci placed the handset down and mixed himself a stiff Campari and soda.

"Alex, what do *y'all* want more than anything else right now?"

"Albassi's fingerprints attached to a dead body with all his missing files on the IEA, on me and on Moro."

"No, you don't. As I said, time's goin' to solve this. Lissen' up. Right now, a dead body would just add to yer foul-ups, Alex. Unfortunately, yer judiciary isn't as corrupt as it once was, an' thank-the-Lord yer rat-infested press isn't interested in Albassi. Let's face it, Alex, who the hell is, apart from you? A corpse in the morgue tagged, *'Mediator in Moro Affair'* on its big toe will get yer investigatin' Magistrate all fuzzed-up an' interested," cackled Barings. "Y'all still with me so far?"

"Yes," replied Cuci meekly.

"Good, as yer vermin press will be barkin' like hog-huntin' dogs, y'all have another chase on."

"Possibly."

"No. Certainly. An' that'd be as much fun as huggin' a rosebush." Cuci remained silent. Barings continued, "Y'all let this get personal, Alex. Big mistake. When y'all did that, y'all lost control an' it's sure outta control now. Albassi is a two-bit lawyer, poor as a sawmill rat too. Y'all can't afford for him to become a liberal crusade." Barings chugged his black coffee. "You're 100 per cent convinced Sentini has Albassi. I'm not. Never have been. Never will be. Don't think it's the Red Brigades' MO. But, if Sentini can really convince Massina that they do have him, then, there'll be nothing to investigate any more. Here's the kicker. Ready?"

"Yes, Judd."

"With Albassi a Red Brigades kidnap victim, the case automatically becomes a 'Terrorist' case, an' the investigation will be sent to Rome 'afore sundown where it can be controlled."

"That's right," replied Cuci.

"Massina's Questura will be one wheel down and draggin' an axle. Outta the game completely. Albassi will be another in a long list of Red Brigades' statistics, an' the Rome investigators will just end up hangin' the wrong horse thief. Case closed."

"And with time on our side..." muttered Cuci.

"Precisely, Alex. W'all know Rome's police couldn't find dogshit on their shoes. Don't have to remind you for fifty-four days they couldn't sniff out Moro from under their noses?"

"No."

"Don't make any more mistakes. Y'all can't afford another one. Down Mexico way they say, *'Paciencia y barajar'.*" Barings let a beat of hesitation pass. "Know what that means, Alex?"

"My Spanish is fluent, my Mexican slang not so."

"Patience an' carry on shufflin' the cards..."

Barings had to loosen his grip on Cuci for this gambit to work, so he let his menace hang in the air.

"Back home w'all would say, *'If it wasn't for bad luck y'all wouldn't have any luck at all'*. Do it my way this time, Alex. Be still. No dead bodies, please." And to appease the psychopath in Cuci he added, "Well, not yet a'while, y'all be OK with that I'm sure?"

"I'll arrange with the governor to have Massina kept waiting until I've spoken personally with Sentini. Satisfied?"

Cuci hung up before Barings could torment him further. For the first time in his life, he felt an emotion akin to dread.

CHAPTER 52

Rebibbia Prison, Rome, Italy.
Thursday, 18th May 1978. Late afternoon.

Massina shifted the passenger mirror to straighten his tie. Having a neat tie-knot was a foible he'd had ever since he'd joined the police. In those days he was zealous in his desire to progress. Nevertheless, the combination of his wife with her ever-present bottle, and the death of his heroin-addicted son had blunted his ambitions. Ironically, his only son's fatal overdose had resulted in his detachment from life itself, which in turn had helped his career to the point where more senior law officers appeared in awe of him. Massina had become, by default, a celebrated and successful investigator with a solid reputation. And no one had sounded more obsequious than the governor of Rebibbia Prison when Massina had telephoned earlier.

Massina's over-starched collar bit into his neck. His tie was straight, but his plans were irredeemably skewed. There was no conceivable way he would be able to catch the last flight back to Milan tonight. Rebibbia's governor had spoken of riots all day long. Riots? Why? From what the governor had said, it had sounded serious too.

"As long as Sentini is in one piece, they can all choke each other to death for all I care," Massina said to his police driver.

"'*Scusate*, Ispettore?"

"*Non fa niente*. No matter," replied Massina.

Massina hustled out of the front seat, closed the door, draped his brown overcoat over his forearm and began to walk towards the prison's foreboding gates. As he did so, his eyes twitched at a dazzle of light sniped by the sun's rays. He turned to look around. A large black Lancia saloon, with Vatican City diplomatic plates, its brightwork gleaming impossibly, pulled up right in front of the gates where Massina was now heading.

A small man, immaculately tailored, walked out of the gates. He stroked his goatee and waited stock still as a powerfully set man with dead eyes – more bodyguard than chauffeur – held the back door open.

"Cuci, what the hell are you doing here?" Massina grunted under his breath, as the Lancia sped away from the prison. He toyed with the myriad reasons why the head of the IEA should be at Rebibbia Prison during a riot. In each scenario, Nicolai Sentini and a corrupt prison governor assumed centre-stage.

Massina pressed the gates' intercom and the security door sprang open. He stepped through it before it banged shut automatically. Massina, deep in thought, was oblivious to the captive, sour prison air that closed in like a noxious fog, only to stay with him all night.

Apart from keeping his options open, Massina hadn't figured out how to exploit the quirk of luck that had just occurred. The tangle of muscle in his stomach felt tighter than ever now.

Usually, an officer of Massina's rank would have interviewed a prisoner of Sentini's category in a guarded interrogation room. Massina, however, had other plans. If there was any chance of uncovering a grain of truth, he needed Sentini to be calm, and the only place prisoners like Sentini were ever relaxed was in the confines of their own castles.

Rebibbia's governor had relented to Massina's demands to meet with the prisoner in his cell, alone, when Massina had made the obvious points regarding the day's riots: Would the governor wish Massina to include the riots in his report? Solely to substantiate the obvious severity of the disturbance of course? Just how many were injured? The guards – anyone killed, wounded or taken hostage?

So, as he had come to expect, Massina got his way and was duly escorted to Sentini's large cell on the upper tier of the prison's southwest wing. A cell that benefitted from the freshest air, the most sunlight and 'cost' the most. A guard opened the weighty iron door, with its peephole and food slot, and Nicolai Sentini, one of the four members of the Red Brigades Strategic Command, stood inside languidly smoking a cigarette.

Massina checked himself and remained in the open doorway: rugs, a solid wood bed, a small mahogany dining table, a TV, a radio, even an antique writing desk below shelves of books. All that appeared to be missing from the comfort of Sentini's cell were silver salvers and crystal decanters; there was a fridge, however. This was a king's castle and a symbol of just how low Italy had sunk. Massina shook his head imperceptibly. He'd been around far too long to be surprised by anything anymore, except, perhaps during the *anni di piombo*.

"I've heard talk of you, Massina, you arrested a friend of mine a long time ago," Sentini spoke in an unusually high-pitched voice.

"Who would be stupid enough to befriend you?" Massina fired back, as he waved away the blue cigarette smoke that poured from Sentini's small mouth. Uninvited, Massina pulled an upholstered dining chair away from the mahogany table.

"Listen to me, Massina. Don't start in. Be nice or fuck off back to Milan. You wanted to see me. I don't remember calling you."

"I have a problem, Sentini..."

"I'd never have guessed."

Sentini's eyes glazed over. He was primed. The IEA had been more than generous. He would have signed a confession in his own blood that he'd personally orchestrated Albassi's kidnap for what Cuci had offered him: use of the recreation cell with hookers, a blind eye turned on his hashish racket, and free rein with harder drugs. As a gesture of goodwill, Cuci had earlier lifted a package out of his attaché case and handed it to him, as a welcome guest might hand over a box of chocolates. It was, in fact, a kilo brick of Mexican Tar – brown heroin – that had been sent to the Vatican City in a diplomatic bag by the Catholic mission in Juarez.

"*Grazie tanto,* Signor Cuci," Sentini had said, as he placed the heroin on a bookshelf. Heroin was not Sentini's drug of choice, but for many inside Rebibbia's walls it was. Heroin was the most valued of all prison currencies, for it conferred power. If all Sentini had to do for Cuci was trade insults with one of the biggest, and ugliest, cops he'd ever seen, then he would, with pleasure.

"The trouble is, Sentini," Massina continued, "you just don't behave like a member of the Red Brigades Strategic Command. Unlike your fellow thugs, Mario Moretti or Renato Curcio, I don't see a messianic look in your eyes."

"Sorry to disappoint."

"I'm here to question you about a kidnapping, one that's alleged the Red Brigades carried out. A Milanese lawyer called Pietro Albassi. Know anything about it?"

"Hang on, Massina, here I am, an unwilling guest of your Republic, without the use of a telephone, without access to the outside world and you want to know if I orchestrated a kidnap that took place last week, hundreds of kilometres north of these walls? You give me too much credit," cackled Sentini, "so I'll save us both time."

He removed a fleck of tobacco from his lower lip.

"A certain faction of the Red Brigades has him, one that doesn't come under my authority. Albassi clouded the waters when we had Moro, that's true, and some comrades are still upset." Smoke curled out of his nostrils. "Massina, you of all people know what barracuda do to people who swim in murky waters."

"I do?"

"They strike at the first thing that glints and catches their eye, whether it's edible or not. Hence Albassi."

"Bullshit, Sentini. Too pat. I'm sitting here opposite you and inhaling your filthy odours. I know you're up to your reptilian neck in something. No idea what it is yet, but for sure it isn't Albassi's kidnapping. You've just confirmed that."

Sentini shrugged. All Cuci had wanted him to do was substantiate the lie that the Red Brigades had kidnapped Albassi. Cuci didn't mention anything about providing incontrovertible proof.

Massina stood up, pulled back his shoulders and knocked on the cell door for the guard. He then wheeled around to face Sentini, who, locked in his stare, couldn't even bat an eye, let alone smoke.

"Sentini, let me tell you something," boomed Massina in his low-pitched voice, "I've found life is either full of coincidences or empty of them. Rarely is it anything in-between. There are too, too many in my life, so I am going to leave you with just one of them."

Massina's presence seemed to fill the cell. He placed his right hand against the cell wall, his fingers splayed out like thick tentacles.

"I'd just joined the police. I was subordinate to a very corrupt senior officer who'd arrested your father for a serious crime. I was there. Your father was a respectable Turin doctor then. It was a long time ago. The senior officer on the case, he's burning in Hell now, took a hefty bribe from your father that day. You didn't know that, did you? No. You were a jumped-up brat at the time, and other than your father, I'm the only living person who knows the 'why' about your father. Now, isn't that a coincidence?"

Sentini stood up, walked over to Massina and ground his cigarette out on the cell wall, barely a centimetre from Massina's fingers. Massina didn't flinch, his unblinking eyes bored into Sentini. Massina banged on the cell door. Before a stunned Sentini could react, the guard had opened the cell door.

"Think about it, Sentini, and quickly. I want the truth about Albassi, not your miserable lies," snarled Massina, as he walked out of Sentini's world. All fifteen square metres of it.

CHAPTER 53

Questura HQ, via Fatebenefratelli, Milan Italy.
Friday, 19th May 1978. Early morning.

Ispettore Massina rubbed his nose and snorted. He felt terrible. His head throbbed and his stomach heaved, as if last night's thunderstorm was trapped inside of it. As for his mouth, well, it felt like fuzzy caterpillars had spent the night there. The beanless coffee and his airless office only contrived to streamline his foul temper.

Due to the brevity of his meeting with Sentini, he'd been able to catch the last flight out of Rome. Flying north had been violently turbulent and the idiots at the sharp end had missed their first approach into Linate, flying through the black anvil-shaped clouds. He should have known better than to fly into Milan in May.

The thought of having to write his report on the Albassi kidnapping this morning meant being careful, yet skilful, neither of which he was inclined to be. On the merits alone, the Albassi case could be handed down to those in Rome who lived and breathed terrorists, namely SISDE, Italy's domestic intelligence agency. He wanted to be rid of the Albassi file. Nevertheless, a part of him, the part that made him a first-rate detective, wanted to keep the investigation in Milan. However, the facts as they were on the ground, with Sentini's 'confession', meant the case was headed south before sunset. The way his head felt, being intelligently economical with all the evidence was going to be as difficult a task as a blind man threading a needle.

"Pezzoli, get in here with the Albassi file," he snapped down the intercom.

He rubbed his nose again and waited.

"How was the Rome trip, Ispettore?"

"Part disaster and part illuminating. I assume nothing has happened since yesterday?"

"Correct. All's been quiet. Even the cranks have stopped calling."

"As I expected." Massina gathered his thoughts. "So, Pezzoli, do you know what happened in Rome yesterday?" He waited in vain. "Of course you don't, so let me tell you. After my original appointment at Rebibbia Prison was mysteriously delayed on account of a fictional riot, guess the name of the first person I saw? You get one try."

"I've no idea," Pezzoli replied, meekly.

"One Alessandro Cuci climbing fussily into the backseat of his chauffeured car. What do you imagine the scourge, maverick, genius, pain-in-the-rear, both literal and metaphorical, power-crazed head of the IEA was doing there?" Massina dithered. "I could guess, but where this puts Sentini, I'm not sure. More to the point I don't think I want to know. If Cuci is somehow involved in this Albassi business, you could bet your grandmother's last egg on the CIA being up to their neck in this bucket of donkey shit too. As for one Pietro Albassi, well, he's no longer orbiting Italy, of that I'm certain."

Pezzoli knew to remain silent.

"Why am I telling you all this?" continued Massina. "Simple, because I can't tell anyone else."

"Do you think Albassi is dead?"

"If he isn't, he soon will be. If he's running, which I suspect he is, they *will* find him. They always do."

"Who are they?"

"Who the hell do you think, *cretino*, the Red Cross!"

"So, what did you learn from Sentini?" Pezzoli asked, picking his gaze up from his grubby shoes.

"Nothing, except that the Red Brigades don't have Albassi. Sentini said they do, but believe me they don't. Trust this nose, Pezzoli, even if you don't like it."

Massina leaned across his desk.

"What are our options then, Ispettore?"

"One: We can write a report that'll leave us hounding Albassi's ghost forever. It's not good policy to have an unsolved kidnapping file hanging around. So that's a solid no. Two: We can write a report that places our heads on platters by stating all we believe. That's a bad call. Never a good idea to reveal your cards. Another definite no. Three: Get creative and let SISDE have the case by telling them what Sentini said.

We'll omit everything we suspect from our report. That's precisely what we'll do."

Pezzoli looked at him quizzically, and then blurted out. "Are you worried?"

"I'm not worried, Pezzoli," replied Massina, looking worried.

"That's good to hear, sir."

"Don't trouble your little head, Pezzoli. I could squeeze Sentini's ugly face until pips shot out of his nose, but I don't want to. Lies have very short legs, and someone, Sentini, the IEA, CIA, politicians, someone will trip over those little legs. Let Rome and SISDE deal with the fallout. From our garret here in Milan we can observe that. Never underestimate the power of silent observation, Pezzoli. Go and write up all the hard evidence we have. Have no fear, I doubt it'll fill two pages." Massina waved his hand dismissively, but managed a smile too. "Goodbye, Pezzoli."

After the door clicked shut, Massina put his head in his hands and held his pulsing temples.

"You're far from stupid, Cuci, but you *will* make a mistake. Even Einstein made mistakes," Massina murmured under his malodorous breath. "You're too clever for your own good sometimes. Don't do it, Cuci, I want a quiet life. Please, please don't do what I suspect you will do."

A part of Massina knew he was speaking with a forked tongue when he said 'please' for the second time.

PART NINE

CHAPTER 54

**24, via Carlo D'Adda, Navigli District, Milan, Italy.
Friday, 14th July 1978. 01:45. Two months later.**

Lorenzo Massina turned on his bedside light. Wincing, he reached over the slumbering mound of drink-sodden flesh that was his wife, and grabbed the receiver.

"This had better be important, it's two in the morning!"

Massina's knee brushed against his wife's unshaven leg. He flinched.

"It's Gianfranco Armedi at the Questura, Lorenzo. I'm on the graveyard shift."

"So why call me, Gianfranco?"

"I'm just doing my job, Lorenzo. You know how it is. The *Questore* gets a call, then *I* get a call, so *you* get a call."

"Get on with it," growled Massina. A hot summer breeze from the nearby park squeezed into the cheerless bedroom. Sweating, he propped himself up against the headboard.

"You remember the Albassi kidnapping?"

"Yes, of course I do. That was about two months ago. Rome has had the case almost since the wretched man was abducted. Don't tell me they've finally received a ransom note? That would be priceless." Massina's tone was as false as his hopes.

"Well, that's one way of putting it. Apparently, a body washed up in Portofino last night. That'll put all those rich holidaymakers off their vongole, eh, Lorenzo. Ha! Ha!"

Massina smirked. Now that was funny. In his experience women behaved at the scene of a crime much as they do in horror movies: they peeked while pretending not to. Yet the more horrific the crime – or the movie – the more their eyes and mouths opened in glee. Yes, women had the edge in the ghoul race.

"Portofino comes under Genoa's command, not Milan's. What the hell has this got to do with us, Gianfranco?"

"No idea. The heroes at SISDE wanted someone familiar with the case who could get there immediately, and that's you, Lorenzo."

"You mean I've got to leave now? Can't it wait until morning?"

"In a word, no. Those are your orders," Gianfranco added, apologetically.

"Has anyone made a positive identification yet?"

"No, but some ID has been found on the body."

"I never met Albassi. How am I supposed to identify him? Call his wife, Gianfranco."

"Are you always this witty, Lorenzo?"

"OK, OK." Massina sighed angrily and then added, "*Vaffanculo*, Cuci."

"What did you say?"

"Nothing, forget it. It's a mantra I invoke when my stomach tightens up."

"Eh? Just get to Portofino. *Buona fortuna*, Lorenzo."

As the line went dead, Massina looked at his wife and cursed his fate. On and on she slept. She wouldn't even notice his absence when she stirred in a few hours for her daily flirtation with the real world.

He struggled out of bed, undid the thick cord that held up his pyjamas and let them fall around his ankles. In the half-light he considered his body. What was it that made the pink blotches that peppered his slush-coloured skin glow so angrily? Perhaps it was the onset of a virulent skin cancer? "No such luck," he said to himself.

He picked up his watch from the bedside table. 01:50. Portofino was a three-hour drive from Milan, even in the dead of night. He decided to skip shaving; was a dead man going to mind? He'd douse himself in the shower, make a pot of coffee, chomp some bread and salami, and leave in an hour or so.

What he hadn't realised was that the clouds on his Ligurian horizon had grown darker with intrigue. Both real and imaginary.

CHAPTER 55

Piazza Martiri dell'Olivetta,
Portofino, Liguria, Italy.
Friday, 14th July 1978. 05:55.

Only Ispettore Lorenzo Massina, Criminalpol, Milan Central, could view Portofino with distaste.

Portus Delphini, Port of the Dolphin, as Pliny the Elder had named Portofino, symbolised to Massina the inbreeding of the five Italian cousins – politics, crime, business, money and religion – which he found irksome. However, what really pissed him off was the preposterous loveliness of it all. He was damned if he too was going to succumb to its charms. Besides, he was only here to examine a corpse.

Massina strolled along the dew-slicked cobbles of the deserted quayside, with only dozy seagulls and the soft glow of a Ligurian dawn for company. The rising apricot light enriched the looming crags and the Castello high above the tiny port; Portofino looked for all the world like a stage set, or a contrived image from a postcard stand. In the small harbour, the varnished mahogany hulls of the playboys' Rivas were glistening like coloured diamonds in Portofino's cool waters, as if they were God's postscript. And all of this was flanked by dense *macchia*, tall sea pines, arthritic, broad-shouldered olive trees and a faded palette of terracotta paintwork houses. It took his breath away. Damn the place.

To compound it all, the Ligurian Sea and the Golfo Marconi were an exquisite backdrop. Not even the warm sea breeze that caressed his tired face like a lover he'd never met, could make him like Portofino. Maybe one day – perhaps in retirement – when he could toss his Criminalpol badge into the sea, might he view the place differently. He doubted it.

Since Gianfranco had called, the only satisfaction he'd had was ordering Pezzoli to join him. It was about time his young assistant shuffled feet rather than files. Bluntly, he had informed Pezzoli to meet him at the office of the Portofino district pathologist.

Massina glanced up at the clock on the bell-tower of the Chiesa di San Martino, a few steps behind the port. 06:25. Even his thirty-minute stroll had evaporated into Portofino's magic. Phoof! Another reason to loathe the place; it could even confiscate time. Anyway, he'd had enough of walking by the hateful yachts moored stern-to at the small quay. Two minutes later Massina found the shiny black door of the district pathologist: No. 7, Vico Nuovo, a minuscule piazza encircled by waterfalls of purple bougainvillaea. He rapped on the brass dolphin door knocker aggressively, only to be taken aback when Pezzoli answered.

"Oh, so you've been promoted to 'Receptionist to the Office of District Pathologist'. So, where's your boss, Pezzoli? I assume he's done his Frankenstein bit? What's his name by the way?"

"Yes, Ispettore, Dr Marco Valente informs me that an autopsy has been performed. The body washed up right along the west quay at about 19:00 last night. After the initial identification was made, Rome pulled all the dental, medical and legal records before contacting us. What we were not told was that they actually had a positive ID before they called you in."

Pezzoli whispered, as if imparting the secret recipe of Coca-Cola. "It *is* Albassi."

Massina studied the young man with a fierce contempt.

"I like you Pezzoli, but please learn from me. Don't believe everything a pathologist tells you. Ever. They're like restaurant staff, they lie and cheat. Why? Simple. Like restaurant staff, they are paid by how many stiffs they administer to. The more stiffs they process, the more money this great Republic of ours pays them. For us to have an 'open' case is different. Our files don't decompose in quite the same manner. Pathologists aren't allowed to have 'open' cases. So, Pezzoli, where is our butcher-man?"

"In the basement. I'll wait for you here."

"No, you won't. Come and get an education. That's an order."

Massina strode off in the direction of the marble stairs. As polite as his mood would allow, he introduced himself to Dr Marco Valente.

After so many stomach knots over the Albassi case, he was curious to see the cause.

Dr Valente was a short, stocky man in his fifties, bad teeth and a pinched face with hollowed-out cheeks, as if he'd spent a lifetime sucking on fresh lemons.

"*Buongiorno,* Ispettore Massina, it's a pleasure to meet such a celebrated detective as yourself." Dr Valente paused. "I don't advise inspecting the corpse. It's not, how to say it… in good condition," he pronounced, with a shrug and a thin smile.

"*Si, Buongiorno,* Dottore. It can't be that bad," replied Massina.

Dr Valente shrugged silently and wiped his gloved hands on his bloodstained apron. Why did these Criminalpol hotshots always think they knew better? Dr Valente's rubber boots squelched as he trudged towards the stainless-steel table. To Massina they sounded as if they were full of dead fish. He winced at the noise. Dead bodies *and* the foul stink of formaldehyde. On an empty stomach. At sunrise. In Portofino. Shit.

"I do have to warn you, Ispettore," implored Dr Valente.

"Get on with it, open the curtains. This isn't *La Traviata*."

"Good choice," Dr Valente murmured sarcastically. "If you insist…"

For a full minute Massina stared, and he knew not to read anything into a corpse's expressions. He paused, before grasping the sheet to yank it off entirely. Stalled in abject horror, morsel by morsel, his mind slowly began to compute what his eyes were telling him. The equation just wouldn't balance. He looked at Dr Valente for help and didn't even notice that Pezzoli was missing.

"As you can see, Ispettore, it's impossible to state time of death. So, I've noted the 1st July," Dr Valente announced, while trying to hide his smug 'I-told-you-so' expression.

"Get out of the toilet, Pezzoli, and get back in here," shouted Massina, "whoever had his hand in this was either very stupid or very cautious. Do you hear me, Pezzoli, get out here now!"

With his hand over his mouth Pezzoli emerged from the adjacent bathroom.

"Thank you for gracing us with your presence, now listen. Whatever Dr Valente's report says, this lump of flesh is no more than a bloated corpse of fish-eaten skin and bone. The trenched sockets where eyes once lived, the blackened stumps of his fingers, his toes from which all the nails have been torn out, these are all tell tales. The first being that all the obvious mutilation you see here is antemortem."

"What's that?" interrupted Pezzoli.

"Before death. That's Latin, *cretino*." Massina continued, "The Red Brigades have no history of South American style torture. So, they aren't the perpetrators. Second, the blood from all of Sentini's and Moretti's killings may run the length of the Apennines, but their handiwork isn't on this dead body."

Massina scratched his stubbled chin and looked down at the hideously disfigured carcass. What had once been a head and face was scarcely a pulped husk.

"Third, this man was tortured to mask any doubt as to his identity. But, if that's the case, then why throw the body at the further mercy of the sea? Why bother?" Massina's bloodshot eyes rounded suspiciously on Dr Valente. "In the final analysis, Pezzoli, there's no hiding from the facts, and the facts, as we are assured by the good pathologist Dr Valente are…"

Massina picked up the aluminium clipboard and read from it.

"Albassi's extremely rare blood type 'AB-' matches the deceased. So too do all the dental records. Unfortunately for us all, the two gaping holes where his eyes once resided have either been eaten by eels, or gouged out by whomever tortured him, thus making a check on his blind left eye, well, not really feasible, is it, Dr Valente?"

The pathologist concurred meekly. Who is this Ispettore Massina he thought.

"So, on paper it looks like our missing lawyer from Milan. It's not even a 'maybe'. Read Dr Valente's sparse report and it's a racing certainty. Pleased to meet you, Pietro Albassi, wish it could have been under different circumstances. Are you with me, Pezzoli?"

Pezzoli nodded his head.

"*Eccolo!* Case closed, Pezzoli! *Andiamo!*"

Despite the facts, as presented by both the corpse and Dr Valente, the knots in his stomach tightened, so much so that he didn't even pay Dr Valente the professional courtesy of *arrivederci*.

Massina strode out into Liguria's early morning sun for a long overdue espresso. He sat down in one of the Piazza Martiri dell'Olivetta's lavish water's edge cafés, and decided to add a murderously priced shot of grappa to his coffee to help settle his stomach from the horrors he'd just beheld. And it wasn't even seven o'clock.

CHAPTER 56

**The Gleneagles Bar,
Mġarr Harbour, Gozo, Malta GC.
Friday 14th July 1978. Late afternoon.**

"Hello, may I speak to Joshua Padden, *per favore?*"

Ruxandra knew the odds of finding Joshua in 'Tony's', as the Gleneagles Bar was known, was her best chance. For whatever his state of inebriation, Tony had always had Joshua's back, and she needed him sober-ish. The line fizzed and she heard noises: garrulous bar-speak noises, above which rose a cry of, "Josh, phone." She'd found him.

"Joshua Padden speaking." His voice was steady. And sober.

"Josh, it's Ruxandra. I have news for you."

Ispettore Massina's earlier call might have been inconceivable if her premonitions hadn't been so strong. Perhaps it was the way he'd delivered the news, his subconscious saying something his vocal cords couldn't? But the facts – and he'd sounded so matter of fact – spoke for themselves: the dental records matched her husband's, as did his rare blood-type, as did the detached left retina, and the remains of his ID cards. Massina had explained calmly that her husband's body had been in the water for many days, possibly a week or more, and the northern currents had carried him a long distance, so physical identification would be impossible. "There would be no point in you attending, Signora Albassi. The post-mortem is complete and the pathologist has signed the death certificate."

'Death certificate.'

She recalled the way Massina had enunciated the words.

'Death certificate.'

The two words ran around her mind like a rabid dog biting everything in sight. Until then 'death' had been a premonition, a speculation.

She'd accepted that Pietro wasn't ever coming back, but his *death* was something the gypsies hadn't quite prepared her for.

She'd readily agreed with Massina that she didn't wish to identify the body of her once handsome husband, especially if it resembled fish bait. All she'd asked him for was the truth about the physicality of his death. Again, she'd gagged on the word, but he'd understood. She took solace in his quiet and deliberate statement: *'It would have been swift and painless, Signora Albassi, that I can assure you. There were two small-calibre bullet wounds to the head, one in the nape of the neck and the other in the right temple. Death would have been instantaneous. There would have been no suffering I can assure you, Signora Albassi. Your husband lived and died a brave man.'*

Massina had grimaced at his duplicity, for the truth was entirely different. Pezzoli had been sworn to secrecy with diabolical threats to his own physical well-being, and the pathologist had been won over, eventually, with plain sympathy. There was no way he could allow Signora Albassi, frosty individual that she might be, to view the body that had clothed her husband's soul. A body that had been subjected to the finely tuned, and passively violent, methods of extended torture perfected over centuries by the murdering Neapolitans.

With bile in his throat, Massina had called her from the anonymity of a motorway café on his return to Milan. His office was polluted enough without having this story adding to its misery. As he had waited for her to answer the telephone, he reminded himself of what to think. The living had a duty to live, and people like him were here to absorb the deleterious film of scum that floated on the surface of the world. He was like a sheaf of pink blotting paper absorbing society's poison. With those thoughts, the lies he had to tell her would run true with conviction. And so, they did.

"You sound well, Josh," Ruxandra said, Massina's considerate words of bravery still echoing in her ears.

"I am. Well, as fit as the demons living in soda water bottles allow me to feel. I've not had a drink since we last spoke. Not bad, eh?"

"I don't know if that's good or bad," she stammered. "Joshua, Pietro is dead. His body has been found. The police called me a couple of hours ago. It had washed up in Portofino of all places. Two bullet wounds in the head. An execution. I didn't think it would happen this way."

Her words were like staccato clips of a musical score, disjointed yet still holding a coherent sense.

"Are the police sure it's him?"

"Yes. They have matched his blood type, his dental records even his blind eye. It is..." she paused "... well, no, it was him."

"Have you been to identify the body?"

"No. I didn't want to. I know how I want him to look for the rest of my life." She checked herself. "There can be no plans yet, I've not even told Toto or Paola."

"How is Paola? I'm almost afraid to ask."

"Still in a coma, Joshua." Her voice dropped and went quiet. He had to strain to hear her. "She may be in a coma, but I'll still tell her. I have to... I have to."

Padden could not even begin to comprehend. He felt unclean. Ashamed.

"Will you promise to come to the funeral?"

"If you tried to keep me away you wouldn't succeed. Just give me twelve hours' notice."

"I will, kind Joshua. Thank you."

"Oh, Rux, just wanted... to, er, add... well, I'll see you."

Not trusting his new sobriety at all, Padden quickly hung up Tony's worn Bakelite receiver before she could ask what he had wanted to say.

CHAPTER 57

**Chiesa di San Marco, Piazza San Marco,
the Brera District, Milan, Italy.
Monday, 17th July 1978. 10:00.**

Ruxandra smiled at Toto as she ran her black-gloved hand through his fine auburn hair, *capelli d'angeli* – the hair of angels – as Pietro used to say. She marvelled at the determined expression fixed on his young jaw, one his father had worn so often. The same jaw that had quivered when she told him the news of his father's death four days ago. She had yet to bargain with the gypsies for the courage she would need to whisper that truth in Paola's ear.

With her dress of heavy black Sicilian cloth, Ruxandra, wearing a gossamer lace veil, was the epitome of an Italian widow. She made a pretence of brushing Toto's jacket in order to study the congregation behind them. How Pietro would have been appalled by the grim theatre of it all: the double standards, the hushed silence, the stale incense, the towering candles, the bullying repression and sickly sweet encouragement of all things ignorant and without sun. She also knew he would have delighted in the unfolding circus in the small, frescoed thirteenth-century church, 400 metres from where they had lived.

There was, of course, a ringmaster. He was an elderly priest with a pinched and unkind face who rocked impatiently on the balls of his feet. Pietro's employer, Dottore Enrico Scampidi, dressed in an impeccable charcoal grey suit, stood apart in a pew of his own, complete with a black armband signalling only his appetite for rife hypocrisy. She had always hated him, in the true meaning of the word; even the gypsies had warned her about him. In the pew behind was Joshua Padden, visibly uncomfortable in an unkempt dark suit and an ill-fitting shirt held in place by a knitted tie that had, once upon a yester-moon, been tartan. He gripped the pew's edge like a man suffering from vertigo. She could all but smell the alcohol oozing from his every pore. Yet she smiled lovingly at him, for his blinking and unfocused eyes never left Pietro's coffin.

Two rows behind Joshua stood a man of a similar age as her late husband. It took a few seconds before she recognised him. So, Victor Salaviglia had travelled north to pay his respects too. Pietro would have loved that his dearest friend was present. She hadn't seen him since her wedding day – Victor had been Pietro's best man – almost ten years ago. A decade that had seemingly evaporated. Victor was taller than Pietro, more rugged and tanned; a man who lived his waking life in fresh air. His attractive moon-like face had aged well; trim chestnut hair flattered his deep-set coffee-coloured eyes. She studied him in a hurry from behind her veil. His tailored black suit accentuated his military posture, and he clasped his large hands in front of him. Despite living different lives – and 1,500 kilometres apart – Pietro and Victor had always been close. And always private. Whenever they had met up in Rome, Naples or Milan it was left unsaid that the reservation was for two, only. She had never minded, for she knew that when they were together, they were far more than the sum of two. There had always been a steady, radiating peace in Victor, who embodied all that was good about her late husband, and she knew that Pietro embodied all that was good about Victor; they brought out the truly noble in each other. Heavy tears of gratitude fell visibly from her eyes which she refused to dab away.

Further behind, and to the left of the aisle, were Angelica and Joseph. Angelica touched her cheek with a white lace-trimmed handkerchief until finally their eyes met. Ruxandra glared at her, not wishing to know whether Pietro had ever slept with her, and swiftly averted her gaze toward the other colleagues she knew hailed from Scampidi's law office.

She did a brief headcount of the remaining congregation before turning around to face the irritable – and irritating – priest who had coughed several times. Over twenty-five people. Pietro would feel honoured.

It was then she heard hinges creak in the manner of all wooden church doors. She swung around curiously. The doors opened a few centimetres, enough for a slim person to glide through before a sacristan tried to nudge them closed. Her expression lightened as she noticed a flushed Ispettore Massina push firmly against the timid sacristan. Leaving the doors ajar, so as not to draw further attention to himself, he took a seat in the back row.

As soon as the priest began to speak, Ruxandra sensed Pietro's presence amongst the congregation. She knew he was there. She could feel him, warm and tactile beside her. He was laughing. She'd believed he'd come to hold her hand one last time. He'd promised her as much, and he'd never broken a promise to her. Ever. Even in death he'd said he would guard and protect her. Besides, she knew Pietro wouldn't miss his own funeral.

Much to the priest's annoyance she continued to wear, for the duration of the service, an expression once removed from sheer joy. In her own tongue she thanked the gypsies for delivering up his body, thereby giving her the very weapon by which to survive.

I love you so very much, Pietro, wherever you are, she thought as she squeezed Toto's hand three times in quick succession.

CHAPTER 58

**1111 Canal Street, Vieux Carré,
New Orleans, Louisiana, USA.
Monday, 17th July 1978. 05:00.**

Anthony Bianchi tossed and turned fitfully on his narrow bed all night. Sleep had been a long time coming, and when he finally dozed, his first light images were as baroque as the July humidity was intense.

A heatwave had gripped New Orleans for more than a week, and the emphysemic breeze which had stolen in from Lake Pontchartrain, had died long before it ever reached his bedsit behind the Saenger Theatre. The all-night hum 'n drum of the French Quarter, just one block south, had made sleep an impossible dream.

He had drifted – alone and sweating – in and out of dreams, until he found himself afloat and refreshed, so much so that he felt human again. A large barrel-vaulted room appeared before him, its darkness illuminated by faces and torsos he recognised, except that none of them matched.

It was as if a malevolently bored God was enjoying a surreal jigsaw puzzle: Ruxandra's lean and attractive face was being worn by a colleague from the office, a man with a hunched body supported Angelica's subtle smile, Scampidi's corrupt stance held Joseph's faint limp, and his childhood friend Victor was wilting in Joshua's old dark blue suit. There was a jaundiced and tired-looking man with a hefty girth who sat alone at the back; he wore the smile of a disbeliever too. Only Toto appeared to be 'himself'. He scanned the cavernous and sinister room for his beloved Paola. She was nowhere to be found. Where was she?

His odyssey continued, unrecognised, amongst the dismembered faces, bodies and limbs.

The more he strained to focus, the more the room closed in around him. There were multicoloured panes of glass on high, and all of them joined with the precision of a kaleidoscope. A robed man, gesticulating to blind eyes and speaking to deaf ears, stood beside a coffin and tried to conquer the chaos with an old leather book. Anthony pulled up a stool and sat, unnoticed, beside the robed man. He studied him. There was something familiar about his manner. He looked like a priest. He had known such a man once, back when time had curled playfully around the smooth edges of day. He remembered the man, a kindly man. A priest too. He looked for his face amongst the faces in the congregation, but couldn't find him. Perhaps the old priest was another disbeliever?

It wasn't until he read a small brass plate with the legend 'Pietro Albassi. 1 September 1944 – 1 July 1978' on top of a varnished wooden box that he knew for certain what he had suspected. He kicked the stool to one side and strode to where Ruxandra was standing. He sought out her gloved hand and squeezed it three times in quick succession. Not in farewell, but with playful welcome: a sensation uniquely theirs, one she would recognise.

This was just a staging post, a celestial warehouse of souls, a place he knew he didn't yet belong. Paola wasn't there, that was why.

CHAPTER 59

Niguarda Hospital,
Piazza Ospedale Maggiore, Milan, Italy.
Monday, 17th July 1978. 12:23.

Ruxandra Albassi was never able to tell her daughter that her father had been killed and they had buried him.

Toto Albassi never did get to show his sister the animal cartoons he had drawn for her every morning since their father had been kidnapped. Although, the ninth birthday card he had drawn for his twin sister the previous month still stood sentinel on her medicine table.

It was as if a phantom had stolen into her hospital room and seized her young life and her soul. Just like that. All the alarms rang suddenly. The lines on all the machines went flat. Just like that.

There could be no earthly explanation. For there was none.

CHAPTER 60

**No. 5, Largo Claudio Treves,
the Brera District, Milan, Italy.
Monday, 17th July 1978. 20:18.**

The duty of informing Signora Albassi that her daughter had passed away while her husband's funeral was taking place, had befallen a Niguarda Hospital nun, not one of Paola's numerous physicians.

She had finally reached Paola's mother at home when she, Toto and Joshua Padden had returned from the funeral. Ruxandra had initially been both stoic and silent upon hearing the news of her daughter's death. She had learned to take care of the living first.

Straightaway, she'd asked Padden to watch over Toto, and shield him from the truth for a little longer, a choice she made in the full knowledge of his recent drinking. It was a choice she was proud of and one – as time would tell – she would never regret. There was still one last night she needed to spend alone with her daughter, albeit in the hospital's morgue. There was still so much she had to say.

After she'd left for the hospital, Toto and Enzo led Padden out of the apartment to the roof where his father used to feed his 'air rats'. The little boy sensed the lumbering man, with his ashen and sweat-drenched face, needed solace too. Only when they had reached the roof did Toto dare speak. Enzo, always alert to the moods of his masters, lay down solemnly at Toto's feet.

"Papà used to come up here every morning, Uncle Joshua. He fed the pigeons over there. Let me show you," he said, pointing to the coop. Smiling, he grasped Padden's hand.

Beneath them, even as nightfall came, the swell of the city's lights cast a deep orangey glow that was exaggerated by the clear, starry night. On the near horizon, carnival illuminations danced under a huge Ferris wheel, its hundreds of lights could have been shooting stars to wish upon. And the hum of the evening traffic was dulled by the shrill of the funfair's excitement. In silence Padden sought out the North Star, and then gripped Toto's hand as if the little boy was the first and last friend he would ever have.

"Mama calls them Papà's air rats. She doesn't like them at all, but every day after school I come up here to feed them, and until this morning I used to say a prayer for Papà. But now he's dead. I'm not sure what to do."

Toto paused, as if to pluck up courage, but it was Padden who tightened his grip.

"What should I do, Uncle Joshua?" Toto asked.

All Padden wanted to do was lie face down on the scummy roof and hold on tight. Instead, he turned away and looked deep into the city. Tears streamed down his rough, veined cheeks. A lifetime of wars, deaths, threats, killers and danger just hadn't equipped him to deal with this crisis. Again, it was Annie who brought him back from the brink. She would have been able to answer the brave young lad. He knew that for sure. He swallowed hard, so the lump in his throat might dissolve. He wiped his cheeks dry, and he turned to face Toto square in the eyes. He knelt down and gripped the boy's arms lovingly.

"I'll tell you what you should do, Toto. You keep coming here every day and feed your Papà's 'air rats', and what's more, you remember to say a prayer every day too. You see, wherever your Papà is, he needs your prayers now more than ever."

CHAPTER 61

**Café Cordino, via dei Condotti, Rome, Italy.
Monday, 17th July 1978. 20:18.**

This time it was Barings who found himself waiting alone at a dimly lit corner table. He'd ordered a large bourbon and a dirty martini for Cuci; he didn't plan on staying one second longer than necessary.

At last, Cuci ambled in. Immediately, Barings clocked that he didn't look his usual crisp self; his tie-knot was askew, his eyes squinted meaner than usual. Cuci stole behind Barings' chair and he slid into the cocooned leather booth, irritated and thin-lipped.

"Judd, *per favore*, to what do I owe this pleasure?"

"Y'all recollect that my forbearance is longer than the Mississippi," Barings drawled, as he held his tumbler, "but whilst here in Rome, it's become shorter than a midget's stream of piss. So, I'll cut straight to it. Have y'all read the cables about Albassi's funeral this morning?"

"Of course."

Barings fisted his knuckles and stared at Cuci's blank response: a response as empty as any dead man's eyes that Barings had ever seen. And he'd seen many. The man just didn't get it. "So, what's yer side of the story?"

"Why? It's all finished. Done." Cuci sipped his martini. "That's the point, Judd. Albassi's death will get added to the list of hundreds of others carried out by the Red Brigades. The pathologist's signature on the death certificate states the corpse is Pietro Albassi. The signature on that document is as good as mine. You'll just have to believe me on that detail." Cuci beamed across the table with genuine pride.

"Y'all are so frickin' low, Alex, y'all look up just to see Hell."

Barings was tired. Tired of Cuci. Tired of Rome. Tired of this mission. "Finish yer tale, Alex, an' *Reader's Digest* only."

Cuci rambled on about myriads of corrupt P2 contacts and Neapolitan murderers he'd hired to deliver a plausibly fake 'Albassi' corpse in Portofino, most of which Barings knew about already. And what he didn't know about just incensed him. However, he kept his counsel throughout by sipping steadily on his bourbon. When Cuci's head of steam had run its course – along with his martini – Barings edged across the table, ever closer.

"I've had enough, Alex, so here's what y'all gonna love."

Barings took a 50,000 lire note from his billfold and slid it under his empty glass. His Southern drawl hit a canyon-deep pitch, and he grinned like a fox in a chicken run. He shunted his chair back and pulled himself up to his full 6'3" height – he appeared taller, such was his anger. He flexed his broad shoulders and leaned forward onto the table, his knuckles taking all his weight. He sucked in all the oxygen around him.

"Don't forget, little fella, Albassi is alive an' kickin' somewhere out there." Barings stared at Cuci like a man would a mad dog. Wild-eyed, he neither blinked nor moved. "An' here's another bone for y'all to chew on, an' y'all don't know this part. I removed this intel from the afternoon cables. Only CIA has this."

Barings dipped his head ever lower. He was right in Cuci's face now, and he breathed out hot southern fumes.

"Albassi's lil' daughter, his Paola, just up an' died this afternoon, 'bout the time her daddy's funeral ended. Her coma just took her away. All without a murmur. The sleep of an innocent child, Alex. Real mysterious apparently. It was as if the life just went out of her, like Casper the Friendly Ghost took her spirit off to go play." Barings bared his teeth and snarled. "Her Daddy's very much alive, yer dumb sonofabitch. An' you murdered his lil' gal. Lord knows where he's at. But he's wounded an' bleedin' very badly. Critters like that get real mean. Y'all don't have a hawk's-eye clue where to start lookin', do you? 'Course not. So, that makes this killin' an imposter plan o' yours as dank an' as dark as the Devil's ridin' boots, now don't it?"

Cuci's expression withered to one of horror. Then white-fear. His jaw went slack and he fought for air, any air, even Barings' air.

And Barings – Texan-tall – turned around and strode out of Café Cordino, as if he was leaving an old saloon, which, in truth, he was.

PART TEN

CHAPTER 62

The Garden District, New Orleans, Louisiana, USA.
Monday, 17th July 1978. Mid-afternoon.

A streetcar, drab-olive in colour, rattled westwards on its iron tracks from Canal Street in the French Quarter, to St. Charles Avenue in the Garden District. Anthony Bianchi yanked on the overhead wire, the bell rang, and he alighted and stood on the southern sidewalk at his destination, his feet wide apart. The muscular roots of the ancient oak trees had long ago buckled the paviours of this most beautiful of New Orleans' avenues.

Overhead, long needles of sunlight pierced the dense foliage only to be softened by beguiling tendrils of Spanish moss which hung from the oaks' branches. He removed his sunglasses. In front of him was a graceful Neo-Italianate mansion built, he later discovered, in 1907. It occupied an entire city block, and yet it appeared to be known simply as 5120 St. Charles Avenue.

Set far back from the sidewalk, on top of its own knoll of manicured grassland, the mansion was the largest private house in the Garden District, if not all of New Orleans. Away, far away, from the oaks and its sprawling lawns, the mansion's cream paint, terracotta roof and green shutters were bathed in sunshine.

Intimidated by its sheer size, he checked his notebook to reconfirm the address: 5120 St. Charles Avenue. That was what the secretary had said when she had called in response to his lineage advert in *The Times-Picayune*: (*'Private Italian lessons given. Bilingual teacher: call 897 4387 for rates and appointments.'*)

She had booked, in advance, three one-hour sessions per week for the next six weeks, and had sent a driver with cash payment in advance that very afternoon to confirm. Clients like that were as rare as a Louisiana snowfall.

WHITE SUICIDE

He scuffed the soles of his shoes on the first step, then ran his hands through his hair. Nerves. He checked the legend on the hand-engraved vellum card which had been paperclipped to the cash: *'Saxon Monteleone, 5120 St. Charles Avenue, New Orleans.'* No Zip code. No State. No telephone. Their absence spoke volumes. It was as if those who knew, *knew*, and those who didn't – like him – didn't matter. He climbed the steps to the front door and rang the doorbell. Before long, a stooped and elderly Negro butler opened the door.

"Anthony Bianchi, Italian tutor," announced Anthony.

"Y'all expected, sir. I'll take y'all 'round to the side door, an' be kind enough to use it in future."

Their eyes met. The butler's eyes were milky with age, and Anthony sensed that born out of a lifetime of only taking orders, the elderly gentleman did not like giving orders. Even his gait was uneasy as he shuffled along the terracotta path to the side entrance of the mansion.

"Y'all here to teach Mr Eddy I s'ppose?"

"I'm not sure. The secretary didn't inform me."

"Well, can't be nobody else. Nobody in the house 'cept Mr Eddy. He's all alone, 'cept us servants o' course." His eyes flickered under heavy eyelids. "Mr Eddy's on vacation and Mr Monteleone, his daddy, is aways at the plantation."

"How old is Mr Eddy?"

"Let me think." The butler stopped dead in his tracks. "His mama gone died when he was eight, an' that was May-time in fact, an' his birthday was last month, June!" For the first time the butler raised his eyes fully; they may have been yellowed with age, but they were clear with joy. "Yessir, Mr Eddy jus' turn' nine years old!" He smiled proudly and carried on walking.

Anthony Bianchi turned away and looked back down onto the grassy strip of neutral ground that bisected St. Charles Avenue. A momentary stomach cramp grabbed his gut. Someone had just walked over his grave; the twins' ninth birthday was in June too. Like all Sicilians, he was fearful of coincidences; and worse, he knew from his own childhood to be wary of whatever followed in their wake.

CHAPTER 63

**Mġarr Harbour, Gozo, Malta GC.
Thursday, 20th July 1978. Evening.**

*T*he telephone rang. Scott Finch had been expecting the call. Men like him were rare: as hen's teeth, as rocking horse shit, as whatever. The phrase 'Short Supply' or 'In Demand' just didn't cut it. Finch knew it too. And the rates he charged shouted it. LOUDLY!

Kidnapping was no longer the turf of a handful of Sardinian shepherds trying to pay the winter fuel bills. Not anymore. In Europe, kidnapping, especially of young kids who played in the Aga Khan's sandpit, otherwise known as the Costa Smeralda, had become big, big business. The sort of business that was run by people you just wouldn't want to do business with. Bodyguards, lone wolf operators like himself, wore their fearsome reputations as others wore socks. They were the new Lamborghini, the new sable coat, the 8-ball of Peruvian flake, the new Benetti, the new Learjet. They were THE only status symbol that counted. Besides, men like Scott Finch kept you alive. Everything else was just going to kill you in the end.

And so began P.J. Fowler's rough and tumble new thriller, *A Man Possessed*. Long before his Milan-Rome-Malta flight had touched down at Malta's shabby Luqa Airport earlier in the afternoon, he'd already scrawled the plot out. More importantly, he'd disinfected his conscience with soda water over the task he was about to embark on.

The three days and nights he'd spent with Toto after Pietro's funeral – and Paola's death – had been too much to bear. He had long understood the symbiotic bond between father and daughter, and he had dreaded Paola's death.

Thankfully, he had no idea where in the world Pietro had ended up, but he was damn sure it was a place where the sun set, not rose. It certainly wasn't a resort on a Riviera somewhere so he could end up in a drunken brawl and dead on a beach. Pietro wasn't exactly going to mimic Caravaggio. No, his friend was long gone, but he wasn't dead, that was certain. The corpse they'd buried on Monday had confirmed to him that Pietro had been right to flee. These people, whoever and wherever they were, would definitely stop at nothing at all. Deaths and executions had been his stock-in-trade in Southeast Asia and this was a carbon copy writ large.

Padden's old limestone farmhouse was perched on one of the many sinewy roads which linked the seven principal Gozitan villages. The farmhouse, alone and sentinel on a precipitous crag, provided a glorious view of the harbour below, the Mediterranean Sea, and the tiny island of Comino in the near distance. He and Annie delighted in their modest home. The memories, even the tragic ones, had warmed its limestone walls in winter and cooled them in summer. Padden had long ago decided that this was where he not only wanted to live, but to die.

He swilled down a tall glass of soda water and arched his back. Writing standing up, and in longhand, had its disadvantages. He opened the weather-beaten doors that gave on to a small terrace where Corinthian vines drooped from a ramshackle pergola. He inhaled deeply on the sea air, undid his fly and pissed on a pink oleander bush. It was one of his writing rituals, one Annie had patiently – barely – tolerated. He zipped up his fly and rummaged in his denim-shirt pocket for a crumpled packet of Italian MS cigarettes he'd scored in Milan. Tobacco was just that, tobacco. He never judged a cigarette by its cover.

The moon was high, and a soothing night breeze had picked up. As always, his home was forever pregnant with Annie's spirit. His memory often jousted with his sobriety, and mysteriously he had no recollection whatsoever of placing a stack of lined school exercise books, next to a beer glass full of sharpened pencils, beside his writing lectern *before* he'd left for Milan. He surely wasn't sober then, but he was now, and would remain so until *A Man Possessed* was finished. All that he had to do was get the lead from the pencil onto the porous paper of the exercise books. That was all. His agent, the sainted Jules, would do the rest; he knew she would.

Pietro was owed the truth wherever he was, however heart-rending his reading of *A Man Possessed* would inevitably be. Padden had promised him that.

CHAPTER 64

**Canal Street, The French Quarter,
New Orleans, Louisiana, USA.
Thursday, 20th July 1978. Early evening.**

Anthony Bianchi glanced at his watch. 18:05. There was just enough time for a coffee and a slice of pizza. Then he'd have to catch the bus and head north to the beach at Lake Pontchartrain, where he worked as a 'ghost' on the Ghost Train Ride at the rundown Ritz Amusement Park. His shift started at 19:30, and his boss, Mr Boudreaux – a Louisiana redneck born 'n' bred – an oleaceous fifty-something huckster had reminded him with a coarse laugh while spitting out a heft of dipping tobacco: *'To be a spook 'round these parts, Tony, y'all need to be punctual.'* Ha. Ha. Very funny, Mr Boudreaux.

Holding down two jobs wasn't easy either. It wasn't so much that working the night shift trying to frighten teenagers who came in search of somewhere to make out, or the daytime hours giving Italian lessons was difficult, it was the travelling to-and-fro from each teaching appointment that ran him ragged.

Built in an almost perfect rectangular grid in the 1730s, the French Quarter covered an area of almost two-thirds of a square mile: it was framed by Canal Street to the southwest, North Rampart Street to the north, Esplanade Avenue to the east, and it was closed in to the south by the long and mighty crescent bend of the Mississippi. About 3,000 souls called the French Quarter, just two or three feet above the water level of the forever brooding Mississippi, home. Algiers was a short ferry ride across the lumbering river, and numerous suburbs branched out both east and west.

He hadn't yet mastered the vagaries of the streetcars and buses, and he wasn't able to call one uninterrupted hour his own, something he desperately wanted to do. Canal Street was wall-to-wall with people. New Orleans was again in the grip of a convention, which meant the French Quarter would be rammed with drunks, out-of-towners and all manner of lowlifes. Momentarily, his attention was stolen away from a newsagent's window by strains of an old Jack Teagarden song – it sounded like 'Mr Miller' – coming from a clip-joint on Bourbon Street. The chance of listening to one of the greatest of all Dixie trombonists deserved a change of plan. Forget pizza. He ran into the shop to buy *The Times-Picayune* and noticed a copy of the *Corriere della Sera*. It had been quite some time since he had seen that newspaper, one of the sentinels of his Milanese mornings. He hesitated. New Orleans was Anthony Bianchi's city; *The Times-Picayune* his paper. The *Corriere della Sera* was Pietro Albassi's.

An elderly Creole lady, perched on a perilously small stool behind her cash register, sneered at him inquisitively, a look she reserved exclusively for those who scanned foreign newspapers for free. The more he dithered, the more her neck craned to one side. So as not to miss the last few bars of Jack Teagarden, he paid for the *Corriere* and ran across the street like a child trailing the Pied Piper.

The bar was grungy and smoke-filled, only the Wurlitzer looked cared for. The burgundy vinyl booths were worn – old gaffer tape was losing the war against sprouting rusty springs – and vacant barstools stood like decapitated guards in front of the beat-up bar. Anthony settled on a stool, closed his eyes and simply lost himself in the strains of Jack Teagarden's soul screeching out of the tinny metal speaker.

"Whatya' havin'?" the barman asked, in a tone that gave off southern vapours of prejudice and ignorance.

"A 7 Up please."

Unlike the lady who sold him the newspaper, the barman held his hostile expression. A 7 Up? Anthony averted his gaze away from his callous, red-rimmed eyes. The booths were, with one exception, all empty. It was the lull in the day when hardened drinkers went in search of more solid nourishment, while the conventioneers pounded pavements and got clipped.

The Jack Teagarden song ended and the Wurlitzer struck up an old Dean Martin song, something about Naples. A cry, as slippery as oil on rubber, bellowed from a corner booth.

"Where'd the hell this one come from, Wayne?"

The barman ignored the remark and turned to Anthony as the only sober ally.

"I just switch the darn machine on, I don't load it," shouted the barman.

"Hey, Wayne, I'm talkin' to you. Thought this was a jazz bar?"

The drunk wanted an answer.

"It is, an' even Dino sober is jazz when you're as drunk as y'all are." There was a fierce authority in the barman's tone which took Anthony by surprise.

Quickly he turned his attention to the two-day-old edition of the *Corriere della Sera*. The last thing he needed was to get embroiled in a drunken debate about Dean Martin and Jack Teagarden. Anthony opened it at the sports section as he always had, and in flicking through the newspaper he caught sight of a familiar face. He studied the small, grainy black and white photograph. There were three short paragraphs underneath.

"Wayne," he coughed, "maybe I'll have a drink after all. Dark rum, no ice."

Anthony began to breathe slowly through his nose.

"Where can I get a packet of cigarettes?"

The barman motioned his jaw silently towards the rear.

Tentatively, Anthony placed the newspaper face down on the next stool and fumbled in his pocket for loose change. He'd given up smoking when he had finished his last packet of corn-paper Gitanes. That was in Sicily, almost two months ago. In a manner never forgotten, he opened the soft-pack of untipped Camels and lit one from a book of matches he found on top of the cigarette machine. He waited for the cottonwool mist of nicotine to fog his brain. Light on his feet, he slowly made his way back to the stool and picked up the newspaper. He'd imagined it. Surely? Or perhaps it was good-old-fashioned voodoo? Or, he reasoned, it was just another three-card-trick his psyche liked to play. Daytime sleight of hand. Yes, that must be it.

'Two Months After Mysterious Kidnapping, Milanese Lawyer Found Dead.'

He re-read the headline word by word. Then he read it again. And again. For an Italian newspaper it was remarkably undramatic. The article was brief, and as far as he could tell, factually correct. Another oddity.

WHITE SUICIDE

The short news story told how soon after Aldo Moro was murdered, a lawyer named Pietro Albassi had been abducted and wounded in Milan, it was suspected, by a renegade faction of the Red Brigades. It went on to describe how as a lawyer Albassi had 'masterminded' the acquittal of two of their members some years before in Turin. The inference for anyone used to reading Italian newspapers, was that the two were connected. It finished by saying a positive ID of the body – *'which had dramatically washed ashore in the harbour of Portofino'* – had been made, and that Albassi had been shot twice in the head, another inference which meant 'executed'. A private funeral had taken place at the Chiesa di San Marco in Milan. End. No mention of Ruxandra, Toto or Paola.

Anthony cautiously folded the newspaper in half, then in quarters and shook his head like a cat caught in a rainstorm. He squinted into his rum and considered that, on balance, this was good news. Cuci had panicked and lost his nerve. Albassi dead meant life for Ruxandra, Toto and Paola. It appeared as if his white suicide plan had worked.

Dean Martin's song quickly dissolved into a repetitive scratching; the needle trapped on the vinyl run off. Only the drunk made a move. Sloppily he leaned across the back of the booth and smacked the Perspex cover. As if by divine providence a second Jack Teagarden record jumped into the machine's prosthetic-like arm. Anthony smiled, it was 'Muskrat Ramble', the old Kid Ory hit, and a favourite.

With the last notes echoing in his head, he climbed down from the barstool, left a five-dollar bill under his unfinished glass of rum and walked towards the door, just as Jack Teagarden's trombone screeched into a wailing climax.

"Hey, mista! Yer paper, yer cigarettes!" Wayne hollered after him.

"I read it, thanks, and I just quit smoking."

"Mista, you OK?"

"Sure, I'm just late for work."

"Whatya do?" The barman called after him.

"You're not going to believe this, but I'm a ghost."

CHAPTER 65

The Vatican State.
Monday, 7th August 1978. 12:15.

Alessandro Cuci wore his black single-breasted (summer weight) suit. And today the Vatican City would be a heaving ocean of black garments after the death last night, Sunday 6th August, of the frail eighty-year-old pontiff, Pope Paul VI, at Castel Gandolfo, the Papal country retreat.

Now, the real work had to begin. There were candidates in the Curia to position, and lobbying to do. He was within millimetres of all he had ever schemed of. The cardinal he was to lunch with later had long ago convinced himself that Catholic celibacy only applied to heterosexuals, and Cuci was up for some lunchtime 'clerical' flirting with this particular cardinal, whose vote he needed to secure.

Cuci hesitated before going through the door which separated his office from his assistant's. In all the years he had occupied this office, he'd paid scant attention to the small, Baroque painting above the interconnecting door. Religious scenes were plentiful in the corridors he prowled in. He squinted up at the scene of *The Martyrdom of St Catherine*, depicted as a wanton romantic beauty, in spite of the awfulness of her predicament. There she was, kneeling with her wrists manacled, her body fettered to a massive spiked wheel, death just moments away. He studied her form and found her manly breasts arousing. The pinkness of her flesh made his neck tingle. He considered the composition to be marred by two angels, who with their overwrought expressions and cumbersome feathered wings, looked like a pair of pale-skinned Neapolitan street rascals. Perplexed, Cuci shook his head as if he had missed the point. The angels had obviously failed to save her, for if they had succeeded, she would not have been canonised and there wouldn't be a Catherine Wheel firework. He toyed at his goatee and walked out of the door with a heavy step. What was the purpose of it all?

The cardinal that Cuci was on his way to meet would probably be wearing the same expression as St Catherine's angels, he thought wryly. Virtually every member of the Vatican Curia (with the exception of himself, and the shady American Archbishop, Paul Marcinkus, Head of the Vatican Bank), had all had their posts terminated when Pope Paul VI's earthly reign expired at 21:40 the night before.

Cuci was only mildly anxious about the *sede vacante*, the period between a pope's death and the Papal Conclave, the gathering of the College of Cardinals. It wasn't so much that the candidate who was set to assume St Peter's chair was in any doubt. The other P2 Freemasons within the Vatican had already chosen the wily Italian from Genoa, Cardinal Giuseppe Siri, as their candidate; a decision taken long before Pope Paul VI's drawn-out death rattle. Ever since the untidy end to the Moro affair, Cuci had wanted this *sede vacante*, and the subsequent transition of power, to go smoothly. There was always talk of a few *papabile* – Cardinals with an outside chance – actually winning, for this was set to be the largest Conclave ever, and Cardinal Siri's third. One hundred and eleven cardinals would be locked in the Sistine Chapel – possibly for days – with a solitary purpose: to elect a new pope by, *per scrutinium*, secret ballot. Anything could happen and the Conclave was not due to start until Friday, 25th August: nineteen days hence.

Cuci stepped out from the cool of the stone building and into the sun and dust of a scorching Roman summer. He eyed the locust-like swarms of tourists who wandered about St Peter's Square. A cripple, his body pitilessly twisted, smiled at him as he hobbled past. Cuci froze. Quickly, he touched his testicles in a ritual act of superstition. Like Mussolini he believed cripples brought only bad luck, and luck was the solitary element in the forthcoming election over which even he had scant jurisdiction.

Cuci quickened his step and made his way down the via della Concilazione towards the Ponte Vittorio Emanuele II and the discreet basement restaurant for his rendezvous.

There would be no slip-up this time, he had covered all points of the compass. Prime Minister Giulio Andreotti and his ilk were mere politicians, commodities to trade and barter with, but to be within a few votes of being the power behind the throne of the Holy See was something else altogether.

Even if a dark horse outsider were to become pope, Cuci's contingency plans – already in place – were faultless. Of that he was certain.

CHAPTER 66

1111 Canal Street, New Orleans, Louisiana, USA.
Friday, 29th September 1978. 23:25.
Fifty-four days after the death of Pope Paul VI.

Anthony Bianchi booted open the thin door to his rundown studio apartment. The Ritz Amusement Park had shut late, despite heavy grey clouds oozing rain off Lake Pontchartrain. He'd been forced to get a taxi home – one he could ill afford – and, dammit, he was hungry again. The lava-flow of junk food he'd consumed earlier made him feel heavy and cumbersome, not replete.

Unhappily, he flopped onto the threadbare sofa and switched on the black and white TV without thinking. Images flicked in and out of his brain as he grazed through the ether. He had little time for television, but it had its uses; the myopic screen often cast him adrift into an uneasy sleep. For not one day had gone by when he hadn't agonised over his fateful decision, and his soul ached. He understood his previous life would never really fade away. Often in despair and loneliness, he would vacillate between regarding himself as either a contemptuous deserter, or a man who had saved all those who had mattered in his world. Deserter or rescuer? He was certain of one thing: if he'd stayed his wife and children would all be dead by now.

A local news channel arrested his attention. The face in the postage-stamp-sized panel behind the anchor's faultless coiffure looked familiar. He lifted his arm wearily and turned up the volume.

And before we sign off, our main story again. The newly elected pontiff, Pope John Paul I, has died unexpectedly in the Vatican after only thirty-three days as Pontiff. Albino Luciani, the Patriarch of Venice, who had chosen the name John Paul I upon his surprise election as Pope on 26th August, had been an entirely unexpected choice for Pope, who had not even been considered in the Vatican as papabile and able to be elected Pope. John Paul I had promised reforms in the Vatican during his brief papacy. After his election, by a strong majority in the fourth ballot of the Conclave, Pope John Paul I had won the hearts of all, including the world's media, who nicknamed him 'Il Papa del Sorriso', 'The Smiling Pope'. Pope John Paul I was just sixty-five years old, and he passed away in the Apostolic Palace in the Vatican City. The cause of his death is not yet known, but our sources within the Vatican indicate his death was due to sudden, and unexpected, heart failure. Good night.

Anthony turned the TV off and stared at the white pinprick of light slowly being sucked into the black vortex. He instinctively knew that the death of the popular outsider, Pope John Paul I, was not caused by the injustice of a clogged artery, or a congenital defect in the heart muscle.

He had understood only too well, but too late, that no one, however powerful, was immune to the satanic conspiracies of others. There was no such thing as total protection. He used to believe that such raw power was illusory, but the cabal that had unified to murder Aldo Moro had reunified to murder Pope John Paul I as well. Powerful enemies indeed.

A flash-flood of despair overwhelmed him. However deep their profane intrigues went one insignificant lawyer and his family would not have been allowed to stand in their way. But he was no longer in their way. Albassi was 'dead'. And in an instant, he dismissed any thoughts of returning to his beloved family. They were only safe because he was 'dead'.

"*Hell is empty and all the devils are here,*" Anthony said aloud, remembering his University days. "Shakespeare would have added, '*... and in Italy too.*'" The impossible decision, and the ensuing, tortuous doubts he'd had after he'd fled, were banished by the news of Pope John Paul I's murder. His pope *had* been murdered of that he was convinced.

A muggy, damp breeze flushed through the poky room. He heard the hoots of a night-owl from a distant park – a Sicilian portend of death. He touched his temple and rubbed his sightless eye. Suddenly, despair gave way to exhaustion, it was as if his very lifeblood had been sucked out of his body. Pope John Paul I. Dead. Will it ever end?

Fully clothed, he lay down on his simple iron cot and closed his weary eyes. For the first time since Friday, 12th May 1978 he slept a dreamless and righteous sleep.

PART ELEVEN

NINE YEARS LATER

CHAPTER 67

**LaBranche House, 700 Royal Street,
The French Quarter, New Orleans, Louisiana, USA.
Saturday, 14th February 1987. Early evening.**

"*Fone! Fone! Fone!*"

Elton, Anthony Bianchi's Amazonian parakeet, squawked as the telephone went unanswered.

"Dawn, can you grab the phone please, I can't leave this risotto."

He peered around the kitchen's white shuttered door onto the *gallerie*, where Dawn Loubiere sat outside sipping her iced tea.

"Sure," she smiled her reply.

She'd met him about six weeks before, at a New Year's Eve cocktail party. They'd been out three times since, but this was the first time she'd visited his home. The storied 'LaBranche House', as it was known, was probably the single most beautiful building in the entire French Quarter. Built in 1840, originally as a row of eleven town houses, it was now all one building, and it crowned the corner of Royal and St Peter's Streets. Anthony's apartment was on the top floor, the third, and she was sure it was the largest in the building. Quite how Anthony came to live here was as much a mystery to her as whether – as local legend told – the ghost of Madame LaBranche, in her blue ballgown, haunted what had been her former home.

Instinctively, upon meeting Anthony for the first time, she'd liked him. Tall, compelling and in his early forties, he was either tanned, European or both, yet spoke with a Mid-Atlantic accent. He possessed an easy smile with green eyes and dark hair greying naturally at the temples. He was undeniably good-looking, in a Cary Grant-ish mien. There appeared to be no vanity to him and their conversation had been small talk polite. However, there was a distance or a shyness about him that she also found attractive. Sitting on the outdoor *gallerie* of his large and graceful home on St Valentine's evening, the answers she'd perhaps hoped to find were certainly not going to be answered. Although in truth, she realised, she had yet to form the questions.

Apart from the rainbow parakeet Elton (whose presence was entirely in keeping with where he lived) she'd sensed that no one else had ever trodden the 1920s wooden herringbone floors and antique rugs of his home. For all its elegance, there was an anonymity which bordered on the anodyne. Nothing intimate, no hints at all, save for the kitchen. The apartment had the feel of a plush hotel suite, with the faint air of a provisional existence. No photographs. Nothing personal. It was how she imagined a nomad, or someone so-light-on-his-feet, might live; someone who didn't wish to be known.

In the main salon, the only tell-tales were a row of seven hardback books, all by the same author. A small marble tablet, with an unintelligible inscription, hung above them. Even the few paintings dotted about were contrived in their ambiguity: Hallmark Hotel-type art. To be able to live at LaBranche meant you were a person of some importance in New Orleans, yet she'd never heard a whisper of his name. A residence at LaBranche could not be acquired by money alone, and especially this apartment.

Dawn Loubiere was a fourth generation New Orleanian who knew only too well the Vieux Carré – the French Quarter – was where *'the city that care forgot'* was founded back in 1718. And it breathed its own singular, and often insular life, every day and every night: from the spectral early morning mist that crept in from the Mississippi, until the sun burned it off to gift its old buildings and pavements a soft and scented light that led to a balmy eventide when all-night revelling would inevitably begin. To a visitor, the Vieux Carré could have been a Hollywood backlot. Yet people had lived, worked and played – and hard too – here for over 250 years.

Within its square-mile grid of alleyways and streets, with their squat European buildings and flowered wrought-iron *galleries*, the Quarter's inhabitants usually had more effervescent personalities: scam artists, Wall Street tykes, junkies – Dixie and chemical – caricature cubs and literary lions – William Falkner had lived in Pirate's Alley, just 200 yards away from Anthony's *gallerie*. She knew there were plenty of sinners and very few saints in the Vieux Carré. This was not a place where seemingly regular men who worked in an office in the Central Business District called home. The French Quarter, let alone the LaBranche, was not a milieu where people like Anthony Bianchi lived. Instinctively, she wanted to understand him better, but his home provided her with no clues whatsoever.

"Anthony, it's a man called Joey Thibodeaux."

She handed him the cordless phone and let her hand linger on his forearm as she did so.

"Hi, Joey, hold on…"

Anthony turned to her open, freckle-dusted face and nodded a silent 'thanks'. Then added, "I need you to please stir the risotto very slowly, and when the rice has soaked up the stock, add these mushrooms and a glass of Madeira. Whatever you do, don't let it dry out. OK?"

"So, just *how* long do y'all plan to keep a gal waitin'?" she teased. "Isn't it easier to cook Creole food, *cher*?"

The words, husky for one so petite, poured out of her as leisurely as molasses from an earthen jug. Her robin's egg blue eyes sparkled, flattered by her fine white-blonde shoulder-length hair. The tang of her citrus fragrance coasted the air. He brushed her hand lightly, nervously, before edging outside to the wrought-iron *gallerie* for privacy. Almost hidden by Chinese bowls of hanging ferns, pots of begonias and forget-me-nots, Anthony leaned against the balustrade facing Royal Street. His top floor *gallerie* was over eighty feet long, and it carried on at ninety degrees, for another thirty feet, to overlook St Peter Street. High ceilinged, and open to the elements, the wicker fans above him moved with the deliberate precision of seagulls over the marshy reaches of Lake Pontchartrain.

"Sorry to have kept you, Joey."

"Mr Bianchi, the boss needs y'all to come over right away."

"How urgent is this?" Anthony sniffed at the evening breeze and detected the faintest hint of rain in the air.

"Well, first he gets a call from Washington, then the fax machine cranks out something from *The Times-Picayune*. That was three hours ago, since then he's been on the phone non-stop. I went to give him his insulin shot an' a sandwich, he just waved me out. The curtains were drawn an' his whiskey glass was very empty. He told me to get y'all to come over. Sorry, y'all got somethin' goin' on?"

"Put me through, Joey."

"He's still on the other line."

"Then go knock on his door and tell him I'm holding."

"Sure, sure, Mr Bianchi."

Anthony shook his head in mild irritation, and let the phone hang at his side to catch the secret street music of sundown in the Quarter: the splash of courtyard fountains, the sound of mules and carriages heading east to their night-stables, and somewhere upwind, a lone saxophonist running through his scales. He loved this area, with all its rhythmic, and often unintelligible, chants – from the 'Lucky Dog' snack-vendor on the corner of Royal and St Ann – to the young tap dancers hustling tourists. Its smells and sounds and music – everything, even funerals, were accompanied by music – were the cogs in the decision-making process that anchored him in New Orleans. A city he only ever left on business and at the direct request of Saxon Monteleone, his employer for nearly nine years.

"Still there, Mr Bianchi?" Joey bellowed. "I'm puttin' y'all through."

The line clicked and Anthony thought he heard a long sigh.

"An-tho-ny," Saxon Monteleone said, drawing out the syllables in an old-school Louisiana accent, "I'm sorry to disturb y'all on a Saturday night, but I'd surely like to see y'all with some urgency." His baritone voice rasped as it always did, but for Anthony it was a languid and warm sound.

"What exactly is the problem, Mr M.?"

"I don't want to discuss details on the phone. All I'll say, so y'all can be thinking about it on your way over here, is *The Times-Picayune* are plannin' to run a profile tomorrow on Khashoggi and Ghorbanifar. Unless I'm mistaken, we made a large shipment of arms to them last year?"

"You know we did, Mr M. It was approved in DC by Colonel North and Admiral Poindexter beforehand."

"Maybe, but ever since this Iran-Contra story broke in DC…" Monteleone sucked air in through his fleshy lips. "I'm sorry, Anthony, Joey tells me y'all got company on Valentine's too. I sure don't wanna fuss you, but I'm not goin' walk you through this on the phone."

"Give me thirty minutes, Mr M. and I'll be over."

Saxon Monteleone swung back in his heavy, buttoned-backed leather chair, content for the first time since the late afternoon. Anthony will clear this up he thought, just like he has most things over the past few years. He ran his hands through his thick, jet-black beard and up onto the dome that was his shaven head. He no longer minded that Anthony had become the keystone in his vast and sprawling corporate life. In fact, he had long ago accepted it and grown to like it. Each of them knew their place, one that had been built over the years on the foundation of mutual respect. After Monteleone's wife had died nearly nine years ago, there was no one else he trusted. He sighed again and pressed the intercom.

"Joey, bring in my shot, an' some speed too."

"Mr Monteleone, it's not good to mix your insulin an' speed."

"Joey, thank y'all kindly for your medical counsel but, please, just do as y'all asked. Then tell Hippolyte Mr Bianchi is expected, an' have Anna-Mae prepare somethin' Italian. I think I disturbed his dinner."

"Yes sir, Mr Monteleone."

Joey wondered just what would happen if one day he wasn't there to carry Mr Monteleone's brown alligator bag of medicines and narcotics. If Hippolyte didn't answer the doorbell. If Anna-Mae stopped cooking, an' the uniformed maids ceased to serve an' clean. If Bertram, an' his fellow gardeners, stopped weedin' the pristine lawns an' nursin' the azaleas, camellias an' all manner of graceful plants each an' every season. If Charles stopped drivin'. If his pilots stopped flyin'. And most important, if Mr Bianchi stopped fire-fightin' calls all day an' all night. Life would, he figured, still carry on. New Orleans' cemeteries were full of indispensable folks. Yes, there were more than enough staff lost in the roomy attics of 5120 St Charles Avenue, an' the out-houses of the family's antebellum estate, the Arbres Plantation, with its one-mile long – arrow straight too – avenue of dynastic oak trees, ready to obey any request from Saxon Monteleone.

Anthony cussed under his breath, pushed the aerial back into the handset and set it down on the mahogany side table. Casually he took the tea-cloth from his belt loops and pulled on a dark blue linen jacket. Dawn would just have to wait for her risotto. His gut told him she would be mildly cross, and who could blame her. In the almost nine years he'd worked for Saxon Monteleone, he'd never let him down once, and he was not about to start. His honed intuition, thanks in part to his own survival *and* to Saxon Monteleone, was pin-sharp.

"Dawn, I'm so very sorry I've got to go out. My boss needs me."

Wooden spoon in hand, she faced him from the kitchen doorway, her elfin figure dwarfed by the tall, white architraves.

"What can I say? I was cookin' up a storm of a risotto!"

She pronounced the word as if it were three – rizz-oh-tow – and her smile tried hard to mask her disappointment. It failed.

"Where I come from, we say *risotto*," he added playfully with an Italian flourish.

"So, just where do you come from, Mr Anthony Bianchi?"

Dawn let the wooden spoon fall to the wooden floor. She crossed the hallway towards him, reached up on her toes and kissed him. He pulled away out of surprise, out of fear. It was their first kiss.

"Why don't y'all go to your meetin' and I'll be here when y'all return?" She breathed the words into his chest as she held him tightly.

"I'm not sure... I might be... I've no idea how long I'll be..." A bachelor for so long, he didn't know how to respond.

Unsure of herself now, she turned to collect her tan leather purse. He looked at her admiringly: Levi's, polished burgundy penny-loafers, a crisp white blouse – two buttons open – and a pastel cashmere sweater draped over her shoulders. It was a wholly appropriate and un-American combination; all that was missing were Persol sunglasses and a Vespa. She looked more Italian than a Roman.

He held the solid mahogany front door open for her, and then shut it behind them. In silence they walked the three blocks to the taxi stand outside the Royal Orleans Hotel on St Louis Street.

"Who calls who?" Dawn asked, one foot in the cab and one on the pavement.

"We both call each other. What are you doing tomorrow afternoon?"

"Household chores probably, it's Sunday. Why?"

"How about we drive out along Lakeshore, then go to Audubon Park for a walk? My Sundays are, well..." again he hesitated "... I always lunch with my boss. It's a sort of tradition."

"Whoever your boss is, well, he seems to own you."

She regretted her words as soon as she'd spoken them.

"Nobody owns me, Dawn," he joked. "So, I'll call for you at three o'clock, OK?"

He kissed her on the cheek and accidently closed the cab door so hard the window rattled. The cab pulled away, and his scarred temple began to throb. So did his left eye. Wearily he looked up into the menacing grey pall just as a heavy raindrop fell. It was going to be a bleak, rain-clogged night and the clouds, thick, wet and swirling, were coming in low over the Mississippi like sinister beings from another dimension. He loathed February. It was true what New Orleanians said: *'There are two seasons: Summer and February.'*

He slipped a $10 bill from his gold money clip – a Christmas gift long ago from Mr M. – and went to hand it to Antoine, the hotel doorman.

"Put the ten-spot away, Mr Bianchi. A cab, sir?"

"Not tonight, Antoine, I gotta drive."

"Don't go too far or too fast, Mr Bianchi, this storm's been ridin' the river all the way down from the Midwest, an' it's goin' to get ugly."

Antoine half waved and half saluted. Everybody knew who Mr Bianchi was.

"Damn your timing, Mr M. but duty first and always," Anthony said aloud, as he trudged home. Raindrops plump and weighty, began to plummet down, but he reached LaBranche before the rainstorm started in earnest. He went to grab his car keys from the silver tray in the hall, but stopped himself. Dawn's scent had lingered; it had moved in. Its crisp, lemon aroma took him straight back to Sicily. He breathed in deeply. Nine long years felt as long as the fifteen minutes since she had kissed him.

He draped his jacket on the marquetry hat stand, walked into the salon and poured a shot of dark rum from the decanter. As he did so, he contemplated the marble tablet which hung on the wall. Chiselled into it were the words: *'L'acqua lu munnu cummigghiava, 'n celu vinea na palaummedda, din ta lu pizzu pinnuliava, na ramuzza d'aliva bedda.'*

The words, in Sicilian dialect, had been carved into the ancient limestone of Bonnera's fireplace. And, as a young boy growing up, he had silently carved them into his soul as a prayer of gratitude for the devotion the Salaviglia family had given him. So, when he'd replicated the verse in New Orleans, he chose the language of his birth, not an English translation – *'Water covered the Earth, then a dove flew across the sky, and from its beak hung, a small branch of beautiful olives.'*

Below the tablet was a neat row of seven hardback books by the best-selling pulp-thriller writer P.J. Fowler. Sipping the rum, he shuffled memories as he would a deck of cards. All seven books – Fowler had published almost one a year – had one principal character: Scott Finch. Anthony looked at the first in the series, the one that had re-established Fowler's name and career: *A Man Possessed*.

Lightly, he touched the book's spine knowing it would bring Paola closer to him. It did, and he shivered.

CHAPTER 68

Mġarr Harbour, Gozo, Malta GC.
Saturday, 14th February 1987. Early evening.

Joshua Padden flexed his aching right elbow. No matter how much he was nagged by Jules, his long-suffering agent, he wasn't going to move from his lectern to hunch down at a desk and start using a new-fangled word-processor machine, with its silent keyboard twinned to a blinking cursor on a TV tube. The very name of the contraption gave the game away! He didn't want to 'process' words. Before a sentence was committed to paper, he'd 'written it', 'edited it', 'punctuated it' and 'proofread it' all in his head. Only then would he write it down. No machine could do that.

Padden was a writer, although he preferred to characterise himself more as a storyteller. Conceit had never been in his suite of beliefs, and the idea that he might be referred to as a novelist filled him with horror. Padden knew precisely what he was; a yarn-spinner who had long ago discovered how to turn $1 into $10 by using a collection of blank school exercise books and a box of HB pencils. He was at the bottom of the literary food-chain for sure, but he (P.J. Fowler actually) was at the top of the food-food chain, so to speak. Moreover, he was a graduate of the, *'If it ain't bust, don't fix it'* school.

And Scott Finch appeared to be getting younger, leaner, fitter and more in demand; six of his seven books had been optioned (although in constant demand, *A Man Possessed* was simply 'not available') and two films were in various stages of pre-production. So long as Joshua Padden drew breath, his right arm would have only three uses: to hold cigarettes, hoist vodkas and beers, and grip pencils. His left arm could atrophy for all he cared.

Routines had become more relevant to him of late. Like many writers he'd developed superstitions to ward off anything which might intrude on the order of his storytelling life. His arcane practices had become disciplined (Padden's doctor preferred to use the words 'compulsive' and 'obsessive') but as Scott Finch liked to say: *'Don't question what melts my butter, or floats my boat. Ever. I'm paying the bill.'*

Padden began writing at sunset. He still pissed onto the same oleander bush before he started working. Alcohol was off the menu during the creation of each first draft; manic pencil-sharpening was his creative bleach. Cigarettes, foul herbal teas, fresh Ħobż – a local sourdough bread – with lashings of Marmite and fresh *bambinella*, tiny locally grown pears, were the only friends permitted across the threshold of Annie's home whilst he turned out each draft. As a rule, he worked through the night. Although drained in the hours before dawn, he *never* completed his last sentence. A half-completed sentence was his lodestar for the next evening: a place to navigate from on the voyage to the end of his story.

Those simple disciplines had served him well during the long, sober and heart-breaking process of writing *A Man Possessed*. But one new ritual had settled in soon after the book's immediate success. The new ritual involved – before sunrise when he collapsed onto his bed – rereading a frayed postcard. The picture was of an impossibly gorgeous Hawaiian beauty: she had a figure like a Coca-Cola bottle, long bronze hair with violet eyes. A *lei* of fifty or more orchids cascaded down from her neck towards her gazelle-like legs. The white powder sand, with a backdrop of gemstone water, served only to distract. The card was postmarked Honolulu, 12th June 1980, Paola and Toto's birth date, and was addressed to him at The Gleneagles Bar. The text was clear. Neat. Ciphered in block capitals. Anonymous. It read: *'THANK YOU JOSHUA. FOREVER YOUR FRIEND. AB.'*

The talismanic postcard would stay on the left of Padden's lectern until the day he dropped. For as far as he was concerned *AB* had saved his life, not vice versa. Just how *AB* had written those words was as much a mystery now as it was then.

Words of thanks in reply to a book which P.J. Fowler had penned about a nine-year-old Italian school girl, who is kidnapped – not for wealth, but for political leverage over her family – and how she had died, alone and in her sleep, whilst manacled to a dungeon wall. Her death, described as mysterious, was against the kidnapper's wishes, and had occurred *after* her father's political capitulation.

The story of an innocent Italian school girl, and how Scott Finch (ex-SAS, part-time alcoholic and full-time gun-for-hire) had hunted down her kidnappers – now murderers – as relentlessly as a Bengal tiger stalks its prey in moonlight. And how Finch had caught and slaughtered – mercilessly – each one in turn, not only redeeming her life, but Finch's too. *A Man Possessed* belonged to him. *AB* that is.

CHAPTER 69

LaBranche House, 700 Royal Street,
The French Quarter, New Orleans, Louisiana, USA.
Saturday, 14th February 1987. Evening.

Anthony discarded his rum and lifted his hand off *A Man Possessed*. He was determined to wrap up this meeting with Mr M. quickly. Grabbing his jacket and car keys, he flashed Elton a grin, snatched an umbrella from the Civil War shell-casing by the door, and ran down the two flights of stairs into the falling rain; he'd never understood the American habit of naming the Ground Floor the First Floor.

His car was parked close by in Pirate's Alley in its own private garage, that rarest of French Quarter treasures. The horses and mules, who shared shelter with his red Alfa Romeo Spider, had sensed the approaching storm. Sweating and nervous, their fecund odour hung like a low cloud as he swung the wooden doors open.

Rain crashed noisily onto the convertible's fabric hood; the car's wipers gunned as he swung out of Pirate's Alley to head west on Royal. He drove south on Toulouse smack into horizontal rain, before hanging a sharp right westward onto Decatur, the road that ran parallel between the Mississippi and the French Quarter. The traffic had thinned, and he motored his way through empty streets under dim, tawny lights until he reached a bleak and rain-soaked 5120 St Charles Avenue, the home of his loyal employer, Saxon Monteleone.

CHAPTER 70

**5120 St Charles Avenue, The Garden District,
New Orleans, Louisiana, USA.
Saturday, 14th February 1987. Dinner time.**

"No need to have the car parked, Hippolyte, I'm not staying long." Anthony hopped out of the Alfa under cover of the porte-cochère.

"Whatever yo' say, Mr Bianchi, but Anna-Mae 'gon cooked some food special for y'all and Mr Eddy."

"What's Mr Eddy doing back from school, Hippolyte?" he asked, trying to mask his surprise.

The butler's hooded eyes dropped to his shoes. Over forty long years of service in a white man's family, he knew better than to look anywhere else in response.

"Don't fuss, Hippolyte, I'll ask Mr Monteleone," Anthony said, cheerfully.

At the same moment he heard a familiar baritone booming like soft Louisiana thunder.

"So, y'all angry at me? Wet 'n hungry with rain fallin' like spent buckshot. The roads all slippery with mulch, an' on Valentine's Day yer lady is madder than a wounded 'gator in a net! Don't forget, Anthony, ladies choose who they love the most, all we men do is favour those who love *us* the most. She a Louisiana gal?" Monteleone stepped into the covered porch with a welcoming smile.

"As a matter of fact, I *am* hungry," Anthony replied, politely ignoring the question. He extended his right hand and Saxon Monteleone shook it. They observed this formal ritual even if it had only been a matter of hours separating a meeting.

"Come straight on through, we've much to talk over," he said, turning to his butler. "Hippolyte, have Anna-Mae bring Mr Bianchi's supper into my study with a glass o' that wine he likes. Inform Mr Eddy I won't be joining him for supper, and Hippolyte, mind the boy dresses properly, wears a tie and eats at the kitchen table, not in front of the darned TV."

Monteleone turned on his heels and marched down the long servants' corridor. He cut, even for those who knew him well, an unconventional figure. He had always been an indisputable force of nature, and like most people with that singular authority, they were woefully unaware of how it governed the lives of those who orbited their universe.

At fifty-seven years of age he still held his college wrestler's physique. Tall, yet stocky, muscular, with large hands and broad shoulders, he was, above all, purposeful. Age had yet to disgrace his body. His heavy build, when combined with his shaven head and hard-boned, bearded face, conferred the air of a rapacious predator with a brutal defensive power. A wide forehead with dark, unsentimental and staring eyes made him look like a hyperphagic bear peering out of its den. While in profile he resembled a caricature of Marlon Brando in *On the Waterfront*: he was all hook nose, claw-jaw with bushy eyebrows above a hidden glare.

In spite of only ever wearing loose-fitting black linen suits, his personality was one of warmth, conformity and flawless ol' Louisiana manners, all furthered by a disarming smile of perfect white teeth. It was this controlled – and it *was* controlled – statesmanlike countenance that won the hearts and loyalty of others: when he engaged with you in a crowded room, you *were* the *only* person in that room. He was not a man who sucked the oxygen out of a room, quite the opposite in fact, he infused a room with not only oxygen, but raw, patrician authority. A man of unknowable wiles, he had preserved a streetfighter's eye for sizing up a potential foe. His adversaries, and there were indeed many, craved the explanation for his successes to be more prosaic; for Saxon Monteleone's dominion of Louisiana was consummate, his Federal influence – from Texas in the west, to Florida in the east, with all the southern states in-between – was beyond envied, his political clout in Washington was coveted, and his untold wealth greater than the sum of all three.

The Monteleone family had arrived in Louisiana from Italy in 1790, a hundred years before the great influx of Italians, and had lived as plantation owners for nigh on 200 years. These were facts of absolute history, all of which he was fiercely proud of. As a direct consequence of this, he was a man who treated the world's inevitable vicissitudes with respect, caution, calculation and intellect. He had two ears and one mouth, and used them thus. A rainmaker he wasn't, and should he decide any circumstance necessitated 'change' he would react with the same decisive – and voracious – speed as the congregations of alligators the family had bred for over two centuries in the bayous surrounding the Arbres Plantation like treacherous moats.

"Why is Eddy home from school, Mr M.?"

Anthony settled himself opposite his employer's leather wing chair. A low Chinese table separated them.

"Because the boy has been a smartass prick again, that's why. Let's not talk about it." Loss crept into his steely eyes. "Anthony, he's seventeen, he's been without a mother since he was eight, nine. What kinda' father have I been? Y'all the one who takes him to football games, y'all taught him to fish, y'all pitched ball for him growin' up. All the things I didn't do. Couldn't do. Don't ask me why. After his mother died, I began to care less, not more." Wearily Monteleone rested his head on the wing of his chair. "The principal sent him home in the hope I'd give him a talkin' to" – he paused – "Anthony, will y'all talk with him, again? Please?"

"You know I will. I'll sit with him before I leave, but I really think you should too, Mr M. After lunch tomorrow, why not take the Cord out of the garage, leave Charles behind, you drive out to the Gulf. Just the two of you. Eddy loves to watch the birds and the men fishing. Walk by the sea, taste the salt air. Try it, Mr M."

"I've never known a gut-wrench like the ones children give you. Horrible. Uncontrollable feelin'."

"I can't imagine it." Anthony swallowed hard. Eddy was the same age as Toto. "What did you need to see me about?"

As he spoke Anthony looked up at the wall behind Monteleone's desk at the framed quote which hung, like an altar's icon, behind every one of his employer's private desks.

'I have found it always true, that men do seldom or never advance themselves from a small beginning to any great height, but by fraud, or by force.' The Prince, NICCOLÒ MACHIAVELLI.

It had taken Anthony some time to realise that the quote was a warning shot, not a welcome sign. Monteleone wanted no truck whatsoever with fraudsters, rogue politicians, corrupt bankers, hoodlums or stupid people. And both men knew that it was becoming harder and harder to do honest business in America.

"Anthony, read these please." Monteleone handed him a sheaf of faxes.

Quickly he scanned a lengthy article about the Turkish arms dealer, Adnan Khashoggi and his Iranian partner, Manucher Ghorbanifar.

"There's only a passing mention of one of your companies, Mr M."

Monteleone leaned forward and hissed in a low murmur.

"True, but this is political now, an' we're not politicians. We're businessmen who *use* politicians, Anthony. Besides, y'all know how much I hate publicity."

"No one is going to run a story without me reading it first, and I haven't had one call," Anthony replied. "We're not gunrunners. You own manufacturing plants for licenced armaments in Louisiana and Texas. Your weapons business is as lawful as your oil, your insurance, your real estate, your cargo airline, you name it. Yes, we sold a considerable quantity of weapons to two US corporations, with whom we've done business with before, and both of their 'End User Certificates' were in order. We are 100 per cent clean."

"Y'all soundin' like a politician, An-th-ony." Monteleone hesitated. "Ssshhh a'while please." His whispered words were delivered slowly, deliberately.

Anthony glanced around the study. "It's not our business to question Washington's approval of EUCs Mr M. I verified everything in DC *before* we shipped so much as one crate of weapons, or banked one dollar. Both Colonel North and Admiral Poindexter agreed the deal, and they inked it too." Anthony focused on his employer. "Why are we talking in whispers? Your study isn't bugged. I had it swept only last week."

"Even the very finest speed induces mild paranoia." Monteleone's cold eyes had the patina of freshly cut slate.

"Mr M., as the auto commercials say, *'Speed Kills'*."

"A minor vice of mine in a world of major ones," Monteleone replied, with dilated, black pupils, and his legendary smile. "Y'all don't be scolding me, Anthony, I'm too ol' an' too smelly. Besides, my daddy taught me two things: never trust a man who doesn't have a visible vice, nor one who signs a contract with a gold fountain pen."

"It's not my place to scold you, sir," Anthony stopped himself short. He'd deal with Joey on Monday in private. For sure.

"Anthony, there's an old Creole proverb, '*Zozo paillenqui crié là-haut, coudevent vini'*." Monteleone loved, and was fluent in, his Louisiana *patois*. "What it means is, '*When the tropic-bird screams overhead, a storm is comin'*.'"

"Go on, Mr M."

"I just heard the tropic-bird scream. I got a call from Defence Secretary Casper Weinberger, not three hours ago. That's why I asked y'all to disappoint the lady tonight. My apologies, once more."

The smile reappeared again, but this time it held a brutal edge Anthony very rarely saw. Saxon Monteleone was right back in his 200-year-old Louisiana ancestors' graves: in tone, in thought and, worse, in his intent. May God have mercy on anyone who stood in his way.

"This scandal is goin' to shake all those smartass, clever-clever suits in DC. The shark hunt has only just begun. The imbeciles in Washington have chummed the waters an' they've scented blood *an'* bait."

"Who's the bait?"

"They've started nibblin' at Reagan's man, his National Security Advisor, oh, what's his name?"

"Robert McFarlane."

"Yup, that's him. A misbegotten high opinion of himself, but he won't satisfy these appetites. Colonel North will be the next one they'll feed off, that's for sure. Just how edible he turns out to be depends on how high this goes. An' I think it goes to the very top, an Oval-shaped top. The Reagan Administration is on full damage limitation after the Grand Jury was empanelled last week."

"Have you got something in mind?"

"I do. Go by our offices and collate the files we have, then before lunch tomorrow go to the Baton Rouge plant and see what's there too. Next, an' most important, check which of our freighter planes ferried the arms down to Nicaragua and Panama. I hear some of our pilots went freelance importin' Class A narcotics on the return legs. Check everywhere you have to. Try our people at the DEA first. If you have any doubt as to the probity of any one of them, fire the entire crew. Immediately. An' then turn 'em all in to the DEA."

"You want to be that extreme, Mr M.?"

"Darned right I do. I know you don't like showdowns, but see this as amputation, not confrontation. I'll not have us anywhere near anythin' illegal, especially drugs. There's goin' to be a lot of blood an' limbs in the water, an' if any more of those fancy Arab gunslingers come a' knockin' for our merchandise again, well, y'all can tell them it's Sunday Hours every day from now on. Got it?"

"I'll check the files for political references, Mr M."

Monteleone visibly relaxed at Anthony's calm reply. "Y'all know it's funny, I often think of how you first came here as a tutor to teach Eddy."

Anthony smiled, and stood up to leave. He held his hand out to shake his employer's. "Goodnight, Mr M. I've got it handled. That means Eddy too. See you at brunch tomorrow."

Out of a combination of respect, loyalty and deep-seated admiration, Monteleone stood up, clasped Anthony's right hand with both of his and smiled again.

Anthony Bianchi, despite his razor-sharp antennae, had not one inkling that his employer had long regarded the younger man as his adopted son, in all but name.

CHAPTER 71

The Vatican State.
Saturday, 14th February 1987. 17:30.

Sunset came early in February, even to the Vatican. Alessandro Cuci paced his lavish office as if it were a cage and he was an angry wild cat. He stared impassively out of the windows at St Peter's Square as he spat out obscenities.

He was forty-eight years old, and for over twenty years he'd worked both inside and outside the Vatican's unique ecosystem; one of untold wealth and global power, with the ability to subtly influence international geopolitics. Vatican Radio, a jewel of pastoral communication, broadcasted daily – in over forty languages – around the world to an audience of hundreds of millions of people.

Then there was the US Catholic lobby, the pared down Kennedy dynasty, the *favelas* of Brazil, the slums of Manila, the drug lords of Mexico… The list went on and on. And all for personal advantage too. The coin of his realm was authority and control, not trappings, per se. The amassing of material wealth was an amusing pantomime, with as much relevance. What mattered was power. If you had *true* power you had the one commodity money could not buy. Power was what he'd always sought, and what he'd achieved, or so he believed. However, one last piece in the puzzle still eluded and ate away, relentlessly, at his insides. The *real* corpse of Pietro Albassi.

The five greatest information gathering networks in the world had so far failed to locate Albassi: the IEA had fallen short, as had England's MI6 and the Soviet Union's KGB. Israel's legendary Mossad (and it had been the IEA who, in 1960, with their Catholic outreach in South America, who had located Adolf Eichmann in Buenos Aires; the IEA had informed a grateful Mossad, who duly kidnapped him, smuggled him to Israel where they hanged the Nazi criminal, a debt Mossad had yet to expunge). Finally, not even the fabled CIA had been able to find Albassi. There wasn't a trace of the man anywhere. Barings had been right all along. Albassi *was* out there. But where?

Barings, after pressure had been applied, was able to shed a ray of light – hope? – some six months ago, with a surprise report that stated Albassi had been killed in a horrific road accident in Zimbabwe in the summer of 1985. Albassi had apparently been living in Africa as an itinerant farm manager, which was indeed plausible. Since then Cuci hadn't heard from either Barings or the CIA. Itchy though he was to seek concrete proof, Cuci knew Albassi was a scab he could no longer ask Barings to scratch.

CIA had distanced themselves from the IEA ever since the multiple Vatican Bank and P2 scandals, and their associated deaths in the early 1980s. The USA had been firmly under President Ronald Reagan's watch since 20th January 1981, and it was his Vice President George H.W. Bush – previously the Director of CIA – who had cooked up the idea of 'removing' Moro. Both Reagan and Bush were set to remain in power until 20th January 1989, almost two years away. And if the polls were accurate, George H.W. Bush would be the 41st President after Ronnie had hung up his PJs. So, CIA were off limits, even to the IEA.

The final coffin nail in the CIA/IEA relationship had been hammered home eighteen months after Reagan's inauguration, at 07:30 on 17th June 1982 when Roberto Calvi, known to all as *Banchiere di Dio* – 'God's Banker'– also a P2 Freemason, was found stone-cold dead, hanging by the neck under Blackfriars Bridge in the City of London's morning sunshine, in an apparent suicide. Calvi's pockets had been stuffed with 11.5 pounds of bricks and almost $15,000 in cash. No one, anywhere, believed any of it. His neck hadn't even been broken. Calvi had been strangled, and then hung from Blackfriars Bridge in a *very* public warning. The graphic pictures of the corrupt member of P2s – aka the *Frati Neri*, the Black Friars – pendular cadaver echoed around the world. This Borgia-like act was *too* baroque, too public a spectacle even for CIA's threadbare sensibilities.

Nonetheless, Cuci was grateful that his old ally had turned up something. However, he didn't quite believe CIA's Zimbabwe report. Albassi was alive. His excruciating ulcer – Albassi's poisoning gift – assured him of that.

Cuci stood over the desk twiddling a pencil. The ulcer jabbed inside him like a needle-gloved boxer. He eyed the water jug and pills on his desk. No. He opened the drinks' cabinet, poured himself a neat Campari and tossed four pills into his mouth instead of two. Exceeding the dosage was the very least of his concerns. He craved for the pain to dissipate.

"Step one in how to aggravate an ulcer," wittered Cuci to himself.

He gulped it down, poured a second, then dabbed his goatee, its grey flecks now dyed to the colour of an espresso. He walked over to the windows and, lost in thought, clinked the ice against the crystal glass. Of late, as darkness fell on misty winter evenings such as today, the illuminated façade of St Peter's Basilica had begun to look like a moonlit iceberg looming out of the fog. Aimed at him. He never had liked it. Too grandiose. Too ambitious. Too Catholic.

A tingle ran the length of his spine, then he shuddered, from his coiffed head to his cashmere-socked toes. Suddenly he felt very cold. He gathered in his scarlet cardigan around his chest.

Someone, somewhere, was trampling around inside his crypt.

CHAPTER 72

**The French Quarter,
New Orleans, Louisiana, USA.
Saturday, 14th February 1987. 23:30.**

New Orleans was both deserted and hostile by the time Anthony headed back to the French Quarter. The city intimidated him sometimes when its tarred shadows dressed in black. Although he loved the cauldron that was New Orleans as he did, he recognised there was something of 'the night' about his adopted home.

Was it the sheer relentless power of the Mississippi, and all that came down with it from the Great Lakes of the north? The river appeared to make the city vibrate and fizz like a giant electricity pylon. New Orleans, regardless of its beautiful architecture, was founded by French buccaneers who had brought ancient fear, and a dark-darkness too, with their cities of cemeteries and the dead buried above ground. Or was it, as it had been often said, that the Crescent City, the voodoo-haunted Paris of the South, was in reality the spawn of Satan and had been Godforsaken?

Driving into the murky streets of the French Quarter at last, the storm's thunder, lightning and pelting rain had shifted south into the Gulf of Mexico leaving in its wake a mean sky streaked in monochromatic hues; a fitting crescent moon spied jealously through scudding cloud breaks. The Alfa's wipers coped, but only just. Gritty rain curled around the car's quarter-lights, and the ill-fitting roof seeped lifeless, pear-shaped drops of water onto the upholstery. Anthony didn't care, he loved his old Italian car.

He should have gone to his office tonight, he knew that, but he wasn't ready for work or for sleep. Either would have meant he saw the sunrise before he saw the inside of his eyelids. Besides, he felt pleasantly replete from Anna-Mae's *lasagna*. In Sicilian lore, good luck comes to those who eat *lasagna* for New Years' lunch, which was a Salaviglia tradition. Both he and Victor had been taught to cook the speciality that was Bonnera's *lasagna* in its vast basement kitchens, and Anthony had shared the same recipe with Anna-Mae almost nine years ago.

What had become of his life – however deep his scars, however profound his sadness – it was a life that somehow worked. Wounded people either survive or die, and he hadn't died. In the marrow of his soul he had felt that Ruxandra and Toto's lives worked too, and that there was happiness there too. That was paramount. That's what it had all been about. They were alive. Not a day went by without the headstrong desire to jump ship and see them, even if from afar, just once more. Always it was the spirit of Paola that checkmated him. Forgiveness wasn't what he sought from Paola. She'd instilled in him from her grave that he'd done his best. Then and now. She was the one who would forever look over him, guide him. That was far more than he'd ever deserved. He'd kept the flames of their Christmases, Easters and birthdays burning bright, rolled into one, which had made it all bearable.

On 12th June each year, Paola and Toto's birthday, he would rise before the sun came up, douse himself in cold water and go downstairs to the chauffeured sedan waiting to take him on the two-hour southerly drive, onto the unpaved, dusty roads out to Grand Isle in Jefferson Parish, where the barrier island met the Gulf of Mexico. There he would board the same fishing boat, with the same Creole captain, and he would spend the entire day slowly ingesting rum, salt spray and reliving his memories and the decisions he had taken.

The 12th of June was his Thanksgiving.

He dabbed the Alfa's brakes gingerly, swung the car into Pirate's Alley and hastily parked up. The horses and mules were calm and no longer agitated; the worst of the weather had passed. Flexing out his cold, cramped shoulders, he walked to the corner of Royal, turned right and headed eastwards to Dumaine and Bourbon. A stiff rum was what the doctor ordered. On the corner of Bourbon and St Phillip, all but a five-minute walk away, he glimpsed the faint lights of Lafitte's Blacksmith Shop Bar.

Lafitte's, an almost square one-storey wood-framed Creole house, had stood at 941 Bourbon Street since 1772. From that day to this, so legend stated, the notorious Lafitte brothers, Jean and Pierre, had used 941

Bourbon Street as a front for their smuggling of 'black ivory' – plantation slaves. Yet, the legend had no basis in truth. Lafitte's was just the old smithy, now turned bar, it always had been. Inside, there were four small rooms, with low ceilings, worm-eaten wooden walls and furniture. It resembled a medieval torture chamber without the implements. All dim lights, open hearth and wrought iron, with a single copper-topped bar of sorts.

Anthony thought back to the first time he had set foot inside. He had almost tripped over the building nine years ago as he prowled the French Quarter's ragged streets on sleepless nights. He had heard noises, animal noises, and so he walked in. A tape recording of hyenas, wolves and all manner of canines yowling and screeching was playing on a tape loop, and loudly too. No one inside so much as batted an eyelid. His second drink finished, he propped himself up against the bar – a stranger in town – and he'd asked the barman, with what he thought was humour: *'This a regular Thursday night set?'* The barman replied, without even raising his eyes from the stained enamel sink where he was cleaning glasses, that the tape playin' was *'for my customer's dogs'*, and he turned his back on him to fix another drink.

Lafitte's had been Anthony's neighbourhood bar ever since. So, what better place to go and try to figure out why his meeting with Eddy Monteleone, two hours ago, could have spirited his thoughts across 4,500 miles back to Italy, and all that had happened to deliver him, nine years ago on a stormy February night, to Laffite's.

He was a man alone. Italy was in another constellation. Another life. One that now belonged to others.

PART TWELVE

CHAPTER 73

**No. 5, Largo Claudio Treves,
the Brera District, Milan, Italy.
Sunday, 15th February 1987. 17:00.**

Streetlamps glowed as feebly as dying fireflies through the thick fog, which Milan's unkempt stone structures carried like a time-worn cloak. The red and green shutters that coloured the faces of many buildings were lost in its shroud-like folds. The streets were ratty from the muddy rains of a long winter. Pavement cafés, their iron chairs rusting with moisture, delayed opening. Newsagents kept their wares indoors to prevent them from becoming sodden. The AC Milan-vs-Naples fixture at the San Siro Stadium had been cancelled for want of light. Milan, it seemed on this cold and dreadful Sunday in February, was a city populated by feral cats, vagrants, junkies and priests: only they stirred in the murk. Even the pigeons had grounded themselves. On days such as this Milan was a lost city, as lost as Atlantis.

"Mama! Mama!"

"Don't shout, Toto! What do you want?"

"I've just spoken to Ferruccio and he says *The Big Easy* is showing at the cinema. May I go please?"

Ruxandra dropped the iron pot into the sink. It sizzled in surrender. She shrugged her shoulders and grinned at Victor Salaviglia, who sat peacefully reading a magazine on a barstool beside her in the kitchen.

"If he wants to go outside in this filthy weather then good luck to him. I've seen the film, it's a thriller set in New Orleans. It's not bad." Victor's wide, brown eyes never left the magazine, but his velvety tone said it all, and more.

"OK, Toto," she replied, "mind you get on the right bus in this weather. *Ciao!*"

She began to scrub scorched tomato from the bottom of the blackened pan as her son crashed through the front door, with a loud cry of, "*Ciao*, Mama! *Ciao*, Victor!"

"Don't frown so, Ruxandra. I was just as clumsy at seventeen. In fact, I think I was worse. Pietro was just as bad too. He and I knew how to run properly amok, it's something we Sicilians do very well."

"You always defend him. You and Joshua are just the same. Toto can do no wrong," she beamed, as she replied.

"As do you!" He paused. "You do know that I love you so very much, don't you?" He put down his magazine and blew her a kiss.

Half-heartedly Ruxandra continued to scrub the ruined pan. What did Victor and Joshua know about children? Zero. And that was the sum total of children they had raised too. She had been the one who had needed to camouflage herself after Pietro had been murdered and Paola had died. In the natural order of life, to bury one's husband is to be expected, but not one's child too.

Sensing her sudden mood swing, Victor rounded his eyes, soft with contentment, at her hastily saddening face.

"Why don't we go to Cortina for a long weekend? Just you and me. How about it? I'm not suited to Milanese weather and I must return to Bonnera before the spring harvests."

"Yes! Yes! What a wonderful idea, Victor. The mountains will blow the winter cobwebs away, and I can curl up in front of the fire while you ski. Toto can stay with Ferruccio," she said, with a seductive look.

She picked up the scarred pan, dropped it in the dustbin and giggled out aloud.

"I used to cook food, but all I do is just burn food. I was never a good cook, was I?"

"In truth, the answer has to be a solid no, *cara*."

He tossed his magazine in the dustbin and held out his arms. She snuck across to where he sat. He hugged her tightly as she ruffled her delicate fingers through his thick brown hair.

"Marry me, Ruxandra?"

"Sssh, Victor, you know I can't," her deep voice lilted softly.

"I do, but you wouldn't love me if I didn't ask you."

They both laughed in unison; a sound the walls of No. 5, and Bonnera, were now accustomed to hearing.

"No, that's true, very true," she whispered.

Her long hair, the colour of lightly burnt almonds, fell about her shoulders as he moved his strong hands up her back to draw her even closer to him.

"How long do you think Toto will be gone?"

He breathed the words through his cream silk shirt – the one she wore so often – into the softness of her breasts. She placed her lips beside his ear and purred, "long enough, my darling Victor, long enough."

CHAPTER 74

The Brera District, Milan, Italy.
Sunday, 15th February 1987. 17:20.

Toto Albassi stood alone in the bus shelter and shivered with cold. The fog hung about his ears like a damp woollen cap. He rammed his hands deep into the pockets of his Levi's. A yellow cashmere scarf, a seventeenth birthday present from Victor, was wrapped around his neck and mouth, and his breath froze in its soft fibres. His best friend, Ferruccio, lived close enough to walk to in spring, but on nasty winter days, or smoggy summer afternoons, he always took the bus. Except when Victor snuck him 10,000 lire for a taxi or two.

For reasons he struggled with, he avoided travelling on the Metro. Going underground made his heart race and his brow sweat. A fear of confined spaces had haunted him ever since his father's funeral; the priest had told him that his father was in the odd-shaped wooden box by the altar. It had looked too small and cramped to spend the rest of your life in. Poor, poor Papà, he had thought then, and he still did. He loved Victor, but it was his Papà he missed every day.

Toto scanned the printed timetable in the shelter and shrugged at his own stupidity. Neither the buses nor the trams ran punctually in Milan, least of all on days like this. On the other side of the road he could just make out the dim numerals on the pharmacy clock. 17:20. He'd give the bus ten more minutes and then at 17:30 he'd start to walk, hoping to catch a bus mid-stop. Standing in the stark shelter was too bone-chilling.

CHAPTER 75

Metairie, New Orleans, Louisiana, USA.
Sunday, 15th February 1987. 14:20.

Anthony Bianchi drove north through backwater streets towards Lafreniere Park, in the New Orleans suburb of Metairie where Dawn Loubiere lived. When he found her house, not far from Lake Pontchartrain's shore, he pulled up, blipped the accelerator and killed the engine. He checked his watch. He was late, but not too late. The regular Sunday brunch with Mr M. and Eddy had gone well, and both had been in an unusually lyrical mood.

The Alfa's black canvas roof nested open behind him. Last night's storm, like so many Louisiana storms, had long passed, leaving a scrubbed, lean blue sky in its backwash. He eyed the big sky and grinned; he was, indeed, a contented man. There wasn't one cloud in sight – all he registered on the horizon was a flight of seagulls – and a clear day was the only excuse he needed to drop the convertible's roof, even if it was a brisk sixty-eight degrees. At forty-three years of age he had butterflies in his stomach. There'd been a few caterpillars in the latter years, but that was all. He blamed himself: a cold, unapproachable workaholic loner, with few social skills.

He had parked just shy of her home, a neat, two-storey affair painted white and daisy-yellow. There was a white picket fence, with a matching gate, which gave on to a baize green lawn, complete with stripes and neat borders bursting with colourful perennials. The simplicity and calm it radiated, even from the curb-side, was almost tactile. Self-consciously he checked himself in the wing mirror, stepped out of the car, unbolted the gate and rang the doorbell. Noises. Dawn's brother perhaps? Then he heard her easy-going voice. She opened the front door.

"Hi, Anthony, it's good to see you." She leaned in and kissed him on both cheeks, then spontaneously she checked to see if her brother was behind her. He wasn't. And with an open smile as gorgeous as a spring rose, she kissed him quickly, lovingly, on the lips.

"I called you 'til after I got home, but when you weren't there I figured, *cher*, maybe it was important y'all work late." She held the fingers of his right hand loosely. "I'm glad you're here now though."

He tried not to stare at her, but couldn't help himself. She looked so fresh in her pale pink Bermuda shorts and crisp white polo shirt, with her blonde hair pulled tight in a high ponytail which only showed off, unintentionally, her perfect complexion. Patently, makeup was for those who needed it; Dawn most certainly didn't. Suddenly he felt very second-hand in his rumpled cream linen suit, Italian-blue shirt and dark-blue tie, recognising that he might resemble a scruffy Sydney Greenstreet in *Casablanca*, albeit slimmer.

"How about Audubon Park…?" he said, while still in the doorway.

She beamed another smile at him and turned up her Louisiana accent.

"Only if we take yer neat lil' red sports car? We don't want to be botherin' for a taxi-cab do we? Besides don't y'all know N'Awlins' drivers look out for their gals on Sundays, but only after Mass of course."

"Sure, let's, er, drive," Anthony stammered, lost for words.

"Fine, y'all wait here while I fetch my purse an' sweater."

He walked her to the car, held the passenger door open, then closed it gently. He walked around the back of the car, and as he did so he noticed her reach across his seat and open his door for him. His heart, literally, skipped a beat.

They headed south towards Audubon Park in silence, with only the fresh air dancing in the car for company. At a set of traffic lights, Anthony faced her and said, "I like it here very much, Dawn. I've been here nearly nine years, so, when do I stop being a tourist and become a local?"

"Y'all never will stop being a tourist, *cher*. I wouldn't worry about it, because if you stay a tourist forever y'all never worry about havin' an Orleanais stamp in your passport."

He pulled away from the green light at a clip, the Alfa's exhaust rasped as he did so, and Dawn held her ponytail in place against the rushing wind.

"I don't follow you?"

"If you're a New Orleanian, it's printed on yer mind. Y'all can move and live all yer life with the sun behind you, or the sun in front of you, in San Francisco or New York, but a part of you will have remained in New Orleans. That isn't always a good thing. It's like being a Catholic, y'all can never quite shake it off, even if you want to." She glanced at him and caught a sad glint in his eye. "Anthony, where is it exactly y'all do come from?"

"I've told you before."

"Y'all have, but tell me again. I like to hear y'all talk."

"Later," he laughed, "I need all my wits about me. New Orleanians are terrible drivers. You don't drive on the left, or on the right, you just drive wherever the sun shines, and today is a beautiful day!"

He took his eyes off the road. Their eyes met. He shot her a wink.

Dawn's sky-blue eyes threw the wink right back at him, subtly too. In that split-second she realised that this man – a man of very few words – had meant all he'd ever spoken to her since they'd first met. She decided that the man beside her was a man of honour. Unseen, she beamed a grateful smile of thanks at Louisiana's sun.

CHAPTER 76

The Brera District, Milan.
Sunday, 15th February 1987. 17:30.

Toto stamped his feet to keep warm and pass the time. The green numerals glowed 17:30. Enough was enough. He peered back down the street to the corner around which the bus would appear. But the corner wasn't even visible. He ran through his three options: telephone Ferruccio to call off the cinema, return home to borrow the taxi fare or start walking towards the next bus stop. The first was not on. Ferruccio was his best friend and would be disappointed. The second was not really a good idea, his mother and Victor were more than generous with him. So, with a shrug of his shoulders, he set off walking eastwards, down via Montebello hoping to jump a bus.

One hundred metres before the next bus stop, a muddy, unwashed blue Lancia saloon drew up alongside him.

"*Ciao*, do you know the way to Piazzale Loreto?" The driver asked nonchalantly as he wound down the passenger window and peered out. His gravelly accent wasn't Milanese; Toto couldn't place it at all.

"Sure, it's the same direction I'm headed. It's next to the cinema I'm going to," Toto answered, as he dipped down towards the car.

"Then jump in and show us. We're lost. We'll give you a ride."

"*Non, grazie*," he wavered, "but I'll explain the route to you as best I can. You're going in the right direction. Keep on straight, and head for Piazza della Repubblica, then ask again. It's not too far."

Toto looked further inside the car. There were three men, all in their late twenties, two of whom sat in the back. He guessed they were travelling salesmen for they all wore shirts with ill-fitting ties. The two passengers turned to smile at him and he noticed a resemblance, all three men could be brothers. Apart from the same leathery features, they had strangely anonymous, stubbled faces, like the ones he saw on gameshows. Torn newspapers and cigarette packets littered the car floor.

"Listen, we're up from the south, Milan is a nightmare, and as for this weather!" The driver sighed, raised his eyes skywards and peeled off two 5,000 lire notes from a wad of cash. "Kid," he said, brandishing the notes to the open window. "I'll give you 10,000 lire to show us the way. Look, the reason we're heading there is to see where they strung up Mussolini and his tart!"

Toto had guessed as much. That was the only reason non-Milanese went to Piazzale Loreto. Once again, the driver smirked at him, this time his stained and chipped teeth made Toto's skin crawl. He peered back down via Montebello. He could just make out the clock's numerals – 17:34 – and still no flicker of any buses' dim headlights.

"*Non, grazie*," Toto repeated. "I'm going to walk." His parents' childhood mantra about cars and strangers still held true.

"OK, thanks for the directions, kid. I'll look for the cinema, that'll be well lit up even in this fog. "Here, kid, take this for your help. Buy some popcorn and enjoy yourself."

"*Grazie tanto*, Signor," said Toto, and swiftly trousered the 5,000 lire note.

"*Andiamo!* Next stop, we spit on Mussolini!" shouted the driver out of the window, as the Lancia sped off into the gloom.

CHAPTER 77

No. 5, Largo Claudio Treves,
the Brera District, Milan, Italy.
Sunday, 15th February 1987. 19:30.

Ruxandra squinted at her clock. 19:30. Naked, and with a sheet half across her, she realised she'd napped and two hours had flown by. It was now dark outside and she quailed in its shadows. As always happened when she awoke, her first thoughts went to Toto. Tonight, he was coming out of a cinema into this filthy, bleak winter weather. Beside her, Victor breathed rhythmically, as a satiated lion would. She lifted her head slowly from his broad chest so not to disturb him. She wanted to look at him again, as if to reassure herself. A part of her heart would always be Pietro's, but she could never imagine feeling anything other than love and gratitude towards Victor. For he had saved her and Toto's lives. She chased away the unease about her son, and calm once more, she nestled her head back into Victor's warm chest and permitted her mind freedom to roam in peace and affection for the man she loved.

After Pietro's death, the money from his insurance policies had numbed her need to leave their home, other than for groceries and to walk Enzo. She'd preferred to clean the apartment, iron Toto's clothes and prepare supper. She had wanted to trap all the molecules that had ever come into contact with Pietro and Paola inside her world. Long after the doorhandles had shone like spot-lit mirrors, and not a moment too soon, did she realise that their world had in fact become their prison.

In 1982, four long years since his father's death, and the death of his twin sister, she saw that Toto had begun to sink, imperceptibly, like a young buck caught in quicksand, beneath the surface of her – and now his – world. Nothing moved any more. Not even the motes in the air, least of all Toto's.

However, the summer of 1982 was to change everything.

Toto was by then a wan and introspective child of twelve, prematurely spotty, with dull, gaunt green eyes, lank greasy hair and inert limbs. All he would do when spoken to was grunt in response. Then one school day morning, as she had prepared his breakfast of fresh fruit and cereal, the realisation that she, and she alone, had done this to him struck her.

Hastily, she'd shooed his slouching, round-shouldered body out of the door to catch the bus to school. She made herself an espresso with Pietro's antiquated machine and sat in quiet contemplation on his old barstool. She reached for a pad and a pen. Her initial intention was to list all her accomplishments over the last four years. The task had not taken long. The espresso was still tepid by the time she had completed her list. There had been no accomplishments. There had been only grief in all its attendant guises: the unending rage of bereavement, the short tempers, the replaying of incidental events, stilted Christmases, the graveside vigils for Pietro and Paola on multiple anniversaries – birth and death – all under skies of varying shades of grey. And of course, there were always the daylight jibes, from the gypsies who lived in the dark nooks of her mind, to contend with.

On good nights there was the torture of unrefreshing sleep. On bad nights there were dreams in which she painted watercolours of impossible happiness only for the mornings to serve up the same void. Then she finally grasped, alone and on Pietro's stool, that she could not weep one day longer. Pietro and Paola no longer lived at No. 5, Largo Claudio Treves, only Ruxandra and Salvatore Albassi lived there. And Enzo, of course.

She had bolted her espresso and went to her neat desk in search of a visiting card. The hand-engraved one which bore the legend *'Victor Salaviglia'*. The same, thick white card which gave his telephone number and an address which read simply: *'Bonnera, Sicilia'*. She'd telephoned him and asked, in as detached an expression as she could manage, if his invitation to visit – some four years ago now – was still open?

Victor Salaviglia had been surprised, pleasantly so (or so she had thought) and he had replied with alacrity that his car would meet their flight at Palermo's airport, whenever that may be. Would tomorrow be alright she had asked, perhaps hastily, and with her small dog too? Would two weeks be an imposition? Yes, of course they could all come tomorrow, Enzo too, and surely two weeks was too short a time, he had replied politely. Was everything alright? Yes, she'd replied. So, he would expect them the next day, and their rooms would be made up and awaiting their arrival. She would travel south with Toto and Enzo to the Sicilian sun. To the land where Toto's father was born and there, together, they might finally lay him to rest.

Two weeks became three months.

Ruxandra hadn't been prepared for Victor Salaviglia, the man, any more than she was for the memories he began to share with her and Toto. The summers when he and Pietro were just two young boys who'd played and laughed together. She hadn't allowed for the exploits of Victor's ancestors, recounted in tones as breathless and warm as the Sicilian evenings.

In the long afternoons she, Toto and Victor would sit together on the grand west-facing terrace at Bonnera, surrounded by terracotta pots, miniature palm trees and Murano vases bursting with wild flowers, whilst Enzo dozed in the warmth. The cushioned wicker sofas they relaxed in sat atop intricate tapestries of Persian and Turkish rugs, all of extraordinary beauty, and they were cosseted from the heat by the gentle breeze wafting down from raffia fans, all of which turned slower than time itself. Views of the Mediterranean stretched out in front of them, and below was grove after grove after grove of broad-shouldered olive trees – all of a biblical age – which descended further than the eye could journey. Bonnera was Heaven on Earth to Ruxandra, Toto and the lizard-chasing Enzo, who'd outgrown slothful pigeons.

Victor had told them of the massacre in the nearby village of San Cipirello in August of 1950: Pietro had been just six years old, and it was in that piazza that Ruxandra's late husband, Toto's late father, and Victor's late friend, had been shot and lost the sight in his left eye. Twenty-seven men, women and children had died on 24th of August 1950. Pietro was the only one shot to have survived. Victor, with a wide and cheeky smile, volunteered that Pietro was always a boy who had made his own luck. Somehow, his telling of the events, tempered and without rancour, had diminished the sheer horror of it all.

The next morning, Victor had dispensed with his driver and bundled them all into an old British Army Land Rover to drive them to the ghostlike village that was San Cipirello. As they set off, Victor smiled at Ruxandra and winked. He then looked over his shoulder and told Toto and Enzo they were going to take the scenic route over rough tracks and terrain, so, hold on! Only later did Ruxandra learn that not once during the entire day had they left Salaviglia land.

She hadn't expected to feel at ease in San Cipirello's small and deserted piazza, where she'd discovered Pietro's spirit entwined in its chiaroscuro shadows. Beside Victor and Toto, she'd sipped thick *ristretto* from what had been Nino's Bar Lombardo, and visited the elderly Father Albert with whom she'd sipped cups of sweet black tea.

With a renewed strength, she accompanied Victor, who'd taken them to visit the simple grave, beside an almond tree and in the shade of tall, sad cypresses, where Pietro's mother, the grandfather Pietro had never known and Nonna were interred. Toto had picked flowering buds from the wild oleanders – white, pink and red – and in his and Paola's name, he had crossed himself and had placed them on his ancestor's gravestones.

As the weeks had passed, and at a slow Sicilian tempo, she hadn't reckoned on Toto becoming a man in the vicious heat of that Sicilian summer. It was as if her son had returned home. He cycled every morning down to the town of Castellammare, and there he swam in its *golfo*. His skin darkened, his northern blemishes vanished, his hair gained lustre, his muscles thickened, his shoulders broadened as his spine straightened and he began to resemble his father in front of her very eyes.

Above all, she had not intended to fall in love.

First with the memory of Pietro, then with the flesh, the blood and the sheer decency of the man, Victor Salaviglia. To her absolute surprise, as well as delight, she discovered that she was able to love the two of them, simultaneously.

On the September day that she, Toto, and a sulking Enzo, were to leave Bonnera, the cloistered heat of Africa was once again on the wind: the *scirocco* wrapped itself around the ancient Castello Ducale, just as it had done countless times before over many centuries. The hard, azure sky – even at its vanishing point – was softened by a reddish frieze of clouds bloated with Saharan sand. Even though hot dust stifled the air, she realised that she could, at last, breathe.

There in the west of Sicily, she grasped the simple fact that she would love Pietro forever. She had promised him as much. In this realisation, she accepted that she was now able to allow Victor to love her in return.

She and Toto had gone to Sicily to bury a husband, a father, a daughter and a sister. They had succeeded.

In Ruxandra's – and Toto's – achievements, the gypsies who had tormented her for so very long, had, at last, forever been silenced. Or so she believed.

CHAPTER 78

**Piazzale Loreto, north of the Brera District, Milan, Italy.
Sunday, 15th February 1987. 20:15.**

Toto and Ferruccio stepped out of the cinema and shivered. The fog had thickened in the two hours they had been inside. It was criminally cold, with dense wintry moisture like the impenetrable white outs he and Victor had sometimes been caught in when skiing in Cortina; his mother barely moved one metre from the hearth for the entire time they were at the Salaviglia chalet.

Flush with the 5,000 lire note he'd earned from being a tour guide – Ferruccio had laughed at that – they stood in the dim glow of the cinema's lobby, as the audience thinned out into the night. They'd both enjoyed the movie. *The Big Easy* was a cop caper set in faraway New Orleans. As far as the two teenagers were concerned, the real hit was the leading lady, a young and beautiful blonde US District Attorney, who fleetingly gate-crashed Toto's thoughts. He smiled to himself as he always did when his late Papà came to mind. His father had been a respected criminal defence lawyer, and Toto wondered if he had ever defended a case against a lady prosecutor as striking as Ellen Barkin was. He very much doubted it. Again, he smiled.

"*Ciao*, Toto, that was a lot of fun. See you at school tomorrow!" Ferruccio called out, as he set off into the murk of the night; his was a short walk home.

Toto waved silently, alone with his memories of his Papà. He turned left and then slunk his head into his yellow cashmere scarf as if he were frightened tortoise. It was bitterly cold after the fug of the cinema, and for sure his 5,000 lire was going on a taxi home. He had much further to go, a solid fifteen-minute cab ride – maybe more. The hard part was going to be finding a taxi on a night like this. He knew a shortcut from the cinema to the Piazzale Loreto, where he'd find a cab. He ducked down an alleyway that would trim five freezing minutes off his walk.

Midway down the alley, and camouflaged in the cheerless gloom, Toto didn't see the grubby blue Lancia saloon, any more than he saw three men steal out under cover of the night's greasy shadows. In a spectral second they had wrestled his young body from the pavement with fiercely strong hands. He didn't catch a glimpse, nor a whiff, of the rag-wad saturated with chloroform which instantly came from behind him. But he did feel himself manhandled by calloused hands as they savagely clamped its sickly-sweet vileness into his nostrils and mouth. He gulped for air and in so doing, the chloroform raked the back of his throat like shards of glass. His body crashed into something hard: concrete wall? pavement? road? He pawed his own hands upwards gasping for air like a drowning cat, his efforts futile against the mind-fogging chemical. A wicked downward spiral of brilliant white and satanic black, a hell-bent helter-skelter of unconsciousness beckoned. It spun around and around in front of his eyes, until a harsh warmth swamped him. His last action was choking, then gasping for air; before nosediving comatose into what was the car's grimy footwell.

Unconscious, Toto didn't know at the time, but six heavy, steel-capped boots stomped his face, and relentlessly pummelled his body into the filth of the Lancia's floor.

PART THIRTEEN

CHAPTER 79

**Cattolica, a town on the Adriatic Coast,
Rimini Province, Italy.
Wednesday, 18th February 1987. 09:40.**

Alone, and with an air of absolute dejection, Lorenzo Massina perched on his uncomfortable green canvas stool. His hands hung idly at his side, almost touching the film of fish scales blanketing Cattolica's harbour wall. Below, the sea was grey and unappealing, and from in-between his fat thighs a fishing rod protruded like an obscenely long, thin penis. He glanced at it with an expression of spectacular disinterest.

He loathed fishing and all the attendant rituals it demanded: Lilliputian stools, idiotic caps, preposterous eight-metre-long rods, outrageously expensive reels, pots of writhing maggots that looked and smelled like foaming effluent from a Venetian sewer. And worse, every item came in shades of one, solitary, colour. Green. Even the variations were unappealing: Khaki. Olive. Teal. Moss. Taupe. Drab. Then there were the wretched hooks. If he hated the militariness of the equipment, then he detested the hooks. Three times now he'd had to have the sneaky barbs removed from his nicotine-stained fingers. Somehow, the hooks slipped into his flesh with greater ease than they did the bait, or the fish for that matter; a number greater than the total of edible fish he'd grappled out of the Adriatic Sea in the two years since his retirement.

Most people who quit smoking remained non-smokers. Not Lorenzo Massina. In his retirement, he'd taken up smoking again as a palliative, a rebellion, a slow act of suicide – he couldn't decide which – either way, he began smoking with vengeance the same day he had returned his badge and Beretta. Thirty-plus a day, and counting.

It was midweek, in winter, and Cattolica harbour was quiet. A dry slush-coloured day, where the sun shone high above the overcast sky as if in a different universe. He could not, nor would not, have lifted one battle-scarred finger to his rod, even if a two kilogram *branzino* had guzzled his bait-less hook. Today, Lorenzo Massina stared vacantly at the dismal horizon, for he was an especially troubled man.

Like everyone else in Italy he had been tracking, with almost pornographic avidity, the ostensibly bizarre kidnap of the teenager, Salvatore 'Toto' Albassi. The frequent news bulletins, all delivered in vague terms, had become as addictive as his Nazionali. Ever since the publication, in the *Corriere della Sera*, of a ransom demand two days ago, Monday 16th February, there had been no further official bulletins or news updates. Intrigue had turned into rumour – via absurd theories – only to end up as bullshit guesswork. All of it spewed out of the media's many orifices, legitimised with bylines like: *'close friend of the family'*, *'informer'* and *'former associate'*. Nonetheless he, like the rest of Italy, except for Adriatic fish, were hooked. He devoured all the constituent parts of the teenager's kidnapping. Greedily so.

With this hunger came his old familiar stomach knot. The one he'd handed in with his police ID when, aged sixty, he knew God had wanted His revenge. He wouldn't be allowed to die on the job. Suffer unto Me. And then some. He, and He alone, demanded that the remainder of Massina's allocated span be spent with her empty bottles of Poland's finest, whilst contemplating a fishless Adriatic Sea. Truly, revenge had been His to savour.

Massina glanced at the almost illegible fridge-note his wife had left him, scrawled in green felt pen. Neither the message, nor the telephone call, had come as a surprise. In truth he had half expected it. Apart from himself, there was probably one other person between the Brenner Pass and Lampedusa who could hypothesise as to who was behind the kidnapping of Salvatore Albassi. Not even his old assistant Luca Pezzoli (now, incredibly, Vice-Questore Pezzoli) could have. In that very realisation, that very privilege (and how he disliked the word) lay his dilemma.

"They can all go to hell in a handcart," he muttered, and began to reel in his limp fishing line.

That done, he crumpled the message in his fist. The note which had informed him Vice-Questore Pezzoli had called, would be as tasty as anything else he had in his turd-green bait box. What was the use? He was an overweight, retired policeman adrift 350 kilometres southeast of Milan. Clumsily, he scrunched the cheap paper onto the hook and recast his line. The emerald and white float bobbed in the light Adriatic swell. The message, and its request, were out of his life forever. It was destined for the gut-sack of an obscurely named fish he would never catch.

He squinted at his watch, and realised his little theatrical charade was a game his mindset had put on just for him. Wait. Who was acting for who? For sure he'd return Pezzoli's, sorry Vice-Questore Pezzoli's, call. There was a chance, albeit as thin and as tenuous as his avocado-coloured fishing line, that Milan Criminalpol might take him back for this one last case.

Suddenly, and with a winner's victory smirk, he stood up, reeled in the line, removed the soggy paper from the hook, and with all the strength he could muster he kicked – one at a time – his rod, his tacklebox and finally his stool into the putrid, sea-green water of Cattolica's harbour.

There was a chance he might actually get killed in the line of duty. Now, that was surely worth a telephone call, no?

CHAPTER 80

Italy?
Wednesday, 18th February 1987. Morning.

Toto's body shivered uncontrollably for ten minutes at a time, only to subside for another ten minutes. It was so rhythmic he could have set his watch by it, if he still had one. It wasn't the cold that caused it, even though that sucked on the marrow of his joints like a greedy rodent, it was the confinement. It was like death itself, and it petrified him.

For the first day he had wept silently out of sheer terror. On the second, he had gone beyond terror and into prayer, and when that had offered him less succour than the tranquilliser-laced hot milk he was given at nightfall, his thoughts had turned inwards. He had regressed. His captors held his body, but not his mind. That alone was still his to nourish until they (and speculating who 'they' were mystified him) found a method to harness that too, like they had his right hand. Crudely, but effectively, it was chained to a rusted iron wall-hook used to tether farm animals.

He had no idea where he was, but on the third day he began to draw a picture to tinker with at will. He was in an old and abandoned cowshed, somewhere high up, but below the timberline. The floor of his jail was hard soil, compacted by decades of hooves. The walls were hewn slabs erected in a dry-stone manner, by hands so skilful that chinks of light never visited him. The massive wooden doors were held in place by rusted iron hinges and bolts. The ceiling was open rafters, and there was a gallery at one end where he presumed fodder and straw had once been kept. The solitary window was covered with black jute through which seeped teasing flavours of pine and woodland herbs.

There was no hint of the soft, comforting southern perfumes of vines, fruits or olives he remembered from Sicily. Was he high in the granite wasteland hills of Calabria? Or was the cowshed in the foothills of northern Lombardy, where the wintry lakes are fed by torrents of Alpine water? Was he even in Italy?

Toto, despite the southern accents he recalled hearing from that fog-bound Sunday evening, liked to dream that he was still in Lombardy. His home. Whenever he thought of home, his mother's face appeared before him like an apparition. Wherever he was, he knew it had to be more than deserted; it must be desolate. None of the aromas that drifted by, at first like strangers and now like friends, had been corrupted by man. There was a chilled purity on the air he'd never experienced before. And three hours ago, as a raw sunrise had signalled his fourth day in captivity, he heard bells in the far distance; the wind had carried the sharp yaps of dogs checking sheep. It was a sound his mind chose to capture. A sound he knew he would replay again and again. The only other noises he had heard were the dismembered commands of his masked captors speaking sharply at him through voice modulators. He was sure there were three. Not even the metallic ungodliness of their devices could camouflage that.

His captors took it in turn, like watches on a ship, to guard him. Three times a day he was allowed out, blindfolded, to defecate or urinate in a pit; it was fifty-three paces away. Then, he was allowed to wash his face and hands in freezing water and stretch his rangy limbs for fifteen, sublime, minutes.

Toto had hollered out torrents of inane questions during the first and second days, and when on the third day they were still greeted by a silence more assured than the security that surrounded him, he'd given up, defeated. For now, he had only himself. His own questions. And they returned him, in body and mind and soul, to those first few years after his father and sister had died.

Then, as now, he felt so alone, as if he were the only person on a faraway planet in a galaxy beyond telescopic sight, out there – where? – far from anyone's reach. The only difference was he was now seventeen. A teenage boy who lay numb and awake in a dead womb of thin blankets on a chill earthen floor. Before, he had been eight years old. Alert, staring and cold, just as cold, in his small bed in Milan, the only warmth coming from the tears on his cheeks and Enzo lying beside him. Tears. There had been so many tears. How he had cried and cried. He was unable to tell his father of his dream; show Paola the cartoons he'd saved for her. Here and now, cold and alone again, he could remember that dream – the adventure dream.

All that had changed was the current predicament in a faceless location. He still had the simple questions of a child. The unanswerable ones.

CHAPTER 81

Cattolica, a town on the Adriatic Coast.
Rimini Province, Italy.
Wednesday, 18th February 1987. 13:30.

"Vice-Questore Pezzoli, *per favore*."
The words stalled in Massina's throat. Was it the words 'Vice-Questore' or the phone box's acrid stink of urine? He lit another cigarette, tapped his nails on the scratched Perspex and watched the smoke spiral sluggishly upwards. He'd been unable to read Pezzoli's telephone number as the ink had run before the fish could devour it, so, here he was in a rancid phone booth waiting on Milan Central's inept switchboard to perform their menial task.

"*Pronto*, Vice-Questore Pezzoli," the voice crackled with authority.

"So, my little assistant has turned out not to be so much of a *cretino* after all. *Incredibile!*"

It was an odd way to greet the man whom Massina hoped would allow him to return to active duty again, but he couldn't help himself, the words just tripped out along with the Nazionali's fumes.

"Ispettore, I see retirement has neither mellowed you, nor neutralised the bile. Good. Good. Because it's just the old cynical Massina I want back in my office on full pay tomorrow morning. How about it? My time is taken up with Rome, Milan and the media." Pezzoli dropped an octave. "Whoever's behind this didn't do their research properly." His voice now a full-on whisper. "Ssshhh. Let me tell you, off the record, Ispettore Massina, the boy's mother is the lover of the now 15th Duke of Salaviglia, the 14th Duke having died just one year ago. She's been his lover since the summer of 1982, almost five years." Pezzoli paused. "So far we've been able to keep that from the media."

Massina cringed at Pezzoli's – now his superior, for Heaven's sake – smugness.

"Wrong, Pezzoli. How the hell did they ever think you had the brains to make Vice-Questore? You're stupider than ever. Listen, whoever organised this kidnap did their research to five-places of decimals. Two billion lire to the Salaviglias is like disturbing a petty cash box. Genius." Massina uttered the last word in a way that it conveyed two meanings: one of sarcasm directed at Pezzoli and one of flattery towards the mastermind.

"What do you mean, Ispettore?"

"Cut this Ispettore will you. I'm a civilian now. If we're going to work together, you'll address me as Lorenzo and I'll call you Pezzoli like I always did. OK?"

Pezzoli felt like the scrawny and insignificant termite he always did around Ispettore Lorenzo Massina, Criminalpol.

Massina continued. "The press is running around like headless chickens only because there appears to be no rhyme or reason involved. Quite right too. Why should anyone kidnap the only child of a widow, who works part-time in a Milanese art gallery? The only bone the press is chewing on is that his father was killed in mysterious circumstances about nine years ago," he said, turning up the sarcasm again.

Massina sucked hard on his Nazionali and kicked open the booth's flimsy cabin door for air.

"You remember the case, surely?"

"Vaguely. It was a long time ago, and I was just your coffee boy then."

"The widow's dead husband was a lawyer, who had the misfortune to have been the principal go-between in the Moro affair. Albassi was supposedly murdered by the Red Brigades. I never believed that, it was the *anni di piombo* after all, and everyone was getting killed or shot at every day. It was like football, a national pastime." Massina held a beat. "Just you wait, Pezzoli, the Salaviglia connection will come out when, and *only* when, the architect of this inexplicable and bizarre kidnap wants us, and the public, to know."

"How can you be so sure?"

"The only reason you called me, Pezzoli, is because you haven't one clue or one theory, and you believe that I may have several. The press is drawing absurd conclusions of mistaken identity. That's all they've got.

Remember the deaf young English girl who was kidnapped in Sardinia back in '79–'80? The kidnappers and the press thought Mr Rolf Schild was Mr Rothschild. Rolf Schild was an English businessman on holiday with his family in Sardinia for Chrissakes! This is the mentality we're dealing with, Pezzoli. You've read the papers. They would rather print rubbish, and spice it with spurious connections to the '73 Getty kidnapping, than admit they've got no news. No news doesn't sell ink or get eyeballs on the TV, now does it, Pezzoli?"

"Does that mean you'll come to Milan?" Pezzoli needed him back, and he let the plea stay.

"It's a bit like the original case with the boy's father. Part of me wanted that case and another part of me wanted it as much as syphilis."

"What kind of answer is that, Lorenzo?"

"It's an 'I don't know' sort of answer. Five minutes ago, I was sure. Now, I'm not so sure."

Pezzoli knew his old boss well enough to shut up at moments like this.

Massina went silent before continuing. "I assume the ransom is *not* going to be paid, and Victor Salaviglia's connections *are* as good as I think they are?" he asked.

"All the duke's Italian accounts we know about have been frozen, and the kidnappers have yet to open up a dialogue. When they do, I'm sure Salaviglia will put a lawyer in to negotiate. The man has a reputation of being honourable, and his connections go as high as you need them to go."

"I don't like that answer. If there's one thing I've learned, there's always someone higher up the ladder no matter how far you climb. You say his connections are first-rate, but take it from me they're not in the kidnapper's league, I promise you. The trouble is, Pezzoli, whatever we do here I'm sensing that the ending has already been written. Sadly, there's nothing you, me or any of Salaviglia's allies can do about it. Nothing at all." Massina's words fizzled out with a mouthful of cigarette smoke which tore at his throat. His heart raced and he felt his chest tighten. It was a combination of deep self-disgust and pumped-up adrenaline.

"Stop talking in riddles, Lorenzo. Are you with me on this, yes or no?"

"Yes, of course I am, Pezzoli." Massina breathed out as he ground the Nazionali butt into the cabin's floor. "But on one condition. We treat this as a shoe-leather investigation. I know it's a curse, but what I'm surmising is, in reality, useless. In fact, it's worse than that, it's dangerous for the Albassi boy."

"You're talking in riddles again. Agreed. Shoe leather. Terrific. So, I'll see you tomorrow morning then?" Pezzoli ignored Massina's ranting as just that, ranting.

"OK. I'll see you tomorrow at Rebibbia Prison, because that's where I'll be."

"Uh?"

"You heard me, Pezzoli. Now, what's your budget like?" asked Massina.

"How deep is the ocean?"

"Excellent. Have a car at my apartment in Cattolica at 15:30 today. It's 320 kilometres to Rome, and I'll need dinner and a night's rest." Massina wavered. "And clear it with Rebibbia's Governor that you alone want to interview Nicolai Sentini. Don't tell the Governor I'll be accompanying you. One other thing, find out everything you can about Dr Marco Valente, the pathologist from Portofino. I want a full background. Whatever you do, do it subtly, do it yourself, don't delegate this to anybody. Dig deep and quickly. You were always a good mole. Are we agreed?"

"Yes, of course. That name rings a bell."

"It should. Years ago you spewed your guts out all over Valente's marble floors. Very embarrassing it was too, Pezzoli. *A domani. Ciao.*"

Lorenzo Massina hung up the decrepit red payphone, kicked the door open and sniffed at the sea breeze. Only now did the Adriatic smell good and cleansing. Not once in the two years since he'd retired to the backwater dump that was Cattolica, had that happened.

CHAPTER 82

Mġarr Harbour, Gozo, Malta GC.
Wednesday, 18th February 1987. 19:55.

"Joshua, you know about kidnappings, don't you? All I see and hear in the papers and the TV is 'mistaken identity' or stories like that. The police won't say anything, and Victor only tells me what he wants me to hear. Please help me understand, what's happened?"

Ruxandra's tone was calm, measured even, however it was the call he'd been dreading since he'd heard the news. He'd thought of getting on the first plane to Milan, but quickly put his eraser to that leaden idea. To see Ruxandra face-to-face, at a time like this, could have catastrophic consequences. Sober as he was (*Bound by Hate*, the eighth Scott Finch book was nearing completion) he just didn't quite trust himself; that was the snag.

He'd gathered that Victor Salaviglia was never so much as one metre from her side. Within an hour of hearing the news (it had been a brief telephone call from the kidnappers) Victor had taken full control. Despite her entreaties to remain in Milan, she was immediately hustled out of the city to his chalet in Cortina with a full Carabinieri escort. There in winter, and in the comfort and security of his mountain retreat, they were able to avoid even the most dedicated of newshounds, and danger. The orders of the Milan police officials were overridden too; Victor had marshalled his – not inconsiderable – influence in both Milan and Rome. All telephone links that would have gone to Milan's Questura were now patched through to his secluded Cortina home. In addition, Victor had thrown a cordon of security – private and Carabinieri – to patrol his extensive grounds. The only humans Victor would permit to get within 50 metres of Ruxandra were ones she wished to see.

Joshua Padden had heard of the outreach the Salaviglia family held, despite having only met Victor Salaviglia once – at Pietro's funeral – he saw in him a man of unimpeachable character and few words. A soft-spoken aristocrat whose breeding ran contrary to the accepted notion that independence of mind (and therefore thought) was a dangerous trait for a Sicilian to harbour. Straight away he'd spotted that Victor could sniff out rats, lies and treachery at a hundred paces. It took one to know one.

Somehow the word 'protective' just didn't quite cut it. The 15th Duke wouldn't flinch at luxuriating in the smell of cordite if anyone so much as thought about harming Ruxandra or her son. The Salaviglia family were Sicilians first; noblemen a distant second. People had long ignored that fact. The Salaviglias were ruthless if needs be. And needs did be right now. With over 700 years of warring foreign bloods in their veins, cold-blooded survival of their family was the totality of Salaviglia DNA.

Ruxandra and Salvatore were Victor's family, whatever the Church Marriage Register didn't state. So, God help anyone who got between that bloodline and those he loved, cherished and had sworn (to himself, Padden figured) to protect. Milan and Rome wouldn't have even thought of, let alone digested, those realities. Salaviglia security would wound whoever 'they' were, and then Victor Salaviglia would fetch his own *lupara*, extract what information he needed, and then calmly blow their brains out without blinking one Sicilian eye. Padden had seen his type before. Silently, he thanked Victor for being Victor.

Joshua had witnessed from afar how Victor had given Ruxandra and Toto a rebirth of life itself. They were Albassi in birth, but they were now Salaviglia in life, and no one was a match for Victor. Padden could bluff, kid and banter his way out of any situation with the very best of them – it had been his life's work after all but not with Victor. Not with Toto kidnapped. Different league altogether. Thank you. Padden decided he was better off staying put in Gozo. If he travelled north to Cortina, Victor would smoke out – that he'd played the central role in Pietro's disappearance, within one hour.

"I don't really know anything about kidnappings, Rux. I'm a storyteller, I write pulp stories remember?"

"Oh, Josh, it's good to hear you," she replied, ignoring his get-out remark.

"Thank you. Is there anything I can do? Do you want me to come to Italy?"

He crossed his legs. Please say, 'No', Ruxandra…

"No. You stay and work, Joshua. Finish your books." Ruxandra added, "You know I've read them all?"

"That's more than I've done," he laughed in an attempt to lighten the tone. "Any time day or night. You just have to ask me for anything. Clear?"

"Yes. I know that, dearest Joshua."

There was no time for him to say goodbye, the line just went dead. He guessed that she had a sub-two-minute attention span before grief and terror snaked inside her again. He'd witnessed just what those two emotions had done to her almost nine years ago, when Pietro had 'died'. They'd all but killed her.

He lit another cigarette to chase away the fraudulent taste in his mouth. The ploy didn't work. So, he went to the deep freeze, found an unopened bottle of Smirnoff Blue and a bag of crushed ice. Fuck *Bound by Hate*. Fuck his agent. Fuck Pietro Albassi. Fuck Anthony Bianchi. In fact, fuck 'em all. He was furious now. Furious at the world, but mostly with himself.

Padden filled the tumbler to the brim and listened to the vodka splintering the ice. He had some very serious thinking to do. And he always did that best when several sheets were flapping into the wind. He stepped outside and gazed out over the calm waters of the Comino Channel to study St Mary's Tower the Knights of Malta had built on Comino's far bluff. The night was gin-clear and star-bright, and the rising moon only made his mood worse. He stared up at it all. The Heavens, the Milky Way, the stars above. Then he drained off his glass in one, long swig without pausing.

"Here's to the coming storm," Padden bellowed at the universe, as he threw the tumbler as far as he could into the creeping night. "Who needs a fuckin' glass?" He grabbed a handful of crushed ice from the bucket, filled his mouth with it and took a deep draught from the bottle, and didn't stop drinking until he needed to come up for air.

CHAPTER 83

Rebibbia Prison, Rome, Italy.
Thursday, 19th February 1987. 09:30.

Massina stared blankly into the taxi's wing mirror. The soot-grey bags under his eyes resembled the folds in his room's grungy net curtains. Strange hotel rooms, especially Roman ones, unsettled him. But it felt good to be back doing what he knew best, after two years of a miserable retirement. He lumbered out of the taxi, paid the driver and looked about the desolate prison car park. Nothing had changed other than the quantity of litter.

There was an eddy of newspapers, cigarette packets and candy wrappers fanned by the biting wind. He stamped his feet angrily and dragged hard on another Nazionali. A whip of smoke stung his eye and he checked the lifeless sky; it had the same unappealing hue as old laundry water, or was it the colour of the sea he had so gratefully left the day before? He didn't care so long as he was back on a case. He pulled up the wide collar of his coat, tugged the belt tightly around his impressive girth and, as he did so, he felt the urge to break wind mightily. Even Roman food seemed to disagree with him.

An anonymous-looking dark blue Alfa Romeo saloon, its windows tinted black, pulled into the car park. Massina squinted, using what little strength he had in his eye muscles to pick out Pezzoli's face.

"Not much has changed by the look of him," groused Massina.

A kilo or two around the jowls from too many long lunches, but he still had that furtive, weasel-ish look about him. The sallow complexion over high cheekbones beneath a mop of curly brown hair, continued to make him look as if he had spent his entire life with his nose buried in a physics textbook.

Vice-Questore Luca Pezzoli got out of the Alfa's back seat, dismissed the driver and strode, with an arrogance that came solely from his unstructured Armani suit, towards Massina.

"Some things do change then, eh?"

Massina remembered how Pezzoli used to slope about the office in brown corduroys and ill-fitting sweaters avoiding people in the manner of a woodlouse avoiding feet.

"Believe it or not," – Pezzoli grinned somewhat sheepishly – "I'm very glad to see you."

Together they set off in the direction of the side security door, through which visitors were screened and signed in.

"I assume you spoke to the Governor?" Massina asked.

"Yes, I did, and I've got bad news."

Massina rounded on him. "Bad news?"

"Yes. Bad news."

"Great," Massina replied sarcastically, "what's happened?"

"The good Dr Marco Valente died in an accident four years ago. Found at the bottom of a ravine in Zermatt. He'd been skiing alone, must have fallen badly and over the edge he went. It was pretty messy apparently."

"I wouldn't call that bad news. If you'd told me that he was still alive that would have been very surprising news, but not bad news."

"I don't understand you, Lorenzo."

"Good, let's keep it that way. Now I suppose you're going to tell me Sentini is dead too, and we can just go and get an espresso and a grappa instead."

"You're warm. Sentini is dying, he's in the hospital ward and in isolation."

"What, right this minute?"

"Yes, but he'll live through the next few weeks."

"Sentini, you old Houdini you." Massina smirked, and lit another cigarette.

"He's got AIDS. He's been a heroin addict for years. He was the main dealer in here and broke the cardinal rule: 'Don't get high on your own supply'. Do you know how they shoot up in jail?"

Massina fell silent and turned away from Pezzoli to face the prison wall. Sure, he knew how they fixed in prison. He'd been a policeman for enough years, and besides his own son had died of an overdose fifteen years ago. Pezzoli's new suit of Armani armour may have given him a swagger, but it hadn't raised his tact level above the Plimsoll line.

Oblivious to Massina's disquiet, Pezzoli continued. "Well, what he was doing was filling an eye drop bottle full of cheap brown heroin, sticking a filament from a lightbulb in the end, and opening his and anyone else's veins up to let the solution in. Makes you think, Lorenzo. He'd been running a profitable shooting-gallery from his cell for years. The Governor told me all about it yesterday."

Pezzoli put an arm on his shoulder, but Massina just fired him a stony look.

"All it proves is that there is a God after all. *Andiamo*, Pezzoli, let's not keep a dying man waiting."

Massina kept the contempt out of his voice, but not his expression. He was beginning to regret throwing his fishing tackle in the sea. Even lunch with his wife had a certain appeal over interviewing a dying junkie terrorist murderer, whilst in the company of a congenital moron, who just happened to be his new boss.

A guard signed them in, took Pezzoli's Beretta and escorted them past the cagelike tiers of cells. Massina rubbed his nose, snorted like a truffle hog and felt a few more arteries strain as he did so. Anything to keep the acrid taste of putrefaction out of his own rotting insides. He hated prisons and what they contained. They all smelt like toxic sewers because they were. Liberal whining about wrongly convicted people really incensed him. Everyone inside Rebibbia Prison had bought their own ticket there, one way or another. No one could convince him otherwise. All that made it different from an underground sewer, he thought, were the turds in here just took longer to decompose in their own filth. Convicts were a super-resilient strain of turd, that was all. If they built prisons underground... Now there was an idea he thought, as the white steel doors to the hospital ward clanged open.

"Follow me please." The guard led the way. "Sentini is in an isolation room."

"So much the better for us, we can swap germs," Massina quipped, as the guard peered through the wired pane of glass.

"The Governor told him personally this morning that he'd better cooperate. Apparently, all he did was splutter a laugh. Strange one that Sentini. When you want to leave, ring the bell on the inside of the door, twice."

Pezzoli had only ever seen old press and mugshot photos of Sentini, and it had been almost nine years since Massina had last interviewed him in his king's cell. However, neither man was prepared for what appeared behind the white door.

Nicolai Sentini had not aged at all, he'd simply disintegrated. He'd become a shrunken corpse that happened to breathe on the whim of a malicious and perverse God. A threadbare sheet covered his ankles as he lay half on his side. He wore only a recently soiled and bloodied diaper. Tubes ran into his nostrils from a bedside oxygen cylinder. Three rusting steel frames, like creaky skeletons, besieged Sentini with IV lines of dextrose, saline and medications. And all were pierced into his parchment-thin arms; the old heroin tracks in his veins still livid.

Expressions, normal everyday ones, such as shame, happiness, anger, had long since left his face, which was now just a screen concealing, and none too well, a death-mask. His eyes had sunk so far into his brow they were black indents in a white cliff-face. Withered skin clung to what had once been a powerful frame, as translucent crepe might cover a shoddy lampshade: elbows protruded nakedly, kneecaps jutted like prehistoric cudgels, strips of hair hung from his scalp, as if an eager raven had pecked out clumps, and his fingers were no more than stumps of calcification. A stream of green mucal gob slithered down his chin and dripped in time with his breathing; the putrid stench of death was unbearable. It struck both policemen that the confiscation of dignity was profane. No crime, not even all of Sentini's, fitted this punishment. Even Massina's heart went out to him, albeit momentarily.

"Been a long time, Massina. Heard you retired." Sentini croaked the words through ripped vocal cords, then he coughed so violently his entire body shook as if it had been electrocuted.

"About nine years. I'm a fisherman now. Believe me, it's easier catching criminals than fish."

Massina imagined he saw a smile crease Sentini's face.

"Listen, I get why you're here. I'm blind in my left eye, just like the man I told you we kidnapped all those years ago, with me it's boils and abscesses. All kinds of worms have eaten my left eye, the right one is headed the same way soon. But I got a radio and I'm not deaf, yet." Sentini sucked in air as if it were a joint. "It's the Albassi story, right?" His guttural rasp was controlled, but he continued to dribble as the words formed.

"Yes, it is." Massina nodded, and Pezzoli looked on perplexed.

"You want to hear something, don't you?" Sentini croaked.

Massina nodded and waited for the dying man to regain some strength.

"We never had the Albassi boy's father, and nor did any other splinter group. The Red Brigades were innocent of that one."

"Agreed. You never had him, Sentini. I knew all along."

"Then you didn't believe a word of what I told you that day?"

"Of course not."

"So, I suppose you want to know who put me up to it?"

"No. I know who did, but I do want to hear you say his name."

Massina saw a flicker of hatred in Sentini's right eye, glinting like a switchblade in a moonlit alley.

"You're a piece of work, Massina." Sentini tried to move his head, to sit up. "You've come all this way to hear me say a name you already know?"

"Put like that, Sentini, yes, I suppose I have."

"Alessandro Cuci. The IEA *Capo*." He coughed up more green saliva and it oozed out of the corner of his mouth. "Want something else? He was the one who turned me on to smack. I've got a lot to thank him for."

"Don't blame him for this, Sentini. Don't look to me for sympathy either. You did business with Cuci. He was always going to kill you. No matter how long it took. That's what he does. There's more patience in Cuci than in a deck of cards." Massina paused. "I suppose it would be a daydream to think Cuci told you why he set you up with me all those years ago?"

"Dream on, Massina. Cuci didn't need a motive. His moolah was all up front. Drugs. Money. Hookers. I was paid to say just what I told you. You don't ask for reasons in prison. You take what's going. Anyway, Cuci couldn't have a reason, reasons are only for sane people."

"Sentini, that's the first, and last, time I'll agree with you."

"Now you tell me something, Massina. Has the boy's kidnapping got anything to do with what happened all those years ago?" Sentini's voice dropped to an exhausted, almost dead whisper.

"Truthfully, I think it might have. I'm not sure. It may also be one of those horrible coincidences that keep fouling up my life again and again."

"Coincidences, eh?" Sentini struggled to raise himself up on his left elbow and muster some dignity, some pride. The effort sapped him completely and he collapsed back into his soiled prison sheets.

Massina took Pezzoli by the elbow and turned to leave without saying a word. He pushed the button twice, and the ensuing silence was broken only by muffled sounds and bodily noises emanating from Sentini's deathbed. Even from outside, the same sounds continued. Massina couldn't decide whether they were sobs, or laboured breaths, or pain from internal organs shutting down. He, for one, had neither the courage, nor the will, nor the desire to find out. Whichever they were they belonged to Nicolai Sentini. It was nobody else's business.

In the stark white passage, made even colder by the nakedness of the strip lighting, Pezzoli took Massina to one side, out of the guard's hearing. He paced uneasily on the tiled floor.

"Why would a man like Cuci want to do something like that?"

"You agreed not to ask me questions like that, Pezzoli. If I told you, you would have me committed." Massina was calm, his rheumy eyes held steady. Aggressively so.

"What do we do now?" Pezzoli inched away from Massina. "I'm not sure a confession of a dying convicted terrorist, implicating one of the most influential people in Italy with Vatican diplomatic immunity, could be counted as useful evidence," stated Pezzoli.

"Evidence as to what? You're white-hot as usual, Pezzoli. There's been no crime committed. All Sentini admitted was he lied to me nine years ago about who the Red Brigades had, or in this case had not, kidnapped." Massina ignored the 'No Smoking' signs and fumbled in his coat pocket. "We haven't got any damned evidence of a crime, and what's more, Pezzoli, we won't have in the future."

"What do we do, Lorenzo?" repeated Pezzoli.

"How the hell do I know! You're the Vice-Questore, you tell me. We wait, and then wait some more. That's what we do. Sometimes it's all you *can* do. Cuci has called all the shots for many years. He'll call the next one."

"So…"

"Pezzoli, apart from not catching fish, I've spent my retirement reading. Ever heard of Edgar Allan Poe? I wish I'd read his stuff earlier. He said, *'When investigating a crime, you have to be able to identify with the criminal.'* I can't do that with Cuci any more than you can. He's not of our world or even this world. That's been his key. He's a chimera. An ever-moving shadow who doesn't fit any profile."

"You're sure he's involved, aren't you?"

"You should know, my dear Luca," Massina grinned as he spoke.

Pezzoli shivered. Massina had never called him by his first name before.

"Cuci had you on his IEA payroll for years, didn't he, Luca?"

Massina leered sinfully at Pezzoli, and managed a knowing smirk as his teeth bit into his Nazionali. His lips tightened around the filter, and he inhaled deeply, as if it was his last breath on Earth. He exhaled a cloud of cheap blue-hazed smoke as he shuffled off down the hospital corridor, leaving his new boss anchored – and speechless – to the white tiled floor beneath his expensive Rosetti shoes.

PART FOURTEEN

CHAPTER 84

Lakefront Airport, New Orleans, Louisiana, USA.
Friday, 20th February 1987. 13:05.

Major Harry Noble eased back on the stick of the Learjet 55C/LR ever-so smoothly. The aircraft's sleek nose edged up over the horizon. Its delta fins, under the aircraft's T-tail, squatted into the chop of turbulent air. He spooled up the Garrett engines and it rocketed forward. Barings felt a surge in the small of his back. He gripped the seat's armrest and peered into the cockpit. Terrified, he switched his attention to the cars speeding along Lake Pontchartrain Causeway. He hated flying. And especially on Fridays, which for some reason he'd always associated with the number 13.

"Harry, what kind of approach do y'all call this?" he bellowed to the cockpit.

"It's the shifting winds off Lake Pontchartrain and a few thunderheads in the area. Don't sweat it, Mr Barings, we're almost on finals, gears down and we've got three 'greens'. I'll have you on the deck at Lakefront in no time."

Major Harry Noble, CIA Special Activities Division, and a veteran of the fabled 160th SOAR, was not just on CIA payroll for his exceptional flying skills.

"Just keep it smooth, Harry, OK?"

Baring's southern tones thickened, as it always did when he flew south, and alas, that was all too rare nowadays. Age had not only caught up with him, it had overtaken him at a mustang's gallop. His rough 'n tumble days in Europe, East Berlin, the USSR and the Middle East were but sepia memories. He spied into the cockpit again as the co-pilot ran through his prelanding checks. Sweating, he looked around at the grey leather interior of the aircraft, the only one of its type in CIA's fleet. His rank entitled him to use any of the 'Company's' infinitely more spacious Gulfstream III's. However, he preferred the fact that his (and it was 'his') Learjet 55C/LR could fly higher than any other civilian aircraft. With a ceiling of over 51,000 feet it could fly in clean air, far above the lumps and bumps which, frankly, unnerved him. NASA had designed the Learjet 55's winglets, which had given the aircraft the affectionate nickname of 'The Longhorn', after Texan steers. He liked that. The heady mix of NASA, outer-space tech, and Southern folklore appealed to him. Anyways, the darned plane flew faster than double-struck lightnin'.

When on finals, his thoughts always drifted back to July 1985. To the microblast and wind-shear that had swatted the Omani government's Gulfstream II out of a starless night sky like a stunned fly, just as they were landing on a darkened desert airstrip after a black op in the Yemen. Only he had been able to run, then crawl, out of the hissing flames of the tangled wreckage into the cold desert sand, straight into a raging inferno of Jet A-1 fuel.

An old helicopter pilot's words rang in his ear then, as it did every time Major Harry Noble announced 'Finals': *'Any landing you walk away from is a good landing, any crash landing you survive is just a high-speed arrival.'* The dumb-fuck US Cavalry helo-pilot hadn't mentioned anything about crawling on all fours, whilst your body crisped like a spit-roasted hog. Where was the comfort in those darned words for the two Omani pilots and three of his best CIA agents who'd all perished that night? Five dead. One survivor. Him.

As part of his iron-willed recovery from a pulped ribcage, two broken hips, smashed collar bones, and worst of all, 60 per cent second degree burns, he vowed through the gauze, the IVs and antiseptics in the Muscat hospital that he would never, ever, fly again.

Nevertheless, when he'd recovered, President Reagan's CIA Director William Casey had pleaded with him to return to Langley, the carrot being the No. 2 position, Deputy Director CIA. Before Barings accepted William Casey's promotion, he'd requested a permanently seconded CIA SAD pilot, and as he'd called it, a 'weatherproof' aircraft. Director Casey had been only too pleased to oblige his new DD/CIA. Anything to keep the brave, cunning and shrewd Judd Barings in Virginia. So, the ice-white Lear 55C/LR, with no – *visible* – tail number and only a small CIA insignia on its solitary door, found its way into the CIA SAD fleet, but only after it had been further modified for even more speed, range and ceiling. The aircraft was the sole preserve of DD Judd Barings and Major Harry Noble. Director Casey had kept his word, for DD Barings was cheap at any price.

Barings looked out of his starboard window at the swept wing. He shuddered as it shuddered in the gusty crosswinds. He felt his hands clam against the supple leather. The belt was as tight as it could go and his one remaining lung was as full of as much oxygen as it could hold. Again, he leaned toward the cockpit as Lake Pontchartrain gave way to the threshold of New Orleans' Lakefront runway. Major Noble flared the aircraft and throttled back. The engines hushed eerily. The wheels seemed to hover over the runway until they grazed the tarmac. Major Noble smiled to himself as he eased in the reverse thrust. The DD would be happy. A 'kiss' landing. He could almost sense his boss's pulse beat a retreat.

The Learjet taxied to a halt and the blades of the Garrett engines clattered as they spooled down. The co-pilot promptly opened the stairway door. Barings wiped his hands on his grey flannel trousers, threw on his blue blazer and touched the puckered, heat-seared skin around his eyes and forehead. To try and cover the multiple facial skin-grafts on his forehead with strands of hair was not his way; dumbass comb-overs belonged on politicians and hucksters. He ducked, and stepped out onto the plane's steps, as Louisiana's heat and humidity rose off the tarmac to greet him. Fifty metres away the rear window of a black Lincoln sedan rolled down. He saw a familiar face, one he hadn't seen in a while. His old friend, Saxon Monteleone.

Monteleone's chauffeur, the ever-loyal Charles, broke his stance of attention and opened the rear door. There were less than five people Barings would fly to see nowadays. His old confederate ally was one such man. Barings knew what he had to tell him could only be done face to face.

"Mr Barings, there's a Comsat call just in from Langley," shouted Major Noble as his boss crossed the apron; he held out the bulky white handset as the DD hustled back as best as he could.

"Barings here," he wheezed, out of breath.

His eyes screwed up into the pink welts where his eyebrows once were. Only when the caller had finished speaking did he comment.

"This became public knowledge about an hour ago? Goddammit. Y'all tell me we aren't a day late an' a dollar short here?" Barings listened intently to the reply over the crackle of the satellite phone. "OK, it could be worse. Y'all have Langley's and Milan's cables encrypted, an' sent to New Orleans station. Do it immediately."

Barings handed the handset over and stroked his chin in puzzlement.

"Darn' it, looks like we're overnightin', Harry. Sorry, please phone yer wife."

Without looking back and deep in thought, Barings limp-walked away from his aircraft towards the black Lincoln sedan.

CHAPTER 85

**Monteleone Group Inc., Central Business District,
New Orleans, Louisiana, USA.
Friday, 20th February 1987. 13:25.**

Anthony munched on his po' boy sandwich. The thick French bread was soggy from the meat's juices: the blood from the ground beef, mixed with spicy local sausage and salted butter formed a thick paste. This wasn't healthy food, but it sure tasted good.

Unless an important meeting took him away from the office, as a man of habit and routine, he passed each Friday lunchtime in one of two ways: he'd either stroll a few blocks east, past the strip-joint spielers and noon-day drunks, to Galatoires on Bourbon Street, with a novel for company, and order a Crabmeat Sardou and sip Chablis, or, he'd remain in his office – all calls cancelled – turn his TV to CNN, and have one of the mail-room crew go to Johnny's on St Louis Street for a po' boy. In truth, he preferred his po' boy Fridays to his Galatoires Fridays.

Lately, he had taken to going down to Johnny's himself, where he'd sit in a corner at one of the red and white check tables. Under the flickering neon beer signs and faded photographs, he'd listen to the lonely-hearts music. Johnny would move between the handful of tables, with a word here, a nod there, always an enamel grin plastered onto his bronzed face. As with the staff at Galatoires, Johnny would leave him alone. All and sundry acknowledged his prominence in the Monteleone organisation, and it wasn't out of naivete that he shut off his mind to his position. As far as he was concerned, he had a senior role, enjoyed the confidence of his employer and was remunerated accordingly. He was loyal and always gave his best. Anthony Bianchi was known to be honest, professional and trustworthy; a rare triumvirate in Louisiana. Life was simple. As it had been for nearly nine years.

An unexpected knock at his mahogany office door startled him. He dabbed his mouth with a linen napkin and put down his po' boy.

"Come in," he said, turning down the volume on the TV.

"I'm sorry to disturb you, Mr Bianchi, but there's a Miss Loubiere in reception asking if you're free. Are you?" Hannah, one of his two personal assistants looked nervous. She moved uneasily on the balls of her feet.

"Miss Loubiere? Sure, ask her to come in please. Thank you, Hannah," he replied with an eager smile.

Dawn had never visited his office before – probably because it hadn't occurred to him to invite her – and he'd not been expecting to see her until tomorrow, Saturday. He quickly rearranged his plate and half-eaten po' boy. Out of habit he scanned the stacks of manila folders on his outsize sheet-glass desk. Nothing confidential. The low French sycamore table, which served as his coffee table, was clear too, as were the two three-seat sofas. None of the nineteenth-century woodcuts of Louisiana life which decorated the cream-coloured walls were lopsided. Even his extensive bookshelves were ordered. Good. He suspected she would notice such details.

"Hiya. Sure I'm not disturbing y'all?"

Dawn peeped around the door, armed with a dazzling sunrise smile.

"Positive, come in, an unexpected pleasure on my late lunchbreak."

Any remaining trace of his reticence had evaporated last Sunday night in the warmth of his apartment. They had made love and talked until the French Quarter awoke to a nippy February morning. They had spoken every day, but they hadn't actually seen each other since she had slipped away, reluctantly, that Monday morning just as the first rays of sunlight struck the bedroom's wooden floor.

"What an incredible office! Oh my, such high ceilings and those drapes, are they French? Are the woodcuts genuine?" She paused for breath. "Is this all yer own office, *cher*?"

"No, it's one of Mr Monteleone's, I'm just the resident caretaker until they find someone who can actually do the job properly."

"Always Mr Low-Key. Well did y'all decorate it?"

"I might have helped. I did choose the TV. Come on, sit down." He hesitated. "I missed you."

He motioned her towards the four wing-chairs arranged around another low table of indeterminate antiquity. She ignored him, and instead walked around his desk and kissed him lovingly on the lips.

"Hug please."

It was a command. One he was willing to comply with.

"I know it's late, but I just came by to see if y'all were free for lunch. It's Friday and I was going to treat you at Galatoires. The darned seminar finished early so I left Shreveport this morning."

"That's over 300 miles! What time did you leave?"

"At sun-up, I guess. Besides, I missed y'all too, Mr Bianchi."

"Why don't we stay here, I'll send out for something and we'll go out tonight, after you've rested up. A plan?"

He squeezed her closer to him.

"Sounds good to me, I'll have what you havin'." She peered over his desk at the remains of his po' boy. "Hot an' spicy too, please. I'm a N'Awlins gal, remember?"

"How could I forget!"

Dawn went to the window and idly pulled back the brocade curtains. From the panorama of his twenty-first-floor corner office, with floor-to-ceiling glazing, the French Quarter looked like a collection of pastel toy houses, all of which had been arranged in a neat fashion by a methodical child. At her feet was the tapestry that was the Mississippi: snub-nosed barges, paddle steamers resembling tiered wedding cakes, small tankers, lighters, tugs, submerged tree trunks and the Canal Street ferry doggedly plying its course across the mighty river to Algiers. They all vied for space as the water, brown, mysterious and thick with mud, moved with an imbued purpose after its 2,400-mile southward journey.

"An English poet, T.S. Eliot, called the Mississippi, 'a strong brown god'. I kinda like that," said Dawn, as she stared down at the Mississippi, mesmerised by its ever-changing waltz. She ran her hand through her fine hair and turned around. How she had missed him.

"What are y'all doing for Mardi Gras? It's late this year, Shrove Tuesday is on 3rd March."

"I always go away. The Quarter is madness before Mardi Gras. Mr Monteleone holds an informal convention at the Arbres Plantation for a week or so. Anything to flee the asylum when the crazies take over."

"Does that mean we won't see each other, *cher*?"

"No, but it does mean I will have to ship out on the Monday."

He felt awkward with his reply. This relationship, new-born, was more than important. The four days and nights she'd been in Shreveport, at her zoology convention, had shown him that. Alone at LaBranche her absence had emptied him.

"So, what have y'all got in mind then?" she asked uneasily.

"I can get away at the weekends for sure."

He saw her try to hide the disappointment.

"I think I'd better leave, Anthony. I shouldn't have barged in like this. I'm tired. I'm sorry."

Her eyes, usually so vibrant and clear, flushed pink with confusion. She walked over to him and kissed him on the cheek. "Can we talk this evening, *cher*?"

She stared at the TV and half listened to the newscaster's clipped pronouncements.

"Sure, we can, now if you want to?"

"Now's not the time. Anyway, I've just realised something."

"What's that?"

"The man in front of me is a mystery, and that frightens me more than just a tad." Her smile was tempered with something he couldn't quite read, but it was a smile nonetheless. "Let's talk about it later," she added, turning her attention to the TV to shift the mood.

"Well, what do y'all think of this Italian news, then, Mr Bianchi?" Dawn asked, pointing at the TV.

"What?"

"The story on the TV, the one about the kidnapped Italian boy."

He turned up the volume on CNN's newscaster.

Here's more on the bizarre kidnapping story which, has gripped all of Italy. Our reporter, Susan Gleepo, live from Milan has the story. What have you got for us, Susan?

An attractive woman stood in a melee of other reporters in front of a building flagged *Corriere della Sera*. She appeared to fidget with her earpiece.

Good evening. It's 7.30 here in Milan, and the city is damp and foggy. Italy has been speculating for some days on the motive for the seemingly motiveless kidnapping last Sunday of a seventeen-year-old boy, one Salvatore Albassi, who was snatched near his mother's Milan apartment...

Anthony dropped the TV remote on the floor. His legs went numb and he leaned on his desk for support. Coincidences didn't happen where he came from, and if they did, death was rarely far away. That much he had never been able to forget.

... until one hour ago the speculation in the media has been that the professional kidnapping was one of mistaken identity. There appeared to be no motive, as the boy's mother is a widow and works part-time in an art gallery. The ransom of 2 billion lire, that's over $1 million US, was deemed comical until, as I said, about one hour ago.

The hot blood that had surged through his body one minute before, now ran ice-cold. His chest felt like someone had put it in a vice.

Approximately one hour ago, the kidnappers sent a motorcycle messenger to deliver three large envelopes to the head office of this newspaper, Corriere della Sera, *just behind me. The first contained an increased ransom demand for 5 billion lire. The second envelope had a hacked-off clump of human hair, ostensibly from the Albassi boy's head.*

Anthony fought to squeeze breath down into his chest. But none of his motor responses answered the call.

Contained in the third envelope is what could be the motive. As with nearly all Italy's kidnappings, it has turned out to be money. Kidnapping has been, for many years, as hallmarked an Italian industry as fine shoes and fast cars. The papers inside the third envelope contained a breakdown of the substantial assets, both here and those held abroad, probably illegally, of the 15th Duke of Salaviglia, the wealthy Sicilian aristocrat. The report goes on to prove a long romantic link between the 15th Duke and the missing boy's widowed mother, Signora Ruxandra Albassi. According to the kidnappers, she has been the duke's lover since 1982. The claims are substantiated with photographs of her, her kidnapped son and the Duke on his Sicilian estate, at his ski chalet and on his sailing yacht.

* * *

An image of a round-faced six-year-old boy, his skin darkened by the sun, jumping up and down in the parched dust of a Sicilian summer, flashed into Anthony's memory. The boy, laughing despite his bandaged eye, held a lizard in his cupped hands that he had just painlessly lassoed with a long blade of grass. His best friend Victor was clapping and laughing too. Then they both knelt down on the earth and looked at each other with broad smiles, as the lizard scurried off into the shade of the large rocks.

* * *

As with every drama in Italy, there's always another question behind the curtain. People are now asking why the police have released all this extra information just one hour after the newspaper had received it. Normally, the police here would take time to verify such information. But the usual channels look as if they have all been bypassed. This is most unusual. As yet we have not been able to speak with Vice-Questore Pezzoli here in Milan, who is heading up the kidnap investigation squad. When we do, we will of course update you. Back to the CNN centre in Atlanta.

The TV crew's lights amplified the particles of Milan's icy February fog just as the picture vanished from the screen. Anthony gripped the edge of the desk so hard he felt his knuckles crack.

"Dawn, can you please get me a glass of water? The bathroom is next to the bookcase. Thank you."

His voice held steady and he found the strength to glance away. He needed time. And one minute ago, he realised that he had always needed time. In Milan it had been time. In New Orleans it was time. In Sicily too. It had been forever the same. But right now, he needed time like he'd never needed it before. How he handled the next two minutes, would – of this he was certain – determine so many things.

The bathroom door clicked shut, her footsteps lost in the thick carpet. Thinking on his feet, and with his left eye blank and staring, he grabbed one of his telephones as if it were a lifeline, just as Dawn returned with the glass of water.

"I was taking her to dinner tonight, Mr M. How about I come out to see you early…" he pretended to pause "… That's fine, that's settled. I'll see you then." Behind his back he caught her footsteps as she began to slip away. "Sure, Mr M., we can talk later? I understand how concerned you are about this…"

Before he could complete the sentence, he heard his office door shut. He put the phone down and reached for the glass of water. Next to it he saw a hastily scribbled note in pencil:

'I missed you stranger. Please know that. D x'

No one heard the sound of the crystal glass shatter the TV screen. No one heard his Sicilian heart being rent apart by the red-razored fingers of evil cacodemons. No one.

CHAPTER 87

Questura HQ, via Fatebenefratelli, Milan, Italy.
Friday, 20th February 1987. 19:35.

"Aaaah!"

Massina drew so hard on his Nazionali it fried the tobacco right down to the filter. Nine hundred degrees Celsius of hot air and toxins scorched his lips. Angrily, he jammed the filter into the ashtray.

"It'll kill you, Lorenzo, and if you smoke much more it'll kill me too. Give it up while we both have time."

"Be quiet, Pezzoli. This case will kill me long before cheap Italian tobacco does."

Massina stood up with the TV remote and grazed through RAI Uno, Due, and Tre. All three stations showed the same images, but from different angles. Only the earnest faces and flaxen coiffures of the news reporters differed outside the head office of the *Corriere della Sera*.

"I don't know about you, but I can't take any more of this speculating. What we just did was supposed to put an end to all that." Massina pressed the OFF button.

"Well, it hasn't, Lorenzo. It's been over one hour since we released all the copy documents to the media." Pezzoli stood up, grabbed his elegant grey cashmere overcoat, Italia green scarf and a dated trilby from the hatstand; he fancied himself as an Italian Philip Marlowe. "Come on, I'll buy you a drink, you're going to need one."

"What's that supposed to mean?"

"We're going to have to change our approach," replied Pezzoli. "I've a suspicion that this is a genuine kidnapping, and not some fanciful conspiracy theory of yours, Lorenzo. As you said, this should be a 'shoe-leather' investigation. So, let's start looking for some real kidnappers, shall we?"

"Pray tell me, Vice-Questore, where would you like us to start? North, south, east or west?" Massina lit up yet another Nazionali. "Here's an idea! Let's put the points of the compass in your hat and draw one out? How about that for an idea? You want to waste good cow-skin when we haven't got one hint of a lead as to where the Albassi boy is? The *Corriere*'s security cameras were mysteriously out of action, and no one even saw the bastard who delivered the envelopes."

"Calm down, Lorenzo. We need to forget about your crazy ideas too, which incidentally you refuse to tell me."

Massina aimed his bloodshot eyes at his superior, who was fussily arranging his Italia scarf around his neck as if it were a silk cravat.

"I'm starting to get pressured, Lorenzo."

"Pezzoli, I told you at the very beginning that other people, ice-blooded professional people, not plodders like us, hold all four aces. All we can possibly hope for is to try and catch them *after* they make *their* move. We have to wait and watch. Trust me. They have to move first and believe me they'll do it soon," added Massina.

"It doesn't make any sense."

"You've just worked that out all by yourself? It's no wonder they promoted you to Vice-Questore." Massina leavened his sarcasm with a pat on the younger man's shoulder. "I'll buy the drinks if we get out of this building in one piece," Massina struggled his bulk into his dog-eared coat. "The very last thing we need is a press comment from you. I implore you, Pezzoli, silence please. We *do* have one big advantage now. It's called 'time'. Whoever is behind this could not, and would not, have schemed that we'd let the hounds pick up the scent so quickly."

"Plain talk please, Lorenzo."

"By releasing the information an hour ago, we've cut short the length of their game plan. We've stolen seventy-two, possibly ninety-six, precious hours they were counting on. Those hours were the ones they were reckoning on for us to verify both their demands and information. Ambushing their game plan could force their hand into errors and mistakes." Massina inhaled deeply before continuing, "It's the only chance we've got, Pezzoli. Unless of course you want to return to Plan A with compass-points-in-the hat?"

Vice-Questore Luca Pezzoli's shoulders drooped in defeat. Massina was right. As always.

"Come on, at last we've got time on our side. Let's make use of it. So to the Bar Jamaica, the drinks are on this pensioner. *Andiamo*, Pezzoli!"

PART FIFTEEN

CHAPTER 88

**5120 St Charles Avenue, The Garden District,
New Orleans, Louisiana, USA.
Friday, 20th February 1987. 18:55.**

Anthony brought the Alfa to a slow halt. Dry thunder rumbled in the distance over Lake Pontchartrain. His thoughts immediately flew to Toto, wherever he was. He opened the car door and caught a glimpse of the full moon. Its raw light spilled through the tunnel of august oak trees. His stomach tightened as it always did when he sensed potential danger to be close by. He checked the moon for a second time, and wondered if it was indeed an omen.

As he was neither expected, nor invited, Anthony had parked on St Charles Avenue and not in the mansion's porte-cochère. In front of him were the flight of wide flagstone steps which bisected the three terraces of verdant lawns. His gut-instinct – always on its guard – beat a retreat when he spied a welcoming light shining from what he knew to be an exquisite Belle Époque Venetian chandelier in the dining hall. Monteleone only ever instructed Hippolyte to turn it on, and strike up the beeswax candles on the hall's tables, on the rarest of occasions and only then if he were hosting a close friend.

Anthony checked his Rolex – another gift from his employer – it was time. He'd waited until the sombre Mississippi had summoned the dusk out of a charcoal sky before setting off from LaBranche. He'd driven in and out of the maze that is the French Quarter for an hour in order to clear his mind.

He scuffed the soles of his shoes on the first stone step of 5120 St Charles Avenue, just as he'd done nine years ago. Better dressed now, he fastened the top button of his white shirt, nesting a steel-grey silk knot tightly into its collar, and smoothed out as best as he could the creases of his dark blue suit. He breathed in deeply and ran his hand over his five o'clock shadow. It sounded like sandpaper on wood and he hoped he didn't look as rough as he felt.

His heart hammered in his chest and he craved black tobacco. He could taste its thick, sweet aroma as he made his way slowly up the steps towards his employer's mansion. He pulled on the brass bellpull beside the mahogany door, heard it peel inside and waited for Hippolyte to greet him.

The Monteleone family had always treated him with the utmost respect, but there was every reason to suspect that its patriarch would cease to afford him the same courtesy. Monteleone would have to sit in his black button-backed leather chair – beneath his Machiavelli quote – and listen to a rambling, fantastical tale of lie upon lie: of kidnaps, terrorists, torture, murders, Italian political intrigue, familial desertion, papal death and far, far more. And then, Anthony would have to explain the absurdity of his own very existence and identity which had been stolen from a dead manufacturer of Antipodean jacuzzis. The very fact that the weaver of this vast quilt of lies, and unquantifiable deceits, had been permitted to oversee most aspects of said patriarch's considerable business enterprises (as well as be privy to every detail of his personal life) was beyond preposterous. Such treacheries might well ensure the Monteleone alligators would be dining Italian before sunrise. So be it, he thought, as Hippolyte opened the main doors.

"Good evening, Hippolyte, is Mr Monteleone engaged?"

"Pardon me for saying so, Mr Bianchi, y'all don't look your usual fine self," Hippolyte replied courteously, ignoring the question. "Oh, don't pay me no-nevermind, Mr Bianchi, jus' go an freshen' up. Let me take yo' jacket an' by the time you've shaved I'll return it pressed. Then y'all to show yourself into the dining hall. Mr Monteleone said y'all be passin' by tonight," he said, with a slightly lopsided smile, and an unusual tone of authority.

"Mr M. said what *precisely*, Hippolyte?" Anthony asked incredulously.

"Pardon me, sir?"

"Did I hear you correctly? Mr M. is *expecting* me?"

"No... No..." came Hippolyte's measured reply. "If I do recall, he jus' said for me to have Anna-Mae prepare summin' extra, *in case* y'all *decided* to pass by." Hippolyte held out both his hands. "Let me attend to yo' jacket please, Mr Bianchi. Y'all know where the powder rooms are."

Anthony, mystified, watched as the oldest Monteleone retainer in 5120 St Charles Avenue shuffled off down the worn oak boards of the corridor that led to the domestic quarters, leaving him to stand alone in the vast panelled hallway. And with no instant explanation – he could only put it down to either a casual remark, or his age – he let himself into the ground floor restroom suite.

The cold water refreshed him and the faint tingle from the menthol shaving cream felt cleansing. He'd forgotten how satisfying a wet-shave could be. But there were many things he recognised, as he studied himself in the gilded mirror, that he'd forgotten on his journey to the here-and-right-now. He splashed cologne on his face and opened the door. Hanging outside on a brass hook was his similarly refreshed jacket. He slipped it on, took a deep breath – he was calm – and strode towards the dining hall's double doors as if he were a soldier leaving a trench. He was in a place beyond courage, folly or heroism; he was in a place of single-minded conviction, where character *is* fate.

Anthony opened the doors without knocking and smiled warmly at Saxon Monteleone, the man he had admired like a father, and served like a dutiful son, for nigh on nine years.

He couldn't read the precise facial expression – or body language – unfurling from Mr M. who was seated at the head of the family dining table, other than to perceive that it didn't appear to be immediately welcoming.

CHAPTER 89

**5120 St Charles Avenue, The Garden District,
New Orleans, Louisiana, USA.
Friday, 20th February 1987. 19:05.**

"Good evening, Mr M. I don't want to interrupt you as I see you have company." Anthony's adrenalin rush was brief. "I was passing and saw the lights on, so I thought…"

"Y'all not interruptin', Anthony, pull up a chair on my left please," replied Monteleone in his slow Louisiana burr.

His voice had been thickened by the wine, and his teeth appeared medievally stained. Barely one glass of the magnum of Latour 1945 remained in the decanter. The coffee cups had been discarded. Evidently, an early dinner had already finished. Monteleone considered Anthony with an unyielding stare, eyes like toy marbles; clear, hard and intense as he pulled out a chair and sat down. A coarsely rolled Maduro cigar smouldered in the corner of Monteleone's mouth, and the dome of his scalp was curiously flattered by the diffused candlelight. Taking a long pull on his cigar, he turned to his new guest.

"Anthony, I'd like you to meet an ol' dear friend of mine, Mr Judd Barings. We were at college in Louisiana many moons ago. Mr Barings had won a scholarship from his town, in truth y'all could hardly call it a town, a speck of a place, isn't that right, Judd?" He coughed, and laughed cigar smoke at the same time. "Remind me, Judd, just what was yer Texas phone number?"

"Y'all know only too well, Saxon. It was Mustang 7." Barings faced Anthony across the table. "That's how small my home town of Mustang was, Mr Bianchi. Tell me, just how small was yours?"

"Pretty small, Mr Barings, but not one digit small. Besides, we didn't have a telephone for years. The island of Malta is only nineteen miles long and seven miles wide." The lie was a conditioned reflex.

"Anyways, Anthony" – Monteleone held court from the head of the table – "CIA came a' visitin' on one of their recruitment drives, tapped Mr Barings' shoulder an' scooped him away from all our fun 'n' games at Tulane. They dropped him plum into whatever they do in Virginia, where the northern weather ain't so kind as here, isn't that so, Judd?"

As his employer spoke, Anthony considered the horrifically burn-scarred face, neck, head and hands of the man who sat on Monteleone's right, where he would usually sit in a meeting. Scars aside (he shuddered at how badly disfigured Barings' body must be) the stranger's almost inert, yet powerful, demeanour voiced only patriotism. Anthony had grasped straightaway that his wounds had been inflicted in war and conflict. He'd read the US jingoism of people like him every day: what's right, the greater good, sacrifice, and blood and treasure expended in pursuit of these goals. Life for Mr Judd Barings was truly Stars and Stripes, but in black and white. There wasn't any sunlight that would strike a shadow in this man's life, thought Anthony.

"Mr M., I apologise, I didn't mean to barge in on a college reunion. I'll pass by tomorrow, there's a matter I'd like to speak with you about" – he hesitated – "in private." Turning to Barings he said, "No offence, Mr Barings, sir, as none is surely meant." Anthony slid his chair back to stand up and leave.

"None taken, Mr Bianchi," Barings stood up too. "I was goin' to retire to my rooms anyway. I'll bid y'all a good night. Gentlemen."

"SIT RIGHT DOWN BOTH OF YOU," Monteleone growled at his guests. Leaning forward, he jabbed his elbows on the table. Cigar smoke clouded out of his mouth.

As if flakes of rust were snared in his throat Monteleone hoarsed out, "Anthony, this man is an ol' trusted friend, who's also Deputy Director CIA. For sure he can tell y'all whether that dumb prairie dog B-movie actor livin' at 1600 Pennsylvania Avenue is wearin' Mickey Mouse or Goofy PJs tonight. An' if y'all ask him po-lite-ly, he'll even inform you what bull-crap his wife Nancy, and her tame astrologer, are gonna spoon-feed our President tomorrow mornin' with his warm milk and cereal. So, may we please work on the basis, that anything y'all wanna tell me, y'all may do so in front of Mr Barings. We good here?" Monteleone sat back in his chair and shot Anthony his disarming grin. "Y'all better appreciate, Anthony, that Mr Barings is as serious as the business end of a .45, an' my bettin' is he's probably a-head of what y'all gonna say."

"Respectfully, Mr M., I doubt it. Besides, it'll certainly keep, so, if you will both excuse me." Anthony again rose from his chair and made for the double doors ahead of him. Both his head and heart pounded. With his back to the table, he opened the double doors. He faltered momentarily in the doorway, suddenly feeling faint and hot. A low sound had rung inside his head. It sounded like Mr M.'s. It was deep, but kindly. It seemed to say: *'Sit down please, Pietro'*. Anthony shook his head to dispel the noise, as if purging his ear of trapped water. The same voice then repeated the same invitation. Anthony's hands froze on the brass door handles. He thought he was imagining it, when for a third time the voice whispered the same words.

"We've been together a long time, you an' I. Honour me please an' sit with me an' my friend." Monteleone slowly prised Anthony's hands from the door handles, placed his hand on his shoulder and led him back to the table where he poured him the last glass of wine from the decanter. Monteleone set it down in front of him. Anthony looked at the glass in silence. The colour of the wine was so deep, so dark, it reminded him of the Tyrrhenian Sea; the very sea in which he and Victor had learned to swim.

"Mr M., I forgot to tell you, it's been confirmed that National Security Advisor Robert McFarlane's overdose, on the 10th February, was indeed a genuine suicide attempt. He took twenty-five or thirty Valium. No accident there."

Focus. Business. Focus. Talk business. Anthony told himself, then the confusion will surely dissipate. Pietro? What was Mr M. saying?

"Reagan's NSA was trying to kill himself because he was compelled to give evidence to the Tower Commission on the Iran-Contra deal. Pathetic." Monteleone stayed on topic, and continued, as if to help Anthony, "No one, least of all you an' I, have ever lost a dollar bettin' on the GOP's bottomless appetite for craven self-abasement an' cowardice. McFarlane is livin' proof, an' I say that as a Republican." He whistled on the lit end of his black, Maduro leafed cigar until it crackled and glowed red-hot. It was the only noise in the room. "Now, what is it y'all want to tell me, Anthony?"

Again, the Monteleone smile.

"*Zaffere qui fine passe narien; laute qui pour vini qui li!*"

"Go on, Mr M., what does this one mean?" Anthony grinned with heartfelt affection.

"'*What's past is nothing, it's what's to come that's the rub!*' or words to that effect. Y'all think about it," Monteleone replied.

Anthony sipped his wine and took a deep breath.

"It's a long story. A complicated one too, Mr M., which doesn't reflect well on me."

"We're not rushin' to get on our a'plane, so take your time, Anthony." Again he blew on the tip of his cigar. "OK, I still call you that?"

"Of course," he responded, off-guard.

"Mr Barings' ain't in no hurry either, are you?"

Barings sucked air into his one functioning lung. He stared across the table and said, "I'm good to stay too, Signor Albassi."

As conspirators do, Monteleone and Barings shared eyes.

"So, Anthony, let's hear yer tale, I already heard Judd's. I'm not gonna rain on your Mardi Gras, but I do have to tell y'all that I knew your true identity a month after y'all came to teach my son Italian. How many years ago was it?" He ignored Anthony's startled expression. "Almost nine years an' no dimes, 'bout right? It was inconceivable that I could *not* know. After coupla' months I realised you could be my eyes, my ears, my hands. Understand, I *had* to know. We are the Monteleone family. Y'all think we let strangers into our livin' lives?"

"Yet you still took me in?"

"Of course! An' this is your story not mine, now git on an' tell it."

Monteleone glanced again at Barings, then ranged his narrowed eyes back on Anthony, who wondered if Mr M. had been too liberal earlier with his speed; his pupils were like small calibre bullet holes. Damn you, Joey, he thought silently as his boss continued to speak. "All I will say, is, what y'all did back in Italy took real courage. More darned courage than I've ever had. You see, I figured y'all had nowhere else to go, you'd run as far, an' as fast, as you could. In fact, further than any man could."

"Is that all, Mr M.? You figured I was desperate and running on empty?"

"Of course not. There were other reasons" – he coughed – "'*C'est le vent ka vente, moun ka ouer lapeau poule*', an' that belongs to the slaves from the West Indies: *'It's when the wind blows that you can see the skin of the fowl'*. I well-like that sayin'. I saw more than skin during those early months back in 1978. Y'all were as naked as a peeled Mojave rattler, let alone a chicken. Let's just say w'all have reasons for our actions *and* our inactions."

With those words, Monteleone lit a fresh cigar. Thick, purple smoke curled up and out of his beard. No one spoke. Both Judd Barings and Anthony Bianchi understood that now was not the time to utter a solitary word.

"Y'all have the floor, Anthony," Monteleone announced, when he was good and ready.

For almost two hours Anthony Bianchi recounted Pietro Albassi's history. Both Saxon Monteleone and Judd Barings listened in a captivated, grim, silence. Not one question was posed, and not one interjection was made, such was their respect for the manner in which the pages were being turned by the Italian man seated at the table.

He told his audience little of what of his life was before Milan, other than that he had been born an orphan in a war-torn Sicily in 1944. His father was, supposedly, a GI in the Seventh Army serving under General Patton fighting their way northwest, and his mother was a Sicilian who'd died in childbirth. But he held tightly inside his heart, the blessed life the Salaviglia family had bestowed on him when he had ceased being an orphan. And during his telling of his narrative, he saw that his life in Sicily was, perhaps, his *only* real life. His story went on to include his wife Ruxandra, their twin children, Paola's 'accident' and her subsequent death, and his everyday lawyerly existence in Milan.

Then, he fast-forwarded to 1978. He spoke of, and speculated about, his involvement as a go-between in the Moro affair with its endless 'cat 'n' mouse' plotting and deceptions between the Red Brigades, the Christian Democrats, the Communists, the Vatican, and so many other players, all of whom read like a cast-list in a Donizetti opera. Then came the inevitable execution of Aldo Moro after fifty-four days of captivity, in its wake trailing the rancid fetor of death, failure and futility. How he was 'set up' by his boss, the shady power-lawyer, Enrico Scampidi. The involvement of the lawless criminals in P2 – with the Vatican's IEA – in the murder of Pope John Paul I after just thirty-three days in the September of the killing year that was 1978. How he had faked his own death and fled Italy, as Paola lay in a coma, in order to protect Ruxandra and Toto, in what was, he admitted, a Sicilian act of tragedy crashing headlong into fate. He had cared not for his own life, only for his wife's and what was then their two children. The ensuing getaway, in a berth on a Malaysian cargo ship he'd bribed his way onto in Lisbon, which had led him finally to New Orleans. And how only later, when in New Orleans, he'd discovered in an Italian newspaper that a corpse, bearing his name, had been buried in what had been his local Milan church, did he know for certain that he had taken the correct decision.

He surprised himself at how remote – detached even – he was during the recounting of the seemingly fantastical story. The only truths he was economical with concerned Joshua Padden, and his conviction that the IEA and its head, Alessandro Cuci – with the help of CIA – were intricately involved in the murder of a First World leader. He was sparing too about his children: Paola dead and Toto now *kidnapped and whereabouts unknown*. Reticently, he confessed that Toto's kidnapping was the sole reason his for presence in Monteleone's dining hall tonight.

The telling and the memories – fresh, raw, and elusive – led him, exhausted, to a silent moment of reflection before he concluded his long narrative with one sentence:

"Gentlemen, 3,206 days ago today I committed an act Italians might call *suicido bianco*."

* * *

Barings was the first to speak.

"Mr Bianchi, let's keep that name please. I've a dime's worth to add if y'all don't mind?" He turned to Monteleone who nodded his approval imperceptibly.

"I was CIA Head of Station in Rome in 1978 at the time of the Moro affair. I knew nearly all that happened, officially an' unofficially. Now, sir, I'm using the word 'nearly', an' I'll come to why later. However, I was aware of Signor Albassi's role. In January 1978, just one year into his term, President Jimmy Carter's Secretary of State Cyrus Vance stated, an' I quote, as I've never forgotten it, *'The US State Department would like to see the Communists hold less power in Italy, not more'*. CIA's mandate is for foreign soil ops only. We're apolitical an' follow orders from our

Commander-in-Chief. As near as dammit, what I just quoted to y'all was a clarion order. Wind the clock back to an earlier time, to 1976 an' '77, before the Moro affair. My then boss, the Director of the CIA, was George H.W. Bush, who today resides at No.1 Observatory Circle, Washington DC as Reagan's Vice President. Some say Bush is the *de facto* President, as good ol' Ronnie is not with us oftentimes. Anyways, I digress. Director George Bush fostered the beginnin' of the American anti-Moro sentiment, because of Moro's diehard commitment to a coalition of his Christian Democracy and the Italian Communists. End o' January 1977, my new CIA boss, who'd been appointed by President Carter, was Admiral Stansfield Turner. He picked up Bush's CIA sneaky leads an' threads. Turner was a naval officer, not a politician, an' he simply ran with Bush's plans. So, we had wild anti-Moro sentiment an' planning from the US.

Washington refused to countenance even one tiptoeing communist into a powerful European government, a US ally an' NATO member. All this Italian confusion an' hostility towards Moro, as y'all surmised earlier, was seized by one Alessandro Cuci, Head of the Vatican IEA. Cuci saw an openin' for his own personal agenda, as well as an opportunity for a power-grab in Italian politics, the Vatican an' beyond. Don't y'all forget the factions in Moro's own Christian Democracy party who also wanted Moro dead an' gone too which only served to help Cuci. I, as CIA HoS in Rome at the time, played second fiddle to Cuci in the Moro affair. I won't deny that within these walls. Outside of 'em, I will. The US *did* want to see the end of Moro an' his plans but, perhaps, *all* yer problems began with the IEA, not with the CIA. It was Cuci who put y'all into bat, Mr Bianchi, his doin' all alone too."

Anthony reflected for a long minute on what the man who'd been CIA Head of Station, as well as Cuci's Confederate in Arms in 1978, had said.

"How so, Mr Barings?" Anthony asked evenly.

"My mama used to say that it's rude to answer a question with a question, an' beggin' her forgiveness, may I ask y'all a question by way of reply?"

"Of course."

"Do y'all recall any specific details about the documents left beside the Alfa Romeo saloon that had been driven by yer office gofer, Joseph, on 12th May 1978, the day y'all disappeared?"

"Impressive, Mr Barings." Anthony frowned in admiration.

"Respectfully, Mr Bianchi, I'd hoped y'all have figured out that I do know the details. However, I was not involved, or informed, of every action."

"To answer your question, no, not specifically. I do remember wiping my blood on various files, the Moro/IEA ones I always kept with me. Mostly they were handwritten notes and schematic threads, some typed and detailed."

"As I suspected. Coincidence got y'all into this."

"What?"

"The papers, the ones y'all left behind, smeared in your rare AB-blood-type…"

"I'm persuaded you're fully informed," Anthony interrupted. Barings ignored him and continued.

"….beside the wounded driver, an' in the car itself, were your extensive Moro notes. However, inside that Moro folder was another one, it was manila and it was empty. But it was marked 'IEA /Alessandro Cuci/ Aldo Moro'."

"More of an explanation please, Mr Barings?" Anthony asked eagerly.

"Well, Alessandro Cuci is kinda like our own J. Edgar Hoover. A wildly paranoid, file-keepin' rabid homosexual, an' neither of their elevators visit the top floor, if y'all get my meanin'? Cuci is even more ruthless than J. Edgar was. Oh, by the by, they both hated communists too."

Barings' pink, rimless eyes bulged from the cigar smoke, and he squinted before he was able to carry on. Meanwhile, Monteleone, oblivious to his friend's discomfort, sat in silence at the head of the table, like a tennis umpire keenly watching a long rally between two top players.

"Go on please, Mr Barings."

"Yer livin' was a direct threat to Cuci's survival. Be under no illusion, Mr Bianchi, Cuci belongs in a padded cell awaitin' immediate psychosurgery. I'm not tellin' y'all this to make y'all feel any better, but y'all were correct that Cuci would, in the end, have had you, Signora Albassi, your twins, an' even Enzo killed at some stage." He paused, not for effect, but more for his own mettle. "Mr Bianchi, Signor Albassi, please hear me now. CIA had no involvement, or prior knowledge, an' moreover we would never sanction an operation like the one we believe Cuci engineered with regards to yer daughter and family. What we found out was *post facto*. Y'all have my solemn oath, sir."

They stared at each other in silence. Anthony intuited that Deputy Director CIA Judd Barings was not bearing false witness.

"As far as we knew Pietro Albassi was simply an honest-to-goodness, hard workin' cut-out an' go-between, albeit in the service of Scampidi an' the IEA, to give the Red Brigades an' the rainbow of politicos y'all have in Italy, some kinda cover. So, Italian crime an' politics as usual, then? But when y'all add into the pot Albassi's bloodstained secret IEA files, an' spice it up with some Cuci voodoo..." Barings let the sentence complete itself.

"I knew CIA were involved in almost every step of the Moro affair, Mr Barings. They had to have been. CIA was the backbone of the operation, even before the kidnap itself."

"How come y'all figured that, Anthony?" Monteleone butted in.

"Simple, Mr M.," he responded steadily. "Anything executed with the precision of Moro's kidnap, and his fifty-four days being hidden, secretly, in Rome, could not, by any definition, be of Italian origin. Italy makes Ferraris, Mr M. They're works of art, but they break down all the time. As for the Red Brigades acting alone. Impossible. Buying black market guns, dynamite and killing capitalists was the limit of their talents."

Anthony rounded on Barings.

"A question if I may, Mr Barings, and I'd like the truth. I am a Sicilian, I have one blind eye, but it sees nonetheless. It knows, believe me." He hesitated. "My daughter Paola. What happened?"

"Shall I answer that with what I know to be fact, or would you like my own personal opinion as well?"

"Both please. I think we have an understanding of each other."

"I have no concrete proof the IEA had a hand in the road accident which befell yer daughter, an' I surely dug deep holes to find out." He lingered. "My personal belief is that the IEA, an' therefore Cuci, were capable of this atrocious crime. My profound understanding of the man informs me that he orchestrated the death of your daughter, Paola."

A tomblike silence enveloped the table. Five eyes met in the middle, as if they too were forging a secret cabal, which in fact, perhaps, they were. The mood shifted in that instant. Each of the three men sensed it in their bones.

Now, and for the very first time, they were equals.

***

"Thank you for your frankness, Mr Barings." Anthony splintered the quiet, it was correct that he should speak first. "Please continue then."

"As you wish. The truth is the day you vanished, Cuci became obsessed with findin' you. Y'all were like a poison to him, a cancer ever flowin' through his bloodstream these last years. Every once in a while, it stops to form another metastasis before it moves on inside him. When that happens, he's off across the plains on another wild goose chase. No one, least of all him, can treat his condition because no one can locate you. Y'all had evaporated into thin air, remember? Y'all were, an' are, the cause *an'* the effect. The cause was in the wind long ago, but he has to keep on cauterisin' its effect." He nodded at both men. "Saxon, Mr Bianchi, y'all have to love the twist Cuci has to deal with, and this is doin' a fine job of dealin' with him."

"A question, Mr Barings. CIA worked alongside the IEA. You knew where I was, and as is apparent, you also knew of my new identity. Why didn't you come after me? You could have told Cuci?"

"I'm not a screechin' bullbat, Mr Bianchi. Y'all are no threat to me whatsoever. Never have been. As long as I knew where y'all were, I was OK with the situation," answered Barings. "I did however throw the Vatican coyote some poisoned meat last year. Langley gave him a fake dossier w'all had concocted. It told how we'd tracked y'all down to Zimbabwe, an' that y'all had been killed in August 1985 in a grisly car crash. Y'all were a roving farm hand by the way. We'd covered all our tracks an' yours too, but he didn't believe our report."

"OK. Am I supposed to thank you?"

"Not at all. Y'all have to grasp that I liked what y'all were doing to Cuci. Your livin' was, an' remains, his dyin'. Your very existence is like eatin' supper without sayin' Grace – it's sinful but sure tastes good. Ah, the irony of it all" – Barings managed a thin laugh – "off the trail again. Back to the matter at hand. I'm of the firm belief that Cuci has coordinated the kidnapping of yer son. Salvatore is possibly the last way he knows of flushin' y'all out, if y'all are still alive. He's had far too many sleepless nights over you. He's as desperate, an' as starvin' as a black vulture in August."

"Nothing is random in this world. Nothing. Where I come from coincidences don't happen, and if they do, as a Sicilian you're born not to trust them."

"If I may say so, Mr Bianchi, y'all bein' mighty controlled here."

"The last nine years hiding in a new life taught me control."

Barings focused his eyes on Monteleone, who had remained steadfastly quiet throughout.

"I see why you hired this man, Saxon," declared Barings, his cruelly disfigured face flashed an expression, one that Anthony read to be one of respect. Behind his cloud of cigar smoke, Monteleone nodded.

"My son's kidnapping was never about money," Anthony announced. "My childhood friend, Victor Salaviglia is wealthy, but is the son of his lover a 5 billion lire target? No. Is kidnapping a big industry in Italy anymore? No."

"I agree," replied Barings. "My gut instinct on learnin' about Signora Albassi's connection with Victor Salaviglia was that it might be a genuine kidnappin'. However, five minutes of considered thought, coupled with my knowledge of Cuci, an' I dumped that idea into the swill."

"Anthony," Monteleone waded in, "I'd like to add that Judd phoned this mornin' an' asked to see me. Never a hardship that. Y'all know how much I detest the television an' newspapers an' all. He'd guessed that I wouldn't have heard about the kidnappin' of your son. 'Fraid to say he was right. Oftentimes, what's happenin' outside the Gulf States irks me. Y'all been my eyes an' ears for a long time. I'm so very sorry."

"Mr M., I've never asked you for anything before, have I?"

"Not that I can think of, apart from havin' Joey feed that darned parrot of yours when y'all away."

"I would like to ask you and Mr Barings for three undertakings, please."

Monteleone and Barings looked at each other and silently concurred.

"Thank you. Firstly, Mr M., I would like two weeks leave of absence. Not once have I requested vacation time. Serving the Monteleone family has been my life for nine years. I've never wished to leave your side," Anthony stated proudly.

"Agreed," Monteleone cut in.

"Thank you, Mr M. Secondly, I would need your word that you will take my secret to your grave. Enough damage has already been done to too many people. Should I not return from my leave of absence, you will need to die with the lie, especially with regards to Miss Dawn Loubiere."

"So that's the lucky gal's name." He shot Anthony that smile again. "Y'all have my solemn oath on that request too."

"Thank you again, Mr M.," he said turning to face Barings. "From you, sir, I need a telephone number and an address."

"A telephone number?" Barings replied quizzically.

"Yes. A man named Joshua Padden. He's a writer. P.J. Fowler is his pen name. Last known residence, the island of Gozo in the Maltese archipelago."

"I heard o' his name an' his pen name. CIA has had an extensive file on him from his Asian, how to say, 'adventures'. Consider it done, Mr Bianchi." Barings concluded with as near a smile as his mouth and eyes could manage.

"By way of explanation, I should say that for the first time since I left Italy in May 1978, I need to be back on Italian soil."

"Y'all not going to try anythin' stupid, now are you?" Monteleone asked.

"Mr M., I am a lawyer in my early forties. I'm in reasonable shape, but I'm not Ronin and the Magnificent Seven rolled into one."

"A man of your obvious intelligence, cunnin' an' instinct for survival would never have thought of offerin' himself up to Cuci?" Barings attempted to mask his sarcasm. He failed.

"I'm not sure that would achieve anything."

"It would actually achieve two things. Two dead corpses floatin' in the Tiber, one bein' yer son. Remember, Mr Bianchi, if y'all gonna run with the big dogs, you gotta be a big dog yourself. If not, y'all will get bushwhacked for sure."

"Judd, tell me something," interrupted Monteleone, "if Cuci is this dangerous, then how come CIA didn't punch his ticket long ago?"

"Easy answer," Barings retorted quickly, "we were so far down a short-assed runway, with an overloaded a'plane, an' by that, I mean CIA had aided in the kidnappin', an' murder, of a First World leader. A NATO Italy ain't El Salvador, Nicaragua or Panama, an' the trees at the end of the runway kept loomin' bigger an' bigger. By then, well, Cuci an' the IEA had ring-fenced themselves with all manner of dossiers on CIA ops. Covert an' not so covert that we, the State Department, an' the US Military had undertaken in Europe, the Middle East an' South America. Fat files, Saxon. A leak of any one of those would have caused more fallout than y'all could shake a stick at. Cuci has an army of more than 750 million Catholics who pay him to be agents. Think on that. Incredible." He leaned forward to emphasise his finale. "No, Saxon, he was, an' is, too hot even for us to handle. The Mossad too. I had two meetins' in Israel an' none of us could find aways 'round the ranch," and without a trace of irony, he added, "Y'all see why I like our Mr Bianchi. He's doin' a fine job killin' Cuci for me, an' that's why I need y'all alive an' outta sight, Mr Bianchi. Clear on that?"

"Yessir, as clear as high noon in Texas," he replied jokily, as he stood up. "One last question. How *did* you find me, Mr Barings?"

"Luck plays a very mean hand in our game. Call it one of yer Sicilian coincidences." He paused. "If y'all hadn't had plastic surgery here in New Orleans, we'd never have been the wiser. Whoever arranged your new legend, an' new IDs, did a mighty fine job. We suspected Mr Padden, but we had no proof. Besides, it didn't matter, we knew where y'all were after Dr Juddah Fogg's carvin' knives were done with you."

With those words, Barings stood up, extended his scorched hand across the table, and shook Anthony's hand as best he could. "Goodbye Mr Bianchi, it has been a very real pleasure, an' I do mean that. By tomorrow mornin' an envelope containin' all the details of Mr Padden's whereabouts will be on the doormat of your splendid apartment at the LaBranche House." His mouth, so brutally deliquesced by flames, just could not camouflage his droll smile.

"Anthony, I'd like your word now," boomed Monteleone, as he stood in front of his dining chair, "no playin' the hero an' no givin' yourself up to this madman. That's my only condition here. Y'all have the full resources of our organisation at your disposal, if y'all decide to use them. That'll be yer call alone. We agreed?"

"Yes, Mr M., You have my word," Anthony replied and extended his hand. Monteleone didn't shake it as usual; instead he clasped it in both his hands and held it tightly for a slow moment. Anthony went to the dining room doors and turned around. "I can't recall who it was who said something like, *'Show me a hero and I'll write you a tragedy'*. There've been too many tragedies and I'm no hero."

Monteleone called after him. "It was F. Scott Fitzgerald, an' he also wrote, *'There are no second acts in American lives.'*"

"I'm not an American, Mr M., I'm a Sicilian," Anthony fired back, as he closed the dining room doors behind him.

CHAPTER 90

**5120 St Charles Avenue, The Garden District,
New Orleans, Louisiana, USA.
Friday, 20th February 1987. 21:05.**

Only after Monteleone had heard the main door of 5120 St Charles Avenue close, did he switch his scrutiny to his old college friend.

"Please can y'all watch over him, Judd?" Monteleone asked bluntly.

"Difficult without showin' my hand. If Cuci found out CIA knew about this, well, I don't even want to contemplate the fallout. But I'm not about to let him walk through the Valley of Death, am I? Anyways, I can't afford for those two to meet." The pink scar-tissue where his eyebrows once were moved in consternation. "I'll assign an agent from the Rome station. There's a real capable Texan gal, fluent Italian, an' quicker than a yaller dog. But, I repeat, no guarantees," Barings added emphatically.

"Thanks, Judd, yer best is always good enough for me. Y'all reckoned he's my adopted son, right?"

"I caught that. Bianchi was in real' tall cotton with y'all tonight, Saxon."

Both men rose from the table at the same time. Monteleone looked at the vacant chairs, picked up a candle snuffer and extinguished each in turn. Slowly, the dining room's golden light dimmed into a melancholy Louisiana night.

"Y'all know far more than you told me, or him for that matter." Monteleone caught a sly glimpse in his friend's expression. "Do y'all know where they have his son?"

"I do know more than I told him, an' you too Saxon. But where they're holdin' his boy ain't clear. Cuci's good. We've only two leads. W'all think he's way up north, in the hills. Brescia, Lombardy, or thereabouts. We also heard Milan brought out of retirement an ol' police Inspector who'd worked on both Albassi's vanishin' act, an' his 'murder'. By all accounts the man's colder than a nun's kiss, an' madder than a wet hen. Great combination in my book. So far, that's all the intel w'all have on the ground from Italy. Gettin' leads outta there is like hollerin' down an empty well. I told y'all that Cuci is as crazy as a cut snake an' slicker than a boiled onion."

"I hear you, Judd. Just keep me informed please."

Barings put an arm on Monteleone's troubled shoulder, and walked with his friend through the mansion's dimly lit corridor into the main hall, where the carved oak staircase awaited them both.

CHAPTER 91

**5120 St Charles Avenue, The Garden District,
New Orleans, Louisiana, USA.
Friday, 20th February 1987. 21:10.**

Anthony leaned on the roof of his old red Alfa Romeo Spider and gazed up at the dining room's bay windows illuminating the front lawns. He waited until the candles and lights had faded, and the two figures had disappeared into the silhouette of the great mansion. The night air was clammy, humid too. Low clouds were pregnant with rain soon to be born. *Benvenuto a febbraio a New Orleans*, he pondered as a full, vibrant moon emerged unexpectedly from a billow of clouds and tendrils of Spanish moss. As he studied the cratered moon, his memory retreated into the earliest days of his Sicilian childhood, and all that he had absorbed over the years, just as Bonnera's soil had devoured the November rains. Suddenly, he realised that all his life had been a journey, a rehearsal, to this very moment in time – the reason he was born. Patience, cunning, calm, timing, planning, courage, dexterity, with his touch and his skills – native, taught and learned – would all be needed if he were to succeed in catching the next lizard.

* * *

"Sssh... Sssh..."

Victor stiffened as Pietro put his finger to his lips. They stood on a rough plateau of hefty stones and rocks clumped together where wild goats often roamed. Bonnera was barely visible in the far distance. This spot, amongst the rough weeds and under a scorching sun, was their favourite place for the 'Lizard Game', a game Pietro always seemed to win. Victor didn't mind, for he loved all games – especially this one – and the company that went with them.

The rules of the 'Lizard Game' were simple: each boy chose three rocks and lifted one after the other in turn until a lizard was found. Then he had to try and catch it, without hurting it, using only his bare hands, blades of grass or small sticks. To win, the lizard had to be held in cupped hands for a few seconds, before setting it down, free to scurry for cover.

Victor liked to use his bare hands, but Pietro only ever used long blades of wild grass. He would pluck one, examine it, and tug at it before making a running noose at one end. He held the primitive lasso in his right hand as he crouched down onto his haunches. With his left hand, he gingerly lifted each stone with a stick until a lizard, with furtive eyes and a body the colour of an olive yet to ripen, appeared. And when one did, Pietro inhaled deeply, held his breath and bored his one eye into the reptile's two eyes. The lizard didn't flinch. Silently, and with stealth and patience, Pietro slowly swung his right hand into a high, wide arc to come up on the lizard from behind. The lizard, hypnotised by Pietro's one eye, registered no movement. Its head squatted lower and its furtive tongue retreated. Frozen in the raw sun, it neither moved nor blinked. And still Pietro continued to stare it into the ground; his look so concentrated, the creature became as solid as the rock that had hidden it. Then, with infallible timing, Pietro unleashed a bolt of lightning in his right arm, and snapped the running noose around the lizard's neck to let the reptile wriggle harmlessly in mid-air. Gently, Pietro cupped it into in his hands and lowered it back into the dust to set it loose.

* * *

Anthony wasn't so sure he'd set the next lizard free.

PART SIXTEEN

CHAPTER 92

Fiumicino Airport, Rome, Italy.
Sunday, 22nd February 1987. 11:05.

Joshua Padden waited anxiously at the International Arrivals gate for Alitalia's New York passengers to be disgorged. A ten-hour red-eye flight can drain anyone, and he was painfully aware that he'd not taken into account what changes nine years on the run could have wreaked on his friend. He was afraid that he wouldn't recognise him.

Padden knew that he hadn't changed that much, more jowly perhaps, aged a bit for sure, but he was counting on Pietro – or was it to be Anthony? – recognising him. So, he'd dressed as he always did: a crumpled dark brown linen jacket with his customary red and white paisley handkerchief stuffed in the top pocket. He wore a blue polo shirt, half-moon reading glasses hung from his neck, and his chinos were creased as usual. The Docksiders were probably the same ones he was wearing the last time he saw his friend in 1978.

Padden needn't have worried. First out of the automatic doors, and carrying a slim black document case under his arm, a tall, broad-shouldered man with gently greying hair strode towards him. He was dressed in a dark blue tailored suit, a mid-blue shirt with no tie. A black cashmere overcoat draped off his forearm. The man, in his forties, had a ramrod straight back and sported a generous smile which creased around his eyes and radiated good health. About right thought Padden. Behind, a porter trailed in the man's wake with three large cases.

Padden grabbed his canvas holdall and lurched forward to bear hug his friend. They held each other tightly and in silence. There were no words that could add anything to their embrace. Even the porter sensed this and kept a few paces back.

"Look at you," Padden said, running his hand over his friend's face as a lover might do. "Is it Pietro or Anthony?" he whispered.

"Anthony, of course. I'm your creation, Josh," he laughed in reply, and found himself comforted by the reek of alcohol on his friend's breath. He wanted, no needed, a predictable ally for what he had in mind.

"Let's get out of here. Airports and hospitals are hateful places," Anthony said, before speaking to the porter in Italian. Padden picked up the word 'taxi' out of the quick exchange.

Once outside the terminal, Padden lit up a much-needed cigarette before saying, "Thanks for calling, and I'm sorry we're meeting like this. Toto's kidnapping has been the only story here. I arrived from Malta this morning." He hesitated. "Where are we going to stay? What's the plan?" Padden's eyes blinked with nerves and questions. "It's been a long time, eh?"

"Yes, 'Prison Time' as they say."

"You must be tired. Sitting down the arse-end of a 747 from New York can't have been a picnic." He toked hard on his cigarette before grinding it into the pavement.

Anthony didn't want to tell him that he'd planned his return to Italy with more precision than he had his escape: he'd worked all Saturday since first-light, before leaving New Orleans in the afternoon on the Monteleone Gulfstream IV. Following his instructions, the Monteleone pilots had filed a flight plan for Teterboro, New Jersey, from where he'd taken a regular Town Car service to JFK to board, first class, the direct Alitalia flight to Rome which left at 19:45. The G-IV, from New Orleans – with a hot-fuel stop in the Azores – would have been quicker, easier and more comfortable. However, Anthony knew, and it was his job to know such things, that all international private aircraft were tracked by different intelligence services. There was also a 1/1,000 chance a plane spotter, or worse, would tag the distinctive green and brown Oak Tree logo on the G-IV's tail above the airplane's N5120M registration. To hide in plain sight on an Alitalia flight from New York was far safer for the homecoming of an Italian fugitive.

Anthony put his arm around Padden's shoulder, and noticed how stooped he'd become. The same irascible expression and warmth still oozed from his very being. Yet age, booze, cigarettes and Annie's ghost seemed to have caught up with him. A Rome taxi pulled up and the driver opened the boot. The porter heaved the three cases and Padden's holdall into the taxi. Anthony peeled off 20,000 lire and thanked him.

"Hotel d'Inghilterra *per favore*," Anthony instructed the driver, and settled back into the vinyl seat. He wound down the window to let fresh Italian air wash over him.

For quite some minutes, all that intruded into the taxi was traffic noise. He'd forgotten just how often Italian drivers used their horns, and how dangerously they drove. The only road law in Italy is the one of survival, even on pedestrian crossings. It was as if the accelerator were an on/off switch: flat out or stopped dead in a jam.

"I'm not sure how to say this, Anthony" – Padden had his elbow on the open window – "but you've no idea how good it is to see you. The torment of not knowing whether someone you care about is dead or alive eats at a man's insides." He turned to face Anthony. "Did you read my books, the codes, the clues I put out there?"

"I learned of Paola's death in *A Man Possessed*, and there wasn't one P.J. Fowler book I didn't devour. All you got in exchange was a postcard from Hawaii." He looked at Padden straight in the eyes. "Without your help all those years ago, Josh, Ruxandra and Toto would be stone dead. They killed Paola. I now know that to be fact. Ruxandra and Toto are only alive because of you. Never forget that, my friend. I don't. Ever."

Padden fished a soft pack of Marlboros out of his pocket, flipped one into his mouth and lit up. He exhaled out of the window, alone with Anthony's alarming statements. Anthony decided not to relay Judd Baring's compliment about his friend's skill; it would only beg yet more questions and he would be honour-bound to answer them. Now wasn't the time. He had to remain focused.

"The last time I had a cigarette was the day I read of my own funeral in an Italian newspaper. I can draw you the picture: a dingy bar on Bourbon Street, New Orleans. Dean Martin on a jukebox and I was late for work," he sighed, "and I worked as a ghost on a funfair ride in an amusement park."

"Whoa! That's a tale!" Padden shook his head. "I tried to quit and failed, although I managed to stop smoking in the few hours I sleep. Smoking whilst asleep is a health hazard." Padden was always ready with a wisecrack when apprehensive, like he was now. "When you called you said that New Orleans was home. That still the case?"

"It was until yesterday morning when the bags were finally packed.

Home is the Hotel d'Inghilterra, Rome." Weariness suddenly came over him like an all-body cramp, as the taxi weaved its way through the one-ways and switchbacks of central Rome.

"After all my years in Southeast Asia, I still have issues with Americans. Not my sort of people. I survived too much of their carnage. I could never settle there. I even said a flat 'no' to the US book tours."

"Josh, it's a simple country. The wide-eyed, big-pawed approach to everything somehow redeems it."

"Does that bullshit mean you actually like it there?"

"Same old Josh," Anthony laughed. "I like New Orleans." He thought fleetingly about his home, the French Quarter, Dawn, Saxon Monteleone, Eddy, Elton and even Joey. "Yes, I do like it."

"You got somebody?" Padden asked uneasily.

"I might have done until last Friday," he replied enigmatically. "I'm not sure today."

"Too soon to ask you what you do there, eh?" Padden sneakily raised his eyebrows and took in the immaculate suit, monogrammed shirt, watch, cufflinks, dark brown suede loafers, document case, all put together with the ease that taste, wealth and authority often bestows. Scott Finch never missed a trick.

"Too soon." Anthony paused. "Later, OK, Josh?"

"Sure. This is your show, not mine. I'm just your old wingman."

They fell into an easy silence. Anthony fixed his gaze out of the open window at the stone buildings ingrained with soot and fumes, and thought how low and bruised they looked after what he'd grown accustomed to. But all was redeemed by their proportions, their symmetry, the architecture, and how the *piazze*, grand and small, the streets, and even the backstreets, were infused with Mediterranean light. It felt like it was his first-ever trip to Europe. He'd missed Italy, and hadn't realised quite how much until the taxi turned into the via Bocca di Leone, a little cul-de-sac sandwiched between the forever glamorous via Frattina and via dei Condotti. Hidden away at the end was a small 5-star hotel, the d'Inghilterra. The ghosts of Byron, Twain, Hemingway and countless others wandered its corridors. His too, after his many sorties in 1978 during the scorch of the Moro affair.

The taxi driver let the meter run as he pulled up at the hotel's front door. Both men remained in the back of the taxi.

"You look exhausted, Anthony, rest up and perhaps we can meet up at the bar later?" His expression was serious. "You do have a plan, right?"

"No, Josh, there's no plan. I'm not on a crusade. Besides, there isn't much I can do. I'm here because I needed to be in Italy. Sounds selfish I'm sure." Anthony despised himself for lying to his best friend, the man who had saved all their lives. He needed time on Italian soil first. The taxi driver hovered beside his taxi as the hotel's doormen heaved the bags out of the boot: 5-star hotel, first class tags on the luggage. The meter could run and run.

"Pity," said Padden, as he struggled out of the taxi. "I was going to have a big bet with you on who was going to end up dead."

"If you'd lost the bet, Josh, I wouldn't have been able to pay up, would I? This isn't political," Anthony added firmly, as he climbed out of the taxi, "this is personal." He glanced at the meter, nodded at the thieving driver and peeled off enough cash to pay the exact fare. He switched his Italian gaze at the still-running meter as if to say: 'Your tip is on the meter, *cretino*.' Anthony was in no mood to be played for a fool.

"Crap! The Catholic Church and Italian politicians have been kidnapping and murdering people for 2,000 years," barked Padden.

"This is a Sardinian gang, Josh. Victor is far too important for anyone south of Rome, or even north of Rome for that matter, to have touched Toto. Victor is legal Mafiosi if you understand me. Very few people are above the law *and* the criminal's law too. The Salaviglias are above it all though."

"So are people like Alessandro Cuci, then?"

"*Touché*, Josh," he said, "but this is Italy – it's crime and business as usual. Toto isn't Salaviglia blood, so, to the Sardinians he's just fair game."

"Are you sure?" Padden asked, as they stood outside the revolving door.

"Pretty sure. Why?"

"I just keep returning to you and the Moro affair."

"Listen, Josh. Albassi is in a pine box somewhere underground in Milan. He's dust, and worms. He's where his enemies wanted him." Anthony slid into the revolving door. "Now," he said, changing his tone of voice, and the topic with it, "I've read all your books so where's my share of the royalties?"

"I've got them here," replied Padden, patting his trouser pocket, "so, let's start drinking them right away."

They both laughed as they exited the revolving door and almost fell into the hushed lobby.

"I'll go and find the bar, and you do the paperwork. Vodka and fresh orange juice is my new drink. Got everything in it. Vitamins and disinfectant. Perfect." Padden threw him a wink and ambled slowly off.

Anthony watched him go in search of the bar, and saw him rest up on the arm of a plush sofa. Padden limped and looked shaky. He scratched his left elbow: for too many years P.J. Fowler had written leaning on his left elbow, whilst holding a pencil and a cigarette in his right hand. To Anthony it seemed as if the routine and the toxins might be starting to win. He crossed over to the reception desk.

"I have a reservation for two, two-bedroom suites for three nights, although we may stay longer. The name is Nicosia for both suites." Anthony spoke only in Italian.

The receptionist smiled at him ingratiatingly, in the time-honoured fashion adopted by the staff of all luxury hostelries, especially Roman ones.

"*Certo*, Signor Nicosia. We have your reservation. How would you like to settle your account?"

"Cash."

"Of course. May I take a credit card imprint for any extras?"

"No," Anthony replied abruptly. "This'll cover any extras." He removed a Manila envelope from his document case, and passed across a thin wedge of $10,000 to the receptionist.

"*Grazie*, Signor Nicosia. That will take care of the first few days I'm sure." Anthony smiled to himself: you haven't seen just how much my friend can drink. He opened the document case and touched a second and much older Manila envelope. He had sealed it in his airless berth on *Straits Star* and it contained Albassi's Italian passport and a solitary photograph of his wife and twin children. As each day at sea, his wilderness sea, had passed his resolve to destroy them had weakened. He just couldn't imagine jettisoning it overboard during the one hour a day he was allowed on deck for fresh air. As the months morphed into years, the taped-up envelope had become his St Christopher.

"Please ask the porter to take all the cases to my suite, and have both sets of keys brought to me in the bar please. *Grazie tanto*," Anthony said, handing his cashmere overcoat to the receptionist. He then strolled to the sofa and offered a helping hand to his friend. Linking arms, like father and son, they sauntered off in search of the dimly lit bar.

CHAPTER 93

**Hotel d'Inghilterra,
14, via Bocca di Leone, Rome, Italy.
Monday, 23rd February 1987. 09:05.**

Anthony Bianchi recalled the morning after his first visit to Tipitina's in 1978. As hangovers went, it was the Holy Trinity of Dire: head, eyes and stomach were all lit up. In 1977, the year before he had arrived in New Orleans, Tipitina's was a neighbourhood juke joint; heavy drinking optional. It had been known as the 501 Club (Louisiana folk, he later discovered, liked life simple; it was situated at 501 Napoleon Avenue, with its toes almost in the Mississippi). Nine years on, it was an upscale warehouse music club, and a cornerstone of New Orleans' cultural life.

Needless to say, Tipitina's success was due in part to the Monteleone family. Saxon Monteleone had heard Tipitina's had started a non-profit organisation to support Louisiana musicians and their music; traditions that were seared into his heart. Anthony had been dispatched late in 1978 to recce the old brothel by the river, and its new charity. Subsequently, he'd recommended supporting – anonymously – both the venue and the charity. Tipitina's, assisted by whispers of Monteleone support, had been set-fair in Louisiana folklore ever since.

Drinking last night with his friend had left him feeling like his first – and last – Tipitina's hangover. His head throbbed. His dry eyes stung. His stomach unworldly. Slumped in his sitting room chair, the minibar buzzed irritatingly. He got up, opened the fridge, took out a San Pellegrino and gulped the cold alkaline water down as if it were medicine, which it was. His next task was to unpack the contents of the two large cases Tipitina's lighting virtuoso, Stevie Conn, had assembled just forty-eight hours ago.

***

Anthony should have known that, *'Come on, just one more road-beer'* was going to be a mistake. They'd remained talking long after the barman had fled. In exchange for 200,000 lire, he'd left his bar 'open' with an honesty pad for Signor Nicosia. It took a lot to impress Padden, but Anthony's sixth-sense gesture with the barman did; Padden evidently had matters to discuss with his friend which required not just privacy, but neutral territory too. Anthony had figured that an empty bar at the d'Inghilterra would cover both bases.

Thankfully, he realised as his headache receded, that it'd been Padden who'd voiced what both men knew had to be said. Yet it'd taken four large vodkas to loosen Padden's tongue.

"You never listened to me nine years ago, so I don't suppose you will now," said Padden as he'd poured himself a fifth, multi-finger shot of Stolichnaya. Honour-bound, Anthony inched a finger of rum from the Mount Gay bottle into his glass.

"Ruxandra has a life. So does Toto. You'd be very proud of him. He's tall and handsome and works hard at school. He has a part-time job at Rizzoli's bookshop too." Anthony had waved his hand in front of him. There were certain details he just could not bear to hear. But Padden had continued relentlessly – justifiably – as Anthony had recognised.

"You have to listen to me. I know this has to hurt. I can see it in both your eyes. She very nearly didn't survive your death. People *do* die from a broken heart. Ruxandra almost did. I mean it. Toto was an inch away from being an orphan like you, *capisc?*"

Padden's eyes had blinked furiously, as fast as a camera's iris, and he kept on massaging the centre of his chest.

"Ruxandra had locked herself away with Toto for almost four, long, years." He lit another cigarette and deep-swigged his vodka. "Victor was somehow able to reassemble a few of the pieces. He introduced her to her son again – your son, in Sicily. You must understand, she was fading away faster than an Asian sunset after you died. She blamed herself, like I did after Annie died. She believed in some eerie Romanian way that she had murdered you." He downed his vodka; Anthony wasn't counting anymore. "If you appear in her life, it will break her in two. She'll always be fragile and need handling with kid gloves. Victor's kid gloves, you understand me?" Padden's tone shifted into an aggressive gear. "Victor is good for her, and he treats Toto like the son he never had. He loves the boy as he would his own."

Anthony's mind flashed back to his own extraordinary relationship with Victor's father. Certain fragments slipped quietly into place.

"I've done my best to keep the faith, and to keep the promises I made to you in Sicily all those years ago." Anger crept into Padden's tone; it wasn't drink-driven. "You hearing me, Pietro, Anthony? Call yourself what you want. It is *their* life. You have *no* place in their lives anymore."

Padden hadn't pulled so much as one punch. He had settled back into his seat, and turned away to chain-smoke in silence.

Anthony didn't respond. He had come far too far to swear promises to anyone other than himself. Even to his friend, his saviour. Here in his suite in Rome, hungover and jetlagged, his gut knew that Padden's four last words – they still echoed in his head – were correct: *'It is their life'*. And he wanted to return to them what he had robbed them of. A life. And if he were able to achieve that, he too might be able to reclaim a portion of his own stolen past.

Room service had rung the bell despite the 'Do Not Disturb' sign on his door, and for that he was grateful. He hauled in the breakfast trolley, ignored the meats, cheeses and pastries but swigged off the two espressos and picked up *la Repubblica* and *Corriere della Sera*. Above the front-page fold in both newspapers he was greeted by different photographs of his son. How surreal, he thought. *La Repubblica* had a head shot, whilst the *Corriere della Sera* had Toto standing beside an olive tree; both were in grainy black and white. Padden had been right. Toto did have his mother's height. The traits he recognised that Toto had inherited from the Albassi gene-pool were broad shoulders, square jaw and a full head of dark hair. Yes, their son was a good-looking boy.

* * *

Anthony unlocked the six padlocks on the two black, custom-made cases. He flipped open their lids and examined the contents with a mixture of awe and trepidation. Stevie Conn, Tipitina's production guru, had explained how to assemble the four ultra-powerful Klieg lights. Stevie, a 6'7" gentle-giant of a man, and as road-safe as anyone could ever be, had quit touring with musicians to put roots down in New

Orleans. These lights, he'd explained, were the best there were. He'd also packed a transformer into the foam bedding to switch DC current into AC. Anthony considered himself handy with the screwdriver, but he was no lighting tech. He knew he would be though, in about ninety minutes, which is the time Stevie had told him it would take to set up the rig. Discreet as always, there's wasn't one question as to why Mr Monteleone's *consigliere* needed: 4 x Klieg lights, 1 x tape recorder, 1 x small Shure microphone, wiring and stands too, and all to be packed in 2 x custom touring cases. All the gear had to work, without *any* hitch, on AC power, and had be ready for collection – backstage entrance – before noon on Saturday.

Stevie had provided all the necessary tools, and Anthony set about assembling the rig. In under ninety minutes the four powerful stage lights were arranged in a semicircle in front of the suite's desk and chair. All were aimed directly at another similar chair, as if they were sunflowers, and the chair the sun. Flanked by the lights, Anthony placed the tape recorder and microphone at the edge of the desk. He checked the telephone's handset cable stretched as far the chair. It did. He flipped the top off another San Pellegrino, quaffed it down in one, nibbled on some Parma ham and admired his handywork before tripping the transformer's ON switch.

In that instant, the suite became a Hollywood backlot set: it was blindingly bright, as if forked lightning had struck and had then been frozen.

CHAPTER 94

The Vatican State.
Monday, 23rd February 1987. 10:55.

Broken people break people and when they're not doing that, they are, invariably, busy being busy. And Alessandro Cuci was busy being busy. He tapped out a drumbeat with the silver spoon against his espresso cup before grabbing a small brown bottle. He dry-swallowed a handful of ulcer pills, then leaned back in his chair to reflect on what was an unseasonably bright, late February morning. The sun shone radiantly through the tall windows, which made his striking office appear all the more regal, if that was indeed possible. The sumptuous colours and textures of the rugs, brocade curtains, priceless antique furniture, archival paintings all combusted in the cheery sunlight, and sealed in him some satisfaction. However, the grandeur of his office served only to amplify his artless labours on possible solutions to two puzzles and one conundrum, all of which had been troubling him over the weekend.

Puzzle 1: Just why had the authorities published all the information he had so painstakingly amassed with such, what was the right word, velocity? They had done so within one hour of the *Corriere della Sera* receiving all three envelopes late last Friday. That was just sixty hours ago. He was banking on the customary four or five days, for the information and increased ransom to do the rounds of the different law enforcement offices in Milan and Rome. The premature release of all that material appeared to have had only one effect; to mess up his meticulous and prearranged plans. But that couldn't be the sole reason, for if it was, that implied someone had foreknowledge of what he had long been scheming. Unless? But there were no leaks in his IEA. Impossible.

So, he moved on to the second puzzle with the conceited expectation that the first would solve itself.

Puzzle 2: Why was the 1985 CIA report of Albassi's death in Zimbabwe so vague? He knew Barings, now unbelievably Deputy Director CIA, to be highly competent, fastidious, professional, and for a CIA operative, as near to trustworthy as they come.

Admittedly, when Almighty God, or whomever, finally decided to give the world an enema the tube's entry point would be Zimbabwe. Information out of that landlocked hellhole was at best inaccurate and often wrong, but that still couldn't account for the paucity of detail – a CIA hallmark – in their report. That troubled him.

The CIA report stated that Albassi had been killed in a gruesome road accident, after having left Harare for the 500-km drive southwest to Bulawayo. There were some skimpy facts about his car (a prehistoric Land Rover) and the TOTAL OIL fuel tanker which had head-on pancaked said Land Rover in true Warner Brothers cartoon style. The accident had, ostensibly, left behind nothing but sky-bound spirals of grey smoke from the flattened Land Rover chassis, as the tanker's 30,000 litres of petrol vaporised it and the black-topped highway. The report had contained timelines and dates of the accident itself, with different farms that Albassi had worked on, but precious little else. Nothing about his actual *life* was in the report. That too unsettled him.

Not long after the alleged accident, in August 1985, Cuci had received CIA's report. Read it. Half-believed it. Filed it. It wasn't until three months later, during the Cold War's death-rattle, Cuci had seen a TV news bulletin in November 1985 of President Ronald Reagan meeting with General Secretary Mikhail Gorbachev in Geneva. It triggered him to reconsider CIA's report.

The Geneva summit of 1985 was the first of many nuclear disarmament discussions between the US and the USSR. Some clown in the US State Department, appreciating how the Russians love proverbs, had taught Reagan to parrot a Russian proverb, one of Cuci's favourites. A delightful three-word rhyming proverb, one that even Reagan could remember: *'Doveryai, no proveryai'*. Reagan had butchered its nuances in the press conference, and the minute he'd heard Reagan's rendition Cuci knew precisely what to do. He would send an IEA team to Zimbabwe. The canny Russians were right: *'Doveryai, no proveryai'* translates as: *'Trust, but verify'*. Cuci did – up to a point – trust Barings, but he was now going to verify his report.

The two IEA agents Cuci dispatched – a man and a woman – returned after three weeks of intense investigative work. Their vague conclusions were: they could neither confirm as fact, nor could they rule out, Albassi's presence, in work, in life, or in death in Zimbabwe. There appeared to be no concrete evidence either way. The two flambéed corpses were unidentifiable, even to the vultures. However, TOTAL OIL was able to confirm the death of their tanker driver, and another driver, in a tragic head-on collision on the date CIA had stated. The Zimbabwe department which dealt with roads, had verified that the portion of the highway where the accident had happened had been closed for over one week, due to 30,000 litres of fuel melting the low-grade tarmac in the middle of August.

So, Cuci was back to square one. The CIA report could be accurate. Albassi *may* have lived and died in Zimbabwe. Nobody knew for sure. Forged intel from the CIA? Possible but doubtful, as the report had Barings' signature and they'd been in the Moro operation together. With no solution to the second puzzle, he decided that the conundrum itself was in fact the easiest to solve. This was merely a binary choice: life or death.

The Conundrum: What to do with the Albassi boy? He couldn't keep him in the northern hills forever. A final decision would have to be taken if his father hadn't been flushed out by next Sunday, some six days away. Since Cuci had been robbed of five clear days by the premature release to the *Corriere della Sera* of the three envelopes which contained: 1) the kidnappers' increased ransom demand for 5 billion lire, 2) sheared off clumps of Toto Albassi's hair; Cuci knew his mother would ID that evidence, 3) a trove of overseas financial statements about the Salaviglia's generational wealth. The envelope also contained fake 'evidence' that the kidnappers were indeed a freelance criminal gang from Sardinia.

Cuci oscillated between freeing the boy and killing the boy. There were solid arguments for and against each option. If the Sicilian Duke were able to liberate the 5 billion lire in US dollar cash, over $3.15 million, from his Lugano accounts – no easy feat – then he might, just might, set the boy free. (The Duke's mediator was negotiating an amount of $2 million in cash, a sum Cuci knew Salaviglia could raise immediately.) Consequently, Cuci's anonymous Sardinian mediator was sticking to the *'5 billion lire or a corpse'* mantra. This ploy was giving Cuci much needed time, if nothing else. So, his conundrum was simply whether or not to spare the boy's life: no more, no less.

All the other contingencies were already in place: the 'who', the 'how', the 'where' of the firebreak-execution of 'his' Sardinian kidnappers. No one was coming out of this alive unless he preordained it. Again, he reflected gratefully, Naples really did have a surfeit of murdering talent for hire.

Cuci decided, on the spur of the moment, to prolong Toto Albassi's life until next Sunday – less than six days – even if the boy's father did materialise. He would wait a few more days to see if his meticulously plotted plan would work out to his satisfaction, as they invariably did. At last, with the conundrum solved, and leaving the two mysteries open, he rewarded himself with a short walk to his French Second Empire drinks' cabinet. Against all his doctors' orders, he poured himself a large measure of neat Campari. He dropped two ice cubes into three-fingers of scarlet reprieve. It was gone twelve o'clock somewhere in the world, he reasoned.

Cuci returned to his desk, clicked the 'No Calls' button on his telephone and sipped his drink, happy that he'd found one solution: Toto Albassi would be dead by sunset next Sunday, paid ransom or not. He had had enough of the Albassi family. His stomach knotted in pain. Cuci edged himself into his chair. Overcome with drowsiness, he closed his eyes: powerful pain medication mixed with alcohol, he suspected. The want of a relieving siesta beckoned and he hoped Morpheus might oblige.

CHAPTER 95

**Hotel d'Inghilterra,
14, via Bocca di Leone, Rome, Italy.
Monday, 23rd February 1987. 10:55.**

Having rigged up the four lights, set up the desk, tape recorder and mic, Anthony stashed their cases in the second bedroom. Next, he unpacked his own suitcase of hastily purchased winter clothes. However bright it was outside he knew from bitter experience that if it reached ten degrees Celsius in February, it would be considered a warm day in Rome.

When all was as he wanted it, he called Padden's suite; the telephone rang off. Padden, he knew, would surface sometime this afternoon, all showered and fresh with a, 'nothing untoward has happened' demeanour. He'd be gripping a vindaloo-hot Bloody Mary in his left hand, a smouldering Marlboro in his right, and he'd be sporting a beefy grin. Padden still gave the impression of being almost indestructible, Anthony reflected.

The adrenalin of his morning endeavours began to wear off and he felt unexpectedly weary. Good weary though. A job well done weary. He went to the door and checked the 'Do Not Disturb' sign on the brass knob. He then opened the minibar fridge. There was a chilled Nastro Azzurro beside the last remaining San Pellegrino bottle. He'd earned a cold beer. He took it to the sofa and flopped into its feathered cushions. He sipped from the bottle with a calmness that he hadn't felt since last Friday evening.

Knowing precisely what his next moves were to be, he finished the beer and closed his eyes gratefully as Morpheus coasted him off into a relaxed *siesta*.

CHAPTER 96

The Vatican State.
Monday, 23rd February 1987. 14:10.

"What is it you want?" snapped Cuci at his assistant, who'd woken him up despite the 'No Calls' (which also meant: 'No Knocking On My Door. *Idiota*') being illuminated.

"I'm sorry to trouble you, sir, but I have two calls holding," he replied calmly. "One is Signor Albicocco, who's called three times, and the second caller refuses to give his name."

Cuci ignored his assistant. His head throbbed from his medicated sleep, so he headed to his bathroom where he splashed cold water on his face.

"What do you mean he won't give his name? People always give their names when calling me," he shouted from his bathroom, and saw that the sun was low in the sky and had taken with it all its former glory. It was cold outside, and with a groggy head he was in no mood for games. He was due at a party later with 'Alfredo the Apricot', as he called his lithe new fancy; Signor Albicocco just didn't sound right. Banishing the idea before it aroused him, he stepped back into his office.

"Sir, the caller asked me to tell you..." his assistant dithered as he reviewed his notes "... *'Where I come from 5 billion lire would be considered cheap.'* That's exactly what he said. I asked him to repeat the message so I could make a note, as it was a peculiar message."

Silence.

The assistant remained mute, awaiting his employer for encouragement.

"Repeat that again. Word for word, and very slowly," commanded Cuci, with equal precision.

The assistant glanced down at his notepad and slowly repeated the message. Cuci felt his heart accelerate with each word. It was Albassi. His plan had worked. Of course it had. Albassi was out there after all. Cuci laughed quietly to himself. Once again, he was back in control.

"Forget Signor Albicocco, and put the other caller through immediately."

Cuci hurried back to his desk. Slowly, he sat down on the padded 'doughnut' cushion his rampant haemorrhoids necessitated. The telephone rang on his desk. He steepled his fingers and let it ring – and ring – savouring each second.

"*Sì, pronto.*"

"I was beginning to think it was real."

"Sorry, I don't understand you?"

Cuci was almost breathless with excitement.

"A real kidnapping. For a minute, I thought I'd come all this way for nothing. So, just how long have you been waiting for me? Nine years, I suspect."

Anthony's mouth was dry; he cupped the mouthpiece to gulp down some water.

"What do you mean?" asked Cuci. His hand was trembling. Was it with excitement or confusion over Albassi's arrogant tone? He couldn't discern which.

"Is that all you can come up with? The fabled head of the IEA asking absurd questions. One of us is up to this job and it isn't you," continued Anthony calmly. He'd taken a betablocker at 13:30 as planned; his heart rate and hands were as steady as a surgeon's. "Get a pen and paper. I'm only going to say this once."

Cuci remained silent. Mesmerised. Spellbound, as if he were being hypnotised.

"Eight o'clock tonight. The bar at the Hotel d'Inghilterra. Don't be late. I hate tardiness in people, Cuci. Come alone and we'll talk. Our conversation will result in the release of my son, and you will finally have what you have long desired. Me, and all my files. Beforehand" – Anthony allowed a beat to pass – "I need to remind you of details which may have escaped you."

"And they are?"

"I know who you are. What you look like. Where you live. Where you work. Where you play." There was a rat-a-tat staccato in Anthony's telling. "I know where your driver lives. I even know who you were planning to see tonight," bluffed Anthony in a calculated deceit; Barings had told him that Cuci was a night-owl who liked to stalk young men most nights. "You, on the other hand, know absolutely nothing at all about me," he continued. "If you decide not to come tonight, then I will track you down, rip open your throat and stare at you as you bleed out. Then, I will discredit your life's work with all the information I already have."

"You wouldn't kill me before I release your son, Albassi. I've photographs of you, and you've a dead daughter you still haven't thanked me for." Cuci had found his voice at last.

"I'm not making a threat, Cuci. I'm making a promise. Death will wake you up one night. He'll have my eyes, so you will get to see me, but only moments before I rip out your throat. You wouldn't believe the skills I've acquired after nine years in Columbia." Anthony took another sip of water. "Do you really want to bet *your* life, not my life, on it? No, of course not. Any photo you have of me is ten years old, and before I had plastic surgery. What matters more to you? My son's life, or your living and your legacy?" Anthony asked rhetorically. "As I said, *'Where I come from 5 billion lire is cheap'*. In my money, that's $3,150,000, and being a gambling man, my 3 million bucks is on the Neapolitan and Sardinian thugs who're holding my son wanting all that money. With their boss deader than Julius Caesar, those animals will get their reward. They'll be rich. They'll be alive. They'll be free."

Cuci remained silent. He was trapped in the words, the speech, the threats, the never-ending calmness of the man who had been his secret adversary for nine, long, years.

"Let me tell you, Cuci," Anthony continued his unrelenting one-act play. He knew full well that he had only one shot at delivering the scripted monologue he had painstakingly memorised. "I live between Cali and Bogota. Killing one man in the centre of Cali, Bogota or Rome is the same. The butchery is simple, it's more straightforward than delivering $3 million in cash." Anthony waited a full second. "Any idea how much that weighs in $100 bills? Go on Cuci, have a guess," he goaded.

"I've no idea," mumbled Cuci.

"Thirty-one and a half kilos. A $100 bill weighs the same as a $1 bill, just one, single gram. When you've split my money into two cases, that's sixteen kilos a case, and I'm not heaving two cases back to South America. So, when you're as dead as yesterday, my money, all thirty-one and a half kilos of it, will be spinning on the black hearts and untold greed of your goons. It's they who will release my son, not you."

Anthony laid the handset on the desk and silently mouthed: Mississippi One. Mississippi Two. Mississippi Three. "I'll be seeing you at eight o'clock, then? Don't be late."

Anthony jammed his finger on the phone's base to click the line dead. He fell back into the chair and began coughing violently, gasping for air. Air was all he needed now.

* * *

Cuci held the handset away from himself as if it were contaminated. All it did was crackle dead static at him like a Geiger counter. Grotesque emotions knotted his face. He stared at the handset with frozen eyes, as if it were the very harbinger of latent doom. It wasn't supposed to happen this way. Where were the pleas? The howling? The begging? Albassi's files?

Cuci realised, with a spinal tremor that only a stolen truth can deliver, that all he had ever had was just a kidnapped teenager, and nothing else. Fleetingly, he thought of calling Barings but dismissed that idea in an instant. Confess to the CIA? Never. In his dreams it only ever happened *his* way. It was ever thus. That was the way the world works. His world. He had conquered and ruled that world. Albassi was scum. Outsider scum. Murdering, drug-dealing scum too, by the sound of it. That piece of Columbian shit was telling him what to do, and when to do it? No. He was the man who had plotted the deaths of Presidents and Popes.

A retort of pain pierced his multiple ulcers like white-hot skewers. Cuci hurled the handset onto the desk and cried out in agony as he nursed his stomach. Gaining some composure, he pressed the loudspeaker button on the nearby intercom.

"Call Signor Albicocco. Cancel my engagement. Tell my driver to leave. I won't be needing him," Cuci snarled out his instructions.

He then rose from behind his desk, as slowly as a man in doubt. He was physically and mentally numb. Doubled over in agony. Again, he massaged the spasms inside him, and in vain. These internal wounds belonged solely to Pietro Albassi, an *avvocato*. He was the *Istituto per le Opere Esteriore*, the IEA.

This torture he was enduring would be visited tenfold on the son. An Albassi.

CHAPTER 97

Questura HQ, via Fatebenefratelli, Milan, Italy.
Monday, 23rd February 1987. 17:44.

Lorenzo Massina sat opposite Vice-Questore Luca Pezzoli, who was fidgeting with a pencil behind his grey metal desk. Massina had been engaged in a long-distance telephone call for more than ten minutes, and Pezzoli was eager to interrupt. In the end, to head off the inevitable bleat, Massina covered the mouthpiece, and shushed Pezzoli. "Please carry on," Massina continued, his forehead furrowed in concentration, "the connection isn't so good." A minute later, the call ended.

"So?" Pezzoli said, before the handset hit the cradle.

Massina didn't reply. Instead, he contemplated the drab office until his eyes fell on its solitary feature. A large wall graph, with a forever upward trajectory which began at the bottom left corner: Point Zero. Massina smirked. Did the graph's mountain-like track denote Milan's crime rate, or the symbiotic relationship between the Vice-Questore's age and his bovine stupidity? Massina checked himself. He was, truth to be told, grateful to Pezzoli for bringing him back from his living hell to his true calling; solving complex crimes.

"Your English isn't as good as mine, Pezzoli, so I'll explain slowly. By the way, my old office was better than yours," Massina added, for no reason whatsoever. "I suspect that call was from a Rome payphone only because that's where CIA Station is. It was a terrible connection, and the caller was an American woman with a strange accent which made her hard to understand. It was only when she spoke Italian, did I understand her." He paused to flame up yet another Nazionali. "In one sentence, she claimed to be CIA and had been given my name, which is why the call came through to me and not you, as she knew I'd worked on Albassi's kidnapping or disappearance, call it what you will, and then his murder. This informs me that what she told me is *probably* true."

"Get to it," Pezzoli cut in.

"I will if you don't interrupt me." Massina drew hard on his cigarette and clouded the room further as he exhaled. "She gave me the location of where CIA believe the Albassi boy is being held. Then, she requested I call a coded number in Virginia to verify her credentials, and to make that call from a payphone," he frowned. "Quite how I call America from a payphone I've no idea."

"What?"

"Precisely, and unlike you I don't believe that if it's sunny when I wake up it'll be sunny all day. In my book, if it's sunny in the morning, it'll piss it down in the afternoon."

"What does that mean?"

"It means that good news is often bad news. We – you and me – are going to keep this between us until we've verified every detail of what I've just been told."

"Surely we should call Signora Albassi right away?"

"No, Pezzoli. I was directly involved with her husband's death. I won't reopen her old wounds," Massina reasoned. "Let's suppose the caller was a crank, an informed crank I grant you, but this could be just another game to make us look even more flat-footed than we already are." Cigarette smoke drifted out of Massina's nostrils as he spoke.

"So, where is the boy then?" questioned Pezzoli impatiently.

"Northern Lombardy, in the hills beyond Lago di Garda apparently, could be as far north as Brescia, even the Austrian border. She offered no further information."

"Lorenzo, we could blanket the lakes as far as the Swiss and Austrian borders with helicopters at sunrise tomorrow, on my command."

Massina choked as he inhaled his Nazionali. "Pezzoli, it's a huge area, and what will they be looking for? A caravan? A hut? A cave? A truck? A barn? A house?"

"OK, you're right. Let's get this intel verified first. There's a payphone next to Bar Jamaica. I've a phonecard that you can use to call the US and I'm buying this time."

"Now that's a plan." Massina stubbed out the filter. "I've investigated many kidnappings in my career and there's always been a snail's trail. A something. A renegade. A jealous wife. A grass. Someone unhappy with their cut of the ransom. There isn't a case I've worked where there wasn't a leak. Even the Calabrian gang who had Getty in '73 had more holes than a lobster pot. Yet in this case, there's not even a lobster to sniff at, let alone its pot. Nothing, not even a whisper of information is leaking. That's why it's all about patience. We'll be airborne if this tip is accurate. We'll have to be. If this checks out, it will be the sum total of our leads. We've nothing else left to go on, Pezzoli. Nothing."

"Don't remind me. I don't know why I asked you to help," replied the despondent Vice-Questore.

"I do. It's because you like having me around." Massina grabbed his packet of Nazionali. "You trust my gut, don't you? So, let's go see if that call from Rome checks out."

"Huh," was all Vice-Questore Luca Pezzoli could manage.

CHAPTER 98

Via Bocca di Leone, Rome, Italy.
Monday, 23rd February 1987. 20:10.

Alessandro Cuci stood under a street lamp, just in from the via dei Condotti. Its dull orange glow cast a spell, like a false dawn, and threw his shadow across the gloomy via Bocca di Leone, 'Mouth of the Lion'. Perhaps he was in the Mouth of the Lion? He doubted it. He was The Lion.

Caught in the lamp's dim glare, a feeble spray of rain spat across his face. Stationary clouds hung low over the city. And somewhere above, the moon threw its iridescent light on other cities, other countries, but not Rome. He wiped his goatee dry with the back of his glove, pulled the collar of his tan Burberry up around his ears, and cursed himself for not wearing a hat. Less than 100 metres away, to his right, were the unassuming glass doors of the Hotel d'Inghilterra.

A thought held him still for a moment. It was an unexpected choice of hotel for a brash, rich Columbian drug hoodlum. From his experience – and he had some – the South American criminal fraternity were all about flash: hooker flash, coke flash, limo flash, noise flash, clothes flash, dollar flash. And the Hotel d'Inghilterra was a tasteful and unobtrusive Roman hideaway. A very un-Columbian mob choice indeed. He glanced at his watch. 20:11. Perfectly late. Fifteen minutes ago, he'd practically inhaled two dirty martinis at Café Cordino's; they'd lifted his spirits, and restored his poise. The earlier conversation with Albassi had knocked him off balance. He knew he held all the aces and that Albassi had supped too long on a plate of Columbian bravado. Big fish-small pond syndrome; he'd exploited that weakness many times.

Before Cuci could give the orders for the boy to be killed, he had to ascertain precisely what Albassi knew and the whereabouts of his files.

Only then could he decide the fate of the father. He'd do that at his leisure too. He licked his lips and set off towards the beacon lights of the hotel. His nose twitched like a bloodhound's and his heart pounded with expectation. He had waited for what had seemed to be an eternity for this meeting.

* * *

Cuci never saw the wooden truncheon crashing into the lower part of his skull, nor truly felt its ferocious impact. His limbs went out and he collapsed into an untidy heap onto the wet cobblestones. Anthony stared down in amazement. Could it have been so easy? Cuci lay motionless on the ground, like a marionette after someone had spitefully cut the puppet-master's strings.

Earlier that afternoon, when Anthony had held the truncheon the New Orleans Police Department had given him, it had felt solid, but so had his own skull when he'd tapped it. The NOPD Sergeant had given him a ten-minute lesson on how, and where, to strike with maximum stun-power and zero blood loss; the NOPD had had decades to perfect their skills. The reality was that the force of Anthony's blow was guesswork, fuelled not by hatred or revenge or anger, but by a sense of justice. His justice. And Anthony was beyond caring whether it meshed with anyone else's. *Grazie*, NOPD.

Via Bocca di Leone was deserted, save for a handful of badly parked cars, one of which was an old grey Fiat saloon Anthony had purchased earlier for cash after his call to Cuci. He'd sat in it, slunk down low in the passenger seat, from 19:00, watching and waiting. Anthony had given himself a window until 20:30 for Cuci's arrival. He *knew* Cuci would come. That was his antennae again. Anthony had Plans A, B, and C in place. There were three ways Cuci could arrive at the Hotel d'Inghilterra, and he couldn't be sure which one he'd choose: by chauffeured car, on foot from the via Frattini end of via Bocca di Leone, or as he in fact did, on foot, from the via dei Condotti end of via Bocca di Leone. On damp nights such as tonight, Romans rarely left their homes, and shunned the idea of walking. But Cuci wouldn't want a third party to know his movements. So, there wouldn't be a driver or a taxi. Even Cuci went 'black' sometimes, he figured.

Anthony heaved a sigh at his good fortune. Holding fast, lost in the shadows and in an anonymous car at the via dei Condotti end of via Bocca di Leone had been his Plan A gamble. His three-to-one shot. The Hotel d'Inghilterra had only three access routes, which is why he had selected it. No other Roman hotel was as hidden away.

Barely audible grunts and moans rose up from Anthony's feet. Swiftly, he pulled a tartan peaked cap and a bottle of Johnnie Walker from his overcoat pocket. He unscrewed the top, splashed whiskey all over Cuci and his own clothes, and rammed the cap onto Cuci's head. They both stank of booze. He felt around Cuci's neck for blood. None. The skin wasn't broken, but an egg-shaped mound was forming fast, just as the NOPD Sergeant had said it would. He lifted Cuci up under his arms. Only once before had he hauled a body any distance, and that was two decades ago: she'd been drunk and he had been fitter, and Ruxandra was lighter than Cuci was. Anthony heaved the inert body upright, and hoisted Cuci's slack left arm over his shoulders. He dragged him towards the hotel entrance, the tips of Cuci's shoes scuffing noisily behind. Twenty-five metres away from the main entrance, he took a deep breath and started to belt out *Volare*. Drunkenly. Out of key. Noisily. The bottle of scotch flailed in his hand.

"Comin' through!" Anthony bellowed at the bewildered doorman. "A clever guy would've sat at your bar. Trouble is, my friend and I aren't smart," Anthony slurred and hiccupped. An inane smile curled around his maw. He waved the whiskey bottle at the astonished receptionist, the one who'd checked him in the day before, and carried on lurching across the small lobby to the elevator.

Once inside the cage-style elevator, he took in a lungful of air and steadied himself. Cuci's face was bloodless, ghostlike, his sagging body flaccid and heavy. The elevator juddered nervously to a halt at the fourth floor. The hotel corridor was tomb-quiet. Anthony's suite was just thirty metres away. All he had to do was get him inside. The rest, he tried to convince himself as he struggled with the tasselled keyring, should be less problematic.

Once safely in his suite, Anthony bolted the door. The 'Do Not Disturb' had been hanging outside all day. He tore off his coat, threw it on the sofa, and positioned Cuci's slumped body in the chair facing the desk; his arms toppled away from his torso as if they were invertebrate eels, dead ones at that. Anthony hoisted him up and let his head drop onto his chest. Cuci was clearly still unconscious, which is exactly how he wanted him.

The eight rolls of gaffer tape he'd arranged earlier were in place. Slowly, and methodically, he wound roll after roll of the silver-coloured tape around Cuci's stomach and chest. It took three rolls. He wound them tight, not so tight that Cuci would have trouble breathing, yet strong enough to constrain any movement. With his upper body secure, Anthony strapped his arms and legs to the chair. Two more rolls gone. Three left. Then he slapped tape across Cuci's mouth, cut a thin slit in the centre – enough for a coin to pass and no more – and wiped the drool and phlegm from his chin.

Anthony stepped back to examine his prisoner, as a painter would a completed work of art. He sought out flaws and imperfections in his work. He found none. In minute detail he took inside himself what had until now, constituted his nemesis: approximately 160 pounds of flesh, blood, water and a few organs. Anthony had suspected all along that it might have come down to this seminal moment in time.

He turned off all the lights in his suite, settled himself calmly into the second chair to allow his one good eye to become accustomed to the curtained darkness shrouding both captor and captive. His sight slowly adjusted to the darkness. He stared at Cuci, and admitted to himself that the price for the death of his daughter, the confiscation of his life, his son's life and his wife's would have had to have been settled someday. *Suicido bianco* was one thing if it was committed voluntarily, selfishly, but something else altogether if ordered with a gun at the very heart of your family. He bit down hard into the flesh and knuckle of his right index finger.

Sweat began to seep down his neck and into his chest hairs. He shivered as the damp shirt chilled his body. He looked around himself, his vision now acclimatised to the suite's shadows. Everything he anticipated he would need in the hours to come were within an arm's reach: towels, shirts, sweater, balaclava, two pairs of goggles, bowl of fruit, water, loaf of bread, straws, thermos of espressos, bucket, torch, blank cassettes. And last, but not least: a grab-bag containing a large serrated hunting knife, ten metres of thin nylon rope and a stash of industrial-size black garbage bags.

Without leaving his chair, Anthony towelled himself off and slipped on a black sweatshirt. He checked his pulse. High nineties. He dry-swallowed 20 milligrams of propranolol. His heart rate would come down soon. All he had to do now was wait a little longer.

Had he not waited long enough already?

CHAPTER 99

**Suite 401/3, Hotel d'Inghilterra,
14, via Bocca di Leone, Rome, Italy.
Monday, 23rd February 1987. 21:28.**

Cuci had been out cold for over forty-five minutes before Anthony heard deep guttural noises – crude and raw – coming from the near-mummified body. He stepped back, placed his hand on the top of the Maglite torch to safeguard his own night-vision, and flashed its beam straight into Cuci's eyelids. He watched them flicker, frantically, like moths at a candle; he was stirring at last.

Anthony hurried behind the desk to Stevie's boxes of *alakazam* and threw the power switch. The four carbon arc Kliegs fizzed momentarily as the carbon-rods in each flared up into their own, terrorising ice-white brilliance. Cuci's eyes opened wide – instantly – like a truck-paralysed Dakota deer. Startled, petrified, he tried to close them. He couldn't, for the hellish light from the four Kliegs, only a few feet away, penetrated his eyelids. Cuci tried to scream. Nothing. He fought against the tape, which bound his hands, arms, mouth, legs, chest. Nothing. He wrenched his shoulders as best he could. Nothing.

At the desk, behind the lights, Anthony pulled on a full-face black balaclava and a pair of Hobart Oxy-Acetylene welding goggles. He poured a glass of water from a jug, dropped a straw in it and went over to Cuci.

"No noise. Drink," he commanded, and threaded the straw through the slit in the tape covering Cuci's mouth. "You won't get another chance for some time. Believe me."

Despite the piercing lights, Cuci's inflamed eyes remained open. They burned with evil. And hatred. And frustration. And, what looked like insanity. Anthony was mesmerised by Cuci's stare, and it checked him where he stood. It wasn't every day you could look the Devil in the eye, he thought, especially when he can't return the courtesy. Cuci continued to suck hard on the straw until he'd emptied the glass. Anthony could sense that he was now alert and focused; the effects of the blow to his head had worn off.

Returning with the empty glass to his desk behind the Kliegs, he removed his balaclava and goggles. For a minute he watched Cuci thrash against the metres of tape that bound him tightly. He watched him recognise the futility of his struggles, and that his sole option was to face a steel wall of bulletproof light.

Anthony knew that his time with Cuci was governed by the damage the crystalline carbon arc lights would do to his prisoner's eyes. It had a name: 'Klieg Eyes' was excessive exposure to such light. The first symptom was uncontrolled watering of the eyes, then conjunctivitis would set in, followed, ultimately, by blindness. A blind Alessandro Cuci wasn't going to be of use to anyone, least of all Anthony.

"Firstly, the rules. Alessandro Cuci, every society has rules and here I make the rules. This is an autocracy of one. Me. So, I'm rather like you and your IEA and your laws which justify killing eight-year-old schoolgirls. Kidnapping teenagers. Poisoning popes. Murdering financiers. Plundering banks. Inciting riots in South America. I could go on, and on, and on..." Anthony spoke crisply from the black void beyond the lights and watched Cuci fighting the glare, dipping his head left-right-up-down as if he were a boxer dodging punches. He knew it was Albassi behind the inferno, as Anthony had made no attempt to disguise his voice. All Cuci was fighting for was a glimpse of the fool who dared to treat him in this way.

"You're securely bound and gagged, Cuci. Don't try and get out of the chair, or hop it towards me. Should you try, and the chair topples over, I'm not going to pick it up. You'll remain prone. It's going to be uncomfortable for you to piss and shit anyway, but it'll be worse on your side. Next, communications. You're able to move your left and right index fingers only. Try."

Obediently, Cuci lifted both fingers upright.

"The right finger means either 'yes' or 'I agree'. The left finger means 'no' or 'I disagree'. Frankly, I doubt the left finger will get much use," he added, "and if you get a hard-on, I'll take that as a 'maybe'. Understand?"

Anthony remained silent until he saw the right index finger move. It did, and in a New York minute too.

"Have you ever heard of a South American arachnid we call the Fear Spider?" Anthony asked. Cuci's left index finger moved. "It's like many of our deadly spiders, but with one exception. Before it injects venom into its prey, it spins an intricate, transparent web to entrap its quarry, often larger than it. Full-blown terror is induced in its victim when it's ensnared, which ultimately leads it to the precipice of insanity. So, a short journey for you then, eh, Cuci?" Anthony went quiet, drank some water and waited, just as a Fear Spider would, before continuing. "When the victim is at the edge of madness, the Fear Spider just ups and leaves until such time as it returns to deliver the final, and by then expedient, jolt of poison." Anthony broke off again. "Cuci, I am that spider. Think of me as the Fear Spider. Understand?"

Cuci's right index finger moved again, hesitantly this time. Anthony imagined he saw the first strand of the web fall across his prey's watering eyes. He fell silent and sat still as he composed himself after his verbal assault.

"You need to remember who exiled me in the first place. You did, Cuci, back in 1978. You knew that, didn't you?" This time there was no hesitating. The right index shot up. "The man you can hear, but not see, is like the son you never had. You created this monster, Cuci. I am your Adam Frankenstein, and now I'm your Fear Spider. Just look down at yourself if you need any proof."

Anthony breathed in deeply, and slowly counted to ten before speaking.

"In your paranoia you'd assumed I had incontrovertible proof that you were behind Moro's kidnapping and his execution. The evidence I had obtained made it impossible to conclude that the IEA and CIA were *not* involved. Finding Giulio Andreotti's fingerprints was harder. Was Andreotti mixed up in your plot to kidnap and kill Moro?"

Again, the right index finger went up.

"I thought so. I couldn't prove anyone's involvement, let alone their guilt, at the time. I can now. Then I was just your and Scampidi's smokescreen, so the IEA, P2, CIA and Il Papa Nero Andreotti, could obscure the facts. A cut-out to be framed? Was that reason enough to kill my daughter nine years ago, and then kidnap my son nine years later?" Anthony shouted furiously.

This time, Cuci hoisted his left index finger.

"No? OK. Here's another question. Were the rumours I'd heard from the Red Brigades and Prodi's Ouija board, enough to sentence my innocent little girl to death?" Anthony shouted again. "Tell me the truth, Cuci, or you're headed straight down to Hades."

Cuci moved his right index finger as deliberately as a sniper would squeeze his trigger.

"I thought so," said Anthony, standing up. Again, he pulled on his balaclava and Hobart goggles and walked over to where Cuci was imprisoned. He knelt beside his captive's right ear, so close that his lips touched Cuci's lobe. He could taste the petrified saltiness of his sweat.

"We're going to make a straightforward deal you and me," Anthony whispered. "Tonight, you're going to call whoever you have to, and order my son to be released at precisely noon tomorrow. The spot where he will be released will be desolate, a minor road, and you will provide the exact details. Six hours after my son has been freed, so, at 18:00 tomorrow, Tuesday, you will be cut free from this chair and permitted to leave this room." Anthony paused. "By that time, I will have left Italian soil. I'll be somewhere over the Atlantic headed home to Columbia." He allowed his words to sink in before hissing into Cuci's ear. "So, what does Cuci get, apart from his insignificant life back? I'll tell you. All the original evidence I've been holding on you and your co-conspirators will be delivered, anonymously, to the IEA office in the Vatican, one week from tomorrow, also at 18:00. None will have been copied or in any way duplicated. None of the evidence has, nor will be, shared with any press organisation. There'll be no investigations, no leaks, no gossiped innuendoes. It'll be back to business as usual for you and the IEA." Anthony took a deep breath. "There is a justice system somewhere out there, Cuci, and you'll just have to square that away when your time comes. Until then, there'll only be one justice system. Mine. Not yours. Not God's. Not Lucifer's. Mine. Remember that. So, you'll need to pray to whichever God you worship for my son's, his mother's and Victor Salaviglia's good health and longevity. If they happen to be in a fatal plane crash, die in an avalanche in Cortina, drown off Capri or get caught in a fifty-car pile-up in the Po Valley fog, I'll blame you. When I am done blaming you, I'll track you down again and I'll kill you." Anthony's lips touched Cuci's ear. "Deal?"

Without any hesitation, Cuci's left index finger shot up.

Without any hesitation, Anthony's teeth ripped into Cuci's ear as if he were a starving *favela* dog with fresh meat, and he tore it from his head. Blood spurted everywhere, filling Anthony's mouth before soaking into his balaclava. Cuci's head snapped back. He screamed, and screamed again, and again, and all in a void of silence. It was as if he were sitting for the artist, Munch.

Anthony stood up, stepped out in front of Cuci and stared him down as you would a mad animal. He knew he was invisible thanks to Stevie's wizardry. Maybe this *was* all about vengeance and retribution after all, he thought before speaking.

"No deal. Fine. There's one other part of the body that bleeds more than an ear, and I'm sure as hell not going to bite that."

Anthony hawked the blood from his mouth onto Cuci, and wiped yet more blood from his face, as if it were venomous. Then, he placed the palm of his right hand under Cuci's chin, and at the same time he flattened his left palm on Cuci's forehead. Through his blue lenses he saw Cuci's eyes widen, fear staining their whites. He began to stretch Cuci's neck back, centimetre by centimetre, until Cuci began to choke and his eyes seeped even more water: he was approaching Stage One of 'Klieg Eyes' and the slow process that would ultimately lead to his blindness.

"I'm going to ask you one more time, or, I will – irreparably – damage," Anthony eased in yet more pressure, "your C1 and C2 vertebra. You won't die, I know what I'm doing, but from your neck down you'll have the locomotive skills of a slug. No arm or leg movements, you'll be incontinent too, and you'll have a tube in your mouth, not a cock. You *will* be alive though." Anthony's palms were sweating as he drove in yet more pressure. "To have all this come to pass all I have to see is the wrong finger move when I repeat the question. If I do, so help me, Paola and so help me, Toto, I'll crush your neck in such a way that you'll be a living cripple. Believe me Cuci, if you believe nothing else. Think about it, but not for long."

Anthony sucked air in through his teeth. He edged Cuci's neck as far back as it would go. The tendons creaked like old floorboards. Cuci spluttered and gagged behind the tape, blood and saliva oozed out of the gap and ran down his chin. Anthony held firm.

"Deal?"

Cuci's right finger moved instantly.

"See, I knew we'd get there in the end."

Immediately, Anthony removed his hands from Cuci's head which slumped onto his chest. He returned to the shelter of his desk and picked up another roll of gaffer tape and the telephone's handset. Quickly, but thoroughly, he strapped the handset to Cuci's left ear, there was too much blood leaching from his right ear. He wound the tape multiple times across Cuci's skull, face and thinning hair. When the handset was secure, Anthony threaded the small Shure mic so it nested in-between the telephone's earpiece and his ear. Anthony then plugged the mic's cable into the socket of the tape recorder on his desk.

"Listen, Cuci," he ordered, "I'm going to remove the tape, but before I do, there's another rule."

With his back to the blaze of the Klieg lights, wearing a bloodied balaclava, Hobart goggles, dressed all in black and standing fully erect, Anthony – unbeknownst to him – cast a sinister and spectral image that panicked even the psychopath that was Alessandro Cuci.

"The rule is this: should you at any instant say anything that I consider to be ambiguous, I will simply crush your neck and this will all be over. I'll have the telephone number of your contact on speed-dial, and I'll leave you here shitting yourself, whilst I negotiate and pay for my son's release with the kidnappers directly. I've already told you, I'm not carrying thirty kilos of change back to Columbia. So, at all times during the conversation you're about to have, my hands will be placed like this." He shoved Cuci's neck back as gentle reminder. "Do you understand me?"

Cuci's right index finger answered the question, and Anthony ripped the tape from Cuci's mouth and chin, taking with it a cluster of the goatee beard.

"Aaaaaah! You CUNT, Albassi," Cuci shouted as loudly as he could, spraying Anthony with spittle.

"Feel better? Good. You only get one of those, and you've just had it. So shut the fuck up and give me the telephone number."

There was a stillness in the room. Anthony's towering black silhouette was partly shielding the blaze of light. Raw power glowed in front of Cuci's suppurating eyes.

"It's a Rome number, 80195." Cuci swallowed hard. "I want water."

"No. Don't say one more word until the telephone is answered. Only an Oscar performance keeps you out of a wheelchair."

Anthony stepped back to his desk, dialled the number, clicked the 'Record' button on the tape recorder, placed a single earpiece into his left ear, so that he could hear both sides of the conversation, and then returned to brace his captive's head.

"*Pronto.*"

"*Buonasera*, Freddo. Alessandro Cuci here. I hope I'm not disturbing you?"

"*Ciao, Capo*, how are you?"

"Never been fitter, never better. You could say I'm on Olympic form."

"Hmm, well you sound a little strange, *Capo*."

"So, would you, Freddo, if you had your head in the position I have mine." Anthony inched Cuci's head back slowly.

"The longest, fattest, most succulent asparagus that you've ever seen is about to slide down my throat as we're speaking," said Cuci. "You see, I'm celebrating, Freddo. I have what I need. The boy is to be released and unharmed. Do you understand me?"

Anthony, in the seconds it took for Cuci to say what he had just said, in the calm and controlled tones that he had just used, began to grasp the man's other worldly reserves of sheer control and power.

"Are you sure, *Capo*?"

"*Si.*"

"You're the boss."

"You tell your men, Freddo, if they follow my instructions to the letter, there's a bonus in it." Cuci's idea of a bonus was to call off the Neapolitans who were lying in wait to put multiple rounds of .38s into their skulls. Freddo included. "What we need is a minor back road. Totally deserted." Cuci was following his captor's orders to the letter.

"*Aspetta un attimo, Capo*. Let me go and fetch a map." The man named Freddo returned hastily. "There's one, not too far away from where the boy is. You're going to need a pen, *Capo*."

"Standing by. I'll get it all down, don't you worry," replied Cuci, icily.

Again, Anthony marvelled at just how extraordinarily composed Cuci was, and with that thought, he realised that he could not continue to play this psychotic, murdering brute for much longer. Was it a part of Cuci's game plan? To do what he was doing now was to be – to own – the persona, the lie, the act. This was not who he was, but he was now so deep *inside* his own lie that he feared his own sanity might never escape.

"On the western shore of Lago di Garda there's a small town called Gargnano. In the middle of the town, a narrow road winds back and forth all the way up to Lago di Valvestino. It's about fifteen kilometres away. When you get to Lago di Valvestino, stay on the east bank of the lake and cross two small bridges. Keep heading north. Pay close attention here, *Capo*, the route gets complicated. Exactly two kilometres after the second bridge, there's a fork in the road. Turn right. It's a narrow road which follows a small river in a valley. The road becomes a dust track. That track ultimately joins up with four other tracks at an intersection. At that intersection is an old, small church. How does that sound for a deserted spot?"

"Maybe it's too isolated, Freddo?" Cuci, as serene as death itself, questioned courteously.

"It'll take the boy some time to get picked up from there for sure, which'll give my men plenty of time to get far away. Time they're going to need, *Capo*."

"You're in charge, Freddo. I don't want any mistakes. Please be clear on that." Cuci spoke with overt menace. No, I'm definitely not going to stand down the Neapolitans he decided, before continuing. "I'll call you in forty-eight hours to make the final payment arrangements. Bonus included, if all goes smoothly. *Arrivederci e grazie*, Freddo," said Cuci, meaning only the first word. Enjoy the afterlife, Freddo.

Anthony released Cuci's head, clicked the telephone line dead and turned off the tape recorder.

"It doesn't sound ideal, but we play the cards we're dealt, don't we?" Anthony said rhetorically. "You'd better pray to the God of Wheelchairs that your man Freddo doesn't fuck up or remove so much as one more follicle of my son's hair."

Before Cuci could even think of a response, let alone speak one, Anthony thrust a pre-cut length of tape across his mouth. This time, the gash of tape had no breathing, drinking or drooling slit; he had a nose, and Anthony wanted total silence.

"You want some water, don't you?"

That right index finger shot up again.

"I'm going for a piss, and I'll think about water whilst I'm leaking," Anthony looked down at Cuci's saturated trousers. "Ah, I see you beat me to it. Don't you even think of trying to move when I'm in the john."

Anthony returned to the desk. He wilted down into his chair to gather his thoughts in the only refuge he had; the black silence behind the furious Kliegs. He removed his balaclava, now all gluey with blood and hooked his Hobarts off. With clear vision, he could sense Cuci's oozing eyes boring into him, penetrating the fortress of light. Somehow Cuci's eyes were eviscerating what was left of Anthony's soul and gutting his stability. His eyes gnawed at his beating heart with the appetite of a bubonic rat; with a look that went far beyond Lucifer's silkiest dream. The tremendous toll this alien situation was taking on his equilibrium was beginning to turn in on him. He had to dig ever deeper and find yet more inner strength. If Cuci detected it...

Just in time, Anthony understood why this man – his prisoner – wielded such power. He was mesmeric, in the purest sense, hypnotic and as irresistible as the serpent in the Garden of Eden. He blanked the potential consequences from his mind. Joshua was next up, although he had no idea what was coming down the pike at him. Another favour to be sought from his ageing friend. He picked up the phone, dialled his suite. Hung up. Dialled his suite again. Hung up. Dialled a third time. Hung up. This was their language-less code for: *'My suite. Five minutes. Bedroom door only. Knock twice. Then twice more'.*

Anthony stood up, and readied himself to leave. His voice was as clear as his head now was.

"You and I have concluded the first part of our 'deal', Cuci. Now comes the second part. If all goes to plan, we'll never, ever, meet again. A man is going to come in and sit right here. He'll give you one glass of water tonight, and one more tomorrow. Tonight, he'll put a pair of goggles over your eyes, otherwise you'll probably go blind before I telephone at noon tomorrow to give him the good news that my son is safe and free. If I don't call, this man will simply butcher you. He accompanied me from Columbia. He's a peasant, a coco farmer, and like you, a textbook psychotic. One of the most ruthless and inventive assassins we use." Anthony took a deep breath. "He speaks no English, no Spanish, no Italian, only a tribal dialect from the Andes. My advice is, don't give him a story to brag about when he returns home with me. There will be no second chance with him. Do you understand me?"

For what Anthony hoped would be the very last time, he saw Cuci's right finger move.

"We'll call this a 'Columbian Standoff', Cuci. No winners. Just survivors."

Anthony's mood tightened with raw anger.

"You murdered my eight-year-old daughter. You kidnapped my son. Go and kill other people, Cuci, but never, ever go near my family again."

He switched the radio on – a talk station – cranked the volume up to a couple of notches below 'neighbour complaint', and marched through the double-doors and out of the sitting room, before the eyes that had pinned him into his desk chair could keep him there, perhaps forever.

CHAPTER 100

**Suite 401/3, Hotel d'Inghilterra,
14, via Bocca di Leone, Rome, Italy.
Monday, 23rd February 1987. 22:19.**

"Ssssh! Whispers only, Josh."

With a finger across his lips, Anthony opened the main bedroom door. In his other hand he held the blood-sodden balaclava and his Hobart goggles. The interconnecting double doors to the sitting room were closed, and he'd left the radio on; he wasn't taking any chances.

"Jesus H. Christ. There's blood all over you. What the fuck is going on?" A belt of Padden's alcohol fumes, mixed with stale tobacco, cuffed Anthony in the face.

"You've got to ease up, Josh, vitamins or not," he said, as he closed the adjoining door. "I need to clean up. Sit down and give me a few minutes to figure out where to begin."

"As a writer I find 'Chapter One' is usually the best," Padden chirped in. He lit a Marlboro, grabbed an ashtray and plopped his weary frame onto the corner of the four-poster bed. He'd seen enough blood to last several lifetimes; it was going to be three or four cigarettes before his friend got out of the bathroom. Dried blood is a bitch to get off.

Anthony stood in front of the ornate bathroom mirror and stared at himself. His blind left eye began to twitch and blink uncontrollably, his hands trembled. He leaned on the basin for support. Cuci's blood, dried to a shade of earthen brown, stained his cheeks, his chin and rivulets had run all down his neck into his chest. He wrenched at his black sweatshirt.

He, whoever he was – Pietro Albassi or Anthony Bianchi – had liberated a demon from deep within that was paralysing him with horror and dread. His whole body began to shiver. What happens now that the demon is out of its hidden cage and free? Memories of his own warm, soothing blood soaking his face, his head, flooded back. He could feel the sensation of the bullet searing into his temple and blinding him, and the memory of, of, of... There were so many buried memories of the summer of 1950.

In an instant, one Anthony had no control over whatsoever, he felt his insides contract as if they were being compressed by a brutal force. And vomit, green and brown and bilious erupted from his mouth and nostrils at an ungodly speed. Poisons, not from his liver, gall-bladder, spleen, bowels, or stomach, but some other unworldly hollow inside of him just kept draining out. He knew, as the acids razored his throat, that whatever he spewed up, there would remain more than enough inside him to nourish the demon he had liberated. Finally, the flow subsided, his eye stopped fluttering and his sweaty body began to compose itself. He rinsed the basin, threw towels on the floor and cleaned up. Then he stepped into the scalding water of the outsized shower, where he undressed. He kicked his clothes into its marbled corner. He let the scalding water cascade over him, painful yet soothing. He concentrated on his breathing until he could scrub himself from head-to-toe. This wasn't over yet, far from it, he thought as he vigorously towelled himself dry. Padden knocked on the door.

"Do you mind telling me what you're up to in there?"

Anthony stepped out of the bathroom in a robe, and swept his wet hair back with a wide-toothed comb. He caught a crease of a smile in Padden's eyes from the edge of the bed, who was dressed precisely as Anthony had instructed. He looked like just another tourist from the Americas: unshaven, wearing ill-fitting Levi's, scuffed white Nike trainers, a loud print shirt over which was a partially zipped, cheap windcheater. A New York Yankees baseball cap was at his side. And a Marlboro smouldered between his nicotine-stained knuckles.

"Josh, you got a cigarette?"

"This must be serious." He tossed him the lighter and a soft pack of Marlboros. Anthony snapped the filter off and lit up. He sucked the smoke in greedily before stubbing it out only after he'd blown-out his two lungs.

"I needed that," said Anthony, as the nicotine buzz rushed to his head. A blue-grey haze billowed out of his mouth as he spoke. He pulled up a chair and sat down to look his friend square on. There was no easy pathway here. A straight on assault of 'the facts' is the language they both understood.

"I've got Alessandro Cuci bound and gagged next door and Toto is to be released at noon tomorrow," Anthony announced impassively.

Equally deadpan, Padden said, "Say that again please. Very slowly this time." For a whole five seconds his rheumy eyes ceased blinking before he added, "Where's the minibar?"

"Banned, Josh. I mean it. You've got a fourteen-hour dry streak ahead of you. Start writing another book."

For fifteen – drawn-out – minutes Anthony explained in precise detail exactly what had happened. The stage set he'd conceived had been built next door. The persona he'd adopted may now have adopted him, he silently feared. The raw brutality he'd had to find, and then temper his own rage and bloodlust for pure revenge. Padden was speechless, but the storyteller in him was beguiled by the intricate and multiple plotlines, the timings, the planning, the execution of it all. It was a near perfect plan if – big if – Padden thought, no one strayed off script. The curtain had dropped on Act I. He was eager to hear his role. Anthony laid out the structure of Act II – the next fourteen hours – and rigorously clarified the persona he had invented for his trusted wingman.

"This takes me right back to Southeast Asia," Padden said in-between cigarettes. Both men stayed silent, but Padden grinned. "You're a son-of-a-gun, Anthony. One slip-up and we could all still be killed, Toto too. When did you hatch up this crazy plot?"

"Precisely. So, pay attention," replied Anthony. "Most of this came to me on the fly whilst I was with my employer and his friend, the Deputy Director of the CIA. He was CIA's Rome Head of Station, and Cuci's point man during the entire Moro affair. The plans fell into place like a narrative."

Anthony reached for another cigarette. He couldn't rid himself of the noxious aftertaste in his mouth.

"Cuci had it coming to him, Josh. You tell me what else I could have done?"

The silence lingered again. Padden glanced down at his ragged trainers, then lifted his head and looked his friend straight on, his eyes steady as searchlights.

"Not disappeared all those years ago," he replied ever so softly.

Anthony crossed the room, stubbed out his cigarette, unable to answer.

"But 1978 was then, Josh. Back to business. I'll call you at 12:45 tomorrow. If Toto is free and unharmed you can leave."

"What, just walk out the door?"

"Yes."

"What about Cuci?" asked Padden.

"When I leave here in ten minutes, give Cuci one glass of water. The glass on the left." Anthony indicated to a side table. "That one has three Nembutal dissolved in it, it's tasteless. He'll go to sleep, which means you can catnap too. At all times you are to remain behind the desk, as I've already explained. At precisely 11:00 tomorrow morning you give Cuci his second glass of water, the one on the right. That has six Nembutal in it. That'll knock him sideways. When you're sure Cuci's out cold, and *only* if I have called you to say Toto is safe, then cut the tape off his right wrist with the boxcutter that's also on the side table. Nothing else. You then leave everything. The lights. The desk, the tape recorder, the mic, everything just as it is. I have the cassette tape with the directions with me. Forget the lot. Put your baseball cap on, go downstairs and walk out the main doors as if you were a tourist going sightseeing."

"You're sure?"

"Positive. All the bills have been paid in cash. Our names and addresses are false. I've asked for our suites to go un-serviced. When Cuci comes around, he'll struggle for a while, but having freed his right wrist he'll set himself free in the end. He's one of life's survivors. All he's going to do, Josh, is melt quietly out of the hotel's service entrance into the chill Roman air. He's shrewd, so he'll say a prayer to Orcus for not having to pay Charon to ferry him across the Styx to Hades where he belongs. He would have survived to live, and to kill, another day." Anthony paused. "I played my role, you're up now, Josh."

"What happens if Toto isn't safe and free?"

"I'll call you whatever happens. So, if I haven't called by 14:00 you must assume I'm dead and leave here immediately. Just go. But do *not* cut Cuci's wrist tape. The hotel will eventually open the suites up, and Cuci will have to answer a lot of questions from many different authorities." Anthony was picking up the smoking habit again. "Lastly, when I call you, if Toto is either dead or still captive, you're to stay here until I return. The drive back to Rome from where Toto is being held is about six hours. Cuci will still be out cold. When I get back, you can then vamoose. Got that?"

"Go? When all the fun is about to start?" An eagerness crept over Padden's animated face.

"As they say in my adopted country, *'This is my call, so I'm making the play'*. Leave it be, Josh." Anthony sensed the demon deep down inside of him stir in anticipation.

"OK. Is there anything else you need from me?" Padden asked.

"Don't look into his eyes, ever. He'll have goggles on, and when you approach him wear your balaclava and your Hobarts too. I've a feeling in my bones that he won't cause you any trouble. I could be imagining this, but I suspect there might be a relief in him that it's finally over after all these years."

"My turn, Anthony," Padden barrelled into their exchanges. "You listen up, young man." He stood up and pulled his shoulders back. "Here's my ten cents' worth. You recall what I said last night, right? Don't you dare forget it. They have a life now. *Their* life. One you abdicated from nine years ago."

"That's the sole reason I'm here," Anthony replied, his voice almost sheepish. "I'm here to give them *their* life back. Trust me. I heard you last night." He paused to stub his cigarette out. "If all goes well, I don't expect I'll see you again, dear friend."

"Cut it out. That's what you said nine years ago, now look at us both. Besides, what would you do without your old 'china plate'? That's Cockney rhyming slang for 'mate', by the way."

Padden wrapped his arms around the younger man and held him very close.

"I've got this, Anthony. Go get dressed, *amico*, and then piss off. You've got a long drive tonight, and I've got another book to write."

PART SEVENTEEN

CHAPTER 101

Woodlands in the area west of Lago di Valvestino,
Brescia Province, Italy.
Tuesday, 24th February 1987. 11:35.

Anthony lay stretched out on a camper's ground sheet in the tranquillity of the Brescian woods; it was so peaceful he imagined he could hear the Earth think. He stared up at the cloudless sky, which was as still as the hour of death. Beside him was a thermos of sweet black coffee and a fisherman's tacklebox he'd purchased three hours earlier in Modena.

A dozen hours ago, about 22:35, he had scurried down the Hotel d'Inghilterra's fire escape, and was soon gunning his way north, through Rome's dark and ominous streets in the old grey Fiat saloon. He knew precisely where he was headed.

Just before 03:00, full-blown exhaustion had ambushed him as he sped north. Bologna was in the rear-view mirror. The *autostrada* was empty, which meant that Modena was only ten minutes away. Yesterday, he reminded himself, as he slowed down for the exit, had begun with a hangover and ended with him capturing the head of the IEA as his prisoner. He pulled off the A1 and headed into Modena. Sleep was mandatory, even if only for a handful of hours.

He knew Modena well, and in the centre of town was the Hotel Canalgrande. It had begun life as a convent in the sixteenth century and, like himself, it too had weathered every storm that had raged. The hotel had been an old favourite of his, and five hours' rest there was worth ten anywhere else. The heavy wooden main doors were bolted closed when he'd arrived. The snoozing night concierge had let him in, handed him a room key and saved the paperwork for the morning; his late-night guest was an Italian after all. Anthony had gratefully taken the key and asked for three alarm calls: 07:45/07:55/08:05 and he watched as the concierge wrote them all down. Modena to Lago di Valvestino was at least two and a half hours. He climbed the stairs to the *piano nobile*, fell onto the bed fully dressed, and was asleep before his head touched the pillow.

Now, awake and alert on his ground sheet, a distant noise splintered the woods' serenity and jerked him back to the present. Approaching from afar – very fast and very low – he caught the unmistakeable clatter of multiple helicopter rotors. The air was brittle, cold and still in the woods. His breath steamed as he counted four dark blue Agusta 109's of the Carabinieri, and an additional four – much noisier – Bell 212's of the Polizia, all flying overhead.

Fleetingly, he thought of Mr M. and the many Bell 212's they'd sold to Central American governments. Shivering and anxious, hiding in amongst the tall pine trees, New Orleans' warm humidity could have been in a different galaxy. Staring up at the helicopters, he guessed they were on a joint training mission, a rare event between the Carabinieri and Polizia given their intense rivalries. All eight helicopters were tracking north, in the direction of the Italian foothills and mountains, and ultimately, to the Swiss and Austrian borders. It was a perfect day for it: the sky was a hardened blue, the alpine air crisp and the visibility seemingly without end.

Then he suddenly realised that this was no joint exercise between the Carabinieri and Polizia. This had to be a CIA search party. His gut had told him last week that Barings had more intel on Toto's location than he had let on. Anthony found a wry smile of gratitude for the slyest fox he'd ever met, and gave up a silent prayer that all the helicopters, with the forty or so heavily armed men on board, would continue to fly ever further north. Destination to be guessed. Anthony had a solid plan with up to the second intel – which they didn't have – and he didn't want any interference at all, however well-intentioned. Like Scott Finch in *A Man Possessed*, had said: *'He didn't need any help whatsoever. He knew precisely what he had to do. And he could only do it alone'*.

CHAPTER 102

**Woodlands in the area west of Lago di Valvestino,
Brescia Province, Italy.
Tuesday, 24th February 1987. 11:50.**

Anthony had chosen his vantage point with great care. A few years ago, a US Navy SEAL had told him that, *'Time spent on reconnaissance is seldom wasted'*. The SEAL was right. Unseen, Anthony had dissected the area surrounding the old church at San Virgilio: four converging tracks, all narrow and dusty, were clearly visible just as Freddo had said they would be.

However, to his surprise and relief, he'd found that the kidnappers could only arrive – undetected – from the western track, the one from Lago di Valvestino. This would be, for sure, the route they would have to take from wherever it was they had been holding his son.

Anthony glanced at his watch. 11:50. His stomach knotted again, this time with a mixture of fear, dread, anxiety and hope. Whatever the kidnapper's escape plan was, they were cutting it finer than prosciutto. Noon, just nine, short, minutes away, was the deadline. The thought of seeing his son, his flesh and blood, churned through his insides. He replayed in his head the conversation Cuci had had with the man named Freddo: there were no hints, ambiguities, codes or betrayals in that conversation. Cuci's instructions were as clear, and unequivocal, as Anthony's promise to crush Cuci into a wheelchair had been.

A heavy rasp, like the sound a truck with a trashed silencer would make, startled him. From his vigil, he reached into his pocket for his Minox binoculars. A white, closed-sided van was wedged deep in a pothole barely a few hundred metres away. Anthony flinched as the driver tried to coax the van free by slipping the clutch and revving the engine. With obvious skill, the driver was able to slingshot the van out of the pothole as if it were a stone. The van rumbled forward towards the church, where the driver speedily hand-brake turned it through 180 degrees, so as to face the direction from which he had come. Skilfully executed Anthony conceded, through the prism of his binoculars.

As if in suspended animation, he then watched three masked men all dressed in army fatigues – he guessed they were late twenties by their muscular build and athleticism – jump out of the van as one unit and recce the immediate area. They wore body armour, and were armed with pump-action Beretta shotguns. They moved with a silent precision, a trained military one, where commands were neither stated nor sought. Cuci had hired the very best, this time.

When the three men were satisfied the area was clear, deserted and no ambush lay in wait, two of the men jumped back into the van's cab. The third man went to its rear doors. Anthony's right eye strained wide and unblinking as he focused on what was to happen next. With a care which seemed wholly out of place, the third kidnapper placed his shotgun on the ground and guided a tall boy, hooded and with his hands bound by multiple cable ties, down the van's step.

The black hood shrouded the boy's head and shoulders, and it contrasted with a bright yellow scarf which hung loosely around his neck. The boy was dressed in jeans and a zippered anorak. The kidnapper led the boy, step-by-step, to a tree stump some fifteen metres away and steered him to sit on it. Again, not one word was spoken. When the boy was seated on the stump, the man took what looked like a microphone from his jacket, placed it against his throat and only then did he speak. Anthony couldn't make out what was said. He did, however, see the boy nod twice at the commands levelled at him.

Anthony's heart skipped several beats as he caught the glint of a switchblade opening in the kidnapper's hand. In a lethally swift move, the blade sliced through the cable-ties. The man grabbed his shotgun, jogged back to the van where he flung open the door and bounced on the balls of his feet right into the driver's seat. So, that was the leader, Anthony said to himself. The man revved the engine angrily, bled the clutch out, and the van shot off in a straight line at great speed, leaving only a rooster-tail of dust in its wake.

The boy remained motionless for maybe ten, very long, minutes. Then, centimetre by centimetre he removed the hood from his head. Free from his blackened prison, the boy began to shake his head from side to side as a chained dog would, in an act, perhaps, of confirmation that he was indeed free, safe and alive. He then licked his palms, and smoothed down his dark, ruffled hair.

Anthony saw through his binoculars that a patch of the boy's hair had been scalped, and the wound showed pink and bloody. Anthony rolled over onto his back again, closed his eyes and let the tears, which fell like millstones, stream down his cheeks. He lay there immobile until the raw, wintry air had crusted their salt into his skin.

His son was alive.

CHAPTER 103

**Woodlands in the area west of Lago di Valvestino,
Brescia Province, Italy.
Tuesday, 24th February 1987. 12:07.**

"Hi!"

Toto's father adjusted his mirrored Aviator sunglasses. The boy, terrified and startled, spun around.

"Where am I? Where exactly?" Toto shouted. He saw only a small church, dirt tracks and trees. Lots of trees. The father watched his son's eyes look up and hold onto the azure, cloudless sky for longer than anyone he had ever seen. That's what almost ten, solitary, days in a darkened and damp cellar, with a gunnysack over his head, would do to anyone he told himself. And for a split second, his inner demon surfaced and whispered in his ear: *'I told you to shatter Cuci's spine, didn't I?'*

"I was kidnapped and I've just been set free. That's what they told me. That I'm free." Toto began to heave and sob and spluttered loudly, "Where I am? Where am I?"

His father dropped his tacklebox and ground sheet into the dust, and walked the few paces towards his son. He went to put his arm on his shoulder.

"Get away from me. Who are you?" Toto recoiled and screamed at his father.

"Hey, I'm just a salesman travelling to Verona. We're at Lago di Valvestino, in Brescia. When I get a chance, I stop here as I like to fish." Toto's father nodded at the tacklebox, "I never catch anything, but I grub around the soil beside the church for live bait. The lake is only a couple of kilometres away" – he pointed at the track – "we're not far from Lago di Garda either."

"I'm sorry I shouted. I want to go home. I live in Milan. My name is Salvatore Albassi, and I really have been kidnapped. I've lost count of the days – nine, ten, I don't know," said Toto, shivering and weeping, his cheeks now bathed in tears. His father didn't offer up the exact number of days his son had been in captivity – nine days tonight – as he passed him a handkerchief.

"I've heard your name, so has the whole of Italy and much of the world too. Come on, let's go and find the nearest police station, young Signor Albassi."

His father picked up his tacklebox and ground sheet, and headed down a different track to a clearing in the trees a few hundred metres away, where he'd hidden the old grey Fiat.

"I just want to see my mother; to go home, to see my old dog Enzo too," Toto said, as he followed a few paces behind the tall stranger.

"The sooner we get you to a police station, the sooner you'll be back home in Milan." So, the air rat chasing marvel that was Enzo was still alive. More good news, thought Toto's father.

He opened the boot, and hurriedly threw his tacklebox and ground sheet in before his son clocked the total absence of any fishing gear. He opened the passenger door for him.

Cautiously, he began to study his son out of the corner of his right eye. He definitely did take after his mother. There was her mouth, and thankfully his and her height. But Toto's green eyes – the same as Paola's – and his wide, arced masculine eyebrows, thick dark hair and olive skin were all his. Toto's complexion was clear, and a weak stubble had furred over his face during his imprisonment. In two or three years, maybe less he thought, the last traces of adolescence would have fallen away, just as the leaves of autumn do. And Toto would no longer be his or Ruxandra's son anymore. He would be his own, proud man. A newsreel of the years he had been with his son flashed onto the car's windshield, as if it were a cinema screen. He smiled at the memories and patted his son on his left shoulder. Toto glanced up with eyes red and puffy.

"*Andiamo!* Your terrible ordeal is over, young man."

Toto blinked, and managed to force a half-grin at the kind-hearted stranger with the gentle smile. "*Grazie*," he said as the old Fiat spluttered into an unenthusiastic life. The gearbox sounded as if gravel not oil was its lubricant, and together, father and son, the salesman and the kidnap victim, motored off slowly down the dusty, potholed track.

"You'll be home in no time. There's probably a Carabinieri station in Navazzo," his father said, knowing full well there was, "and that's well before Lago di Garda."

They drove in silence until the track turned into a road.

"So, tell me all about yourself, Salvatore?" his father asked, looking straight ahead.

"Everyone calls me Toto and I live in Milan," he stammered. "Do you know why I was kidnapped? Is my mother alright? Was a ransom paid? Is that why I am free?"

"I'm afraid I don't have any answers, Salvatore. My job takes me to Ticino and the only thing more boring than Swiss newspapers is Swiss cheese. I haven't followed all the story. I'm sorry."

"I can't imagine why anyone would want to kidnap me. My mother is not rich. She works in an art shop in Milan."

"Oh, I see." He kept his eyes glued to the road, lest he inadvertently give anything away. "So, what about your father?"

"He died when I was a boy, nine years ago, and my mother never remarried," Toto replied matter-of-factly.

"Do you have any brothers or sisters?"

"No, my twin sister died too, the same time my father did. But my mother has a boyfriend, if that's the right word." Toto giggled, showing his true age, which made his father crease a smile.

Neither the Fiat – with its grinding brakes and gearbox – nor its teenage passenger, much liked the twisting road down to Navazzo and Lago di Garda. Toto opened the window for fresh air before continuing. He hesitated. "My father was Sicilian and so is my mother's boyfriend."

"Let me get this right, so, you're half Italian and half Sicilian? You get they *are* different countries?"

"No, no, sorry, my mother is Romanian, so I guess I'm half Romanian and half Sicilian."

"If you were born a hundred years ago, that's what you'd be. Today you're just an ordinary Italian like me," his father told him, as a furrow crept across Toto's forehead.

"I think I prefer being half Sicilian and half Romanian," said Toto, nodding his head.

"Good choice! Any idea what you want to do in life?" his father asked with genuine curiosity.

"Well," he paused, "my father was a lawyer and my mother's friend, well, he's a farmer in the west of Sicily. He grows olives, grapes, lemons and the sweetest blood oranges ever." The father knew only too well just how sweet Bonnera's blood oranges tasted; as children he and Victor had devoured a lifetime's worth. And he sensed the animation on his son's face as he spoke about Sicily, but he dared not look. "I suppose I shall become a lawyer like my father was," Toto concluded dolefully, and with resignation in his voice.

"Why so?"

"It is a good profession. What do you do?" Toto asked.

"I'm a photocopier salesman for my sins. I have a good friend who is a lawyer, and he said to me once that if he had his time all over again, the very last career he'd choose would be the law. Know why? My friend told me lawyers are the same as hookers, they both have clients and they both screw for money." Father and son laughed in unison. "Don't be a lawyer, Salvatore, be a farmer."

"I would much rather work on the land in Sicily." Again, he heard his son's soul come to life. "The harvests are exciting, there's always something to do. I love working outside with my hands. The weather is better, I swim every day in Castellammare and there's no fog like there is in Milan!" Toto laughed again.

"What's stopping you?"

"School at the moment, and my mother too I suppose. She says, *'One husband is all one is meant to have in life and I've had mine'*."

"Maybe your kidnap, and you now being safe and all, will change that. I'm sure your mother's friend would give you a job on the land after university. You are going to go to university, aren't you?" he asked his son a little too sternly.

"Yes, I hope so. My mother and father met at university in Milan. It's funny, I often wonder what he'd think, what he'd advise me if he were alive today. I still miss him" – Toto took in a deep breath of fresh air – "and when I wake up each day, I hope I will miss him less" – his father heard his son's pitch waver – "but that hasn't happened yet."

Whoever the man, the one with dark hair, greying lightly at his temples, was at that precise moment in time, he swallowed very hard. He wired his jaw shut and remembered his oath to himself and to Joshua Padden.

"I'm a father too. A boy about your age," he said warmly, "and I think your father would say to go to where your roots are. You can't go to Romania, so you go south to Sicily, young man. It sounds like your mother would like that too. I'll tell you something else, Salvatore, my father died many, many years ago and not a day goes by when I don't miss him."

And all too soon they passed a road sign which indicated the beginning of the village of Navazzo. He took his right hand off the steering wheel and touched his son's shoulder lightly.

"Hey, look up ahead, there, on the right, there's a Carabinieri station." He stood on the brakes and pulled right up in front of the building, on the opposite side of the road. Despite the lunch hour, it looked as if it was open for business.

"It's been good talking with you. Think on what I said. Head south to your Sicilian homeland, where the weather is at least free. I can't stand the cold in the north! Good luck, Salvatore!"

The father held out his hand to his son as he opened the passenger door. The son took the stranger's outstretched hand and shook it firmly. A man's handshake.

"You never told me your name, sir?" his son asked with a wide smile.

Yes, his son really did have his mother's smile.

"You never asked. Anyway, my name is Signor Cuci. *Buona fortuna e vai con Dio*, Salvatore."

"Thank you for finding me and helping me, Signor Cuci, and for all you have said too. Toto crossed the narrow pavement and headed up the stairs, and for some reason, known only unto God, his son stopped, looked back, waved, and blew his father a kiss before he disappeared into what would be the arms of grateful Carabinieri officers.

Before the father ground the gearbox into first gear, he sat quietly letting the old engine clatter on. In peace and solitude and sorrow, but most of all with a crushing sense of relief, he allowed his tears of pain, of pride, of grief and of joy to fall freely down his cheeks.

They were tears, not just for all the lost years, but for much, much more.

CHAPTER 104

The road from Navazzo to Linate Airport, Milan, Italy.
Tuesday, 24th February 1987. 12:54.

Anthony wound his way back down the corkscrew road from Navazzo to Gargnano, where, at the water's edge of Lago di Garda, he turned sharp right. He heaved a sigh of relief knowing he would have a calm twenty-minute drive beside the lake before hitting the A35 to head plum-west: direction Linate. There had been a time when he'd called Linate his second home. Thankfully, the airport was to this side, the east, of Milan, and he'd be able to avoid the city, the traffic and worse, its haunting memories. Linate was as close to Milan as he dared go. From the town of Salo, where he would leave Lago di Garda behind him forever, the drive to Linate would be no more than ninety minutes, even in the increasingly reluctant and emphysemic Fiat.

He stopped at the first petrol station on the A35 *autostrada* for fuels – petrol for the Fiat and two caffè corretti for him. He had to gather his thoughts, just as the night gathers the dew. He was late for his promised call to Joshua too. He shunted to the back of his mind the inevitable call to Mr M. He just wasn't up for that now. Again, he checked his watch. 13:54 was 07:54 in Louisiana. Far too early to call the amphetamined night owl that was Saxon Monteleone. Relieved, he vowed to call him when he had landed in Rome's Fiumicino Airport later that afternoon, and before he departed Italy for the very last time, on Alitalia's New York flight.

Sipping his espresso topped off with grappa, his mind turned to the immediate issue: when would his son's freedom be thrown to the hyenas that were the Italian press? His best guess was about 17:00–17:30 tonight, in order to make the TV news headlines and the front pages of Italy's self-important newspapers. Quite how precisely Milan's Criminalpol were actually going to spin his son's release was food for his next caffè corretto.

Anthony downed the dregs in one, took a phonecard from his money-clip, slotted it into the payphone and dialled the Hotel d'Inghilterra.

"Josh, you want the good news or the bad news?"

"Bad first. Always."

"None of the kidnappers are dead. Yet. They were all ex-military. The best. They'll be killed for sure when Cuci is safely back in his Vatican lair."

"What's the good news, Anthony?" Padden asked.

"Toto is safe. He's free. I drove him to a Carabinieri station not far from Lago di Garda. I'm at a filling station on the motorway heading to Linate to fly to Rome for my connection to New York." He faltered for a second. "Before you ask, I kept my word. An anonymous photocopier salesman from Ticino who was out fishing for the day, found Toto in exactly the spot Cuci and Freddo had decided upon. All's fine, Josh. So tell me about your end."

"God alone knows who brewed Nembutal, but they sure work. Cuci came-to with the cock's crowing, then I gave him the second glass of water as you'd instructed. He's comatose now."

"He will be until evening. The second glass had enough to knock a horse sideways," said Anthony.

"I spent this morning stewing, and I got fed up and wanted my vitamins, then my old Asia training kicked in. So, I cleaned the suite, wiped down all the surfaces and cases. I've packed your suitcase, and I'll lose it this afternoon where it'll never be found. You can't be too careful."

"Thank you, and what's your next move, Josh?"

"As you ordered. I'm going to return to my rooms, sweep them clean too. Then I'll cut the gaffer tape securing his right wrist and leave." Padden wavered. "I've decided to hang around in Rome. Do some research, eat too much, drink too much. You were right, I did get an idea for a new yarn during the long night as I stared at our man. Writing is 90 per cent perspiration and 10 per cent inspiration, and I hit a sweet spot about 03:00 hiding behind these incredible lights. And I was as sober as some priests I've known too!"

"By the time Cuci comes around, Pietro Albassi and Joshua Padden will have collapsed their tents like Arabs in the night, and vanished back into being Anthony Bianchi and P.J. Fowler," Anthony stated with certainty. "Don't forget, we beat him at his own game. We held him to account. The irreparable damage we inflicted was to his psyche, not his ear. The world had been his playpen until now. Not anymore. Cuci will never go near Ruxandra or Toto again. Even wounded and angry, he's too canny to tackle Victor who'd only ever show the bastard true Sicilian mercy." Anthony laughed to himself at the thought. "Cuci will never speak of anything that happened. The reputational damage would cripple him, just as I would've done if I'd had to, Josh."

"You're right. There's not a bloody thing he can do. I thought about all the angles. Just who's he going to scream and shout at? No one. Not even his Pope could find us. We'll be in the wind long before those horse pills wear off."

"We did a good deed, Josh, and I couldn't have done it without you, and your trust. Thank you again."

"You go with your own God, Anthony, back to your home, your life, your boss and the lady you think you lost. Stay safe, and don't ever return to Italy again. Got it?"

Before Anthony could respond, all he heard was the fuzzing of a dead payphone, and the roar of traffic on the *autostrada*. Slowly, he replaced the handset, and returned to the cash till to order up another caffè corretto. He was far too hungry to eat anything.

* * *

As Anthony approached the long-term car park at Linate Airport, the road sloped off into a shallow, watery ditch. He pulled over and opened the boot. He took out the fishing paraphernalia and put them on top of the boot. He walked back 100 metres and threw the ground sheet into the fetid water. He then returned to the car, grabbed the tacklebox and walked 100 metres beyond the car, upended its contents and dumped them too. Next stop the car park. He drove up, snatched the ticket from the machine and drove to the very farthest corner. He parked up beside the fence and began his own thorough clean sweep of the interior. Mysteriously he'd grown rather attached to the old grey heap of soon-to-be-rust, he was sure that it was the fact that its interior was infused with the lives of a father and a son. He'd never known anything about his own father, other than he'd been, according to local hearsay, a soldier in the US 7th Army as they'd swung through the west of Sicily, liberating Italy from Fascism.

Anthony rubbed the car keys clean on his trousers and chucked them under the footwell mat. He gathered up the thermos and his leather document case, which contained about US$15,000, an equal amount in high denomination lire notes, his US passport, his Alitalia New York ticket, and his real treasure: a solitary photograph of his wife and twin children, and Albassi's long-expired Italian passport.

Content, he sauntered away from the car and jettisoned the thermos in a dustbin. Later rather than sooner, knowing Italy, the car would be found, months probably. He'd risked the car being uninsured. The seller hadn't asked for a Rome residency permit; he'd been busy licking his fingers as he'd counted the thirty crisp $100 bills he'd been handed. Besides, what were long-term car parks for if not for parking cars, long term?

The faithful old Fiat was a phantom, just like him. He mulled that over and over as he strolled towards Linate's terminal, gleaming in the distance.

CHAPTER 105

Linate Airport, Milan, Italy.
Tuesday, 24th February 1987. 14:45.

"*Buongiorno*, Signora. I'd like to book a one-way ticket to Rome *per favore*. I'm connecting with your flight to New York," Anthony told the young brunette with a pixie haircut at the Alitalia desk. "I have no luggage, so can you please check me in here?"

With a flirtatious smile that sailed right over his head, she took his cash, and handed him a boarding pass with an invitation to the first-class lounge.

There were no queues, and in minutes he was in the airside shopping mall. He checked the Departure Board. His flight to Rome was due to leave at 17:00, which gave him all the time he needed: a shower, a shave and a new set of clothes. Time to rid himself of the 'uniforms' the Columbian narco and the Ticinese photocopier salesman had worn. He hoped that a showered, clean shaven and stylishly dressed Anthony Bianchi would be able to eat something at last.

A dark blue, single-button jacket, with a faint beige box-check wound into its cashmere, caught his eye in the Hugo Boss window. Anthony nodded at a young salesman and rattled off a list of garments he required: The jacket in the window, 1 x white cotton Oxford shirt, 1 x pair of cotton boxer shorts, 1 x pair of navy cotton socks, 1 x pair of the best quality brown loafers – size 44 – a matching leather belt, a white cotton pocket square and 1 x pair of the darkest shade of denim jeans available. *Per favore*. And yes, he was pressed for time. So, in under ten minutes, he walked into the lounge with two large Hugo Boss bags and headed for the showers.

Another ten minutes passed before an entirely different man looked in the mirror. He ran his hands through his hair and Anthony Bianchi smiled back at Anthony Bianchi. There was absolutely no self-congratulation in his expression, just one of unadulterated relief and an amnesty with the world. He exited the extensive washrooms holding only a slim black leather document case under his arm. Everything else, including the clothes, the Aviator sunglasses and the personas of the murderous Columbian and Ticinese salesman, had been discarded in Alitalia's bins.

* * *

It was now 15:20, and 09:30 New Orleans time – in ten minutes – would be an acceptable hour to call Mr M. It was vital, and respectful, that Anthony be the one to deliver the news. He suspected Barings would have stayed his hand.

He found a seat near the window and sat down to rehearse what he was going to say to his loyal employer. He would keep it brief. To the point. The details – which he would surely edit – would be shared with Mr M. upon his return. Today's executive summary would be: Dear Mr M. my son is free and safe, as am I. Alessandro Cuci is alive and will never be a threat ever again. I'm leaving Rome later for New York, and I'm looking forward to returning to work. End.

At precisely 15:30 his time/09:30 New Orleans time, he inserted a phonecard into the payphone and gazed out blankly through the large windows at the aircraft and the bee-like activity of the busy airport. He dialled, as if on autopilot, 001 504 767 1958 and let it ring. And ring. No answer. Very bizarre he thought to himself. Perhaps a typical Italian technical SNAFU? He tried the number again.

"1958, hello, Dawn Loubiere here, who's callin' please?" She sounded out of breath. Anthony was dumbstruck. He had dialled the main line at 5120 St Charles Avenue. The home of Saxon Monteleone. Dawn had answered. What was going on?

"Hi y'all, who's calling please?"

"Dawn, it's me, Anthony. What are you doing at Mr Monteleone's house?"

"Anthony, *cher*, what y'all talking about? Y'all just called me at home."

And then he grasped what had happened. It was Dawn who was, subliminally, foremost in his mind. It was her he was returning home to, not Mr M. Love, like virtue, honesty, truth and morality was its own reward, and he recognised in a split-second that he owed a very substantial debt to her; one that had to be honoured.

"Dawn, do you have a minute or two?" he asked cautiously. His question was met with a silence.

"Sure, if y'all tell me you're safe an' well. Are you?"

"Yes, in a word."

'Tell three people a secret and you've told the World'. Anthony had already told Saxon Monteleone, Judd Barings and Joshua Padden, so, what possible difference would there be if he told a fourth?

"I'm in Milan and I'm flying to Rome to connect onto a flight to New York," he hesitated before adding, "then I'm returning home to New Orleans."

"Sounds like one heck o' a lot of flying, *cher*. New Orleans is still home then?"

"It is, and I'll be back soon. I've a story I need to tell you."

"I figured that, Anthony. I promised myself that if y'all ever came back, I'd sit with you an' listen. I hoped you'd come back. I knew all along somethin' was up. Y'all terrified me when y'all just vanished."

Light-headed with relief he said, "It's not an easy story, but it'll be the truth."

"Y'all remember one of our dates. It was a Sunday, 15th February, just nine days ago. Goodness, seems like nine years. Y'all picked me up from home in your neat little car an' we went to Audubon Park. Y'all were a tad nervous by the way." She laughed her laugh, and Anthony *saw* her. "We had a swell time, an' when y'all drove me home, the roof was down, it was chilly an' I realised that only secrets kill love." Her voice wavered; he could hear her breathing. "So, if y'all are ready to share those secrets, well, I figure there'll be as much chance of killin' my feelins' as y'all would have puttin' socks on a rooster." Anthony laughed. "Now y'all run along an' catch all of yer 'planes. I'll put a red-line through Saturday *an'* Sunday in case what y'all want to tell me is as long a tale as *Gone With the Wind*. Fly carefully, darlin'" – a beat passed – "y'all are my forever, Anthony." And before he could reply, Dawn had clicked the line dead.

He stood still and thought about what she'd said, and so calmly too, that the knot in his stomach unravelled at last. He decided he would call Mr M. after he'd eaten his first proper meal since he'd landed in Italy sixty, long hours ago.

CHAPTER 106

Bar Jamaica.
23 via Brera, Milan, Italy.
Tuesday, 24th February 1987. 17:45.

"Sometimes I can't believe you, Pezzoli. If stupidity were a crime you'd be sentenced to death." Massina, out of breath after the five-minute walk from the Questura HQ, shook his head in despair.

"Thank you for the compliment, and from you, Lorenzo, I take it as one. Remember, in Italy it doesn't matter how a crime is solved, so long as it is solved," Pezzoli pointed out. "Today it's all statistics, targets, political pressure," he leaned across the small wooden table and whispered, "and today we solved a crime, Lorenzo."

"Bullshit, Pezzoli! Never believe your own press. Remember what I'm telling you and don't ever forget it." Massina lit another Nazionali, and blew the acrid smoke towards the ceiling. "When your face smiles back at you from the TV tonight, and from the front pages tomorrow, don't ever forget that we didn't solve anything, apart from a few crossword puzzles. All we did was sit in your office wondering what the hell to do next. We most certainly didn't solve Italy's most complex kidnapping since Getty."

Massina tried to flag down one of the sullen waiters. Yet another graduate of 'The Deaf & Blind School of Service', of which there were plenty in the Bar Jamaica. He then waved both arms in the air, as if he were a drowning sailor, and accidently burnt a neighbour's jacket with his cigarette. "Damn," he muttered and headed to the L-shaped zinc counter. He'd be his own waiter. He'd never understood why Bar Jamaica was so popular: low ceilings, cramped floor space, a noisy crowd of would-be artists, intellectuals, photographers and left-wing 'poets'. It may have been around since 1911, and seen off a deuce of wars and squadrons of Blackshirts, but it wasn't his idea of a bar. Massina squeezed his bulk through the three-deep crowd and demanded two glasses of Tuscan gut-rot. Criminalpol had changed he pondered, and slapped down a 10,000 lire note on the counter; the only thing that hadn't was the location of the HQ. As he waited for his change – no tip today – he helped himself to a fistful of peanuts from the congestion of bowls and ashtrays. He caught Pezzoli's eye. Massina signalled him with a raised eyebrow. Pezzoli read the room instantly and nodded back. Massina wanted to spy and to eavesdrop. The bar was a buzzing hive of journalists, all of whom had attended Vice-Questore Pezzoli's impromptu press conference at the Questura HQ, just forty-five minutes ago. Massina's radar wanted to 'read' those headlines right now.

Pezzoli's press conference had been a PR coup. Massina had been standing at the back of the crowded hall, and had listened in awe as his assistant of yesteryear fielded tricky questions and bluffed a coherent story out of thin air. It could have been a Cinecittà Studios production: flash bulbs zinged, motor-drives whirred, TV boom-mics prodded the raised dais where Pezzoli stood and questions were shouted aloud, and then shouted again. During all this commotion, Pezzoli, the circus ringmaster, kept a semblance of order. He took questions in turn – with fixed-eye contact – he knew the faces of those journalists who actually *mattered* and he answered their follow-ups too. Pezzoli had been masterful, Massina admitted, and he realised just why, and how, his dull, timid assistant had achieved the rank of Vice-Questore. Pezzoli was a man who could kid-the-kidders with the best of them; he had what Rome referred to as 'crossover potential' for any career in public service. In Massina's language that meant he knew how to bullshit and lie: the politicians, the press of any stripe and, of course, the lamentably gullible public would suck up anything Pezzoli said. Victims and criminals didn't seem to matter anymore.

The barman slopped down two wine glasses and a dish of coins. Massina shot him a sarcastic *grazie* and decided to stay put. Pezzoli was engrossed in conversation with a senior reporter from *Corriere della Sera*.

There were only three incontrovertible facts which Pezzoli could deploy:

1. The precise location where Salvatore Albassi had been deposited: Navazzo's Carabinieri station in Brescia.

2. Having easily identified the small church at the intersection following a description from the Albassi boy, Criminalpol had sealed off the area. They now had the size and make of the kidnapper's tyres, courtesy of Niki Lauda's high-speed getaway.

3. The purported name of the mysterious photocopier salesman from Ticino. A tall man with dark hair, greying at the sides, who'd never removed his sunglasses, who'd stumbled across Salvatore Albassi whilst out fishing. After much persuasion, Pezzoli had finally agreed not to release the name of the salesman, on the sole condition – and Massina's sworn oath – that he would reveal the secret he had so long guarded.

Leaning back on the bar drinking the second glass of red, Pezzoli's in fact, he admired the justifiably smug expression on Pezzoli's face. Massina knew then that he'd made the right call to insist on withholding the man's name. The *Corriere*'s reporter was enthralled with Pezzoli's verbal wizardry, and his own proximity to greatness.

Massina knew precisely what Pezzoli was saying, as the two of them had earlier cooked up the story themselves: non-existent informers in the kidnapper's gang, Sardinian of course, coded tip-offs from phone booths in Olbia, the massive Carabinieri and Polizia air search combing the area as far as the Swiss and Austrian borders, which had resulted in the discovery of recently deserted farm buildings in the low-mountains. There were veiled implications, and vague hints, that Criminalpol were hot on the trail of the gang's present whereabouts as a result of the air search. And no ransom had been paid at all. Ask the 15th Duke of Salaviglia yourself had been the final Massina/Pezzoli throwaway bluff for the press. Sure, try getting within 500 metres of him or his family. No, it had been Criminalpol's solid detection work that had solved the case, and freed the Albassi boy. Massina knew that the web of lies would be enough to keep crowing politicians and the insatiable press more than happy. Add in also the photographs of an ecstatic mother hugging her son while a patrician aristocrat looked on two paces behind her. And this being Italy, the story as told would suffice. Italians always fell for neat solutions.

And in a few months, no one would care when a handful of wretched, and ill-fated Sardinian sheep herders known to be part-time, low-level kidnappers, would be rounded up, charged and framed. The story might make the inside pages, a paragraph above the lottery results perhaps, but it certainly wouldn't make the evening news. Justice would have been seen to have been done. A Sardinian gang had been arrested, tried in open court and all sentenced to lengthy jail time. This was just one of the many kidnappings they hadn't committed. So what?

Massina was uncommonly skilled in the delicate art of fabrication and falsehoods. With Pezzoli high on his adrenalin of luck, success and ambition – a Senate run was already being floated by the centre-right press – he would digest any story his trusted and revered ex-boss would feed him about the salesman from Ticino.

Massina had the confirmation he had long sought and always, intuitively, believed. Until now he'd had no proof, other than his own instinct. Pietro Albassi was out there somewhere, and he had been all this time. *Buona fortuna a lui.* Albassi had done the right thing by returning from God knows where to free his son, however he had achieved it.

Bravo Signor Albassi. All was good according to the Gospel of St Lorenzo. Cold justice had been served. Pietro Albassi's secret was bulletproof safe with him. Massina would travel with it as far as his burial plot in the cemetery in Cattolica. And no further.

EPILOGUE

'If we want things to stay as they are, things will have to change.'

**Giuseppe Tomasi Principe di
Lampedusa
Palermo, Sicily.**

33,000 ft above the Tyrrhenian Sea, Italian airspace.
Tuesday, 24th February 1987. 18:25.

It was only when Anthony was heading south to Sicily, at 33,000 ft above the Tyrrhenian Sea, that he realised the enormity of what he'd done: switch his Rome flight to Palermo at the last minute, missing his New York connection. The two gates were side by side, and it was another gut instinct decision. He trusted them, doing so had saved his life.

Before he'd set off for the Rome gate, he'd called Mr M. Their conversation had gone better than he could have hoped: Mr M. had neither probed with questions, nor pressed for answers. He'd listened intently, on a scratchy transatlantic connection, with what sounded like relief. He'd instructed him to stay the night in Rome – *'... eat good Italian food and enjoy yourself, Anthony...'* – as he would be sending the Gulfstream in the next two or three hours, so that he could fly straight home to New Orleans on Wednesday evening. Anthony protested. Mr M. insisted. Anthony surrendered. It was ever thus between them. He knew the battles to fight, and an 'insisting' one with Mr M. wasn't one of them.

Gazing out of the window into the setting sun, there was, as far as he was aware, no reason for him to visit Sicily. He'd achieved everything he'd set out to accomplish: Toto was alive, unharmed and free. Ruxandra had their son returned to the safety of his mother's arms and those of Victor too. What more could he possibly wish for? Nothing. After all this time, he'd been able to keep the oath he'd sworn to uphold as Paola lay in a coma. The family would live on, even if it had meant he'd had to sacrifice himself.

The one-hour-forty-minute flight landed at Palermo just before 19:00, in that last breath of mellow daylight – those few precious minutes between twilight and dusk – an unruffled Tyrrhenian Sea sparkled out of the window as they approached the airport. *Only* in Sicily, he reflected.

Palermo, Sicily.
Tuesday, 24th February 1987. 19:15.

Clear of the terminal, he took a taxi to the Villa Igiea. Once a turn-of-the-century palazzo at the foot of Monte Pellegrino and the water's edge, it was now a fine hotel. He checked into a large suite overlooking the sea. From the Villa Igiea, it was a short distance to the port, and he knew that such a walk in the salted air, would be both cathartic and invigorating.

The docks were just as he'd remembered them as a boy. For years he had accompanied Victor and his father to Palermo to oversee the safe loading of Bonnera's harvests. The Salaviglias deemed it a duty, one he was sure Victor continued. Some things never change, he realised. And as he wandered aimlessly in and out of the wharves and jetties, with as many memories ricocheting inside of him as there were starlings in the cloudless, twilight sky, an idea came to him.

Back at the Villa Igiea, he called the concierge, ordered a chauffeured car for 09:00 and ensured his clothes were laundered overnight. Then he began the slow process of running a deep bath. He removed both miniatures of Captain Morgan from the minibar. Sipping the neat rum on the terracotta balcony, he stared wide-eyed at the chatoyant stars which reflected back at him from the sea he had known since the day he was born.

Was it the twenty minutes in the deep, warm bath, the fresh air or the rum that had soothed his weary body? He didn't much care which. It was probably the sum of all three. The wake of the stalled ship had not only caught up with him, it had overtaken him. Exhausted, he crawled under the cool linen sheets and woollen blankets. He left the curtains and windows wide open to draw the sea air into his suite. As he drifted off to sleep, he knew he would be woken in the morning by the soft light of a Sicilian sunrise, fortunate and hungry, just like the Sicilian orphan he was.

San Cipirello, a village in the west of Sicily. Wednesday, 25th February 1987. 10:15.

Nothing had changed, and yet everything had changed.

Pietro Albassi let his eyes lead him around the small, and still irregular, piazza which now bore a name, Piazza Umberto II. King Umberto II had been their king when he and Victor were children. If they had to name the piazza in San Cipirello after anyone at all, the very last king of Italy was a fine choice indeed. Pietro looked at the sign again and chuckled. He knew who would have chosen the name.

Memories he had thought had long been consigned to the inaccessible reaches of his subconscious began to tumble out, bright ones as well as opaque ones. Was his subconscious an open treasure chest crammed with too many gems, or a casket pregnant with only dark spirits, one where the latch, for better or for worse, refused to remain fastened?

This piazza was where he had been shot almost thirty-seven years ago. Twenty-seven men, women and children had been killed that day. He was the only one who had been shot to have survived. Even if it were a solitary atom, Pietro Albassi's blood was to be found somewhere in the earth of San Cipirello.

He crossed the piazza, and as he did so, he gazed up into the sky imagining he could see Paola looking down on him approvingly. Retribution had not been a motive, saving her twin brother's life had been the singular focus of his discipline. But Alessandro Cuci had made it personal the day he had ordered Paola mown down. Even so, vengeance *had* tasted good. Too good. And that, Pietro supposed as he wandered around the perimeter of Piazza Umberto II, was why he had chosen to return to San Cipirello this morning. There had only ever been one score to settle and it had now been settled.

He fastened the button of his cashmere jacket, and studied what had once been Bar Lombardo, Nino's bar. From far and wide people would come to Bar Lombardo, for everyone had loved Nino. Not least because he had been born with two thumbs on his right hand, which he delighted in showing off. The shrewd, three-thumbed bar owner that Nino was, knew his audience: Sicilians are not only a superstitious race, they are drawn to the peculiar.

Bar Lombardo was where it had all began. The old men of the village, their complexions marbled by coarse wine and a lifetime of toil in the searing elements of Sicily, had played *scopa* and gossiped amongst themselves about everything and nothing. Nino's was the precise spot where the notorious San Cipirello massacre had taken place. The sign above the Bar Lombardo was still red, but the café had been renamed Bar Ferrari. Its tables and chairs were no longer nailed together from fallen cypress trees, and the compacted earth and split bamboo mats were gone too. Cheap ceramic floor tiles, a stainless-steel bar and chairs made from extruded white plastic were the replacements. A solitary, time-worn picture of the Virgin Mary still hung above the bar's door. He saw that.

Some things never change.

The proprietor of the Bar Ferrari shot the classy-looking interloper a flinty look, his po-face all twitch and bone. He did as the man had politely requested and laced his espresso with a hefty slug of grappa. Pietro picked up a plastic chair and moved it outside into the sun. The fountain in the centre of the piazza, the one that had made the women blush and the men laugh, was all boarded up: posters for toothpaste, washing powder, tyres, and old films long since viewed, clung precariously to the flimsy plywood.

He sat gazing at what had been the fountain, reliving a game the children used to play: they would all stand around the fountain – their backs to it – until its ancient pump randomly ejaculated a tall jet of water skywards. The second it did so, you had to run away as fast as possible, for if even a drop landed on you, well, then you were out. Pietro, always nimble and fast, was usually the winner amongst the fifteen or so children who played. Water, fountains, chasing lizards and a piazza full of laughter were yesterday's tales too.

Some things do change.

The cobblestones of the piazza had been worn away over many years by donkeys and their carts with steel treads, the occasional working horse, old tractors, and latterly cars, vans and scooters. The buildings were neglected and unloved. A glum little *pensione* – who would wish to stay here, he wondered? – stood in place of the old regional office. Tucked away in the far corner a small cinema had been built on the site of the village dung-heap, where the birds used to feed. He wondered if the cinema proprietor knew that fact? He doubted it. Pietro couldn't decide which he preferred: the dung-heap or the cinema? On balance, the cinema, but only by a donkey's nose, and solely because the cinema didn't attract the flies like the dung had. The alcohol-spiked espresso tasted both bitter and strong. He bolted back the last chewy dregs, took his cup inside, placed a 5,000 lire note under the saucer and left without saying a word.

Pietro stood on the step of the Bar Ferrari and took it all in again. Something was troubling him, and he wasn't sure what it was until he noticed a lonely old lady crouching alone on her front steps. That was it. No one sat on their front steps anymore and shared stories. There was no laughter. There was no laundry hanging from the small, pot-bellied iron balconies. There were no people. San Cipirello was properly deserted; a ghost town. Circling the piazza, he spied a teenage girl in the shade selling – or hoping to – wild flowers from an aluminium pail. Pietro strolled over to her, asked her name – Sofia – and how much for all her flowers? Shyly, she responded 5,000 lire. He handed Sofia 20,000 lire, nodded a grateful *grazie tanto* then cut down the side street to where Nonna had lived.

Some things do change.

The small street off the piazza where he had lived with Nonna for a time now bore a name: he bowed his head in disbelief which was followed by an indignant laugh. The irony was too much. Yes, the naming of *corsi, vie, viali* and *piazze* was an Italian 'honours' system, but to call this urchin side street in a poverty wreaked Sicilian village 'via Aldo Moro' was too much. His pained laugh turned to a hearty one, and he saw that Nonna's old dry-stone-built house was still standing. This was Salaviglia land. Of course, it was still standing. He took it in his stride, and carried on down the ragged via Aldo Moro towards a path which he knew would lead him out of town. The secrets of San Cipirello, it would seem, were destined to remain with him forever.

Some things never change.

Having reached the path, it was exactly how he remembered it. No more than a sandy track, bordered on both sides by tumbledown stone walls, enigmatic prickly pears, accidental hedgerows and harsh, wild cacti. The old homesteads, where pride had once resided, hadn't been replaced with modern low-slung hovels. His spirits lifted at this discovery as he walked towards the cemetery, the sole purpose for his being in San Cipirello this morning.

He navigated a steep downhill bend and as he did so, laid out in front of his eyes, some forty years later, the same wide-open vista appeared which, went from the Tyrrhenian Sea in the south, to the Heavens in the north, and to the east and the west; a never-ending panorama of such incredible, unspoiled beauty, that it took his breath away. A time capsule from centuries ago opened up before him: olive trees older than Moses, groves of scented oranges and lemons, wild pastures where hardy rock-scrambling goats roamed free. This was just the backdrop. Industry, local speculators, the Mafiosi could only encroach so far, and San Cipirello was one of the many Salaviglia bulwarks in the west of Sicily. For no one dared build high, low or close to the country, and it was a country that the Salaviglias had ruled over, and preserved, since the eleventh century. Even the sea – as far as the vanishing horizon – was their land.

Some things never change.

Minutes later, Pietro came upon the cemetery of San Cipirello to find its wrought iron gates open, as he'd remembered they always were. An infirm caretaker, dressed in old grey trousers and a thin, blue woollen cardigan over a white vest, dozed peacefully on a stool inside the cemetery walls in the shade of an olive tree. The caretaker nodded politely. Beside him was a rusty tin box full of lire coins. Pietro slid a banknote under the coins and the caretaker, who he guessed to be in his late seventies, smiled appreciatively in return.

Pietro wandered methodically up and down each of the well-tended gravel paths which separated the many rows of graves and simple headstones. The cemetery was full, unlike when he was a child. The twenty-seven souls who were murdered on the 24th August 1950 had an area set apart. Haughty cypress trees surrounded their graves as sentries would a citadel. He stood solemnly at each grave, and out of respect he crossed himself and read each name out aloud before moving onto the next. He noticed that Nino Camporele was buried, not surprisingly, beside his best customer, Dr Carlotto, the Salaviglia's personal physician who'd helped deliver him and had tried in vain, with Nonna, to save his dying mother's life. The names of those killed that day would always resonate with him, and here for the very first time, he understood what 'survivor's guilt' meant. A few of the headstones held sepia photos which peered back out at him. He doubted he recognised any of them, but he liked to think he did. Beyond *i ventisetti*, as they were known locally, he saw a communal *congregazioni*. For as the elderly passed away, the needs of the dead had changed too, as there appeared to be no more burial plots.

Far beyond the *congregazioni* the cemetery's sole almond tree was beginning to blossom. The white and pale pink petals wept into the flowers' deep magenta centre, and the few petals that had already fallen to the ground could have been large snowflakes, if it were anywhere other than Sicily. There were yet more protective cypress trees surrounding the graves, and Pietro knew full well that tucked away in this serene nook – a secret garden – he would find the sanctuary where his mother, his grandfather and Nonna had been laid to rest.

Some things never change.

Chiselled into his mother's granite headstone was her name and the years of her birth and death. Sadly, there was no sepia photo, but her grave appeared to have been lovingly cared for over the years. A handful of colourful wildflowers lay in front of a lit candle shielded by red glass. There were no weeds or extraneous plants. In the grave to her left was the grandfather he had never known, and to his immediate left, Nonna was buried. Three graves, and a small plot to the right of his mother's, were guarded by oleanders. Pietro knelt down and placed Sofia's flowers on the ground, and he proceeded to divide them into three equal bunches. Ritually, he placed the flowers on each of the graves. Someone, perhaps Father Albert, if he was still alive, had honoured the graves over time. Somebody had.

All of a sudden he shivered in the February sun and felt that Toto had been shown San Cipirello's cemetery, where their meagre history lay. He was sure of that. Pietro rocked lightly backwards on his heels. He could sense Toto's presence beside his grandmother and great-grandfather. He was certain it was Ruxandra who had brought Toto to this hallowed place. As silent as a bursting bubble, he intuited that Victor had accompanied them too. He hoped so.

Pietro solemnly believed that everything he constituted as a man had stemmed from the kindnesses, education and love he had been freely given by the 14th Duke of Salaviglia, and his only child, his son Victor. To have Toto and Ruxandra loved and shielded by his dearest childhood friend Victor, now the 15th Duke of Salaviglia, was far, far more than he deserved in this life.

Some things never change.

Pietro breathed in the unseasonably warm air and the honeyed fragrance of the oleanders. High above him he caught, anchored in the cobalt sky, a red hawk as it hovered, its eyes locked onto a prey. Lost in his own reverie, Pietro studied his mother's grave once more. Just as he was about to stand up, he felt a hand tap him gently on the shoulder. Startled, he jumped up and saw the old caretaker.

"I apologise if I alarmed you, Signor, I was behind the almond tree," the caretaker stuttered nervously. "Such a beautiful tree, no? In Christianity, the almond implies divine favour and divine approval. A perfect corner for these souls, no?"

"Yes, beautiful. Very beautiful indeed," Pietro mumbled in reply.

He took in the caretaker's eyes and then his expression, the old man's smile held a stillness. Somewhere in Pietro's subconscious was a glint of recognition. The caretaker returned Pietro's stare, and he did so in compelling silence. Uneasy now, Pietro bent down to run his hand through the fine, white stones carpeting his mother's grave.

"They're pretty flowers. Thank you," the caretaker whispered.

Still with his back to the old man Pietro asked politely, "Sorry, but do I know you?"

"You should do. I'm Father Albert. I helped Nonna bring you up." The old man took his time, as if he had all the time in the world. "Please tell me, why you are here, Pietro?"

"What are you saying?"

"You're Pietro Albassi. Why are you here?" he asked again.

Silence again engulfed them both. In the end, it was Pietro who broke the quiet.

"I wanted to see my mother for the last time." The child within surfaced. "My first breath was her last breath, we shared that if nothing else."

Father Albert faltered, then coughed. "You're a young man. You've many years ahead of you. Why do you say such things?"

"Why all the questions, Father Albert?" Pietro queried. "I may not be old, but my future years will not be spent here. My time…" Pietro raised his chin towards the magnificent landscape in front of them both. "No, I don't belong here anymore. I've done my duty."

"I knew you didn't die in 1978," Father Albert said softly. "We priests are permitted to understand things that others aren't. I knew you would return, even if it was for just one day." His elderly voice held firm. "I loved her too."

"Who?"

"Your mother. She was a fine young woman. Strong, with a free spirit. You inherited that side of her. Like you, she wasn't born to spend her life in Sicily. She didn't belong here either."

"Well, she did spend her short life here."

"Yes, she did." Father Albert opened his arms wide, as if giving a sermon and gazed down at the dynastic Salaviglia estates surrounding both men. "The stench of death after the massacre in 1950 was everywhere, in our nostrils and our souls, it was even in our clothes. It has stayed with us all forever."

Father Albert knew only too well how those words would resonate with Pietro and he continued speaking as if his life depended upon his words. "This land has a life of its own: it takes the weak and makes them weaker, and the strong, well, it makes them stronger. It's the clever ones who take from the strong, and *then* they escape just as you did."

Pietro wondered what Father Albert was leading up to.

"You were born strong and clever, Pietro. I saw it in your eyes the day we buried Nonna and your blind eye burned into my soul."

* * *

The pallbearers lowered Nonna's coffin into the grave. Despite the anger of the August sun, there was a coldness in Pietro's blind eye and his seeing eye. He looked all around him. His stare rested on Father Albert, and his heartbreak and turmoil only retreated when his eyes met Victor's, who was standing beside his father. Before the service began, Pietro walked over to Victor and his father.

Father Albert held up his prayer book as a sign that the burial was to start. As he did so, Pietro interrupted. He had a question to ask out aloud, and it would be the only time in his life that he would ever ask it.

"If this is Nonna's grave," he said, stepping to its edge, "then where is my father buried?" His voice was quiet, still, almost silent.

"He was a soldier, Pietro. One who fought alongside God for what he believed was right," answered Father Albert.

Pietro stepped back from the graveside. Victor reached out and took hold of his friend's hand and grasped it as if he'd never let it go. Together, they heard the words, the unintelligible words, the ones Father Albert droned out in Latin, until the gravediggers heaped clods of earth noisily onto Nonna's plywood coffin.

The funeral was over. The old lady who had nurtured him was now dead, and buried next to his mother and grandfather. His father's grave would forever be unknown. As unknown as his father. All that had remained in that Hell-sent heat of a Sicilian August in 1951, were a child's simple questions. Ones Pietro would never ask again.

* * *

Father Albert carried on with a relentless passion. "You'd have ended up a criminal, in prison or dead, or all three, if you'd stayed here. Pietro, there is a long dusk in your soul."

Pietro nodded in tacit agreement. The last three days had surely confirmed Father Albert's insight.

"This land, this sea, they were not for you. Sicily's unending decay was too much for you. I saw it, Pietro, believe me, I did. That's why the old Duke took you under his wing at Bonnera after we'd buried Nonna. I asked him, and he did so willingly, for he had always wanted a second son. You were his child as well as mine. It was he who sent you north to Lombardy for your later education. He was right. If you need proof, just look at yourself now. You learned enough to come back for your son, Pietro. So, our intuition wasn't wrong. The clever do take from the strong. The Salaviglias understand these lands better than God himself."

Father Albert's eyes held far more than forty-three years of pleas as he spoke. Pietro was numb, confused and tongue-tied. He stepped closer and gently placed his hand on the old priest's shoulder.

"Enough, it's history. Whatever happened all those years ago is as dead as Paola, Nonna, Nino, my mother, the old Duke, all of them," Pietro said with finality. "We've all had to call a truce with our own devils, haven't we? *Arrivederci*, Father Albert."

"Fear not, Pietro, I will guard your secret forever. No one will ever know," he concluded.

"*Grazie*, Father Albert. We'll keep this between us, my mother, my grandfather and Nonna."

Pietro extended his right hand, which Father Albert ignored. Instead, the old priest leaned in and kissed him tenderly on each cheek. "*Buona fortuna e vai con Dio.*"

Pietro nodded solemnly and slowly wheeled around to walk up the path to the cemetery gates. When he reached the gates, he looked down at the cemetery once more. Father Albert remained at peace under the almond tree beside the graves of his mother, his grandfather and Nonna.

The poised, and always resolute, cypress trees moved gently in the breeze. The concentrated stares of hundreds of souls bore down on him, just as the tranquillity of the cemetery rose up to him. He knew then he would never return. For the last time, he smiled at his mother's grave and vowed that one day he would plant an almond tree somewhere. Louisiana, perhaps? Once a year, when the white and pink petals carpeted the ground wherever that tree stood, his mother would come back into his life, albeit briefly, and they would again share a lost embrace.

* * *

His driver, Guido, was parked up two streets behind Piazza Umberto II screened in the shade of what had been the Carabinieri station. He opened the rear door of the Mercedes. After one last stolen glance at San Cipirello, Pietro slid into the car's leather cocoon.

"We're going to take a different route, Guido, the back roads," Pietro instructed, "through the Salaviglia lands."

"That will take forever, Signor?"

"Today, I have forever," Pietro replied cryptically. "I know these roads like the back of my hand. This is my land, Guido. We won't get lost. Trust me. *Andiamo.*"

Without a further word, Guido shrugged his shoulders and executed a U-turn to head eastwards. Forty-five minutes later, Pietro recognised a knot of dusty crossroads.

"Guido, pull in here for a few minutes. I'm going to get out and walk."

Pietro took off his jacket, left it on the seat and rolled up his shirtsleeves. Ahead of him was a steep climb, even for a wild goat, to the top of the barren hill. At its peak, he knew he would find a tabletop plateau of rocks that had been, in another life, a favourite place for the 'Lizard Game' he and Victor had loved to play. A vista would also open up, where he knew he could glimpse – just – Bonnera. To leave Sicily, and not say *arrivederci* to Bonnera would be to trespass against all that was right in the world.

Some things never change.

Angry at himself for the cigarettes he'd smoked in the last few days, he wheezed his way to the top, and let all that lay in front of him restore his body and soul. Bonnera stood custodian far away in the distance, yet he could feel its presence from here. This was what he needed to calm his troubled mind. Father Albert's words kept replaying over and over in his memory. He could neither be rid of them, nor decipher them. He had rambled on about many things: God, Nonna, his mother, Sicily, the Salaviglia family, the massacre in 1950… and all with different explanations and beliefs. Yet three remarks remained lodged in Pietro's subconscious. He couldn't translate any of them.

'I loved her too.' What on Earth did Father Albert mean by that? The statement had nagged at him as if it were a mosquito in the dead of night. Unexpectedly, and in an instant as he contemplated Bonnera framed in the hazy foreground, did he grasp what it was that had been buzzing in his mind.

Who would wish to be laid to rest, for all eternity, in a small plot to the right of a young woman, a shamed one too, who had died giving birth to a bastard, and who had all through her pregnancy refused to reveal the father's name? Pietro shook his head at his realisation. How had he not grasped this before, even as a child? The signs were there all along. The space to the right of his mother's grave was waiting for Father Albert Fiero. A vow is never a vow until it's a broken vow, no?

The second confirmation came immediately into focus: *'You were his child, as well as mine.'* Father Albert had said of himself and the 14th Duke of Salaviglia. He was Victor's blood-brother for sure, but he was *not* Victor's brother.

Then there was the third, and final, statement that convinced him of what his left eye should have seen all along.

'Buona fortuna e vai con Dio.'

These were the exact same words Pietro had declared to his own son – only yesterday – as he had watched him leave forever.

* * *

Pietro scrambled down the rocky hill and rested up against the car to catch his breath. Then, with a grin as wide as the Golfo di Castellammare, he bowed his head, closed his eyes and stood very, very still. All he took in was the chirring of the Salaviglia's cicadas. The last pieces of his Sicilian jigsaw – his life's odyssey – had fallen into their rightful places. He smiled in gratitude at the Parcae – The Sicilian Fates – who had returned him to San Cipirello today.

"*Guido, prendiamo la strada veloce per L'Aeroporto di Palermo, per favore, devo prendere un volo questa sera.*"

AFTERWORD

In 1978 I was living in Malta and followed the gruesome account of Aldo Moro's kidnapping closely. His pitiless execution, some fifty-four days later, became Europe's John F. Kennedy & Robert F. Kennedy assassinations combined, especially if you lived, as I did, between Malta, Sicily and Italy. The late 1970s were indeed the *anni di piombo* – the years of lead: terrorism, bombs, and the endless, seemingly relentless, random slayings of civilians and law enforcement. It was a civil war in all but name, with multiple acts of terrorism from across the political spectrum. In 1978, urban guerrilla actions throughout the country were running at a rate of five/six attacks *per day*. In 1980 Robert Katz wrote in *The Days of Wrath*: 'There was plenty of law that year [1978], but not much order'. And all the while, the Cold War growled on, dictating Soviet, American, European and UK foreign policies.

White Suicide spans the period from 1944–1987. A central theme in the book is the 'master and servant' relationship between Italy, Sicily and America. There are numerous theories over the genesis of the sometimes fraternal, sometimes fractious, sometimes ideological but always political connection between Italy and America, and all in an era before CIA was even founded.

One thesis, germane to the US/Italy bond, involves a Sicilian, Salvatore Lucania, better known as Charles 'Lucky' Luciano. It has long been accepted that with his Jewish partner, Meyer Lansky, this odd-couple of ruthless career criminals were the fathers of modern organised crime in America with their creation of the National Crime Syndicate.

In 1936 Luciano was convicted of running prostitution rackets in New York and New Jersey. A guilty verdict (and a thirty-to-fifty-year sentence) was duly handed down to the thirty-nine-year-old, who continued to oversee his crime family unimpeded from within the walls of various New York prisons.

WHITE SUICIDE

Before Pearl Harbour, Luciano and Lansky controlled the New York and New Jersey docks and their waterfronts. Not long after the US declaration of war on 7th December 1941, the Office of US Naval Intelligence *approached* Lansky with an extraordinary proposition: the US Navy (and its Office of Naval Intelligence), with The State of New York, would offer a *full* commutation of Luciano's prison sentence in exchange for Luciano and Lansky providing not only protection but assistance at the docks, including no labour union strikes. A further condition was Luciano would collaborate in 'Operation Underworld'. This US operation required Luciano to deploy his Sicilian Mafiosi connections, intelligence and 'soldiers' on the ground in Sicily to both the Office Naval Intelligence and US military, prior to 'Operation Husky', the planned Allied invasion of Sicily.

It is accepted that the success of 'Operation Husky' was due in part to Luciano's Sicilian Mafiosi. After the war, the US Navy and The State of New York kept their side of the Devil's bargain: in February 1946 Luciano was deported from New York on a ship bound for Naples, whilst, incredibly – the ink barely dry on the WWII surrender documents – Lansky was awarded the US Medal of Freedom by President Harry S. Truman in 1945 in a secret ceremony at the White House. And in September 1944, *White Suicide*'s fictional protagonist – a Sicilian, Pietro Albassi – was born into the dark heart of this US/Italy relationship.

Following the abduction of a First World leader in broad Roman sunlight, it didn't take much reading between the lines to perceive that US fingerprints *might* be found all over Moro's kidnapping; Washington had long been making statements about Italian domestic politics. Moro was both the architect and driving force behind the *Compresso Storico* (Historic Compromise) to form a governing alliance between his Christian Democracy (DC) and the Italian Communist Party (PCI). But Washington had other plans for its ally. They had clearly semaphored their views on the idea of permitting a Kremlin-funded communist party into an Italian – and by default NATO – ruling government. And Italy ignored all the flags.

White Suicide is a book where fact, fiction and, perhaps, conspiracy theories are intertwined. It weaves in many true-life players and events: Aldo Moro, Giulio Andreotti (twice and seven times prime minister of Italy, respectively), Romano Prodi, venal P2 freemasons, Vatican corruption, US presidents Carter and Reagan, the Iran–Contra affair, CIA Director George H.W. Bush (later 41st President), the 'sudden death' of Pope John Paul I in September 1978 after he'd discovered extensive financial malfeasance within the Vatican.

Real people – Italian, American and Vatican – appear throughout and are woven with the fictional characters. All instances where they and/or their institutions appear – and there are many – may be relied upon to be as correct as research, in both the public and private domains, can be. Where quotes, in italics, are used, they too may be relied upon as accurate.

* * *

The following paragraphs (in a loose chronology) will hopefully add context to where some of the extraordinary factual aspects of this book intersect with Pietro Albassi's fictional story.

'Operation Husky', as the ambitious Allied invasion of Sicily was named, began on the night of 10th July 1943, and the island was recaptured on the 17th August with a comparatively small Allied loss of life (5,749). Mussolini's fascist government subsequently fell from power on 25th July, and the Armistice of Cassibile, where the Kingdom of Italy surrendered to the Allies, was signed in Cassibile, Sicily on 3rd September 1943. General Patton's 7th Army had landed on the south coast, his 3rd Infantry division sweeping northwest through the towns and villages towards Trapani, Marsala and the capital Palermo. It was believed that Pietro's father was one of Patton's infantrymen.

The International Herald Tribune news report on the San Cipirello Massacre, which happened fictionally on 24th August 1950, is based on an actual massacre during the May Day celebrations in 1947. At 10:15 on 1st May at Portella della Ginestra – a village in the mountainous hinterland behind Palermo – the true-life bandit Salvatore Giuliano and his men shot and killed eleven men, women and children and wounded twenty-seven more, including a little girl who had her jaw shot off. The Portella massacre is still regarded as one of the most violent acts in modern Italian political history. For the purposes of narrative and timelines I have changed both the date and the village. In my IHT article Giuliano's cousin, Pisciotta, was murdered in December 1950 in Ucciardone prison in Palermo (*'with enough strychnine in his coffee to* *kill 40 horses'*) but in reality, he was likewise poisoned in February 1954; again, this date change is for narrative purposes. At the time, the real-life Interior Minister Mario Scelba played a shadowy role in the aftermath of the Portella massacre. The 14th Duke of Salaviglia is a fictional character, however, the Salaviglia family tree is a composite of several Sicilian aristocratic patriarchs.

The kidnap of Aldo Moro, and the entire operation – the hapless Roman flower vendor, the minutiae of Moro's morning routine, to the execution of the kidnap itself (streets, vehicles, terrorists, the murder of his five-man security detail, munitions used, shots fired etc. may be relied upon as facts). Fifty-four days after his abduction, the manner of Moro's death at the hands of the Red Brigades commander, Mario Moretti, may also be relied upon as factual. Moro's private funeral, and his unwanted State funeral, are recounted according to the timelines as the events unfolded. Mario Moretti was arrested in 1981, given six life sentences and was inexplicably paroled in 1997 after serving only fifteen years; he remains alive, whereabouts unknown.

Romano Prodi's role in the Moro affair may at first seem to be incredible, comical, even fantastical. But the Ouija séance on Sunday 2nd April at Professor Clo's country home in Zappolino (thirty kilometres from Bologna) did take place; Prodi was one of eight university professors present. Prodi has stated on numerous occasions that 'Gradoli' was indeed spelled out by the 'spirit' they'd 'contacted', apparently it was the 'soul' of Giorgio La Pira, a previous leader of the Christian Democracy party. What follows is a more detailed timeline of Prodi's implausible story, and for pacing reasons is not in the body of the text. Prodi did contact the Christian Democracy HQ in Rome on Monday 3rd April and passed on the address from the séance (in our story, he offers up the address to Pietro). Four days later on the 6th April, the village of Gradoli was raided and searched by Italian forces who unearthed nothing whatsoever. There is some (unproven) evidence that 'outside' forces instigated this raid; for narrative purposes, Barings does that. 96 via Gradoli was, it turns out, a Red Brigades safehouse/base where Moro was indeed being held by Moretti and others. Not long after Gradoli village was upended, Moro *was* moved; 8 via Camillo Montalcini (where he was later executed) is most likely. On 18th April, 16 days *after* Prodi had received his paranormal intel – and had passed it on to *his and Moro's* party HQ in Rome – 96 via Gradoli was finally searched. Other than clues – specifically running bath water taps, a Red Brigades confirmation calling card of their one-time presence – Moro was not found. If Prodi's tip-off from the spirit world had been deployed better, and more swiftly, Moro would probably have been freed and Moretti and his *brigatisti* arrested. Later, in the 1990s when Prodi was prime minister of Italy for the first time, the Ouija séance issue resurfaced; two other attendees vouched for the mystic saucer and Prodi's 'Gradoli' statements. In 1999 Prodi was summoned by the Italian Parliamentary Commission into Italian Terrorism. He had just been elected President of the European Commission (served: September 1999 – November 2004) and to have refused to testify could well have posed yet more embarrassing questions. Prodi stuck to his story, and did so again in May 2006 during the General Election, when he was running neck-and-neck against then Prime Minister Silvio Berlusconi – once a P2 member – who accused Prodi outright of lying and withholding the truth about the Ouija séance. Prodi defeated Berlusconi and was elected prime minister for the second time, and the Ouija séance story again evaporated into the ghosts' ether. Romano Prodi, now in his eighties, lives beside the sea in Tuscany. His role, and the truth of it in the Moro affair, remains under debate to this day.

Statements made by the US regarding Washington's views of its NATO ally, as the Cold War stalked on and on, are far too numerous for the narrative. George H.W. Bush was appointed CIA Director Central Intelligence in January 1976, and in the Italian General Election that year, the Italian Communist Party (PCI) – openly funded by the Soviet Communist Party – won 34.4 per cent of the popular vote. The PCI's astonishing result was a clarion warning for Washington. Moro and his plans were clearly a threat to the Western Alliance. The fear of an Italian government being able to pass on NATO military tactics, installations, and scores of NATO intelligence agents and secrets directly to the Kremlin – and its Warsaw Pact allies – were a clear and present danger as far as the US was concerned. Furthermore, a Communist governing coalition in Italy also represented a significant cultural failure for its long-time ally, the US. A postscript that indicates how strongly the US Government, State Department and CIA felt is an account by Moro's widow, Eleonora, of a meeting between Henry Kissinger (Secretary of State for presidents Nixon and Ford) and an unidentified CIA official in early 1978. According to Signora Moro, her husband was informed at this meeting (which has the aroma of an American 'Hail Mary' pass, after all else had failed) that he should not continue to pursue the strategy of bringing the Communist Party into his Cabinet: *'You must abandon your policy of bringing all the political forces in your country into direct collaboration… or you will pay dearly for it…'* Moro thought – fleetingly – of quitting politics. However, he remained resolute, and a month or so after the Kissinger/CIA meeting, he was kidnapped and later murdered.

The Institute for the Works of Religion (IOR), or more commonly known as the Vatican Bank was founded in 1942. Secretive and shrouded in controversy, it only released details of its operations for the first time – and then under duress – in 2012. It has (declared) global assets of €3 billion. Its mission statement remains the same: *'To provide specialised financial services to the Catholic Church worldwide'*. However, it has been dogged by scandal since 1945 after hiding in excess of 200 million Swiss francs ($1 billion-plus in today's money) of *Raubgold*, 'stolen Nazi gold', in the Vatican's Swiss vaults. The Vatican Bank was beset by further financial and political scandals in the early 1970s and 1980s, culminating in June 1982 with the almost theatrical murder in London of Roberto Calvi the Vatican banker, another prominent P2 member. Several works published in the 1980s and 1990s allude to the Vatican Bank's further involvement in anti-communist movements in Europe during the Cold War, and that the bank was used by the CIA as a funnel to supply the right-wing Central American Contra rebels from 1979–1990 during the Reagan/Bush presidency years 1981–1989. There has been an endemic drip-drip of more financial scandals for the Vatican Bank during this century too: the latest in 2018 when Vatican prosecutors indicted the head of the Vatican Bank, Angelo Caloia, for embezzling $62 million in another real estate scam. He was found guilty in January 2021 and sentenced to eight years in prison.

The death of Pope John Paul I on 28th September 1978, only thirty-three days after his election, caught the entire world by surprise. What followed was a litany of missteps, statements and cover-ups; the Vatican couldn't even agree on the time of his death. There is no doubt there were motives a-plenty: money, scandal, rife Vatican corruption, and a surprise 'outsider' with reformist and liberal views elected Pope. In David Yallop's 1984 bestselling book, *In God's Name*, he states that three senior archbishops (including Marcinkus, then head of the Vatican Bank) conspired with three P2 members (including Calvi) to murder John Paul I. However, his theory (dismissed by the Vatican) remains unchallenged. David Yallop died of natural causes in 2018.

* * *

In the final analysis, and returning to Pietro's 'first principles', the inexplicable truth is that Moro was not found *alive* during the fifty-four days of his captivity in Rome. Was it actually incompetence, confusion, lies and obfuscation by right-wing Italian powers? Was it really the staunchly pro-US and NATO prime minister Giulio Andreotti, P2 and others – the US included – all of whom had fierce anti-communist agendas – who conspired to bury (literally and metaphorically) every aspect of the Moro Affair? It would appear so.

Carabinieri General Carlo dalla Chiesa, who led the investigation into Moro's murder, was later dispatched to Palermo as *prefetto* (Prefect) and was shot dead (with his wife) whilst driving on 3rd September 1982 just five months after he'd landed in Sicily. It was believed that whilst investigating all aspects of the Moro Affair, he'd *'learned far too much'*; his assassination was predicted by the crime reporter Carmine 'Mino' Pecorelli. Described as a *'maverick journalist with excellent secret service contacts'* Pecorelli was, in early 1979, set to publish the latest in a canon of articles about Moro's death; he was going to allege that a *'lucid superpower'* (read: USA) was responsible, and he too was shot, and died, on 20th March 1979 whilst driving in the Prati district of Rome.

Former Christian Democracy prime minister – and Italy's most senior statesman – Andreotti was later charged in 1993 in Perugia (alongside two Sicilian Mafia bosses) with complicity in Pecorelli's murder. Andreotti (and his two Mafia co-defendants) were acquitted in 1999. However, Perugia's prosecutors successfully appealed the verdict. At Andreotti's retrial in 2002 he was convicted of complicity in Pecorelli's murder, and was sentenced to twenty-four years in prison. Inexplicably, his two Mafia co-defendants were acquitted.

At the time of the second guilty verdict Andreotti was eighty-four years old, and remained at liberty pending his final appeal to the Supreme Court. This was a man who'd helped draft the First Republic's Constitution and went on to become the most powerful politician in the byzantine world of Italian politics. Andreotti served as prime minister in seven governments between 1972 and 1992 during his sixty years in parliament, and was a Senator for Life.

The following year, 2003, the Supreme Court heard his appeal. This being Italy, Andreotti was, of course, acquitted (again) but this time 'definitively'. He died of respiratory failure in Rome in 2013, aged ninety-four.

Forty-six years later, the Moro Affair remains unsolved. His kidnap and murder will remain one of the 20th century's enduring mysteries. There is every reason to believe that forces far more powerful – and potent – than the strapped Red Brigades were involved. Not one political – or judicial – investigating commission into the Moro Affair has ever been able – or seen fit – to provide explanations, let alone answers.

ACKNOWLEDGEMENTS

Any writing endeavour is a highly collaborative affair, which couldn't happen without the time, spirit, opinions – and plain hard work – of many disparate talents. My name is on the cover, but an awful lot of folks helped put it there.

The late Christopher Little was at the genesis of *White Suicide* (WS) and had long championed (and later corralled) the many different ideas for this book. He was a loyal, clever and witty friend. And as the world knows, a phenomenal agent. I had the privilege of knowing him for what seemed like forever. I first met him in the Gleneagles Bar in Mġarr Harbour in Gozo with Philip Nicholson (pen name: A.J. Quinnell) discussing a manuscript Philip had just finished called *Man on Fire*. Philip wanted Chris – an old friend and business associate from Hong Kong – to sell his first stab at writing a book. Despite not being a literary agent – but an exceptional salesman – Chris agreed, and then sold it. And then he sold it again. And again. Chris' career was, and will remain, the stuff of publishing history. One is permitted to wonder where certain of Chris' authors might be without his years of dogged work and support.

At the beginning of the hateful lockdown in March 2020, and at Chris' behest, I revisited the WS manuscript. Knowing that he was dying, and probably wouldn't see the finished rewrite, he urged me to consult Celia Hayley to edit the book. Thankfully, she agreed despite a hefty first draft. And if I could rededicate this book, it would be to her. Quite simply, Celia is the most remarkable editor and mentor I've had the pleasure of working with. I wouldn't be writing these acknowledgements if it hadn't been for her skill sets and patience.

Recognising a shift in publishing, Chris guided me to John Bond and Whitefox, where Julia Koppitz, Chris Wold and Jess King drew in all the disparate threads and talents needed: media, cartographers, typeface, cover designs, copy and line editors, and all seamlessly. Jessica Fry was much more than my amanuensis as the manuscript went through Celia's edits, tasks and rewrites and finding pesky split-infinitives; she sketched the initial endpaper map ideas too. Before (and after) Chris passed away Jules Bearman – his gatekeeper – was always there to organise lunches, dinners, just about everything really.

Thank you to those who simply offered encouragement and/or read early drafts: Mike Mount, Phillip Roberts, my eldest son Hamilton, Carolyn Beegan, Michael Bianchi, Hamilton South, Steve Cohen and Gordon Wise of Curtis Brown all gave opinions and observations which honed the final/final manuscript. Charles Glass also somehow found the time to read it whilst finishing his latest book, and then offered his own generous endorsement. Riccardo Saraceni (a Roman and future son-in-law) proofread – and corrected – my agricultural Italian, and placed *scopa* playing cards next to a *scacciapensieri* on my desk. The late Philip Nicholson lent me his ears in bringing Joshua Padden to life and also introduced me to personnel (who must remain nameless) at Malta Special Forces who assisted with Pietro's *suicido bianco*. Steve Cohen, who's designed and lit stadium shows across the planet *('Simon, you can't consider yourself a stage and lighting designer of any worth until you've been fired by Fleetwood Mac, which I just have been...')* signed off the Hotel d'Inghilterra dénouement. Jamie Cowie MCSP MKDE demonstrated, in grisly detail, just how to crush vertebrae. The late Jeffrey Mizzi became Saxon Monteleone's Creole teacher; I still can't fathom how, as Jeff was Maltese. Any and all errors throughout are on my slate.

Countless people in hotels, B & Bs, bars, diners and restaurants across Italy, Sicily and the American South, specifically, Milan, Bologna, Rome, the Vatican, Modena, the Northern Lakes, Portofino, Cattolica, Palermo, Castellammare, Erice, Trapani, Marsala, Corleone, Syracuse, Catania, the Maltese archipelago, Lisbon and New Orleans freely gave time and advice on how to identify – and avoid – pot holes during multiple research trips. In a time before Hurricane Katrina destroyed New Orleans, Vicky and Max Loubiere walked the backstreets and cemeteries of their city with me. My PA and dear friend of 23-plus years, Toni Eggar, somehow put up with all that's gone on too.

A *grazie* to Harriett Jagger Gaul who read the prehistoric draft. All five of my children – Hamilton, India, Orlando, Cameron and Imogen – had inputs too as this book came together. Thank you all.

The final word has to be for my late father, who swam with his young son in Golfo di Castellammare, and for many years afterwards we continued to sail the compass rose of the Inland Sea together: he instilled in me its beauty, its traditions, its lore and its dangers.